THE REVOLUTION AND THE FOX

Book Four of The Calatians

by Tim Susman

Argyll Productions
Dallas, Texas

CONTENTS

To Laura,

whose art breathed life into these stories

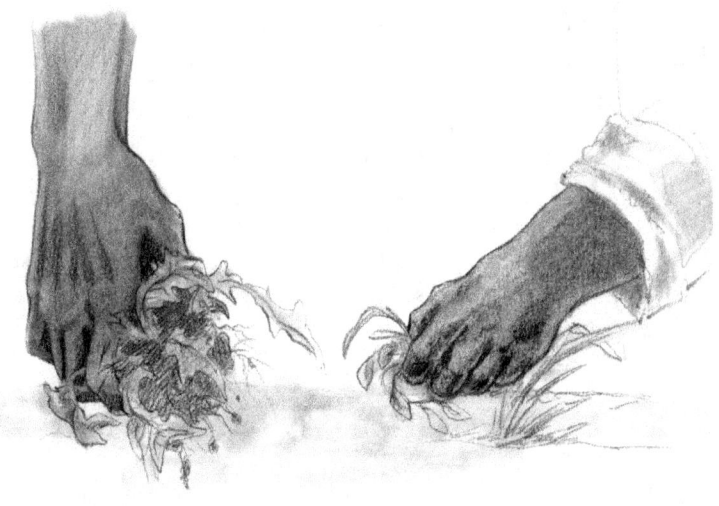

CHAPTER ONE: THE EXPOSITION

Kip stomped into Emily's office in the Lutris School brandishing a small bound pamphlet, his fox's ears flat back against his head, his tail bristled out despite his efforts to control it. "Have you seen this?" he asked, and threw the pamphlet down on her desk.

The large raven on the windowsill behind Emily jumped and fluttered her wings at the noise. Emily didn't react to the pamphlet until she'd finished adding a column of numbers, and then she pushed aside the ledger she was working on and turned the thin booklet to face her. "'The Softest Fur,'" she read from the cover. "Is this supposed to be you and me?"

"Yes." Kip stared down as she flipped to the first page and read. "Abel brought it back from London. It's—embarrassing."

"Oh, I don't know. 'His claws traced the milky-white her breast.' Apart from the hideous grammar, it's actually not bad." She set the pamphlet down and slid open one of the drawers of her desk. "Have you seen the one about me and Abigail Adams?"

Kip's ears came back up as she handed him another pamphlet, smaller than the one he'd brought. "'The Comfort of a Beast'? Am I in this too?"

"I think that's meant to be 'breast,'" Emily said. "My former husband gave it to me when he came to one of Abigail's lectures."

"Did he write it?" Kip searched the pamphlet for an author's name but found none.

"Honestly, it's too inventive for Thomas. Besides, whoever wrote it, I don't think he's seen a woman's body. He has a very curious idea of where things are and how they work." She picked up 'The Softest Fur' again. "Does this one have sorcery in it?"

"Yes," Kip said. "But they have no idea how that works either." He gave her pamphlet back to her. "You may keep it if you like."

"I shouldn't let it worry you," Emily said as she slipped both pamphlets into the drawer and closed it. "Thomas wanted me to be embarrassed and it quite took the wind from his sails when I accepted the thing cheerfully. It's a sign of respect. Not everyone gets made into the subject of a penny dreadful, you know."

"I think it's another tactic of Victor's."

Emily tapped fingers on her desk. "I would think he would at least know how sorcery works."

"I'm serious." Kip slumped into the chair on the other side of her desk. The warm breeze from the window brought scents of flowers from the peach trees that had given the town its name. Usually he enjoyed the sweet smell as a reminder of the territory owned by Calatians, but today he was more than usually aware of how precarious their school and that territory were. "He won't give up, ever."

"All we know for sure that he's done is write some columns in the Boston papers that were not very well received."

"Enough people talked about them."

"I know you think he was behind the protests against the Lutris School and the movement to deny us the Master rituals—"

"I'm certain of it. The language in the complaints was the same as he used in the columns."

"—but you have to admit that he's hardly the only one who thinks we don't deserve to start our own school."

"When Alice and I went to visit her parents, I paid a visit to Master Jaeger and I asked him, and he said he doesn't believe anyone at the American school was behind it, and Victor is in London now. Who else would do it anonymously? He knows he has no position of authority."

"Even if it is him," Emily said tiredly, "what are we to do about it? Go to London and have a stern talk with him? Believe me, I would love to drop him in the ocean somewhere and be done with him, but if he's under London's protection, that could—"

"I know, I know." Kip's tail lashed. "It would almost be worth an international incident to be rid of him. I just worry about what he'll do next. It's been two years since the war ended and he hasn't stopped."

"If his best remaining tactic is a penny dreadful, then I think you can sleep more soundly. About him, anyway." Emily pulled the ledger back toward her. "Did you come up here just to show me that? I've got several more pages of numbers before I can officially tell you whether we're going to run out of money in three months or four. And that has nothing to do with Victor."

"I know that." Kip craned his neck to look at the figures. "No, I came to tell you that Alice is expecting, so she won't be coming with us to the Exposition of Sorcery."

"Oh!" Emily brightened. "Congratulations. Are you nervous at all?"

He shook his head. "I'm anxious to get back to Amsterdam. I know not all the Calatians there like me, but—what?"

Emily was glaring at him. "I meant, are you nervous about her health, or about becoming a father?"

"Of course I'm worried about her health," Kip said. "In New Cambridge we always had a healer nearby for the births. It's not just as a teacher that a healer is lacking here, so we must find one at the Exposition. If not, we haven't any hope. Unless you want to reconsider allowing Peter to teach."

"We can't risk the school's only guardian," Emily said. "And I'm not sure he would agree to teach anyway."

Kip nodded. "As for becoming a father…" He smiled tightly. "I will be the best father I can, but Abel will be there, and my father and mother, and Aran and Arabella, so Alice and I will have plenty of help. Her parents are talking about coming down from New Cambridge, but they would have to sell the farm and buy a new one, and I can bring them back and forth as they like, so they may settle for extended visits. They'll be here for the christening, at least."

"Better you than me. This tedious work gives me a new respect for our disgraced Master Patris. I'd never be able to do it and then tend to an infant as well."

"What, Malcolm wouldn't help?"

Emily looked up over the rim of her spectacles. "My dear Irishman has many excellent qualities, but progressive ideas about the responsibilities of child care are sadly not among them."

"I suppose nobody's been reminding *you* every day about your duty to produce offspring."

"No, Mother gave up on me when I ran off to become a sorcerer, which she equates with becoming a man." Emily tapped the ledger. "And if she could see me now, she would be even more convinced of that. Speaking of… we should discuss how we intend to approach nobles at Amsterdam, now that it's only a couple days away."

Kip nodded. "Can we just tell them we need money to keep the school open?"

"Abigail says that it's not wise to confess how much you need money. It puts them off."

"How does one approach them, then?"

"You talk about how you'd like to do more for the students, but sadly, you haven't got quite enough, and while you don't need their money, it would certainly help. Even though we only have four masters technically employed by the college, that's four masters we have to provide room and board and salary for—stop, I know you don't want to take money, but Alice isn't working and you have a family to support. So unfortunately we will probably have to offer sorcery in exchange for money."

"That doesn't feel right." Kip got up and swung his tail back and forth.

"What, selling sorcery for money? You did as much with Old John."

"That was different." He stopped and stared past Emily, as though they were in New Cambridge and he could see down the hill to the Founders Rest Inn. "I was doing work, little jobs, and John was giving me a place to live. What sorcery could I do that would be worth the amount we need? These moneyed people should be contributing because they want to invest in American sorcerers and help make us great."

"They've got the New Cambridge school for that." Emily made a face. "I guarantee you that Master Colonel Jackson, the great hero of the Revolutionary War, has no trouble getting his friends to contribute."

"Hasn't Mr. Adams said more than once that these two colleges are his best hope for keeping the confederation of states from all going their separate ways? That everyone needs our protection?"

"I suppose one college fills that need as well as two. At any rate, whenever I'm invited to meetings, which isn't often, I have to speak up to remind them that we exist, and I'm afraid that this government of men has come to think of me as a nag. Mr. Madison advised me to seek money closer to home, but did not offer to provide any of it, naturally." She scoffed. "Virginians are very quick to propose solutions that do not involve them doing any work."

Kip tapped his foot. "I asked Bryce again about money yesterday. He said that until we get a harvest this fall, they won't have much to spare, but after that the East Georgia government might be able to contribute a little."

"That'll help. But it doesn't sound hopeful to keep us going even through the winter."

The fox shook his head. "And with no promises from our country, even though we helped end the war—"

"The position that East Georgia was our reward is a not unreasonable one." Emily smiled.

"I know, I know." Kip heaved a sigh and stood, then walked over to Emily's window and set his paws beside her raven, looking out over the entrance to the school, where large wrought iron gates leaned against the nearly-complete posts, waiting to be hung. Beyond the gates, a short brick path led to the town of Peachtree. Already the memory of the village when he'd first come to visit his parents felt disconnected from the large, sprawling town below him.

"Hallo, Sleek," he said to the bird, and she bobbed her head in response. He half-turned back to Emily and said, "The school went up quickly and we're all established here, and I have to admit that it's been more peaceful than I'd imagined possible."

"Then don't worry. Come with me to Amsterdam and find some healers to pay with the money I'm going to raise."

He lowered his head, looking inward now. "Do you think Victor will be there?"

"It's a place only for those who can do sorcery," Emily said. "Of course he will find a way in. And so what if he is?"

"It's Victor. I know he's up to something. He won't stop until—"

"Kip."

The fox turned from the window. Emily had turned sympathetic eyes on him. "We all know who he is and what he is. Need I remind you that Albright is gone?"

"'Gone.' Nobody will say whether he's dead, in prison, or simply living at the King's pleasure in hiding somewhere. Perhaps still instructing Victor."

"If you keep obsessing over him—either of them—then they're winning a battle without lifting a finger. Let him go, Kip." Emily waved at her ledger. "Now, if you don't mind, I do need to finish this."

Kip leaned back against the window. "Did Malcolm decide whether he's bringing the students to the Exposition? If he's not going, I don't mind sharing a room there with you if it would save the school some money. We've done it before."

She raised an eyebrow and pulled out the drawer from her desk, where the pamphlet he'd brought in still lay. "Have you forgotten this so quickly?"

"Oh." His ears flattened, and he shook his head. "You're right."

"Not that I'd let a penny dreadful stop me from saving the school money if it was important," she said, closing the drawer, "but for one, Malcolm and the students are going, and for another, I rather suspect Alice will want some privacy even from me."

"Alice isn't going." Kip went on in the face of Emily's growing smile. "She's pregnant. She can't. What?"

"Oh," Emily said, "I was just wondering whether I should send Sleek to follow you home so I could watch you try to tell her that.

Back at the house he shared with Alice, Abel, and Abel's cubs, Kip called Alice's name from the small foyer. "In here," she replied from the main bedroom upstairs, and a moment later Kip's raven Ash sailed in from the back of the house to land on his shoulder.

The house, newly built by Calatians from the town in the past year, followed an open floor plan for the warmer climate and its Calatian residents. The foyer led directly to the wide staircase, and to the left and right, large open doorways led to the dining room and parlor, respectively. Both the great oak table in the dining room and the plush blue chairs of the parlor sat empty as Kip passed them, then walked up the stairs and to the main bedroom.

When he walked in, he breathed in Alice's scent and his heart quickened a little, as it often did. She looked lovely in her plain white nightdress, and though each of her paws held a gown, he walked forward quickly to rub his muzzle to hers and rest a paw on her hip. He might have held the kiss longer but for the presence of nine-year-old Arabella sitting next to the bed, who said, "Hallo, Daddy Kip," as he entered.

Alice kissed him back with a bright smile and held up the gowns. "Which one do you think is better? I like the blue one because it's more comfortable, but the yellow one goes better with my fur and also I think it's more formal. Oh, but the blue one would look better under a purple robe."

"I like the blue one," Arabella announced, swinging her legs and tail. "I like patterns better than flowers."

"I do too, but the flowers are more elegant, and there are only a few of them." Alice weighed them and looked again at Kip.

He smiled and shook his head. "There's no point in asking you not to go, is there?"

"None."

"You're—"

He gestured at her midsection, but she cut him off before he could say it. "Yes, I am, and what of it? It'll be months still until that slows me down. After that, yes, there will be a long time where I won't be able to travel or go anywhere interesting. But that time hasn't started yet, and I'm not about to allow it to start now."

Arabella frowned, looking between them. "What's going to slow you down?"

"Remember, you're going to have a new sister or brother?" Alice asked. They had talked, the three of them, about whether to call Alice's cub a "stepsibling," and Kip and Alice had both told Abel that they wanted their cubs to be considered full siblings to Aran and Arabella.

"Ohhh." Arabella put a paw over her own stomach. "It makes you slow?"

Kip walked over to the gowns and touched the yellow one. Ash clicked her beak. "When Aran was little and you carried him around, didn't you have to go slower? And be careful with him?"

Arabella looked back to Alice. "Yes, I see."

"I'm not carrying around anything like Aran's weight yet," Alice said, "and it's only a few days in Amsterdam. Emily will send me right back if there's any trouble. Besides," she added, "there's more likely to be healers there than here. And if I'm to be a sorcerer, I should be a sorcerer whenever I can and want. And I can, and I do want."

"All right, all right." Kip had little desire to pursue the argument; being in her presence reminded him that he did want her to come along.

"Speaking of…" Alice paused. "Do you think you might ask one of the sorcerers there about your dream?"

"I'm done with that." He pulled the sleeve of the yellow gown up. "I like the pattern on this one better. Where's Abel? Have you told him we're going?"

"Not officially, but I'm sure he's worked it out."

"Daddy's out in the garden," Arabella said.

"Do you want time with him tonight?" Alice asked. "I don't mind. I'll be busy packing, and we'll be together over in Amsterdam."

"Thank you," Kip said, turning to the door. "I know it's out of turn, but I think so, if that's all right."

"It's fine. Ara, darling, would you fetch my petticoats from the chest there?"

Down the stairs and behind them led Kip to the back door, which opened onto a wide porch. Beyond that lay the garden, only now starting to show results of the planting they'd done a month ago. Abel and Aran knelt in the dirt, pulling weeds from between the small shoots, the smaller fox mimicking his father's motions with frequent looks for reassurance. A warm earthy smell with notes of green and of the two foxes filled the air.

"Is that a weed?" Aran asked as Kip approached them.

"I don't think so." Abel examined it. "But we can wait until Mrs. Pole comes around tomorrow and we'll ask her." He saw Kip and stood, smiling, ears perked. "We'll learn in another year," he said, "and I wager Aran will be a better gardener than any of us."

The nine-year-old cub wagged his tail and showed Kip the weeds he'd pulled. "That's wonderful," Kip said. "Our plants will grow tall and strong for sure."

"And have lots of strawberries!" Aran said.

"The strawberries are over there." Abel pointed. "They should be ready in another month or two."

The cub clapped his paws, sending pieces of weed scattering over the ground. Kip laughed. "I hope they're as good as the ones we got from Savannah last year."

"They will be." Aran touched his nose. "The plants smell sweet."

"Go take a look at them." Abel gave the cub a pat on the shoulders.

Aran needed no more encouragement; he ran along the garden to the shady patch of ground where the dark green strawberry plants spread their leaves. Ash took off from Kip's shoulders and soared over the cub, circling around him once and then landing on the nearby shed. Kip shifted to Ash's view for a moment out of habit, and then back to himself when Abel said, "Alice was packing, so I presume you couldn't talk her out of going to the Exposition?"

Kip shook his head. "She pointed out that there would be better healers there anyway."

"Hopefully not for long."

"That's part of the idea." Kip smiled.

Abel looked at him for a long moment. "Maybe someone there can explain your dream?"

"If I feel the need to be laughed at in Amsterdam as I was in Boston, I'll ask." Kip smiled. "I'm sorry. I know you mean well."

Abel looked neither offended nor amused. "It's not an ordinary dream. You've said that."

"I know. Maybe you're right. Maybe there will be someone there who can help."

"All right." The other fox met his eyes. "It's a lot of weight you're carrying. Can I help with any of it?"

Kip draped an arm over his shoulders, breathing in Abel's scent. Though very different from Alice's, it also reminded him of the joy that was present in his life. "You can look after Aran and Arabella, and help with Alice's cub when it arrives. And spend tonight with me. Alice said it was all right."

"That I can do." Abel answered Kip's smile with one of his own.

"And keep talking to the Isle Calatians. If you can find us two more students as good as Jorey, that'll be a great start to the next class."

"I can do that as well. Jorey himself will be the best ambassador, though. Take him back to the Isle to show them what he's learned."

"Maybe we'll stop there on the way back." Kip squeezed Abel and then dropped his arm.

Aran had finished inspecting the strawberries and now ran back to them, into his father's arms. "They look healthy," he announced.

"Good." Kip reached down to rub between the cub's ears; he flattened them and smiled. "I'll be gone for a few days and I'm counting on you to keep them looking healthy until I get back."

"You're taking Jorey with you?" Abel asked.

"We're taking all three of the students," Kip said. Ash flew back from the shed to land on his shoulder. "Malcolm thinks it'll be good for them, and it'll show people that we're a real school. We won't tell them that three is the entire class. Though they might figure it out. Why else would we bring a Calatian and a woman? Never mind that Jorey and Charity show more promise than Richard."

"I imagine Master Vendis will be pleased to have a break." Abel smiled. "Whenever he comes to dinner, he looks as though he's been trying to chase them all around the town."

"I wouldn't be surprised if both he and Argent spend the whole week soaking in a bath. I only have the children for one class and they're exhausting. I don't know how he manages every morning. In our classes with Patris, we were so quiet. Is it something we're doing wrong?"

"They're not afraid of you." Abel gave a slight smile.

"I'm not afraid of you," Aran echoed. "I think you're a very nice second father."

"That's good." Kip crouched down to be at the cub's level. "Because you're a smart, wonderful little fox, and I love you very much."

Aran detached himself from Abel to go hug Kip. "Do you think I'll be magic too one day?"

"We'll see." Kip had watched, but neither he nor Abel nor Alice had seen any sign that Aran or Arabella had any more access to magic than their father. "Maybe in a couple years we'll play some games and see how you do."

"Good." The cub's little tail wagged.

Kip let go and stood. "I suppose I should get ready to go, too."

"Come on, Aran," Abel said. "Let's help your second father pack."

CHAPTER TWO: AMSTERDAM

The Dutch school of sorcery, the Athæneum Maleficis Artibus, had a translocating room for visiting sorcerers in the basement. When Kip heard this, he thought of the basement full of moldy paper that he and Coppy and Emily had been assigned to upon matriculating at Prince George's College, but this basement smelled clean and fresh and the floor felt slick and clean under his feet. Someone had even placed fresh-cut tulips on small tables around the edges of the room, which had given the air a light honey scent.

"Come on." Emily pushed Kip and Alice forward. Ash fluttered to keep her balance but stayed on Kip's shoulder. "We can't stand here in the center."

"Nobody's going to translocate on top of us," Kip said, but hurried toward the door.

"No, but the point of this room is that it's big and empty and it's supposed to be easy, so let's keep it easy. Hendrik keeps telling me that it's busier than usual because of the Exposition."

Scents underlay the flowers, a composition Kip remembered from previous visits to Amsterdam. The plants and dirt and water and people contributed to a smell unique to this city, one that grew stronger as they stepped from the translocating room out into a small foyer where a clerk sat behind a small mahogany desk.

Alice wrinkled her nose, dropping back as Emily stepped up to give their names. "What's that…that kind of <*mintbit*> smell?" she asked Kip.

He inhaled and sorted through the scents. "Coriander," he said. "It grows around many of the gardens here."

"I like it."

"Me too." He stepped up to Emily's side to face the young woman behind the desk wearing purple apprentice's robes similar to Alice's. "Good morning," he said.

"It's evening here, sir." She spoke excellent English with a Dutch accent. "Would you be so kind as to sign our ledger please?"

Kip took the proffered quill, dipped it in ink, and signed his name on the indicated space below Emily's. Alice reached out at his side to take the quill when he was done, signing quickly so that the ink didn't have time to dry.

"Thank you so much," the woman said, taking the quill back. "Welcome to Amsterdam. Is there anything I may assist you with?"

"I'm to talk to Master de Wees," Emily said. "Is he upstairs in the common room?"

The woman beamed. "Just so. He is welcoming new arrivals. If you are with a group, you will be assigned an apprentice to show you to your quarters."

"We're from the Lutris School in America," Emily said. "I'll be right back with the others."

Her raven, Sleek, took off from her shoulder to land on Alice's, and a moment later Emily vanished. The apprentice cleared her throat. "Excuse me," she said, and tapped the ledger, her eyes wide. "Could you please tell Master Carswell how much I owe to her?"

"Owe to her?" Kip frowned. "Did she loan you—"

Alice put a paw on his arm. "Of course we can," she said, "but you should tell her yourself. She is quite pleasant. How long have you been an apprentice?"

"Oh!" The young woman sat up at the sound of Alice's voice and looked quickly at the ledger, "I had not realized—Apprentice Penfold? I thought you to be Master Penfold's brother."

"I'm his wife." Alice smiled. "It's all right. In robes, we foxes look very similar to you."

"I have met many Calatians. I did not think—" Her cheeks reddened.

"What's your name?" Kip asked, in as friendly a voice as he could.

"Apprentice de Groot, sir."

Malcolm and Jorey, a young red squirrel in student's robes, came through the door in that moment. Corvi, Malcolm's raven, looked alertly around the room from his perch on the sorcerer's shoulder as Malcolm reached back, feeling for the door to close it behind them.

"Good evening," Apprentice de Groot said. "Please sign the—" She gasped, seeing Malcolm's eyeless face for the first time.

Malcolm walked confidently to the desk and put his fingers on the ledger. "This book?" he asked.

"Y-yes, sir."

As Malcolm signed, Jorey came up beside him, bushy tail twitching. The squirrel glanced at Kip, who gave him an encouraging smile, and then spoke to Apprentice de Groot. "Master O'Brien's appearance may be off-putting," he said, "but don't let him startle you with it. He has sorcery to allow him to see as well as anyone—better, even."

The young woman seemed grateful to have another face to focus on. "I—I meant no—"

"He knows you didn't." Jorey took the pen from Malcolm and added his name to the ledger.

"He can speak for himself, young student," Malcolm said, though he smiled.

"Sorry, sir." Jorey put the quill down. "I'll hold my tongue."

"Aye, well." Malcolm put a hand on the squirrel's shoulder and guided him to one side. "Let's set our sights on something attainable before we go reaching for the moon, shall we?"

Before Jorey could reply, the other two students arrived, followed by Emily. The taller, a fair-skinned boy whose white robes bore dirt on the sleeves and hem, strode first to the table, smiling under his mop of red hair as he stuck out a hand to Apprentice de Groot. "Good day," he said. "I'm Richard Farmer, student at the Lutris School of Sorcery. It's a true pleasure to meet you and visit your country. May I have the honor of knowing your name?"

"Oh, ah." Apprentice de Groot's cheeks reddened further. She took his hand. "It's Jan, thank you."

"Thank you for welcoming us to your lovely city." Richard brought her hand briefly to his lips. "It's so inspiring to see another woman joining us in the ranks of sorcery."

"I only just became an apprentice last month," she said.

"What area are you specializing in?"

"I'm going to be a translocational sorcerer."

Emily nudged the third student, a young girl with light brown skin and black hair, up to the table as Richard said with genuine enthusiasm, "That's wonderful! I would love to be able to travel, but I fear my talents lie more with the physical."

"Oh, there's so much to learn with physical magic," Jan said. "I couldn't master very much of it myself—" She noticed the third student and composed herself. "I'm so sorry. Richard, can you please sign the ledger, and then..." She inclined her head to the girl.

"Charity," the girl said. "It's lovely to meet you. I'm to be a translocational sorcerer as well."

Emily came to stand beside Kip, both of them watching Richard as he signed the book. "He reminds me of Victor," Emily said in a very low voice, "but not in the bad ways."

"He means the things he says," Kip said. "And he actually has magical talent."

Emily nodded. "Still, I worry a little about him."

"I worry about all of them. But they'll watch out for each other."

Richard watched as Charity signed the ledger, and then the two of them joined Jorey off to the side, whispering to each other while keeping an eye on their teachers for guidance. Kip smiled. "They remind me of us," he said. "The three of us, I mean."

Emily nodded. "Except they don't have other students to fear."

"No." Kip put an arm around Alice's shoulders. "We've done that right, at least."

Apprentice de Groot gazed at Richard for a moment and then came back to herself and raised a hand to Emily. "If you please, Master Carswell, Master de Wees will be awaiting you."

"Yes, thank you." Emily smiled. "Come along, everyone."

Master de Wees, a tall bearded sorcerer who looked to be Kip's father's age, greeted Emily with a very rehearsed, "Welcome to the International Exposition of Sorcery. We are delighted to have delegations from all over the world given the chance to visit our lovely city and share knowledge of sorcery." He didn't introduce himself to nor ask the names of any of the other six people trailing behind Emily.

They left the Athæneum, which gave the students a chance to look back at it. Charity gasped, and though the other two remained silent, both of them stopped with her to stare at the ornate mansion's elegantly curved roof, coming to a sharper peak than they were accustomed to seeing, below which ran a band of gilded reliefs depicting acts of sorcery. Below that, a series of windows, each framed in a small stone archway, looked out over the plaza they stood in. But the most striking feature was the door through which they'd just passed, a great ebony slab with gold handles, and the gold inscription across the stone above it.

Emily had told Kip that the inscription meant, "From the world of the spirit by our will into reality," a quotation from the famous Dutch Master Hoeneck, who had financed the building in the 1700s. But Kip liked the look of the Dutch words: "Geestkracht maakt macht."

"Crikey," Richard said. "Why doesn't our school look like that?"

"Cause we haven't any money," Jorey answered promptly.

"That's enough," Emily said. "This building was built three hundred years ago on the orders of the King of Holland. Our school was built by our own hands and our people. If one of you turns out to be an accomplished sculptor, you may feel free to add your designs to the walls. Until then, you're here to learn about sorcery, not buildings."

"Yes'm." Jorey put his ears back, and Richard and Charity might as well have. They hurried on with Malcolm guiding them behind Master de Wees, who had folded his arms at the delay and now strode quickly forward again.

The Hotel Drijvende Bloem, not nearly as elaborate as the school, still looked more elegant than any building in Peachtree, with a bright clay brick facing and light sandstone trim. It jutted from the street into the canal with a flower-lined walkway around it that burst with color—though this close to the canal, Kip and Alice could definitely smell the water even over the flowers. On the street side, the hotel wall stood mostly flat with sharp peaks to the roof, but the end closest to the canal curved to match the U-shape of the walkway, and where it rejoined the main body of the hotel, the building bore interestingly sharp corners.

In the stark marble-floored lobby, Master de Wees cast about the crowd of people going back and forth and finally waved down a harried-looking balding man in a well-appointed suit. "Heinrich," he said, "These are the Americans."

"Ah, a pleasure! I am the concierge," the man said, shaking Emily's hand. "Heinrich Schmidt, at your service. I'll just call a bellhop to show you to your rooms. Have you any luggage?"

"We do," Emily said, "but I'll fetch it to the rooms directly once we know where they are."

"These are sorcerers," Master de Wees explained, and turned to Emily. "Are you situated? I apologize but I am awaiting three more delegations."

"Yes, thank you. I look forward to seeing you…" She trailed off as Master de Wees turned and walked away in the middle of her sentence. "Later, I suppose."

"Rude," Alice said.

"He's busy." Emily turned back to Schmidt. "We'll wait until a bellhop is available."

Ten minutes later, a boy of fifteen led them up two flights of stairs to three adjacent rooms. Each looked the same except that one room had an additional set of cushions on the floor next to the two simple beds. "We're in this one," Malcolm said, ushering Richard and Jorey into it. "You two may share one of the beds or take turns on the floor, as you like."

Emily and Charity took the second room, and Kip and Alice the third. The bellhop told Emily, "Facilities are at the end of the hall, shared with all the rooms. There's a pot if you don't wish to walk down there in the night."

"Thank you," Emily said, and then, because the bellhop still stood expectantly, she dug out her purse and put a ten-cent coin in his hand.

He looked at it with puzzlement, then shrugged and slipped it into his pocket. "Much obliged," he said, and departed.

While Emily went back to Peachtree to get their luggage, Malcolm sat the three students down on one of the beds in his room, with Kip and Alice standing behind him. "I want each of you to make the most of this time," he said. "The school is paying for you to have three days in Amsterdam because we believe you have a lot to learn here at the Exposition, and I've personally told Headmistress Carswell that you'll make it worth the school's money."

"Yes, sir," they chorused. Both Charity and Richard sat very still, but Jorey couldn't keep from kicking his legs, and his bushy tail kept twitching.

"All right. Now, you've all got your specialty, so I want you to go find an exhibit relating to your specialty from another college, study it, take notes, and make a report to me on it. One for each of the first two days. Understood?" They nodded. "On the third day, I want you to find an exhibit relating to another area of magic, one that isn't yours, study it, and write a report."

"Sir?" Jorey raised a paw. "Are the reports to be written while we're here?"

"No. You'll have a week to write them once we return. So take good notes."

Charity raised a hand. "May we write about the same exhibits? I mean, there will be some that fit the first two days for one of us and the third for another."

"Yes, excellent," Malcolm said. "Aye, if you like, you may write about the same one. You may discuss it, but I want you to take your own notes."

Jorey raised his paw again. "Sir, what if the sorcerers won't talk to me or Charity?"

"Explain politely that you are a student of sorcery at the Lutris School. If you need to talk to someone and they refuse, come get one of us."

They had no more questions and were about to be dismissed to go to bed when Kip thought of something. "If any of you encounter a man named Victor Adamson, of King's College probably, do not speak to him, and come report it to one of us immediately."

"And be on your guard," Malcolm added. "Don't let another sorcerer touch you. That's how spiritual sorcerers cast spells on you."

"Yes, sir," they chorused, eyes wide.

"Are we going to be taught spiritual sorcery?" Richard asked.

"We're hoping to find an instructor to take on that task," Kip said. "At least the basics—learning to defend yourself and so on."

Though they told the students to sleep, none of the four adults were very tired, and Emily thought the college could afford to buy them each one drink, so Kip, Alice, and Malcolm followed her downstairs to the hotel's bar. The ravens (save for Corvi, who always stayed with Malcolm) remained behind in the room with a small basin of water, perched by the open windows so they could come and go as they pleased.

"I haven't seen your classes in a while," Emily told Malcolm as they walked. "You've gotten even better at teaching."

"Ah, it's kind of you to say." He smiled. "But what is teaching but talking, and talking I've been doing all my life."

"It's not just talking," Alice said. "You have a good sense for how to get people to pay attention to the right things. I wouldn't have thought to ask them to look at exhibits outside their specialty."

"Me da used to say, if a man isn't well-rounded then he's well flat, and I've always thought that a wise thing to keep in mind. Haven't we all benefited from learning in places we never might have thought?"

"True enough," Kip said. "But also they all really like you."

"Well, that's easy." Malcolm turned to smile. "I'm quite affable by nature, and my disability instantly elicits sympathy, so everyone is well-disposed to me on first meeting and I've a good touch for not making them feel otherwise as time goes on. With my classes, I try to remember the teachers I liked best and learned from best, remember what they said and how they acted, and do the best I can to imitate them."

"You're doing a lovely job," Emily said, "and I'm saying that as the headmistress."

"Oh aye?" They'd reached the foot of the stairs, where Malcolm stood aside so that Emily could walk through first. "And what does Emily Carswell say of it?"

Emily stopped on the other side until Malcolm had come through and then threaded her arm in between his arm and his side. "She says you're lovely as well."

CHAPTER THREE: DIERENPARK

Over drinks—a warm milk for Emily, a more exotic cocoa for the foxes and Malcolm—they discussed their own responsibilities for the following days. Emily had made a list of wealthy nobles who might be willing to sponsor the school, and she and Kip had made a list of questions for him to ask healers who might be interested in coming to teach at the Lutris School.

"You're not bad at this administration job, come to that," Malcolm said with a smile. "What's my homework?"

"And mine?" Alice asked.

"Malcolm, you help Kip in his search and be available if the students need you. Alice, if you don't mind, I'd like you to accompany me."

"Of course." Alice rested her paw on Kip's.

"As one of the heroes of the American War, you'll be very helpful. Be ready to tell your stories of the battles."

"Kip has better stories," Alice said.

"Not true," Kip protested.

"Kip needs to talk to healers, and any other interesting sorcerers who might be willing to teach Calatians." Emily smiled at both of them. "Kip's reputation as the sorcerer who destroyed the Road—"

Kip let out a long sigh and rubbed his eyes with a paw. Emily went on.

"Though we all know the truth of it, Kip's reputation is great enough that he needn't be present. Having another sorcerer there will add to the strength of our pitch."

"And I'd much rather not have to tell that story again." Kip raised his head. "Nobody wants to hear any of the other ones."

"All right. I can tell the story of the Thames escape. After all, Kip slept through part of that." Alice smiled and put on an earnest tone. "'You know about the destruction of the Road, but did you know that there was an entire adventure simply to get to that point?'"

"Excellent." Emily sipped her milk. "Even just one wealthy patron could change our fortunes substantially."

"Cheers," Kip said, and lifted his cup.

The cocoa had a nice earthy sweetness to it that coated his palate and built in his nostrils before subsiding after each sip. Kip liked it and Alice seemed to as well; though it was strong, it wasn't overwhelming, even though it had not been diluted for foxes.

When they'd finished their drinks and the attendant conversation, they got up to leave. Kip turned and came face to face with the manager who'd greeted them when they arrived. "Begging your pardon, sir, but would you be Master Kip Penfold?"

"Aye," Kip said. Alice took his arm and perked her ears attentively as well.

The manager produced an envelope and held it out. "A gentleman brought this and was most insistent that we relay it to you at the earliest possible opportunity."

Kip took the envelope. "A gentleman?" Alice asked.

The manager nodded. "A Calatian of the rabbit persuasion."

The letter inside the envelope, a single sheet of paper, bore writing in a familiar hand. Kip didn't need to read the signature before he said, "It's from Charles Cotton." To the manager, he said, "Did the gentleman wait?"

"No, sir."

"Thank you for finding me so quickly." Remembering the bellhop waiting for a tip, Kip leaned over to Alice, who had charge of all their money. "Have you, er…" Ten cents seemed too little for the manager, but a whole dollar? "Have we any coin?"

"Sir." The manager held up a hand as Alice dug into her purse. "There's no need." But he smiled, and it seemed to Kip to be a genuine smile. "We are most grateful for the service you have provided to our country." He bowed and then, as though flustered by his own display of emotion, hurried back to the lobby.

Malcolm and Emily joined them as Kip read the letter. "Dear Kip," he read aloud, "Please excuse the forward nature of this letter. I learned that the visitors from America would be staying at the Drijvende Bloem, and so I delivered the letter here. I do hope that tonight, if possible, you will be able to come visit Dierenpark again. It has been far too long since your last visit and I would be delighted to show you the progress we've made here before the Exposition takes all your time and attention. Should you receive this letter in time, please come to The Glade at any time before midnight and I will meet you there. Very sincerely yours, Charles Cotton."

"What's 'The Glade'?" Alice asked.

"A public house in Dierenpark; that's the Calatian neighborhood."

"Oh! Can we go?" Alice rested a paw on Kip's wrist.

"It would be rude not to," Emily said.

"I suppose so." Kip had hoped to put off seeing the Calatians until he'd settled a bit, but Charles was his closest friend here, and keeping their friendship in good order was important. Besides, he could feel the rabbit's impatience behind the restrained wording of the letter, and the prospect of seeing Charles again did lift his spirits. "What time is it now?"

"Just past ten-thirty," Emily pointed to a showy gilded clock in the hotel lobby.

"Well, it's only fifteen minutes to walk there, as I recall. My knowledge of Amsterdam is not exhaustive, though."

"If you wouldn't mind some company," Malcolm put in, "I can have Dar guide us."

"Are you sure you wouldn't rather get a good night's sleep?" Emily asked Malcolm. "After all, there's the address to open the Exposition in the morning."

"And I'm sure you'll give us all a splendid report on it." Malcolm smiled. "A little joke, there. I'll be back with Kip before the clock's struck one, and sure, isn't it just going on dinnertime by the clock we woke to this morning? I'd lie awake until one in the morning anyway."

Emily gave a theatrical sigh. "Very well, I suppose only one of us need be responsible."

"Fostering good relationships with the Calatians—" Kip said.

Emily laughed, interrupting. "I mean of me and Malcolm. Of course you must go, and Alice too. Find us some more students."

"To that end," Malcolm said, "what would you say to bringing Jorey? Provided he's not yet asleep."

Kip nodded. "It would be good for him, and for them."

Jorey was not asleep, it turned out, and was eager to meet more Calatians. "Richard wanted to come too," the squirrel informed them in the lobby, "but Malcolm said that one human was enough. How many Calatians live in Amsterdam?"

"Somewhere between seventy-five and a hundred and fifty," Kip told him, ushering the squirrel to follow Malcolm and Alice outside. "I only brought the first community over two years ago and I know more have arrived since then."

Daravont, Malcolm's demon, knew Amsterdam no better than Kip did but, unlike the fox, was able to fly forward invisibly and find The Glade in relation to where they were. Besides being a guide, the demon whispered to Malcolm where people lurked in the shadows, possibly meaning them harm, and guided them around those spots. Their ravens remained on their shoulders, hunched against the mist and shadows around them.

Kip kept Jorey close to himself so he could send the squirrel home at the first sign of trouble—not that he was particularly worried about cutpurses, nor even cutthroats for that matter. Sorcery could handle even the worst of them, and no mere human with a knife could scare Kip after the things he'd faced. But he did not wish to draw any extra attention to himself, and getting into a street fight, however lopsided, would certainly do that.

Though Kip could see well enough in the monochromatic moonlight, he preferred to explore the streets by the odors that presented themselves to his nose. At night, the smell of the harbor carried over that of the flowers, but Daravont led them away from that miasma. The smells of yeast and bread signaled a street of bakers, and fermented yeast on the next street a series of public-houses. (These also announced themselves via the muted roar of conversation and laughter emanating from the brightly lit windows.)

Besides these smells, there were smells of meat and of pastries, of clothing and simple machinery, and people, so many people, more than Kip could distinguish. Odors flitted through his nose like stars in the sky, each one distinct and then immediately lost among the others. He'd walked through streets in Boston and New York, but only London's crowded neighborhoods could compare to this.

Someday, Kip thought, there will be a city of Calatians this crowded. Street after street of narrow houses, thousands of Calatians in one place, and not for a strategic reason.

(There was a movement to name the inlet where he'd taken thousands of Calatians during the war, "Calatian Bay," but the movement was complicated by the fact that Australia was still a British holding and the British were not particularly inclined to commemorate the single event that had most contributed to their loss.)

Finally they came to a crossroads where a large sign proclaimed "Welkom bij Dierenpark." Jorey said, "Dierenpark," as they walked past the sign. "That's a pretty name. Do you know what it means?"

"It means, 'zoo,'" Kip said, and Jorey fell quiet.

From here, he knew the way: one street in and a right-hand turn. Alice walked quietly at his side, Malcolm a little behind. The scent here changed; Alice caught it too. Rather than humans, there was rabbit, badger, weasel, mouse, and fox. There were still scents of clothing and of food shops, less meat and machinery and more bread and pastries and vegetables.

And there was the smell of ale, and there was the sound of conversation and laughter. The windows of The Glade weren't brightly lit, because many Calatians saw well at night, but they stood out from the rest of the darkened street as though they'd had a half-dozen lanterns blazing behind the glass.

Ash fluttered on his shoulder as they walked in, muttering annoyance at the light and sound. It took Kip a moment to make details out of the wash of brightness that his eyes saw at first, and in those seconds the conversation dipped and muted. He thought that it was because he and Alice had walked in, strangers, and then he heard someone say, "What's the furless doing here?"

"Now, now, now!" That cheerful voice he recognized. Charles Cotton bounded up to the three of them. "It's only been two years; can you not recognize the sorcerer O'Brien, the one who stood watch over us while we waited for his friend…"

He paused dramatically. Kip's adjusted eyes now saw almost the entire clientele of the public house staring at them. Though a small community, there was only one public house, so every table was occupied, nearly thirty people all told. "Master Kip Penfold," Charles said in a ringing voice, "to win the war for us!"

A pumped fist concluded this declaration, and the audience responded with a great cheer, and with even more excitement than Charles may have intended. Several of them came up out of their seats to greet Kip and Alice and even Malcolm.

But there were those, Kip noted, who turned away, and some of those muttered to each other. Then he occupied himself with the people who did want to greet him, and he shook paws and smiled. Alice, like Kip, had had a good deal of practice being an object of interest, and she greeted people as much as he did.

Jorey provided some chatter behind them. "Master Penfold's wonderful," he said, and, "I'm one of his students, you know," and other things in a similar vein. He continued even when these statements went mostly unheeded by the Calatians seeking to meet Kip and Alice and Malcolm.

"Come, come," Charles cried, and guided them over to a table against one of the walls. Someone at one of the tables they passed said, "Go, go," too faintly for Kip to identify the voice; he did not want to show them it had bothered him, so he didn't even turn around to see who was at the table. He knew there were those who disliked him for bringing them to Amsterdam. There was nothing he could do about it.

"I have been wondering," Kip said, "how you mean to show us Dierenpark this late at night. Surely all your shops and schools are closed?"

"They are." Charles stopped and gestured to the table, where sat another fox, two mice, a badger, and a weasel. "But the people who have made them the successes they are sit here before you. Letitia Trewel you know."

This was one of the mice, a dormouse. Kip had met her two years ago when he had to tell her of the death of her brother Thomas at the Battle of the Road. "Of course," he said. She smiled back at him. At the time, she hadn't held him responsible for Thomas's death, though he felt acutely that he could have saved him, and he was glad that time had not altered her disposition.

"And the rest of them are," he pointed around in quick succession. "Martin Canno, Donna Lyle, Esau Brock, and Lifkin Quick." These were the fox, the other dormouse, the badger, and the weasel, in that order.

Each of them murmured a greeting as the four sat down. Kip repeated the names to himself to try to impress them into his mind. While he was doing that, Malcolm said, "And the one of us you haven't met yet is Jorey Birch, one of our students at the new school."

"Thank you so much for inviting me—I mean, us—well, you invited Master Penfold and he allowed me to come along—"

Alice broke in with a smile. "It's such a pleasure to meet you all. As we build our town in Peachtree, I wonder how you all are faring in building your community here."

Martin Canno, the other fox, set his ears half-back. "It's a rather different enterprise. We here are not creating a new community out of whole cloth. We have moved into houses from which human occupants were evicted, and we are trying to build relationships in the place of that damage."

"We had to evict human residents too," Kip said. "Well, not 'evict,' but they were granted land elsewhere and I wouldn't think they would want to live on land they didn't own anymore. But many of them weren't happy to leave. A few still refuse."

"But the people left behind." Martin turned to Kip. "You're all Calatians, there in East Georgia."

"And you all got to bring your families with you." This was Lifkin the weasel.

"I thought—" Alice turned to Kip and then back to the table. "You were supposed to be allowed to bring your families."

"Immediate families," the weasel said. "Not my brother and his children, not my aunt nor my cousins."

"We only had room—" Kip started.

"Aye, I know the reasoning. I'm not blaming you." Nearby grumbling; Kip turned his ears away from it. "Simply pointing out the differences between our situations."

"I'm sorry," Alice said.

"I left my family too," Jorey piped up. "I'm from London but I moved to Peachtree to be a student."

"You wouldn't have expected your parents to come, would you?" Lifkin asked.

Jorey flicked his ears back. "They live in a dirty house with six other squirrels," he said. "I'd have liked them to come. But there wasn't room. Maybe next year, I'm told. Once I learn to translocate I'll go see them more often."

Letitia Trewel, closest to Alice, reached out a paw. "I'd love to visit Peachtree someday," she said. "But when we talk about what we've done here, it's important you understand what surrounds us. The school, for example. Back on the Isle, I had my pick of helpers, people to take care of the children as well as help with the lessons. Here I only have one helper, and often we have to take care of the children after school when their parents are working. But we've held regular classes for the last six months, and last month a Dutch teacher came to observe and help us."

"So having the humans around isn't always a bad thing?" Kip asked.

"Not always." Esau Brock grinned widely. "I've taken a good deal of inspiration from the bakeries here." He patted his belly. "As you can see. The bakers, at least, are pleased to teach me a few new tricks. Many of the people understand that our presence here elevates their country into the top tier of world powers again and are grateful for that."

"Aye," Lifkin said. "And we're not having disappearances like back in London."

"What?" Kip and Alice said it at the same time, ears standing straight upright.

"I'd have thought you'd have heard about it." The weasel gestured with a paw. "My brother told me two healthy fellows have disappeared in the last two months."

Malcolm, too, had leaned forward with interest. "The British aren't fighting a war they haven't told us about, are they?"

"We wouldn't know if they did," Alice pointed out.

"They weren't calyxes that disappeared," Lifkin said.

"Ah." Malcolm rested his elbows on the table. "Kip, hasn't Abel mentioned it?"

Kip shook his head. "Well—he did say that people were worried about the safety of the calyxes, but not why, and..." And that had been Grinda, and she was always worried about sorcerers, and had Kip discounted her worries because of that? He bit his lip. "We should have been told."

"Perhaps they don't wish to call on you to solve any more of their problems," Lifkin said.

"Lif," Charles said reprovingly.

"No, that's fair." Kip sighed. "It's not mine to worry about."

Malcolm elbowed him. "Not that that's ever stopped this fellow in the past."

"We've plenty to worry about," Alice said, but her voice was uncertain. Below the table, her paw touched Kip, a reassurance that the matter was not closed. "But if there is anything we can do to help, should you hear..."

"Or for you here," Kip added. "Our purpose in coming was to see what you've accomplished, and I did not wish to assume you needed anything from us, but it's freely offered if you do."

"I should like to take the cubs we teach to Peachtree." Letitia looked around. "For a visit, to show them more of the world. Is that something you can do?"

"Of course," Alice said. "It's not something I can do easily, but Emily specializes in it and Kip and Malcolm can each do some as well."

"And Master Argent," Kip said.

"And Charity," Jorey reminded them. "She hasn't actually translocated yet, but she will."

"One of our other students," Kip clarified. "How many cubs?"

"Only ten."

"Then we could take them in three trips, perhaps four. It would not be a great imposition."

Lifkin spoke up. "Could you also bring some of us back to London from time to time?"

"Have you not asked the masters at the college here?" Malcolm asked.

"Didn't know we could." The weasel sat back. "They're not Calatians."

"I'll speak to them," Kip said. "It's not an unreasonable request."

The conversation turned to the other shops: Lifkin was a tailor and Donna Lyle, the quiet mouse, a carpenter. She'd learned from her father and here in Amsterdam had opened her own shop because there were no others with the skill. Surprisingly, she did a good deal of business with the humans of Amsterdam. "They think I'm a man," she said with a laugh. "So I deepen my voice a touch when they come in."

Alice laughed at this. "There are some advantages to being a Calatian, I dare say."

Kip kept his ears perked, but if there were more abusive comments directed his way, he did not hear them, and eventually he relaxed and enjoyed the rest of the conversation. But the disappearances from the Isle weighed on his mind even after he, Alice, Malcolm, and Jorey had taken their leave and returned to the hotel.

CHAPTER FOUR: TRIPPENHUIS

I did warn you." Emily couldn't keep the exasperation from her tone.
Kip yawned again, and Alice rubbed her eyes. Malcolm appeared as awake as he ever did, except when he too stifled a yawn. "Woke too early," he grumbled. "Surely there must be a spell to help one get a reasonable night's sleep?"

"That'd be a healer's spell," Emily said, "and God willing, Kip won't be too tired to find us someone who can cast it."

"I'm fi-ine," Kip insisted, his assurance belied by the yawn that interrupted it. "Once we get there, I'll find the energy."

"What did you all talk about last night, anyway?" Emily set a quick pace as they left the hotel to walk along the street toward Trippenhuis, the palatial hall where the Exposition was held. Malcolm and Alice trailed behind them, and their students brought up the rear of their little party, Jorey yawning as much as Kip and Alice were.

"The Calatian community in Amsterdam. There are some people still angry with me for the arrangement, but Charles and his friends are doing well. Oh," he remembered, "and there have been Calatians disappearing in London."

Emily's frown deepened. "I don't like the sound of that."

"Nor do I. Charles didn't think much of it, but it worries me."

"Didn't Abel tell you about it?"

"Not all of it," Kip hedged. "Of course, they said that there were two in the last two months, and he was last there a week ago, so he might not have known how many there were. And he and Charles have different sources."

They strode on in silence, and Emily's mouth tightened. "Do you think…"

"Victor? He'd be my first thought."

"And Albright did say that thing about his 'experiments.' Oh, Kip." Despair crept into her face. "Picking on us is one thing, but if he's harming Calatians…"

"He's always harming Calatians one way or another."

"If he's here," Emily said, "maybe I will send him to the middle of the ocean."

"Have you been to the middle of the ocean?" Kip asked.

"Sleek has." Emily touched the raven on her shoulder.

"Whyever for?"

She raised her eyebrows. "In case I want to send someone there. Do try to keep up."

They turned a corner and came in sight of the great mansion Trippenhuis seated neatly between two other large houses. Built after the classical style, the broad face of it featured flat reliefs mimicking great wide columns between which four stories of windows looked out. Atop the columns, a small cornice rose above the roofs of the abutting buildings, setting Trippenhuis apart from them in height as well as design.

At street level, two sets of double doors stood open, and at each, two liveried footmen greeted the stream of people and took their names. Emily led the small group to the nearer doors and produced a small sheaf of papers from the purse she carried.

Even before they met with the footmen, music from inside reached Kip's ears, a light melody on strings. "I don't know this music," Kip heard behind him, and half-turned to see Richard tilting his head, trying to catch the tune. "Maybe when we get inside."

"How could you know the music?" Jorey asked absently, tail twitching as he tried to see past the footmen.

"I know most of the famous works of European composers," Richard said.

Malcolm turned his head. "It's likely a Dutch composer. When you get inside, you'll be able to hear it better."

Kip had not learned any of the composers beyond some Bach and Beethoven, whom he'd thought might be Dutch because of the name. But Richard wrinkled his brow and said, "I don't think I know any Dutch composers," and Richard certainly knew Beethoven if Kip did, so he kept quiet. Before he turned back to where Emily was handing their invitations to the footman, he caught Charity's eye. When she saw this, she rolled her eyes at Richard, and although Kip wanted their students to support each other, he gave her a smile anyway. And then he lifted his nose at a slight tingle, the kind that he felt when a demon was nearby. Not a powerful one, but certainly a demon.

"Come on," Emily said, "let's not linger in the doorway."

She ushered all of them into the first room, where the students gawked at the beautifully painted frescoes and elegant velvet drapes and Kip tried not to. The tingle grew briefly stronger and then faded as he entered the building. A demon watching the doors, then; that made sense.

"Gather round," Malcolm said, but before they could all turn their attention to him, a purple-robed apprentice joined them.

"Hallo," he said in Dutch-accented English, and held out a piece of paper. "Would you like a map to the Exposition?"

"Yes, please." Malcolm's raven turned to see the paper, and Malcolm's hand found it a moment later.

"I can explain the map, if you please."

"That would be delightful, thank you."

The young man took the map back, preoccupied enough that he didn't notice Malcolm's face. "Now, here's the ground floor, where we are right now. To the back you'll find the Salon, where there are a number of tables for visitors to enjoy refreshments and speak to each other. The stairs to the first and second floors are also located from this room." His finger moved along the map. "Beyond the Salon on this floor is the First Exposition Hall, the largest room in the Exposition. Here is where the special events will take place. Tomorrow, Master van Dijk will perform a feat of sorcery that has never been done in an Exposition before!"

Alice half-turned, and Kip put a paw on her shoulder. The students similarly seemed intrigued by this pronouncement, but remained silent. The apprentice, oblivious, went on. "On the first story, you will find exhibitions from European countries. Holland, Spain, France, England, Prussia, and Russia have all sent sorcerers."

"Whom did England send?" Kip asked before he could help himself.

The apprentice glanced up. "I'm afraid I haven't memorized all the names," he said. "But there is a Master Woodhall from England scheduled to perform a feat at the First Exhibition Hall on Wednesday."

"I don't know him," Kip said in response to Emily's look.

"Nor do I." She brushed a strand of hair from her face. "Please, do go on."

"Yes, very good." The apprentice pointed. "On the second story you will find sorcerers from outside Europe. Persia, India, China, Indonesia, and Egypt have all sent sorcerers to the Exposition."

"Now there's a thing," Malcolm said. "I'll have to go talk to those good fellows."

For the first time, the apprentice looked at Malcolm directly. To his credit, he only flinched, and his words came out smoothly. "They have some very interesting sorcery," he said, "though I have not had the chance to explore it fully."

Malcolm took the map back with a smile. "I hope you get the opportunity," he said. "And we appreciate the work you're doing to help others find their ways."

"Yes, of course." The apprentice bowed. "Enjoy the Exposition." And he hurried off without another word.

"What a helpful chap," Malcolm said. "Eh, Corvi?"

His raven clacked its beak in amusement. "All right," he told the students. "You lot, first floor and then second floor. I'll meet you here in the Salon around lunchtime and you'll tell me what exhibits you're going to write about."

"Yes, sir," they chorused, and set off for the Salon.

"Right." Malcolm held out the map. "I think I have a clear picture of where to go. Anyone else want this?"

"I'll take it if nobody else will." Alice reached out, and Malcolm gave it to her.

"Alice, why don't you and I start in the Salon?" Emily said. "I've arranged some meetings, but not until this afternoon. We might as well take this opportunity to be seen."

"I'll go to the second floor with you," Kip said to Malcolm. "I'd like to see the sorcerers from outside Europe."

"Don't forget why we're here," Emily said to Kip.

"The British sorcerers aren't likely to want to come to America," he said, "and we'll ask the Dutch headmaster directly, and the Spanish and French at least are convinced that they are already part of a great nation. They are likely here to take the measure of potential enemies more than for the joy of exploration. Whereas any sorcerers who voyaged here from China or India most likely did so out of curiosity. They may be more open to joining a frontier school."

"I wasn't questioning the order in which you do your task." Emily smiled. "Simply reminding you of it. Don't get lost staring at the fancy sorcery from China and trying to figure out how it works."

"I'll keep an eye on him," Malcolm said. "Or Corvi will, at any rate."

Emily's smile broadened. "I can't imagine what trouble the two of you might get into. All right, I know you know what our mission is here, and what's at stake."

"Of course we do." Kip kissed Alice on the muzzle. "Tell good stories."

She nuzzled him back. "Ask someone about your dream."

The Salon held not only tables, but the string quartet producing the music that filled the building. Alice and Emily found an empty table and sat there, while Kip and Malcolm chose the nearer side door and climbed the stairs behind it. Their ravens flew ahead of them up the stairs while Kip helped Malcolm through the crowd to the first floor and up the empty stair to the second.

The first room they entered was empty enough for the ravens to rejoin them without worrying about being jostled by crowds. Kip lifted his nose to the scents in the hall and caught many new ones, while Malcolm murmured, "So many colors."

Red paper lanterns hung all along one side of the room, below which hung the Chinese flag and another flag with three concentric circles on a black background: red the outermost, then green, and a bright gold at the center. Men—Chinese sorcerers, Kip presumed—stood near the flags in black robes with red trim, and each one bore a gold pendant around his neck. One was in the process of casting a spell that created a beautiful pattern of frost in the air.

On the other side of the room, the green, red, and white of the Egyptian flag hung behind a trio of men in green robes. Unlike the Chinese sorcerers, they had two tables in front of them draped with green cloth and bearing a pair of elaborate white birdcages at either end that held green parakeets with red bills. Between the cages lay some books, a bottle, and a few small glasses.

What few visitors were in the room had gathered around the Chinese sorcerer, and while Kip did want to see the display, he couldn't pass up the opportunity to talk to the Egyptian sorcerers.

As he approached the table, one of them gestured, and the bottle lifted from the table and poured a sweet-smelling liquid into one of the cups, which then rose to Kip's chest height. "Would you care to try some sugarcane juice?" the nearest of the three asked in perfect King's English.

"Thank you." Kip reached out and took the cup, which came free from the spell easily. The juice smelled even stronger close up, and when he took a sip, the sweetness overwhelmed him. "It's very strong," he said.

"Ah." The man smiled. He brushed his mustache with a finger. "We have none of your people in our land. It must be that your taste differs from ours. My apologies."

He reached out, but Kip kept the cup. "I like it," he said, aware that refusing or disliking the drink might give them offense. "I wasn't expecting how strong it is. Like taking many sugars in your tea."

The man's smile grew. "Indeed. My name is Nephi."

"Kip." Kip extended a paw, and the man shook it. "It's a great pleasure to meet you."

"This is Moise and Femi." The man indicated his compatriots. The one called Femi came up and whispered something to Nephi in a language Kip didn't understand. "Ah. Femi says that you are Master Penfold. Is it so?"

"Yes, that's me." Kip took another sip of the sugarcane juice.

Nephi bowed. "In that case, it is a very great pleasure indeed. We stand in awe."

"Oh," Kip said, "there's no need for that."

The smiles remained fixed on Nephi's face, as well as his two colleagues. "What questions have you for us?"

"Tell me about your school," Kip said.

They did so, speaking very generally, of course, and explained that the parakeets were their familiars, in cages more for their protection than for any fear they would escape. Nephi and Femi were what Kip would think of as Masters, and Moise was an apprentice, but more advanced; they called him a "journeyman sorcerer," and from what Kip gathered, this was not a stage to be advanced from necessarily. A sorcerer might spend his whole life as a journeyman and not be thought less of.

"Journeymen," Moise explained, "do God's work among the people. For some, it is a calling. For others..." He brushed a hand modestly down his green robe. "It is where we feel most comfortable. But surely you in America have something like this."

"Er. We used to. Sort of. In New Cambridge, where I grew up, there was a sorcerer's school nearby, and for a while the healer would come down to the town, and sometimes another sorcerer would come as well. But the sorcerers all worked for the Crown—the King—and the government would tell them where to go. Some work on roads and buildings, big projects that benefit everyone, and some work for the military, and we..." He included Malcolm, who was talking to one of the Chinese sorcerers, "study sorcery and educate new sorcerers."

"Yes, we know this." Nephi smiled. "We thought that perhaps having rid yourself of the Crown, you might also have made other changes."

"We have. We have a representative system of government and we're striving to make sure that everyone's interests are balanced. But at the same time, we are a young country and we know that many of the other powers of the world view us as an easy target."

"Surely not," Moise said. "Your colleges of sorcery and your military sorcerers are among the finest in the world."

"Yes, but..." Kip stopped himself before reciting a list of his country's weaknesses to a foreign sorcerer. "I certainly hope the rest of the world shares your views, but the countries that surround us now have a bloody history of taking from one another."

"That surround you in America?" Nephi looked puzzled.

"No, no." Kip made a wide circle with his paw. "Here, in this palace. Holland, England, Spain, France, Prussia."

The sorcerer's face cleared, and he laughed. "How correct you are. My own country has had those periods in its history. Now, I fear, we struggle not to be one of the things taken. But surely you live on a new continent far from the Old World?"

"Far in some ways," Kip said.

"Ah, I take your meaning." Nephi smiled. "Indeed, we had to send a bird on ahead, and then we could jump to the palace."

"And now," Kip said, "you may return whenever you like."

"With each jump, the world grows smaller."

They talked a little longer about how the Egyptian sorcerers found new students, and Kip determined that none of the three was a healer. The healers they knew had little interest in exploration and advancement, and none wished to spend the better part of a week in Amsterdam when they had people to attend to.

Kip gathered from this that their healers treated disease as well as physical injuries, which he had thought only a few healers in the British empire could do. He didn't want to press further; both he and Nephi engaged in the conversation while also holding back important details of their respective colleges and education, and he respected those boundaries. Besides, his main goal was to find a healer, and learning about Egyptian healing practices was helpful but no more so than reading a book about water when you were thirsty.

Two Spanish sorcerers came up as Moise was showing Kip some simple spells he could do with sand. Living near a desert shaped their study of physical magic, and Moise was more skilled with sand than even Alice was. But the Spanish sorcerers barely looked at the sand. "Excuse me," one said to Kip. "You are...Master Penfold, yes?"

"Yes." Kip flicked his ears back. Neither the scent nor the features of the dark-skinned men were familiar.

"If it is not a disturbance," the Spanish sorcerer said, "may we trouble you for the story of the Road?"

From Moise's expression—unsurprised, polite—Kip understood that Moise had known who he was and had been politely refraining from asking him. "I'm sure you've already heard it," he said. "I can't tell you—"

"Of course we would not ask how you did it." The man smiled. "But what was it like, when it disappeared?"

So Kip told the story of the Road between Bristol and New York, how beautiful it had been, how strange it felt to walk along the surface of the ocean with no land in sight anywhere. He talked about how salt had encrusted the surface but you could still see the shimmer of magic, how the waves splashed your feet, how fish swam into view and birds wheeled overhead. He told them how when it disappeared, magic vanished from the world for a moment as though in protest. He left out that the Road had been destroyed by his former mentor Cott, who had perished in the incident, and that Ash, who sat on his shoulder, had been Cott's raven, her binding undone by the destruction of the Great Feat and reformed in the surge of magic returning in its wake.

Ash fidgeted as he told the story. Their bond was strong, and he did not feel anything like fear from her, but all the same he couldn't help thinking that the story upset her a little whenever he told it.

"It is quite incredible," the sorcerer said. "Nobody else alive today has even witnessed the destruction of a Great Feat."

"I suppose not," Kip said, although several of the sailors on Cott's boat were still alive, as far as he knew. "If you'll excuse me, I must go find my friend."

Malcolm had moved to the far end of the room, talking with one Chinese sorcerer. As Kip approached, Corvi turned on Malcolm's shoulder. Without turning himself, Malcolm said, "Ah, here's my distinguished colleague, Master Kip Penfold. Kip, this is…just a moment, I'm certain I won't get it right, and I do apologize for that…Master Li?"

"Li is my family name." The sorcerer bowed to Kip.

Unsure how to respond, Kip bowed back, trying to approximate the motion the other sorcerer had made. It seemed to suffice. "It's a pleasure to meet you," he said.

"Please excuse my imposition," the sorcerer said, "but is it true that you have witnessed the destruction of a Beautiful Miracle?" When Kip frowned, Master Li said, "I apologize. A wondrous magic, one that remains in the world. I do not know the words in English."

Kip's ears went back. "Ah," Malcolm said, "it's true as true can be, and I dearly wish we had time to tell the tale, for it's a grand and stirring one. But Master Penfold and I have agreed to travel through the entire Exposition in a single day, and so sadly we haven't the time to stand and tell the tale again. Should we happen by here tomorrow or the day after, then of course Master Penfold will be delighted to tell his tale, I'm certain."

"I shall eagerly await your return." Master Li bowed again, and again Kip tried to return the bow.

"They have no healers," Malcolm murmured as they left the room.

"Neither did the Egyptians." They passed through a short hallway and then emerged into a larger room, this one housing three countries' delegations. The entire left hand wall had been hung with the flag of India, colorful tapestries showing white-robed Indian men riding elephants, standing among peacocks, and casting spells, often in the presence of tall, blue-skinned men who sometimes had multiple arms.

To the right, two flags Kip didn't recognize shared the wall: one red over white, the other plain white with a gold lion in the center and a sun rising over the lion's back. "I'll take those, shall I?" Malcolm asked, walking to the right and leaving Kip to join the crowd of people talking to the nearly dozen Indian sorcerers.

One of them was casting a spell on a bowl in front of him which appeared to be filled with sugar. The brownish-white granules darkened and flowed together, and a rich sweet smell filled the air. "There you are." The sorcerer raised his head and smiled, speaking with just a trace of an accent. "It is a traditional Indian candy, much like your toffee, I think? But the spices are different. Please. Please." He broke the mass into pieces and held the bowl out to the crowd.

Kip reached forward to take one along with everyone else. On the far side of the crowd, a sorcerer who hadn't noticed him before grabbed the edge of the bowl and pulled it away from Kip's paw. "Sorcerers first," he said.

The Indian sorcerer looked an apology at Kip, but only said, "Please sir, do not touch the bowl."

The other sorcerer let go, grumbling. By this time, several others in the crowd had noticed Kip, and one of them recognized him and elbowed the one who'd pulled the bowl away. "He is a sorcerer, you idiot."

"What?"

"Don't you remember the stories of the war?" From their accents and white skin, Kip judged that they were English, but he didn't know either of them. "That's Penfold. Er—Master Penfold." The man executed a clumsy bow.

Two more Indian sorcerers came over and stood by Kip, examining him with great interest. The sorcerer who'd pulled the bowl from him stared. "Penfold? The one who—?"

"Yes, the one who." His companion pulled him away. "Come on, go make an ass of yourself somewhere else."

At least they hadn't asked for the story. If they were from King's College, they probably knew it well enough already. The remaining sorcerers, however, looked greatly interested, and so Kip, to forestall, asked the Indian sorcerer with the bowl, "I do beg your pardon, but are any of you trained in healing? I have a few questions."

One of the two who'd come up, a middle-aged man with some grey at the temples, stepped forward. "I am a healer," he said. "Have you an ailment?"

"Not exactly." Kip gestured to the side. "May I take a moment of your time?"

"Of course." The sorcerer inclined his head and walked with Kip to a quieter section of his table.

"Thank you." Kip let his tail swing free as he left the small crowd. "My name is Kip Penfold and I come from the Lutris School in America."

"I am Vijay Chakrabarti." The man smiled. "You may call me Vijay if you have difficulty with the surname."

"Chakra-barti," Kip repeated. "Chakrabarti. I will try to remember."

Chakrabarti inclined his head. "Most kind of you, sir. How may I be of assistance?"

"Do you heal the mind as well as the body?" Kip asked.

"To the best of my ability, although that rests more with experience than with sorcery, you understand."

"Yes." Kip smoothed his whiskers back. "The other question is—" He took a breath. "We are looking for a healer to come teach at the Lutris School. Would you, or any of your colleagues, consider that?"

Chakrabarti's eyes widened. He glanced back to the rest of his colleagues and then leaned in, lowering his voice. "Is this a true offer, sir?"

Kip's tail swished, but he kept his excitement otherwise under wraps. "It is."

Chakrabarti considered for a moment. "I must confess to you, sir, that I have not yet attained the rank of master."

"Oh." Kip studied the lined face, the grey hairs among the black. "Did you begin your education late in life?"

"Oh, no, sir! Quite the contrary. I began my studies at the age of fourteen. I have spent thirty years as a minister."

"A minister? A preacher?"

"No, no." The man smiled, making his mustache flare up at the ends. "I minister to people in the city of Calcutta. Myself and Master Kosaraju and Master Agrawal are from Calcutta. Our colleagues are from the colleges in Delhi and Bombay."

Kip took in the whole of the Indian exhibit. "How many colleges are there in India?"

"Of sorcery?" Chakrabarti smiled. "Oh, many, many. There are small schools, perhaps thirty or forty, where students may go to learn whether they can perform sorcery. When they graduate from these schools, then they may go to one of the colleges. Delhi, Calcutta, and Bombay are the largest, but there is one in Agra and one in Jaipur and I have heard that one has just been opened in Bangalore."

"Six colleges." Kip shook his head. "The British Empire has only one now."

"Some might consider the Indian colleges part of the British Empire." Chakrabarti's smile faded.

"Oh." Kip didn't know what to say to that.

"There is more and more interference…" Chakrabarti shook his head and his smile returned. "This is not a complaint I should be making to you. After all, Kip Penfold, you have also felt the heavy hand of the British and you have shaken it off with great success. In fact, I am very pleased to be speaking to you, although it was Master Kosaraju who most wished to see you. It was he who told you about me."

One of the other Indian sorcerers kept sneaking looks at Kip. That one was probably Master Kosaraju. "I'm glad I was able to attend," he said.

Chakrabarti leaned in again. "I wonder if you might tell me…"

Here it comes, Kip thought, and prepared to tell the story again.

"How one such as yourself came to study sorcery. It is my understanding that your people are not…sorcerers."

"Ah." Kip's ears stood up. "You don't have Calatians in India."

"No, sir, we do not. We know of them, of course, and among sorcerers there is much curiosity. Among the people of India, your people would be regarded perhaps with fear more than curiosity. I am sad to report this."

"I understand. I am pleased that there is less fear among sorcerers." Kip smiled, and told Chakrabarti about his father's relationship with Master Vendis, the procuring of a spellbook, his discovery that he could do sorcery, and his acceptance into the college. "There were many who did not want me to attend, but I worked as hard as I could to prove them wrong."

"With admirable success." The other sorcerer inclined his head in a sort of bow. "It must have been very difficult being the only one."

"I wasn't." Kip hesitated. "My best friend Coppy—he was an otter—he joined too, and he died trying to protect the school. Our school—the Lutris School—is named for him."

"I am sorry to hear it." Chakrabarti looked like he meant it very sincerely.

"It was several years ago." Kip cleared his throat. "But tell me about your work as a healer in Calcutta. Do you treat disease as well as physical ailments?"

"I can treat some of the symptoms of disease," the sorcerer said. He told Kip of his work, how he kept thinking that he should go back to the college to finish his coursework and teach others, but there were always more people who needed his help. "Often I would go to bed exhausted and wake four hours later to a new line of people at my door. But last year, two new healers came from the college, and now I have time to myself. I started taking instruction at the college toward becoming a Master, and I have time to come here and meet new friends from other countries."

"Are you interested in coming to Peachtree?" Kip asked. "I mean, to America?"

"I would greatly enjoy that." Chakrabarti turned to his colleagues. "I must consult with the ones in charge of my instruction to gain their blessing."

"As soon as you can confirm that, it would be very helpful. And if you might be able to secure a recommendation from the master who instructed you, or the head of your college, we will need that."

"I am sure I can procure that."

"And I would like you to meet my colleagues…" Kip sent Ash to go find Malcolm and bring him over.

Chakrabarti's eyes flicked to the raven as she left. "This raven is yours?"

"Yes. She bonded to me—we have a practice of having a companion. Some call them familiars. I can see through her eyes and speak through her mouth."

"That is exceedingly interesting. I know of familiars; many sorcerers have them. The British attempted to introduce them to our practices, I am told, but we regard it among our people as enslavement of an animal that has a soul as much as we do. The practice has never been undertaken among Hindus."

"Are all Indian sorcerers Hindus?" Kip asked.

"Not all. Some are Muslim. But we have a long tradition of respecting each others' beliefs. The College of Calcutta was founded by Shah Jahan in 1639 and although he was Muslim, he specified that the college would always welcome sorcerers of every faith." He paused and smiled. "You might know Shah Jahan best as the ruler who commissioned the Taj Mahal."

"I've heard of the Taj Mahal," Kip said, "but never seen it."

"Ah! We have a picture here somewhere. I shall find it for you."

Malcolm arrived at that moment with ravens on both shoulders. Ash hopped from his shoulder to Kip's as he drew nearer. "Lazybones," the fox said affectionately. "Didn't want to fly all the way back?"

In response, she croaked and rubbed her beak against his ear. He smiled and said to Chakrabarti, "I'm not sure it's enslavement. She takes advantage where she can."

"Yes, I am sure." The man didn't smile, but turned to Malcolm to introduce himself, and Malcolm extended a hand as he said his own name. Chakrabarti only briefly flinched when Malcolm faced him, but did not ask about the Irishman's eyes, nor did he react in any other way.

"When would you be able to sit down with us for a bit and talk about the college?" Kip asked. "Our college, I mean. Our headmistress is here but is occupied today."

"I am required to be here this morning into early afternoon," Chakrabarti replied, "but tomorrow I have a large portion of the day to myself. I would be happy to meet with you then."

"Fantastic," Kip said. "I mean it."

They spent a little longer speaking with Malcolm, Chakrabarti telling him about India and Calcutta, and their debt to the East India Company. "We have fought back armies," he said, "but what good is sorcery against trade and tariffs and economic power? We may strike down the great Khan's armies as they ride south to conquer us and yet we have no spell to combat the greed of men when promised riches, no sorcery to tear up unfair contracts signed years ago."

"My people are similarly afflicted," Malcolm said, "though we haven't the might to fight back armies. We had to strike one by one, a little at a time."

By now the crowds had grown, and one of Chakrabarti's colleagues signaled to him. "I do beg your pardon," he said, "but I am needed."

"Of course," Kip said. "Thank you so much for speaking to us."

The sorcerer smiled. "It had been my very great pleasure. Oh! One moment."

He hurried away and then returned carrying a small plate on which two small brown lumps rested. "I do not believe you were able to try our sweets. Please."

He held the tray out. Kip and Malcolm each took one. "Thank you very much," Kip said, placing the sugary treat on his tongue. Sweetness and a profusion of spice burst into his senses. He sorted out cinnamon and perhaps saffron, as well as at least two other fragrant spices he did not have names for. They remained on his tongue even when the candy itself had dissolved.

"Lovely," Malcolm said, and Kip nodded agreement.

Chakrabarti acknowledged their thanks with a nod. "Until tomorrow, gentlemen," he said.

CHAPTER FIVE:

UNWELCOME MEETINGS

Kip and Malcolm visited the rest of the exhibits without finding another healer, and by the time they descended to the first floor by the far stair, both were feeling a little hungry. So they returned to the Salon to get something to eat and to see how Emily and Alice fared.

The women were deep in conversation with a very well-dressed couple, so rather than disturb them, Kip and Malcolm each took a small luncheon plate of bread, cold meat, and cheese, and as the tables had filled, they stood near the back and ate. Everything was delicious, and the cheese had a rich nutty flavor that was almost too strong for the fox's palate.

When they'd finished, they wiped their fingers on the cloth napkins provided and gave plate and napkin to one of the uniformed attendants who wandered the Salon collecting them. Before they had a chance to talk to Emily and Alice, however, Jorey came down the stairs and stopped just inside the Salon, scanning it. As soon as he spotted Kip, he came hurrying over.

"How's your work going?" Malcolm asked gently as Jorey skidded to a stop in front of them.

"I'm trying," he said, and switched to Kip. "Please, sir, would you come with me?"

"I've got my own work to do," Kip said. "What's the problem?"

"None of the sorcerers up there," he jabbed a clawed thumb at the ceiling, "will talk to me. They'll talk to Richard, and sometimes Charity because she's pretty, but when I ask questions they just ignore me."

"Have you told them you're with the Lutris School?" Malcolm asked gently.

"Oh aye, of course I have, sir, but it makes no difference! I might as well be reciting Keats or times tables, for all they care."

"All right," Kip said. "We need to go through the first floor anyway."

"There are so many rooms, I don't know if I saw all of them," Jorey said as they walked toward the stairs. "There's tables for England and Spain and France, and another room with Russia and Prussia—I thought that was funny, Russia and Prussia, but they're very different it turns out—and then a room where people are doing different kinds of physical magic and alchemical magic and I hoped someone would be doing spiritual but I haven't found anyone yet. What was on the second floor?"

"Egypt and Persia and China and India," Malcolm said. "Perhaps one or two others, but Kip and I got hungry."

"And we found a healer, maybe." Kip climbed the stairs, Malcolm beside him, Jorey behind. "At least one possibility."

"So quickly!" Jorey bounced along behind them. "Is he a Calatian?"

Kip laughed. "No. I think the only Calatian sorcerers are in Peachtree for the moment."

"I came from London," Jorey pointed out. "There could be Calatian sorcerers in—well, in Spain, I suppose. And here. Where else are there Calatians? India?"

"No. We are hoping to start a town in Australia, but we don't even have sorcerers there," Kip said.

"Some say that's an advantage," Malcolm murmured.

"There are a lot of politics involved." Kip smiled back at Jorey as they reached the first floor. "It won't happen tomorrow, that's for sure. But I think this kind of," he gestured around the first room they entered, "international cooperation feels promising."

"Let's visit the British table before you make such grand pronouncements." Malcolm stood still while his raven surveyed the first room, which was entirely given to the British sorcerers.

"Are you going to try to get one of them to come to Peachtree?" Jorey asked, hopping up next to Kip.

"Shh. No, probably not." There weren't any sorcerers Kip recognized, but then, he only knew a handful of the King's College residents, and that had been three years ago. One bored-looking trio wore robes over military uniforms, four eager young sorcerers engaged visitors, and the rest stood behind the tables talking among themselves and looking put out whenever one of the visitors asked them a question.

"Should I ask the military sorcerers about physical magic?" Jorey asked. "I don't see anyone else here doing complicated physical magic. They're levitating bowls and such, but I can do that."

"You should go see the Egyptian sorcerers," Kip said.

"Hush a moment." Malcolm pulled them to the side so they weren't blocking the doorway, but didn't move toward any of the sorcerers. He bent his head, listening, and Kip perked his ears to catch the young sorcerers' words as well.

"They're recruiting?" he asked in a low voice.

"Aye, sounds like it to me. 'Send your children to King's, oldest sorcerer's college in the world'—well, our Chinese friends might have something to say about that."

"Who would go to King's if they weren't born in the British Empire?" Kip asked.

"You brought me from London to America," Jorey said.

"That's because King's wouldn't take Calatians," Kip said. "If they would, would you have gone there?"

"Maybe." Jorey's tail flicked. "They still don't have Calatian masters, and I'd rather learn from you. No offense to you, Master O'Brien."

"None taken," Malcolm said, "but have a care."

"I wonder if this is because we're taking Calatian students from them? Maybe they realize they can take students from anywhere, any other country. If they gain the best students from other countries and take them to King's, then…"

"Aye." Malcolm nodded before Kip finished his thought. "Now I'm wishing we'd paid to have a table here as well. We need students more than they do."

"We need teachers more." Kip kept his voice low.

Someone stepped up behind him. A moment before he recognized the scent, Victor Adamson's voice said, "I'm available, if the price is right."

Both Ash and Corvi fluttered with the dismay that Kip and Malcolm were able to otherwise contain. Kip put a paw on Jorey's shoulder and pulled the squirrel back between himself and Malcolm. "We're not speaking to you," he said.

Victor walked forward and turned to face them. Dressed in a sharp ice-blue vest and coat, his blond hair perfectly coiffed (with a lavender-scented oil), he looked as wealthy as a nobleman Emily might solicit for donations. "I'd heard that Americans are all uncouth ruffians, of course, but I'd hardly expect it of someone with a good British education."

"Funny thing," Malcolm said, "you can never tell how someone will turn out even with a good British education."

"No, I suppose not." Victor smiled and his eyes flicked past Kip. "Who's this handsome fellow you're trying to hide from me? Hallo there. You know Kip and I were at school together?"

"We were also at school with Matthew Chesterton," Malcolm said. "Kept up with him, have you? What's he been doing lately?"

Victor kept studying Jorey. "Still apprenticed to Warrington last I heard," he said. "Taking him a while to earn his master's robes. Perhaps he should've tried being a war hero."

"Master Penfold is brilliant," Jorey said indignantly, "and so is Master O'Brien. They're quite excellent teachers and there's nothing they cannot do."

Victor stooped, hands on the knees of his finely tailored pants, to bring himself to Jorey's eye level. "Teachers? I see, this is one of your students."

"Yes, and we're taking him around to learn what he can from those who can do sorcery," Malcolm said, "so if you don't mind?"

Victor straightened and looked Corvi in the eyes. "I would not presume that I could learn nothing about seeing from someone with no eyes," he said.

"Then you're exhibiting here, I suppose." Malcolm met the comment about his eyes with equanimity. "Showing off all the things you've learned."

"Oh, not here. Ha ha! Can you imagine?" Victor gestured to the tables. "Old men and parlor tricks."

"So your experiments aren't ready for the world to see yet?" Kip couldn't resist a jab of his own.

"Ah, I didn't say that." Victor's smile made the fox uneasy. "Who knows, if you're here on the last day, maybe you'll learn something."

"Going to stand up and introduce someone with real magic, are you?" Malcolm asked.

A shadow passed across Victor's face. "Don't think you're so special with your master's robes and your ravens and your sorcerer names. I've got a sorcerer name too."

"Right." Malcolm steered Jorey forward. "We've got many other things to learn, so we'll take our leave of you."

Victor caught Kip's arm as the fox made to follow. "I do think my demonstration will be of great interest to you," he said.

The touch on his arm, the attempted restraint, brought the bright hot siren song of fire to Kip's mind. *A small burn*, it whispered, *just enough to sear his hand. That would make him let go.* He tamped the impulse down with the ease of years of practice and twisted his arm in Victor's grip instead. "How's Farley?" he asked. "Murdered anyone lately?"

Victor let go and exhaled, a dramatic sigh accompanied by a pitying expression. "If only you could let go of the past, you might be able to glimpse the future."

"Those are just words that sound elegant and don't mean anything," Kip said. "I have an excellent view of the future I and my friends are building—

despite your best efforts—and you and your murderous crew are not part of it."

"Well," Victor said, "then I'll bid you good day." But his face went cold, even the false friendship falling away from it. He studied Kip a moment longer and then turned on his heel.

The temptation to create a fire surged even stronger. He could spark a small one that could sit in his paw for a moment and help burn away his anger and frustration, and then it would be gone. Maybe nobody would even see.

At that moment, Jorey looked back at him, and Kip remembered that he was a teacher too, and a guide for these young students. He put the idea of fire away with not a little regret.

"Master Penfold?" Jorey said. "What's a sorcerer's name?"

"Sorcerer name," Kip corrected, and drew Jorey away from the rest of the crowd to speak quietly. "You know the phrases we teach you to help you access magic?" The squirrel nodded. "When you attain the rank of Master, a spiritual sorcerer examines your connection to magic and—with your permission, always with your permission—reads the name that magic knows you by and gives it to you. You can use that to access magic after then."

"Why don't they give us sorcerer names then? It would make magic easier."

"It's only done for masters," Kip said. "I don't know why, but that's the way it's always been done."

"What do they sound like? What's your sorcerer name?"

"You're never to reveal your sorcerer name to another." Kip put his finger to his muzzle. "And you're not even supposed to know about it. I didn't find out until someone did the ceremony for me. So hush, and don't tell Richard or Charity."

Jorey looked away, so Kip said, "I'm serious. Promise you won't tell the others."

"Yes, all right." The squirrel kicked at the floor. "We promised not to keep sorcery secrets from each other."

"This isn't a secret that will matter. It's just a thing Victor was using to puff himself up."

"Then why can't we tell anyone about it?"

"Because it's tradition, that's all."

"You told us to question tradition."

"Yes, yes." Kip smiled and shook his head. "But you have to learn them first. When you all get your master's robes and your sorcerer names, we can discuss the tradition further. I'll tell them I made you keep the secret. Now come on, let's finish your tour."

Kip was glad that his job for the next hour was simply to give Jorey access to the European sorcerers on the first floor, because his mind kept going back to Victor. What could he be working on? What kind of demonstration was he going to put on? He walked absently behind Jorey up to the Spanish sorcerer doing physical magic and nodded when the sorcerer asked if he was Master Penfold, the famous Master Penfold. "I'll be glad to tell you a little about the Battle of the Road," Kip said, "if you'll give my student here a small amount of your time."

So the sorcerer answered some of Jorey's questions and then Kip gave his practiced account of the battle, drawing a small crowd to listen. A few asked questions about details Kip had omitted, or tried to get him to say that he'd destroyed the Road, which he had pointedly not admitted to. He'd learned to navigate these questions without seeming like he was avoiding them, and Malcolm had learned to pull him away so that he didn't seem rude. "Master Penfold," Malcolm said after three questions, "we really must be moving on."

"So sorry," Kip said to the crowd, and escaped with Malcolm and Jorey to the next set of tables.

This same general pattern repeated at the Prussians, the Russians, and then at the alchemical magic table that two of the Dutch sorcerers had set up, which Jorey had decided he wanted to write about. This was likely because the alchemical sorcerers were the friendliest they encountered and did not even wait for Kip to introduce Jorey before asking if the squirrel was a student of sorcery (Kip still promised to tell them his story).

While they were talking to Jorey, Kip spotted a familiar face: Master Janssen, the headmaster of the Dutch College. The tall grey-bearded man had just left a conversation with one of the Dutch tables and strolled through the room, hands clasped behind his back.

Kip caught his eye and smiled, and the sorcerer changed direction to come over to Kip. "Master Penfold," he said in his deep bass voice. "We are so delighted you could come see our Exposition. What do you think of it?"

"It's wonderful," Kip said. "To have so many sorcerers here in one place talking about sorcery is like a dream come true."

"Have you had the chance to have many productive discussions?"

Kip smiled. "A few. I greatly enjoyed meeting the sorcerers upstairs. Here I find myself mostly talking about myself."

Janssen nodded gravely. "That is the risk of doing great things."

"I was in the right place at the right time..."

Janssen's smile returned. "With the risk should also come the reward. You did those things, after all, and nobody else did."

"So everyone keeps telling me." Kip swished his tail and stood straighter.

"I have a question for you, as it happens."

"Of course." Janssen guided them over to one side of the room, away from the crowd. "How can I be of assistance?"

"You know that we are trying to build up our school. We currently have masters to teach alchemical magic, translocation, defense, and physical magic, but we are still lacking a healer. I have been enquiring here but have only found one who might be willing to come teach for us. If you know of any masters—from your school or elsewhere—who might desire to teach in America, I would be very grateful to be introduced to them."

"Ah." Janssen stroked his beard.

"It needn't be permanent," Kip added quickly. "A span of five years, perhaps; enough time for us to find another teacher."

"Or perhaps a rotating post, to be filled every two years by a different master?"

"Yes, that would suit." Kip exhaled. If Janssen were willing to help them, his task would be far easier.

"There is a small difficulty, which is that our healers, most of them, did not work with you during the war and do not know you well, so they lend a small amount of credence to rumors of your inexperience and incompetence, which I am certain are lies spread from London." Janssen fixed Kip's gaze with his. "However, we have a newly robed master in healing who is both less opinionated and less empowered to choose his own posting. It is usual for new masters to continue to work with an established healer for a year, but de Koning is quite skilled and we could shorten that time."

"I would greatly appreciate it. If he's willing to come, of course."

"I don't think you need worry about that." Janssen straightened to his full height and met Kip's eyes with the air of one sharing a secret. "He's still beholden to the Athæneum, and we owe you more favors than a hundred healing masters could repay. If he is not eager, he will certainly at least be willing."

"Thank you. I hope he will be eager as well." He chose not to pursue the matter of rumors, nor the irritation he felt at how widespread they had become, and focus instead on the possibility of having two healers at the school. He would have to ask Emily how to pay both of them, but hopefully she would have a solution to that problem by the time the Exposition ended.

"I'll speak to him. In the meantime, may I introduce you…"

Janssen guided him to a table and introduced Kip to two sorcerers practicing translocation, then to a foursome showing off demonstrations of physical magic building elaborate sculptures from sand and mud, and finally back to the alchemical magic table where Jorey remained talking to one of the two sorcerers.

"Please," Janssen said, "I hope you will attend a dinner tonight at the Athæneum as our guest. Master de Koning will be there and I will prepare him to discuss a temporary appointment to the Lutris School."

"Of course." Kip looked around for Malcolm. "May I bring guests? My wife is here, and two other masters."

"We would be delighted. You know I wish to have excellent relations between our two schools." Janssen offered a hand.

"As do I." Kip shook warmly. "It is nice to feel that we have an ally here, at least."

"Ah, yes." The headmaster released Kip's paw. "The newly-named School of the Americas, isn't it? Headmaster Jackson? They have sent representatives here, although like you they declined to present an exhibit."

Whom could the school have sent? Probably not Jackson, although he might appreciate the chance to visit Amsterdam on official business. Master Jaeger wouldn't travel, Master Splint wouldn't be allowed to (Kip had made enough enquiries about getting Splint to come to Peachtree that he doubted Jackson would let the healer out of his sight), and none of the others, to Kip's memory, had shown much interest in travel. The ones who might have, Masters Vendis and Argent, now taught at the Lutris School.

He didn't care enough to ask, and anyway Master Janssen was making to depart, so Kip thanked him and bid him good-bye. Malcolm had gotten Jorey the attention of a friendly German sorcerer, so Kip told him about the evening's invitation and then returned to the Salon.

Emily and Alice sat at the same table, alone now. Kip took a glass of soda water from one of the attendants and joined them. "How successful has your day been?" he asked, reaching out to Alice as he sat.

Alice squeezed his paw and then reached for his soda water, so he gave it to her. "A mixed bag," Emily said. "A good deal of 'we are so excited about what you are doing, and just as soon as we're able…' and a little bit of 'how much land is available in America these days?' And one person who asked Alice to tell war stories."

"And one who wanted to know if you were about," Alice said. "Not to hear stories, but because he was scandalized that I would be here without you."

"There were several people who didn't want to talk to two women." Emily rolled her eyes. "Mostly they came around when I introduced myself as the headmistress of the school, but two walked away again."

"How many people did you talk to today?" Kip asked.

"Twenty or so, I should imagine. The nobles aren't as interested in the actual sorcery so much as who's here, and so they all linger here so they can see and be seen."

"So," Alice continued, setting Kip's soda water back in front of him, "they like to find new people to talk to so it doesn't seem like they're only staying here to see who else is here."

"Did you have any luck?" Emily asked.

"A little, perhaps." He told them about Chakrabarti.

"Only the one healer?" Emily asked. "You went through our questions with him?"

"Yes. He seems a competent and decent fellow. We might also have a Dutch healer, but if possible I'd like to retain them both, if this de Koning is also good. Headmaster Janssen has invited us to dinner tonight and said we might meet him there and discuss our proposal."

"How lovely of him." Alice smiled.

"We've put Holland on the world stage in terms of sorcery." Emily lowered her voice. "I'm pleased that they remain grateful."

"They also helped us become independent," Kip said, matching her tone. "Not just America, but the Calatians."

"And better rights for women," Alice added.

"We've helped each other, then," Emily said. "So it's good that we continue to do so, and I'll leave it at that. Speaking of world stages, though, it sounds like things are not going so well on the Continent here. Holland is fine—the people are happy with their role in the war. They feel they got a great benefit while giving up very little. But in Prussia, there's a good deal of agitation between the Kingdom of Prussia and the other German states, which as far as I can tell comes down to how closely their alliance works and what they call it, but I'm sure at the root it's more than that. And Spain is somewhat stable by virtue of being ready for war with England at all times, but France is suffering from what Napoleon demanded of it to create its empire and then from the penalties taken from it when that empire fell."

"So there aren't any French nobles here?" Kip asked.

"There are." Emily looked a little put out that he hadn't asked anything else. "Some of the nobles kept their family lands and still have a good deal of wealth. But I feel our best hope is with the Dutch nobles. They're currently our closest allies on the Continent."

She went on with some other point about politics, but Kip's mind had skipped to the British Empire, and in the middle of one of Emily's sentences he blurted out, "I saw Victor."

Alice stiffened while Emily merely pursed her lips, but Kip could read her well enough to understand her annoyance. "Did you," she said. "How does he look? Disheveled and filthy, I hope."

"Alas." Kip shook his head. "He saw Jorey."

Emily's lips tightened further. "If he interferes with our students in any way, so help me…"

"You'll drop him in the ocean?" Kip asked with a smile.

"He'll wish I'd only done that." Emily's eyes darkened. "Sleek has been to a great number of unpleasant places."

"Where is Sleek?" Kip only then registered that Emily's raven wasn't with her.

She pointed up. "On the roof. I thought it would be off-putting for nobles if I had a bird on my shoulder."

He nodded. "I was accompanying Jorey because the sorcerers up there wouldn't speak to him otherwise, and Victor saw me and Malcolm. We made him feel most unwelcome."

"I'd expect nothing else." Emily's mouth did curve into a slight smile. "All right, then, we've all got to be on our guards a little more. If he has the chance to sabotage us, you can be certain he'll take it."

"But why?" Alice asked. "He's got his post at King's doing whatever he's doing, and we've got our school. Why can't he leave us alone?"

"Because we've got magic," Kip said, "and he doesn't, and he doesn't think that's right."

Emily nodded. "Women and Calatians doing sorcery while the proud son of a respectable shipbuilder—"

"—who knows more about sorcery than all of them put together—"

"—can't so much as lift a single pebble."

"It's just not fair!" Kip imitated Victor's cultured tone as best he could.

"It's more than not fair." Emily sighed. "It's a great wrong in the world."

"Is that what his experiments are about?" Alice looked between them.

"To be honest, he's never said as much to us." Kip lifted his eyes to the ceiling, decorated with beautiful paintings of the old Greek and Roman gods.

"But he oozes it every time he talks to us. The entitlement drips from him like sweat."

"Though I've never seen him sweat," Kip said.

"He might be a demon." Emily rubbed her cheek thoughtfully. "One his father summoned and bound and never let go."

Kip laughed. "He's too coherent to be a demon."

"Besides," Alice put in, "if he were a demon, he'd be able to do magic."

"Only when his father commanded it."

"All right." Kip stood and leaned over to kiss Alice. "I'm going to talk to the British sorcerers and see if I can find out anything about Victor and his experiments. Good luck the rest of the day. I'll find Malcolm and we'll meet down here to go to the dinner."

"Good luck yourself," Emily said, and Alice ran her fingers along his paw.

For the better part of an hour, Kip walked around the British sorcerers on the first floor, engaging them in conversation here and there. They all knew who he was, even if he didn't know them, but unlike the rest of the attendees at the Exposition, they weren't interested in hearing his story of the Battle of the Road. One of them told him stiffly that he'd known Cott and had been a good friend of his, which Kip found dubious; he'd been introduced to all the Masters Cott was on speaking terms with during his time at King's. There weren't many. But the mention of his former master brought back memories of his death, so he left that conversation quickly.

Others ignored him and spoke very loudly near him about "that upstart school" and the "ragged urchins and animals pretending to be real sorcerers." He walked away from those people and kept his ears forward, ignoring the little urges that called him to start a fire at their table, or to find Victor and start a fire on him.

A couple of the British sorcerers were bored and therefore more talkative. They said variations on, "No hard feelings, jolly good work on your part," so he spent more time with them. But even these more forthcoming men knew little about Victor and his experiments. "Rum fellow," they agreed. "Struts about like he owns the place, and no more magic in him than in the stones of the college."

"At Prince George's," Kip said, "his father had donated quite a lot of money to the school."

"I don't know as King's needs his father's money," the first sorcerer said. "He knows someone, likely the headmaster, and that someone is very interested in what he's doing."

"Is he going to show something of it here?" Kip asked. "He told me he was going to present something on the last day."

"Oh, you've spoken to His Nibs?" The sorcerer laughed. "We was told to mind our tables, do our little sorcery, and tell people King's is the greatest college of sorcery in the world."

"Who doesn't know that already, I ask you?" the other said. "But it's a sight better than runnin' errands for Martinet."

"Oh, I know him," Kip said. "Rather, I've met him. Had supper with him one night."

"Lucky you," the sorcerer said sourly, while his companion nodded. "That you only had to sup with him one night, I mean."

"He wasn't too bad." Kip smiled. "But I was a novelty. A Calatian who could do sorcery."

"Fire sorcery, no less." The other sorcerer shook his head. "I wouldn't want that. They say it eats you up inside."

"Like spiritual magic," his companion said, "but of the soul, not the mind."

"It can be controlled, like anything else. I don't feel like starting a fire right now. And even when I do…I can stop myself."

They both laughed. "I'd hope so. This old place would go up like kindling," the first one said.

"You've no idea what Victor's doing, then?"

"No. Why d'you care so much?" He turned to his friend.

"Aye," the other replied. "None of us do."

Kip didn't want to mention the missing Calatians, which might not be related. There were a lot of reasons Calatians might go missing in London. "The last time I saw him was during the war," he said, "and he talked about experiments he was doing." Although it hadn't been Victor, actually; it had been Farley, who'd said that Victor was doing experiments to help him. Presumably that meant reversing the demon's curse that had made the bully a marmot-Calatian, which would explain why Farley—and Albright—had said that Kip would be "useful." He rubbed his whiskers. "He and I have fought in the past, and he's enlisted other sorcerers and bullies to try to get the better of me."

The sorcerers exchanged a look and uneasy grins. "Ay, I wouldn't want to be on that one's bad side."

"Can't help it, I'm afraid." Kip held out his paws and swished his tail around. "I was born on his bad side."

"Aye, but it's profited you well enough. Got your own territory and all."

"Wish my family could have our own territory."

Kip took a breath in, already formulating a question about whether the young English human men in front of him would also like to be looked down on their whole lives, prevented from owning property or participating in government, and casually beaten or killed, in exchange for that territory. But it was not an argument worth having, not here any more than back in the newly-built corridors of power in America. "It's been very nice," he said. "Thanks so much. I'll let you get back to your work."

They protested that talking to him was the most interesting thing they'd done all day, which might have been true but also felt like courtesy. At any rate, people were streaming downstairs for the first great exhibition, so Kip went to join them.

That first public exhibition, by a Prussian sorcerer, held little interest, but Kip watched it all the way through anyway. The Prussian summoned a water elemental and levitated it, broke it into pieces, absorbed part of it into cloth and then let it separate itself again, and showed how it might carry ink to write on paper. All of these were things Kip knew to be possible and had seen done, but for many in the crowd, the feats inspired gasps and cheers. Across the large room, he was pleased to see Jorey, Richard, and Charity clustered together with Malcolm nearby, all watching avidly. None of the sorcerers currently at the Lutris School had an affinity for water elementals, so this was good for them to see, if not particularly useful for him.

He searched the crowd for Victor, but the pale young man was nowhere to be seen. Emily and Alice had remained in the Salon talking to the most fancily dressed pair Kip had yet seen: a man and woman in white powdered wigs, with skin so pale it had to be made up with a cream of some sort, dressed in multiple layers of shimmering finery, blues and lavender and cream with gold trim and jewelry. If anyone at the Exposition could spare money, it looked like they could. Just one of the rings from the man's fingers would probably keep the school going for six months.

Toward the back of the crowd, on the opposite side of the large room, a figure in a hooded cloak watched silently. Nobody else's face was hidden, so the figure intrigued Kip and he watched it for a few minutes. Then it made a movement and the hackles on his neck rose. It couldn't be, could it? His casual attention turned intent as he looked for the shadow of a marmot's muzzle below the hood.

From where he was, he couldn't make out any details, but the longer he watched, the more certain he grew. So he made his way through the crowd, slowly, trying not to look like a hunter, but keeping the cloaked figure in his sights the whole time.

He'd made it halfway across the room, perhaps forty feet from the figure, when a Dutch-accented voice behind him called, "Hey Calatian, put your ears down, we can't see!"

Another voice laughed, and then someone else said, "That's Master Penfold of America."

Kip turned to see a sorcerer talking to two well-dressed young men who reddened upon meeting his eyes. They mumbled apologies and looked away, and Kip shook his head and returned to his path.

When he looked back toward the hooded figure, it was staring directly at him. Twin gleams shone from the darkness. And then it turned and made for the far exit, close behind it.

Kip cursed inwardly and hurried his pursuit, but his quarry had clear space to traverse while the fox had to make his way through people trying to follow the presentation at the front of the room. He told the raven on his shoulder to follow the figure, and Ash launched herself from his shoulder, causing a small panic around him that slowed him further.

Through Ash's eyes he watched as the figure reached the door and pushed through it. Ash darted through above his head, clearing the door a moment before the figure turned and slammed it shut.

This door didn't lead back to the Salon but to the street outside. Ash soared above as Kip navigated the crowd of people, a task made more difficult by his double vision. The hooded figure hurried along the street to the canal front where there was a crowd of people, but paused at the corner and looked back.

Ash's view jerked in Kip's sight as the raven stopped dead in mid-air. Recognizing the effect of a spell, he stopped just as quickly in the midst of the crowd, gathering magic even as Ash was driven toward the ground. Panic flooded his link with the raven, but Kip cast the simple spell easily and caught her a man's height above the street. For a moment his spell wrestled with the other for control, Ash trembling against the restraints of both. Kip resumed his hurry toward the door, worried that the figure—it was Farley, he was even more sure—would come back toward Ash, but then Farley disappeared around the corner, and Ash was released into Kip's spell.

She squawked a protest and so he let her fly in pursuit of their quarry. Cautious now, he directed her to the roof of Trippenhuis where her keen eyes could scan the crowd in front of the great building.

Kip finally got to the door and out into the cool air, filled with the scents of the city rather than of hundreds of people. He breathed in and then kept close to the wall as he trailed Farley, watching primarily through Ash's eyes. She perched on one of the cornices atop Trippenhuis, and when Kip had determined that there was enough room for him, he translocated himself up beside her.

"Now," he said, "let's see where he goes, and if we can keep out of sight while we follow him."

The latter proved moderately difficult, as Farley was now aware he was being followed. Ash kept to rooftops and tried to fly only when he wasn't looking back. Once she lost him in the shadows, but flew over the surrounding streets until she found him again.

Kip hadn't seen a great deal of Farley Broadside since his demon-cursed transformation to a Calatian, but that had not affected his lumbering gait nor his quick reflexes, which showed as his hood snapped around to look from side to side and even behind him. And it was in one of these looks that Kip finally got the confirmation that he was right, when the cloaked figure's hood turned into the sun and for just a moment, the fox saw Farley's familiar muzzle.

Something was different, though; the last time he'd seen Farley, the man had shaved all the fur from any visible place on his body, leaving pink skin and a criss-cross of angry cuts and welts. But now the short brown fur appeared to have grown back, at least in the brief glimpse Kip caught.

Then the muzzle was hidden again, and perhaps he hadn't seen Ash, because his steps slowed. He appeared to be heading for Dierenpark, but then diverted down a different street and across a canal. In this open area, Ash and Kip wanted to remain cautious, so he held her back, and indeed, on the other side of the bridge Farley turned again to scan the sky suspiciously. Then he continued forward, directly into a small, shadowy street.

Go, Kip urged, and Ash took off, gliding across the canal and to the roof of the house on the corner. She looked up and down the small, relatively quiet street, but the hooded figure was nowhere to be seen.

"He must have gone into one of the houses," Kip muttered to himself. "One of the ones near the canal; he didn't have time to go far."

Ash, disappointed that the hunt was over, tried to peer into the windows of the houses, but Kip stopped her and called her back. Years ago, when they were children, Farley had been very good at setting ambushes, and that worry prickled the back of Kip's neck. At this distance, if Farley caught Ash in a spell again and tried to kill her by smashing her into the ground, Kip couldn't stop him.

"Let's remember that street," he told himself and Ash as she flew back to him.

A raven appeared in front of him, and he thought for a moment that it was Ash before realizing that he could still see through her eyes, several streets away. The other raven alit near him and spoke in Malcolm's voice. "Good heavens, man, whyever are you all the way up here? Is it the smell? I know the crowds are thick."

"No," Kip said. "Farley's here. I was following him."

The raven croaked, indignant, probably feeling some of Malcolm's emotion. "Ah well, where the master walks, the hound stays close behind, me da used to say," it said. "All right, come down to the Salon when you've finished. I'm going to bring Corvi back because I can't see a thing down here and people keep elbowing me."

"I'll bring him down when Ash gets back," Kip said.

"You're a gentlemen and a true friend." Corvi squawked and then hopped onto Kip's shoulder.

This lasted only until Ash returned, when she flew at the other raven and drove him from the shoulder she considered hers with a flurry of wings. "Careful!" Kip called, averting his muzzle, but in a moment Corvi had flown away and Ash had taken his place. She rubbed her beak against Kip's cheek and then nipped his ear.

"All right, all right," he said as Corvi landed on the other shoulder and he prepared to descend. "Let's all get along, shall we?"

It was nice, he reflected as he stepped into the muted murmur of the exposition hall, to walk around with fewer suspicious looks than normal, and as tiring as it was to have to tell the story of the Road over and over, it was better than walking around Philadelphia and being told he wasn't allowed in certain places (when he wasn't completely ignored).

The moment he stepped into the Salon, before he'd spotted his wife and friends, Corvi took off from his shoulder and flew directly to Malcolm. Kip followed the raven's flight and took the last seat at the table, between Alice and Malcolm and across from Emily. "Everybody ready for supper?" he asked.

"Quite." Alice smiled at Emily. "It's been a trying day."

"Tomorrow will be no better, I'm afraid." Emily reached out and squeezed Alice's paw. "You did wonderfully, though. As for supper, please make my apologies. I'm rather weary of talking to people and I think I will make my own way tonight."

"Would you like company?" Malcolm asked.

"No, no." She gave him a wide smile. "You go on to the dinner, eat the lovely food, make the acquaintance of this Dutch healer. I would prefer to be alone tonight. Well, me and Sleek." She reached up to the raven, who took her finger gently in her beak.

It would be nice to have Emily there to meet the sorcerer, but Kip couldn't deny that she'd earned a respite if she wanted one. "All right," he said, and then rubbed his fingers along the wood grain of the table and looked toward Malcolm. "Did you tell them?"

"About Farley? No, I thought I'd leave it to you to cast such a pall over their day."

"Farley's here?" Emily's brow lowered. "You should've let him drown."

"You should've sent him farther away," Kip replied mildly.

"What was he doing?" Alice perked her ears.

"Watching the water elemental exhibition, and then running away when I spotted him."

"If he's here and Victor's here, we need to be doubly careful," Emily said.

"Four times as careful, for either one of them is bad news and together they multiply rather than add." Malcolm kept facing Alice, but Corvi turned around on his shoulder, surveying the room. "Where are the students?"

Kip's fur prickled again. "I haven't seen them since Jorey was with you at the exhibition."

"I sent them in here while Corvi went to find you."

"I sent them back to our hotel," Emily said. "We know Farley hasn't taken them, because you were following him, but it's worth sending one of the ravens along to keep an eye, I suppose."

With Emily not accompanying them to dinner and Malcolm needing Corvi to get around, that left only one option. "I'll send Ash." Kip stood as he said the words. "Shall we go?"

Once outside, Ash took off from his shoulder and soared over the streets leading back to their hotel. She knew what Jorey looked like, so Kip didn't have to watch through her eyes, but he did check in from time to time.

"She's found them," he reported to Alice and Malcolm when Ash spotted Jorey's bushy tail beside the other two students. "They're fine, walking back to the hotel."

"Good," Malcolm said. "Sets my heart at ease to know that, it does. Would you mind keeping Ash on them until they arrive safely?"

"Of course not." Kip told Ash this and promised to save her some morsels from the dinner they were about to attend.

Because Ash was curious, she remained close enough to the students for her, and therefore Kip, to hear their conversation. Richard spoke about the sorcerers he'd talked to and how nice everyone was. He had also somehow, in the midst of taking notes for his homework, found the time to talk to a Dutch girl he was going to meet later. Jorey filled in his experiences with the European sorcerers when Richard had to pause for breath, also asking Charity what her day had been like.

"I talked to a few people," she said. "Most of them were very pleasant, although some were surprised that a woman was studying sorcery, and a woman of my race at that."

"Was that up on the second floor?" Richard asked. "I don't know if the Chinese have any women sorcerers, or the Egyptians."

"No; they were all very nice to me," Charity said. "Well, not the Chinese, but they were very busy. One Persian translocation master talked to me for quite a while and told me he believes I have the makings of an excellent sorcerer."

"You do," Jorey said. "You'll be translocating people in no time."

"He told me the same thing." Charity sighed. "But no, the rude ones were more the Europeans."

"You would think they would be more enlightened."

"Same with me," Jorey said. "Until Master Penfold took me around."

"Most of them were fine," Charity amended. "Just some of the British and Prussian ones. And even they were far nicer than I'm used to in America."

"Oh, well, them." Richard waved a hand.

That was when Charity happened to look back and catch sight of Ash. She stopped for a moment, then hurried forward and whispered in Jorey's ear, then Richard's, and from then on they kept their conversation quiet.

Kip chuckled to himself and then told Alice, to whom he'd been relaying the conversation. "I'm glad they're at least somewhat vigilant," she said, and pulled his muzzle to hers for a kiss. "And now I'm glad you can talk to me for one minute until we arrive at dinner."

At the front door of the Athæneum, an apprentice directed them to the dining hall, staring at the three of them with wide eyes. Headmaster Janssen greeted them and showed them to one of several round tables laid with white linen tablecloths and silver candlesticks. The candles filled the air with a waxy floral scent that almost covered the scents of the several dozen people in the room.

By the number of empty seats, more were expected. But the table where Kip, Alice, and Malcolm sat down was full save for one seat that Janssen said was saved for Emily. Kip made apologies on her behalf and Janssen said he completely understood.

He introduced them to Master de Koning, a young man with straw-blond hair, plump red cheeks, and an enthusiastic manner. The others at the table, all older, were professors at the Spanish school and their English, though functional, was limited.

Janssen had told de Koning of Kip's request, and the cheerful young man at least put up a good show of being excited at the prospect of traveling to America. Once Kip had asked all his questions and received very satisfactory answers, de Koning asked a number of questions about the college that Kip tried to answer honestly, though he worried that he was making it sound like a backwater town compared to the metropolis de Koning was used to.

Alice helped him quite a bit, jumping in to offer the benefits of Peachtree: clean air, fewer people, fresh produce, and lovely weather. After a little while, Kip let Alice do most of the talking because de Koning responded much better to her words than to his. He focused his ears toward the Spanish sorcerers, but his Spanish wasn't good enough to make out more than a few words.

They noticed his attention, though, and toward the end of the meal the youngest of them leaned forward and said, in accented English, "Would you be Master Penfold?"

"Yes." Kip knew what was coming.

"My others and I speak not so good English but we would be most grateful to hear your story," the sorcerer said. "My name is Galena, and my other Iglesias," here he gestured to one of the older sorcerers, who nodded at the mention of his name, "can cast a spell from mind to mind to understand you. If you will permit."

Allow a Spanish sorcerer to link to his mind? As recently as a year ago, the idea would have been unthinkable. Half a year ago, though, he'd met an ambassador from Spain in Philadelphia; they were there to negotiate a relationship with the newly-formed country. America was already on good terms with the Dutch and French, and the Spanish did not want to be left out of any alliance.

Kip's main worry was that he didn't have a spiritual sorcerer to monitor the spell from his side. The only one he knew well enough, Peter Cadno, was a spirit trapped in stone who currently resided in the walls of the Lutris School.

"You hesitate." Galena—Master Galena?—nodded. "I understand. How if we have one of the sorcerers of this country assist us?"

"Aye," Malcolm said. "That'd put us all more at ease for sure."

So one of the Dutch spiritual sorcerers was found, and agreed to serve as the conduit between Kip and the Spaniards. Through his spell, Kip told his story once again, and the Spanish sorcerer relayed it in Spanish to his comrades.

After the story, Kip left his table for a time and mingled with their hosts. He wanted to get to know them better, but he also wanted to find out if any of them had an idea of what Victor might be planning at this Exposition. Farley's presence meant that there might be a hidden motive, but Kip had no idea what it might be.

Unfortunately, none of the Dutch masters did either. The one who had the most knowledge said that Headmaster Cross of King's College had vouched for Victor's presentation and had assured the Dutch school that there would be no dangerous sorcery practiced.

"No sorcery at all, more like," Kip muttered, and returned to his table with his curiosity and unease intact.

CHAPTER SIX: ON DEMONS

While Kip had been meeting Dutch sorcerers, Malcolm had befriended Master Galena and Alice had de Koning ready to pack his bags that very night. On the walk back to their hotel, Kip was inclined to say that he'd had the least productive night of any of them—"all I found out was that Headmaster Cross knows about Victor's research, and we could have guessed that."

Their rooms were empty when they returned, and none of them knew where Emily could have gone. The students, at least, were all safe in their rooms, watched over by Ash. The raven returned to Kip's shoulder when he opened the window in his room and fluffed herself up importantly. "Good job," Kip said, and fed her several morsels of cheese he'd taken from the dinner.

All three of them were too exhausted to stay awake waiting for Emily, so after Malcolm checked in with their students, all of them fell soundly asleep. And in the morning, Emily had returned and told them about her evening over breakfast.

"There's a pub in London whose food I was missing, and since it's dinnertime here and there both, I thought I would pop over," she said. "And then being so close, I went over to the Isle to talk to some of the Calatians about the disappearances."

Kip's ears shot straight up, and Alice's did too. Emily had that satisfied smile—smug, Malcolm called it—that she got when she'd done something she was proud of. "Who did you talk to?" Kip asked.

"Whom," she corrected him. "I talked to Wilton Blaeda in his home. Poor fellow can't get around well anymore. And I talked to Dotta Lutris, and Ella, and some of their friends. Not Grinda," she added to Kip. "It isn't just you she distrusts."

"I know." Kip sighed. "What did you learn?"

"Not a great deal. But everyone seemed very grateful that anyone was interested. They've complained to the constables once, and they laughed and said Calatians must fall in the Thames every day. It seems as though none of the calyxes have been taken, at least."

"So it's someone who doesn't want to anger the sorcerers," Alice said.

"I rather think that points to a sorcerer." Emily sipped her tea. "How else would they know who the calyxes are? Anyway, Dotta took me to see an old polecat named Chesser who doesn't sleep well and walks around at night. He swears he saw one of the vanished Calatians being carried across the Thames by a hooded figure. Of course, he reasoned that it was Death come to take them away and wouldn't hear any other explanation, but I suppose we four can think of one or two."

"If it was Farley, I don't know that he's that far off," Malcolm said grimly.

Kip had been thinking the same thing. "Surely the others don't believe it was actually Death?"

"No," Emily said. "In fact, before I talked to him, Dotta said, 'Now don't you mind his talk of Death and all,' and said that when he first told people, it was just a hooded figure, but since then he's added a scythe, and she wouldn't be surprised if there's a pale horse in the story soon enough."

"Did he mention the scythe to you?"

"He did." Emily rolled her eyes. "But it was useful to hear. At least someone saw one of the missing Calatians actually abducted, so that's something."

"We figured that's what was happening." Kip couldn't put his finger on why this annoyed him. Emily had gone and gathered information on a problem facing his people. Was it that she'd put herself in danger? Or was it that she'd gone without him?

"There's a difference between figuring and knowing," Emily said, "and that difference might mean getting some more powerful people to look into it."

"Who's going to look into it if the headmaster of King's condones it?"

"I suppose we'll have to find that out." She returned to her tea.

"We have to do something. All of us." Alice looked around the table.

"Of course." Emily brightened at Alice's determination, which made Kip feel even worse about his own behavior.

"Thank you for going," he said. "And yes, we'll do something. But if it is Farley, at least we know they won't be kidnapping anyone else while he and Victor are here."

"Don't be sure about that," Malcolm said. "They could pop back as easily as Em here did. Well, perhaps not as easily, but easily enough."

"Could they, though? Farley never learned translocation. If he had, he wouldn't bother flying Calatians across the river, or running down streets to get away from us."

"If the headmaster is indeed approving their research, he'll have given them a sorcerer for that." Emily rested her elbows on the table. "But you're right. And besides that we still need to worry about the survival of our school."

"And the safety of our students," Malcolm said.

Alice's ears lay back. "Do you think we should send them back right now?"

All three of them looked at Malcolm, while Corvi returned their gazes. "No," Malcolm said at last. "We'll keep an eye on them, sure, and if the four of us can't keep them safe here, then how much safer will they be back in Peachtree with fewer sorcerers, all told? No, this will be a good experience for them and we'll warn them to be on their guard."

"They're already looking out." Kip told them about Charity spotting his raven the previous night. Ash made a clacking noise on his shoulder. "It's not your fault," he assured her. "It's hard for ravens to hide."

"It would be nice if we could have a raven trail Victor. Or Farley," Emily mused. "Not that I think they'll be stupid enough to try anything here, but I'd feel better if I knew someone was keeping an eye on them."

"We'd have to be very careful," Kip said. "Farley tried to kill Ash and would have succeeded if I hadn't been nearby."

"Ah, of course." Emily shook her head. "Foolish of me. All right, we'll do the best we can without putting anyone in danger."

"What about a demon?" Alice asked.

"They've demons at the entrance to the Exposition," Kip said. "Probably checking to make sure no other demons get in."

"You didn't tell us that." Emily's voice regained a little edge.

"It only registered for a moment, and anyway, none of us were going to summon demons there."

"All right. We can summon them out here, though. I'll do that and have them keep a watch for either Farley or Victor outside Trippenhuis. Inside, I suppose we can't do much."

Kip didn't answer, even after Malcolm said, "Aye, we need to make sure we have as much protection as we can muster." He hoped he wouldn't have to say anything, but Emily noticed his reserve.

"Kip?" she said.

"If you need me to summon a demon," he said slowly, "then I will. But if you and Malcolm can do it, then I would prefer not to."

"I know." Emily sighed. "I wouldn't be asking if it weren't important. There was the one you used during the war; do you still know their name?"

"I'll find one," Kip said. Only Alice and Captain Lowell knew that he'd promised Nikolon he wouldn't summon her again and had burned her name out of the book of demon names. Neither of them knew why he'd done that, because he hadn't told anyone how Nikolon, unbound by the destruction of the Road, had continued to obey his orders and had saved Calatian lives in the process.

He had told Malcolm that he felt less comfortable summoning demons than he had prior to the war, and Malcolm understood his concerns a little, but Kip himself hadn't worked through all the ramifications of his beliefs. Were all demons capable of empathy? Nikolon had also implied that she'd taken advantage of being unbound to curse Kip, though the only change that might be a demon's curse was his recurring dream, a patchwork of emotional resonances and sun-drenched places he'd definitely never been, and that hardly felt like a curse.

If everyone started to treat demons as though they were people, would demons take advantage of that? Some demons, certainly, but would all of them? How would you know which ones without taking a dangerous chance? It seemed that it would be impossible to find a working relationship. And yet, demons were so important to the world powers that nobody would ever agree to simply stop summoning them.

This was not the place to have that conversation, so although Emily gave him a long, questioning look, he didn't elaborate. "Fine," she said. "If there are demons watching Trippenhuis, I think we are safe there. But outside, we'll have at least one demon active at all times watching Victor or Farley, and one of our ravens on the students."

"Ash can watch the students," Kip said.

"I'll summon the demon, then." Malcolm smiled Kip's way.

Charity, Jorey, and Richard joined them after breakfast, and Emily herded the seven of them out to the street. They spent the short walk to Trippenhuis talking about what they'd seen and what they intended to visit today. The students seemed genuinely excited, and Jorey asked Kip whether he would be able to spend part of the day with him. "It was so helpful yesterday."

"Of course," Kip said. "I can walk around with you in the morning. In the afternoon I'm going to meet the Indian sorcerer and talk about bringing him to Peachtree, though."

"When do we get to meet him?" Charity asked.

"If we convince him to come teach for us, you'll meet him before we go home."

They'd arrived at Trippenhuis, and Emily said, "We'll do our best to bring him along, but that will depend on how Alice and I do today."

"We believe you can do anything, Headmistress," Charity said, earning a smile.

They passed an old man who had set up a table in the street across from the corner of Trippenhuis and called out from behind it to the people walking by. "Hear the secrets of Divination!" he said in French-accented English. "Learn the discipline that nobody dares to teach!"

Jorey hurried up to walk beside Kip. "Can he see the future?"

"No," Kip said. "There are some sorcerers who think they can, but they can't."

"Why do they think they can, if they can't?"

Malcolm laughed shortly. "Dear boy, if you can solve that problem, then the human race, yes, and Calatians too, will be ready to take the next great step forward."

"I mean…" The squirrel's nose twitched. "I know when I cast a spell to lift something that it worked because I can see it lifted. If their spells don't work, why do they think they do?"

"Because when you cast spells predicting the future, you can be very vague," Kip said.

Alice chimed in as they walked past the table, ignoring the man. "I could predict that you will have lunch today. Or I could predict that at some point in the future, you will eat cheese. But I don't need to cast a spell to do that."

"Or," Kip said, "they predict things like the King of England falling, and whenever it happens, they can say they predicted it."

Jorey absorbed this. "So they just make everything up?"

"Sometimes so much that they believe it." Kip gathered all the students in front of him as Emily presented their list of names at the door.

The footman examined Emily's paper but did not move aside for them. "Ah, my apologies," he said, "but the birds may not be permitted in the building."

"What?" Emily's tone had her raven lift its head, and Ash stirred as well. "They came in with us yesterday."

"I am aware, ma'am, but they are not allowed inside today."

"Whyever not?"

"I am sorry, ma'am, I only know they are not allowed inside today. Please." He gestured to the people waiting behind her.

Kip told Ash to fly up to the roof, and when Emily heard the rustle of wings, she whirled on them. "Don't—all right," she said, seeing Corvi still on Malcolm's shoulder, and turned back to the footman. "Do you see Master O'Brien?"

"Of course I do, ma'am, but—"

"His raven is how he gets around. If you take it away, you're leaving him with no way to get around, no way to see the exhibits. He might as well not even come in."

The footman shifted. "I am very sorry, ma'am. You may speak to the director of guests if you care to. He is in the Salon at present. But I cannot allow the birds into the building."

Malcolm placed a hand on Emily's shoulder as she took a breath to argue further. "It's all right," he said. "I'll wait out here while you go sort it out."

"I'll wait with you," Kip offered.

"Don't worry," Malcolm said. "Out here, I won't be alone." He nodded his head toward Corvi.

"All right. But be careful. Ash is up on the roof if you need anything."

"Thank you, my friend." Malcolm reached out and shook Kip's paw, and then stepped back against the wall as Kip, Emily, and Alice—without ravens—entered the building.

Emily disappeared into the Salon, leaving Alice behind, while Kip escorted Jorey around some of the exhibits they hadn't seen previously, facilitating his conversations but then stepping back to allow the young squirrel to talk by himself. He did well, Kip thought; more forward than Kip himself would have been, but that was good. He asked smart questions and thought about the answers when they were given.

After lunch, Richard and Charity took Jorey off to see some of the exhibits they wanted to talk about before doing their homework, and that left Kip free to talk briefly to Emily. "Did you sort out the business with the ravens?" he asked.

Her expression told him the answer even before she snapped, "No. Someone lodged a complaint, and they say that a raven was used to commit a 'most grievous violation of privacy,' and nobody here will tell me who it was. I don't want to suspect Victor of everything, but—"

"But I did send Ash to follow Farley yesterday."

"Yes." Emily sighed and unclenched her fists.

"If I'd known—"

"You couldn't have. You did the right thing and you should do it again if there's the chance. They can't forbid ravens outside the school."

Kip nodded. "So is Malcolm coming in?"

"He says there's little point if he can't have a raven or a demon to see, and he has a point. I asked him to keep an eye out for Farley and he said he would do that and I didn't need to invent a task to make him feel useful." She rolled her eyes. "I think there are things he could learn here, and I told him that we don't know for sure that demons are forbidden. He said it wasn't worth the risk."

"I'll check on him now and then," Kip promised.

"Do that. He'll hate it." Emily smiled.

"But now I should go make sure Chakrabarti can join me for the afternoon. I'd like you both to meet him."

"Of course. We'll be down here. We have a French noblewoman to meet with and then..." She turned to Alice.

"Russians," Alice said.

"Yes, Russians. Everyone seems at least politely interested to get on the good side of the Americans in one way or another, and that should benefit us even if we are the fifth or tenth best way to do that."

"In their minds," Kip said.

"Of course."

He hugged Alice and kissed her good-bye. "Back in a moment, I hope."

Chakrabarti was behind his table talking to visitors, but met the fox's eye and gave a brief nod, so Kip waited until he'd finished and then walked up. "It's pleasant to see you again," the Indian sorcerer said, extending his hand.

Kip took it and shook. "The same to you. Are you free to come meet our headmistress?"

"Of course. I look forward to it." He stepped out from behind the table and walked alongside Kip as the fox returned to the stairs.

They had to wait for Emily and Alice to finish their other appointment, which gave Kip time to answer questions about the Lutris School and to find out that Chakrabarti had asked permission from his headmaster to take some time off to work in America. The school was reviewing his request. "There may be a question of whether the Lutris School will make some kind of gift to compensate for my absence," he said. "I am sorry about that but it goes according to our traditions."

"Of course," Kip said. "We can discuss that with Emily when they're free."

At that moment, Emily shook hands with the nobleman and they both stood, He departed a moment later, so Kip and Chakrabarti walked up and took his place.

Kip introduced them, and apart from Chakrabarti asking Emily if it had been difficult for her to take on a man's job ("it's a woman's job now I have it," Emily replied), everything went rather smoothly. They soon got down to talking about facilities at the Lutris School and compensation, leaving Kip and Alice to sit together with clasped paws and listen.

About thirty minutes into this conversation, an official of the Exposition came into the room and announced that the Athaeneum's demonstration was about to begin in the large exhibit hall. Fully half the people in the Salon got up to move to the back room.

"Do you know what they're demonstrating?" Alice asked. "I feel like they told us."

None of them did. "I would be pleased to accompany you," Chakrabarti said. "If you care to find out."

"It depends on how long it takes," Emily looked at Alice. "The French woman was the best prospect we've had yet."

"The French love us," Alice said. "I believe we could go see for a short time. It would be nice to be able to talk about it with our hosts, should they ask."

"Very true." Emily rose. "All right, let's go see what it's about."

Despite the warnings, they had to stand for almost half an hour before the demonstration actually began. As soon as the curtain rose, the crowd quieted, and Kip knew what the Dutch masters were going to demonstrate. Next to a Dutch sorcerer on the stage stood a weasel-Calatian, eyes downcast to the wood of the platform. Kip didn't know him specifically, but he was clearly a calyx, and so: "They're going to summon a demon," he murmured.

"What?" Chakrabarti sounded more startled than Kip had yet heard him.

"He's got a calyx up there," Kip said. "They're going to show off their calyx magic. What's the most flashy calyx magic? Demon summoning."

"That's right," Alice said. "One of the nobles mentioned it yesterday. I'd forgotten until now."

"This is not good." Chakrabarti pressed his fingertips together.

"Why not?" Kip asked. "Because of the binding?"

"The summoning of spirits is forbidden in India," the other sorcerer said. "It is considered to be blasphemous."

"To Hindus?"

"To all faiths!" Chakrabarti bowed his head. "My apologies. I understand that it is a practice in the British Empire and in other European countries. If I were to come to America, I would restrain my objections to the practice, though I hope I would not be asked to cast such a spell myself."

"Of course not," Emily said. "Honestly, we don't summon demons very much anymore."

"But may I ask why it's blasphemous?" Alice asked, which Kip had wanted to ask but didn't feel comfortable enough to.

"Spirits exist beyond the world we know, and some are gods," Chakrabarti said. "It is as if you could cast a spell that would summon your God to manifest in your presence and follow your commands. Would you do that, or would your Church prevent you?"

"The Church would prevent us," Kip said, "although they don't seem to mind the raising of demons."

Chakrabarti had calmed. "Your church believes in only one god. We believe in hundreds. When there are many, who can say whether a spirit from another world might be a god or might not? The great Hiravijay Suri said, 'Do not trouble another living being from its home, be it the smallest insect or greatest spirit.' We sorcerers do not all follow his religion, but his work on the spirit world is unmatched in our history. There is one sect that believes even sorcery itself to be immoral as they say that our power is drawn from the spirit world and the act of drawing it may harm the spirits there." He bowed. "If you will excuse me, I would prefer not to watch this."

Kip was certain that the weasel on stage had seen him and was continuing to avoid his gaze, so he was happy to leave along with Chakrabarti. Emily likewise had little desire to see a demon summoned, but Alice wanted to wait and see if anything went wrong. She remained behind while the others returned to the Salon.

CHAPTER SEVEN: SPECTACLE

B ack in the Salon, Chakrabarti apologized for his "outburst," which Kip thought rather an exaggeration. "I knew when I came here that we might be witness to a summoning," the Indian sorcerer said. "I do not know why I was not prepared to see it thrust in front of me on a grand stage, something to be admired."

"The Dutch only got calyxes two years ago," Emily said. "They have an interest in showing off to the great powers that they know how to use them. This is a very political demonstration." She looked around the Salon and gestured to the Dutch flags hanging in the corners. "This whole Exposition is very political, come to that."

"Yes," Chakrabarti agreed. "We were pleased to be invited. Quite often, European interest in India is limited to what spices we can trade them, or what gems they can take from us."

"But don't you have sorcery?" Kip asked. "Surely they can't just come in and take things."

"There are more ways to take over a country than by force." Chakrabarti laced his fingers together and looked down over his mustache. "I have told you how the East India Trading Company has insinuated itself into our government. Now its directors are consulted on some government decisions. Presents are made to them of the sort one would give to neighboring maharajas. I would not be at all surprised to return to India and find that one of the East India Company directors has been given an official station in our government."

"That doesn't seem right." Emily frowned.

"Their money raises them to those levels," Chakrabarti said. "Many of us worry about where it will go. Your revolution has been an inspiration, and yet perhaps the British have learned from it too. There has been no destruction of a college, not even an act of violence, so if we were to begin a conflict, we would be the aggressors. In addition, India is made up of many many states, who would all have to agree to work together. The ones who do not get money from East India Company are very keen to attack. The ones who are rich, they are not so interested. And there are remote states who do not care."

"We are starting to have some of those problems," Emily said. "Each of our states was once a colony with its own government and people, and they want to preserve that identity, but we also know that none of us is strong enough to be a force in the world alone."

Chakrabarti nodded. "This is one reason I would like very much to travel to America. I think there is much we can learn from you. But more than that, I have lived in Calcutta my whole life, and only visited a few of the states that make up India. This travel, to Amsterdam, is the first time I have been to Europe. I would like to see more of the world, and not only see it, but understand it. To understand a place, you must live there."

"Lucky for us," Kip said with a smile.

"Oh." Chakrabarti turned to him. "I believe that if you asked my colleagues, half of them would give the same answer. Many of them wished very much to come with me, but I told them that a healer was what you were looking for. Still." He turned to Emily. "Should you wish to add more sorcerers, I can recommend some."

She laughed shortly. "That's good to know. Right now we have only enough money to bring on one healer, perhaps two, and those are our greatest need. We have physical sorcerers, alchemical, and translocational, but—" She met Kip's eye. "No spiritual."

"Spiritual sorcerers are very important." Chakrabarti leaned forward and spoke earnestly. "I am not trained in many advanced spiritual techniques, but our spiritual sorcerers are used often to help protect government officials, preside at public meetings, and raise the spirits of armies."

"Raise the spirits of armies?" Kip hadn't heard this. "Here, we have strict rules about spiritual magic being used on people."

"Without their consent," Emily reminded him. "If an army consents to be…uplifted, then there's no ethical problem with it, I suppose. It seems a very large undertaking, especially without calyxes."

"Four spiritual sorcerers working together may affect the spirits of an army of one or two hundred men," Chakrabarti said. "So I am told. I have not worked that magic myself. I know only a few spells purely of the mind. My specialty is the connection of mind and body."

Alice walked up during this remark and sat at the table with them. Without looking at Kip, she addressed Chakrabarti directly. "Do you have any experience interpreting dreams?"

"Dreams?" He looked startled.

"Yes." Now she looked at Kip.

He put his ears back. "It's nothing," he said. "We don't want to bother Chakrabarti with—"

Alice interrupted. "Kip's been having the same dream quite often. It's troubling."

"Alice, really. There will be plenty of time for this if Chakrabarti comes back to Peachtree with us," Emily said.

"There's no harm in asking."

Chakrabarti smiled and held his hands out. "There are those in Calcutta who will explain the meanings of dreams," he said. "But not in the schools of sorcery."

"You see?" Kip gestured. "You might as well ask that old man yelling on the street about Divination."

"Just because you don't want it to be anything serious doesn't mean it isn't," Alice retorted.

"Oh, please," Chakrabarti said. "I beg your pardon. I did not mean to make light of this. A dream that returns may be a message from one of the gods. I only meant that those who could interpret it would be found in the church rather than the school of sorcery."

"Oh." Alice's ears perked up. "We haven't gone to a priest."

"We aren't going to," Kip said firmly. He'd only just met Chakrabarti and didn't want to explain the "feelings of betrayal" in the dream to him any more than he wanted to talk about them to a priest. "There's nothing but the same images, no premonitions of death or anything. Besides, if something were going to happen, it would have happened by now."

"You've been having this dream for two years and you won't go see anyone about it. How do you know what's going to happen or when it might happen?"

"Master Chakrabarti," Emily said, standing, "it's been a great pleasure meeting you, and I hope we can bring you to Peachtree with us. I'm afraid Alice and I have to meet with some other people now."

While Chakrabarti explained that he had not attained the rank of Master in his country and Emily responded that they would have to call him that if he were going to teach, Alice gave Kip a look that meant that this discussion wasn't over. He pushed back his annoyance and reached over to take her paw. "I know you're concerned," he said. "I promise that when we get back, I will ask someone to look into it."

She rolled her eyes in a very Emily-like way. "I'll believe that when it happens," she said. "But thank you for thinking to say it."

Kip and Chakrabarti spent the rest of the afternoon together talking about India and America and about sorcery, a discussion Kip thoroughly enjoyed. After a walk through the first floor's rooms, they went outside to join Malcolm.

Chakrabarti pulled his robes more tightly around himself as they stepped outside, but the brisk, pleasant chill invigorated Kip. Through the eyes of Ash, he found Malcolm easily, an island of calm in the crowd of loud, boisterous sorcerers, and led Chakrabarti to the edge of the canal where Malcolm sat on a stone post with the cool breeze from the canal in his face. He didn't seem to mind the smell of garbage that lingered around the water, but Kip wrinkled his nose and held a paw in front of it.

"Hallo, you two," Malcolm said as they approached. Chakrabarti looked taken aback at this, so Kip reminded him of Malcolm's raven, perched above them on the roof of Trippenhuis. The Indian sorcerer felt comfortable enough to ask Malcolm what had happened to his eyes, and when Malcolm began by telling him that a demon was responsible, Kip encouraged Chakrabarti to explain his country's beliefs about demons. He had to speak up to be heard over the sorcerers around them, even to Kip's sensitive ears.

Malcolm asked many questions along the same lines that Kip had. When he'd finished, though, he asked, "And has Kip told you that he has some of the same ideas about demons?"

"Ah." Chakrabarti turned to Kip. "He has not."

"We haven't talked much about it, but he doesn't like to summon demons anymore. He thinks perhaps they have more humanity than we give them credit for."

"They at least seem like living beings," Kip said. "I'd never thought that we draw magic from their home, or that it might be harming them."

"That," Chakrabarti said, "is considered rather extreme. That sect also will not wear footwear for fear of harming insects. And yet, there is something to the idea. If too many towns drink from the same pond, the water quickly becomes foul. And how can we know the effect if we cannot see the place we draw magic from? We—my branch of Hinduism—believe that the good we do with magic outweighs the imagined ill, but can we be sure?"

"A demon offered to take me to the demon plane once," Kip said. "To the spirit world. I just didn't know how I'd get back."

"Or if it was a trap," Malcolm said.

Kip smiled and explained, "Malcolm and I have had very different experiences of demons."

"Aye," Malcolm said. "If you'd seen the one that did this to my eyes… would you like to hear the story?"

Chakrabarti said he would, and so Malcolm told it, how Farley Broadside had wanted a demon and Malcolm had casually dropped the name of a fourth-order demon, telling Farley it was second-order. How Farley had kidnapped Kip and intended to show his superiority in sorcery by killing him with a demon, but found himself unable to control it once summoned. How Farley had been turned into a marmot-Calatian and had gasped out Malcolm's name so that the demon summoned him and removed his eyes. And how Kip had somehow found the strength to banish the demon. Here the Indian sorcerer's eyes flicked over to Kip, studying him, and Kip splayed his ears and looked away.

The sun sank lower in the sky, and their conversation moved on to comparing weather, food, and other local customs. Chakrabarti's easy manner made Kip even more sure that the sorcerer would work well with the rest of them in Peachtree. If Emily could get enough money to pay him—once they found out what he would want to be paid—then everything would work out.

Their students came out of Trippenhuis as the day ended, talking amongst themselves and still holding their journals. Charity saw Kip and Malcolm and interrupted the chatter of the other two to guide them to the adults. Richard came up to Malcolm first. "Master O'Brien," he said, standing tall, "we were able to complete our reports even though some of the sorcerers didn't want to talk to Charity and Jorey. I vouched for them and there was almost a fight."

"A fight?" Kip's hackles went up.

"It wasn't exactly a fight," Charity said. "One of the Prussian sorcerers got rather loud and told Richard he hadn't learned enough to be speaking that way, and Richard said—" She looked at him.

"That respect and courtesy didn't require any kind of scholarly learning," Richard said. "And he glared at me and I said I could defend myself and my friends, and then one of his colleagues took him and pulled him back."

Corvi soared down from the roof and landed on Malcolm's shoulder to glare at the students. "Standing up for your classmates is good," Malcolm said, "but have a care how you do it. Not every battle that presents itself to you is one you're obliged to engage in."

Richard's face fell, but Charity and Jorey nodded, and after a moment he joined in. "I know, but it just wasn't right," Richard said stubbornly. "What he was saying."

"Perhaps not," Malcolm said. "Surely not. But what if you'd started a true fight and been expelled from the hall, or, God forbid, injured? How would you be able to present me with these lovely reports then?"

Charity stifled a giggle, and even Richard smiled. "Yes, sir," he said.

"You've a good heart," Malcolm told him, "and that's a fine thing to have, and not something we can teach you. Aye, and I know well it hurts to bridle it sometimes, but fine hearts can run away with you just as wicked hearts can, and sometimes more easily as their motives seem good and just. Now, let's hear those reports."

Malcolm introduced Chakrabarti and then listened to their reports, looking through the notes they'd taken and giving a good deal of praise along with ideas for what to look for on the following day. While they were talking, Kip and Chakrabarti drew back farther down the canal to talk quietly together.

"Your students seem very intelligent," Chakrabarti said. "I had heard that many in the British Empire are too proud for instruction, but that does not seem to be the case."

"No," Kip said, "although when I was in school a few years ago there were certainly some of those."

Chakrabarti asked him about his schooling, but at that moment he noticed Jorey trying to catch his eye, so he beckoned the squirrel over. "What is it?" he asked.

"I'm sorry to disturb you, Master Penfold," Jorey said, "but I thought you should know that Charity was very brave as well."

"Oh?"

The squirrel nodded. "When Richard said that to the sorcerer, it was because he made a very rude remark to Charity, but she stepped back and didn't say anything. And then when Richard made ready to fight, Charity came up with me to hold him back even though it meant coming under the eyes of those sorcerers again."

Kip nodded. "That's brave indeed. Why did she leave that out?"

"She didn't want to have to say what the sorcerers said," Jorey whispered. "I don't want to tell you. It was very cruel."

"All right, we'll leave it at that. But thank you for telling me," Kip said.

Jorey remained by him as he told Chakrabarti a little more about the classes at the Lutris School, but in the middle of it a loud argument approached them through the crowd. He tried to ignore it, but the two men's voices increased in volume and sharpness until he couldn't shut them out even by flattening his ears. From the roof, Ash showed him two men moving toward the canal, not directly at them but definitely in their direction.

They were loud enough that even Chakrabarti noticed. He saw Kip's ears go down and said, "With your sensitive hearing, it must be difficult to keep your concentration in public places."

"You learn to filter things out." Kip smiled tightly. "But sometimes you just can't."

"I would worry in a place like this." Chakrabarti looked back toward Trippenhuis. "When sorcerers have disputes, it is the innocents who suffer.

There is an old story that there was an ancient village called Hanumana where two sorcerers fought over a woman. They fought for twelve days, it is told, and at the end of it there was no sign that the village had ever stood, and everyone in it was gone."

"I hope there are enough sorcerers here to stop these two before they erase Amsterdam." The two did look as though they might come to blows, and at least one of them sounded drunk. Kip readied himself in case someone needed to intervene, very aware of his students so close by. In the crowd around him, a few other sorcerers watched the argument intently as well. They were talking in what sounded like German, so he couldn't make out what they were saying, but the louder one's words slurred into each other while his companion spoke more precisely.

As they approached the canal, the drunk sorcerer shoved his companion away, pointed at Richard, and yelled something in German. Richard looked startled and said something to Malcolm, but a moment later he rose into the air. His arms glowed with ruby light, but before he could cast a spell, the drunk sorcerer had thrown him into the canal.

While this was going on, Charity had lunged toward the drunk sorcerer but Malcolm gripped her arm to stop her. The drunk, noticing, turned his attention to them while the sorcerer he'd been arguing with tried again to hold him. This time the drunk shoved his companion away and yelled something at Malcolm, at which point Jorey took a step forward and Kip grabbed his robe. "Malcolm has wards up," he said, casting a spell himself to pull Richard from the canal and keeping his awareness heightened. It would do no good for him to enter the fight now, not when he had students to protect, but he could not help wishing that Emily were here to translocate the drunk.

Richard, feeling Kip's spell on him, had focused his magic elsewhere. Water rose in a great wave from the canal toward the shore. Kip cursed. He summoned magic to try to cast a second spell, but before he could, the drunken sorcerer pushed the wave back toward Richard with a jeering yell. Kip only just lifted him out of the way in time.

By this time, several sorcerers had formed a circle around the drunk, but he wouldn't let anyone get close enough to translocate or cast spiritual magic on him. As they closed in, he shot up above the crowd, laughing, and then his laughter turned to a startled yell as he arrowed toward the canal himself, his physical magic no match for the combined spells of several of the people below.

Kip relaxed; it looked like the fight was over. But he did not let go of Jorey, and it was a good thing, because a large tree that stood beside the canal toppled over unnaturally quickly with a loud rumbling as the roots broke the surface, dislodging stones that fell into the canal. Most of the people below got out of the way, but a few were struck by its branches. Whether the drunk had done this from the canal or someone else had used the fight as cover wasn't clear.

Richard came safely down beside Kip and Jorey. "That was the Prussian sorcerer," he said, dripping and breathless.

"Are you all right?" Jorey ran to him before Kip could get the question out.

"Only my dignity was harmed, but the rest of me is quite wet," Richard said.

"There are wounded." Chakrabarti gathered his robes about him. "I should go. They have restrained the sorcerer now, I see."

Indeed, a Dutch sorcerer Kip recognized had come to the edge of the canal and another had translocated to the middle of it, one hand on the shoulder of the drunk Prussian. A moment later, the two of them stood on the canal's edge where the other sorcerer met them, and together the two Dutchmen led the Prussian away.

Kip followed Chakrabarti to watch him minister to the wounded, leaving Richard and Jorey with Charity, who looked upset. "I tried to translocate to Richard so I could send him to safety," she said, "but I couldn't do it quickly enough. I couldn't follow him as he was moving."

"That's advanced," Malcolm said gently. "It was well thought, though. You'll learn that skill soon enough, and we will be working on wards and defensive magic that will also serve in a situation like this."

Hopefully there wouldn't be more situations like this, not for the students. Kip sighed and trailed Chakrabarti as the sorcerer, along with two or three other healers, attended to the half-dozen wounded. It looked like the worst injury was a deep cut to the forearm of a Dutch sorcerer, who kept saying over and over that they shouldn't have allowed liquor at the Salon even as Chakrabarti mended his wound.

When everyone had been healed, Kip and Chakrabarti walked back to Malcolm. "I should've expected," Kip said, but his words trailed off as he saw Victor Adamson lounging outside the nearer doorway of Trippenhuis. The young man surveyed the crowd and then met Kip's eyes and smiled, lifting a glass as though making a toast.

"Expected what?" Malcolm asked.

Kip shook his head. "Oh. There's alcohol here. That's all." He scanned the area around Malcolm, where Charity and Jorey were at the canal's edge. "Where's Richard?"

"He went to help with the tree," Charity called.

"Of all the…" He must have gone around behind them while Chakrabarti was healing. Kip excused himself and pushed through the crowd toward the tree, which now stood upright amid a circle of sorcerers—including the still-dripping Richard.

The tall boy looked satisfied until his eyes lit on Kip, and then he saw right away that the fox was mad at him. He stepped away, his expression changing to confusion. "I was only trying to help," he said as Kip strode up and grabbed his arm. "It's partly my fault the tree's knocked down."

"You've got to stay with us or with your fellow students." Kip looked around again, but Victor was gone. "This fight wasn't your fault. It might have been provoked."

"What?" Richard looked genuinely startled.

Kip stopped, still some twenty feet from Malcolm and the others. He lowered his voice. "I don't want to alarm any of you, and I don't want you to say anything to Jorey. But you deserve to know why you shouldn't go off on your own. There's someone here who has a particular interest in magical Calatians. This fight might have been a gambit to separate you two from Jorey, and if he hadn't been talking to me at the time, it would have worked. So if you see a hooded figure or that blond man standing by the door, and we're not around, take the others and get away as fast as you can."

Richard absorbed this and then looked about for either of the people Kip had warned him about. It didn't take long for him to spot Victor, but to his credit, he didn't point. "Is the blond man this Adamson fellow you warned us about?"

"Yes," Kip said. "He's very dangerous, even if he doesn't appear to be."

"I think if we saw a 'hooded figure,' we should quite definitely run the other way," Richard said. "But would someone really kidnap Jorey? I'd have thought our greatest danger was drunken sorcery. That fellow disliked me from the start, and liquor fed his anger."

"Liquor that someone might have given him. And how would it look for our school if our students were seen publicly brawling? We're trying to convince teachers to come work with you, so you must be on your very best behavior."

Richard lowered his head and didn't answer. Kip pulled him back toward Malcolm, going on as they walked. "I know you want to be a hero, but you must choose the right time."

"I helped with the tree. That wasn't bad, was it?"

"No. And let's be clear: he attacked you. There was no fault of yours there. But the wave out of the canal—that wasn't necessary."

"It could have been anyone," Richard protested with a smile. "There were half a dozen people trying to control him."

Kip laughed shortly, arriving next to Chakrabarti. "It could have been anyone, but I know it was you. Now stay here with Charity and Jorey and we'll all walk back to the hotel together in a moment." Ash kept an eye on Victor, who'd watched Kip without any change in his amused expression.

"I've just been explaining to Master Chakrabarti here," Malcolm said as Kip and Richard arrived, "that alcohol is not permitted in our colleges, as he's been telling me it's forbidden in his."

"I am surprised that sorcerers are permitted to indulge here," Chakrabarti said.

"For my part, I'm surprised it was only two." Malcolm gestured at the crowd. "All these people, and wine flowing freely in the Salon. Mind you, it takes a good amount of determination to get that drunk on wine. I prefer a nice whisky myself, or did, back when it was allowed."

"Neither of you drink at all?" Chakrabarti looked between them.

Malcolm shook his head as Kip said, "No. I can't ever lose control, or I could do more than just drop a tree on someone."

"Ah, yes. The Road." Chakrabarti nodded and clasped his hands in front of himself. "I have often thanked the gods for blessing me with the power I have. I would not trust myself with the capacity for destruction."

"Some of us have no choice," Kip said, though he was thinking about all the harm a spiritual sorcerer might in fact do.

"Yes, of course, of course." He turned to Malcolm. "And what sort of sorcery do you practice, Master O'Brien?"

"I'm a defensive specialist," Malcolm said. "I cast a ward over myself and Charity, and you two as well."

"Malcolm kept me alive during the war, for sure," Kip said.

"Ah, maybe I spared you a concussion or two." Malcolm smiled broadly. "'Tis nothing, really."

Chakrabarti inclined his head. "I look forward to hearing many stories about the war."

"Ah, you're asking the wrong people, sir," Richard said. "These two won't give us any war stories no matter how much we ask to hear about their valiant deeds of heroism."

"Aye." Malcolm swatted playfully at his shoulder. "Almost as though war is a terrible, grim enterprise and not a fantastic adventure."

Richard bore the swat stoutly, standing before Charity and Jorey. Charity spoke up. "But if you won't tell us the stories, how are we to know how to act in situations like these?"

"I'm right here," Kip said. "You could have asked."

"Sometimes there isn't time." This was Jorey, standing on Richard's other side.

Malcolm laughed. "All right, it's wonderful and admirable that you all stand up for each other. It warms my heart, it does. But for the moment, your best course of action is to avoid these situations, at least until you've a little more training."

"How much did you have when you kept all the Calatians safe in Australia?" Jorey asked.

"More than a year and a half. Now let's all get on back to the hotel."

They walked off with Malcolm, grumbling good-naturedly. Kip and Chakrabarti followed a short way behind. As they passed Trippenhuis, Kip looked for Victor, but the blond man was no longer there. "We're very proud of them," he said to Chakrabarti, "as I expect you can tell."

"With good reason." The Indian sorcerer smiled. "I can also understand that you would need help with discipline."

Emily and Alice arrived back at the hotel that evening with some good news: the French nobles they'd been talking to had agreed to help the school. "Provisionally," Emily said as everyone cheered, sitting around the hotel's parlor area.

"What does 'provisionally' mean?" Malcolm asked, his arm already around her shoulders.

"It means they're going to talk to some more people tomorrow and if they find someone they like better, we won't get anything." Alice stuck her tongue out.

"Mmm." Malcolm stroked his chin. "Can we kidnap them? Just for a day?"

Emily laughed. "If only. We've made our case and I did lean rather heavily on my association with the Adamses, so I hope they'll find that convincing enough."

"We don't have any other donors?" Kip asked.

Emily shook her head. "Not of substance."

"What about that von Bismarck?" Alice asked.

"Oh, yes. He pledged to send us some money, but it's really only enough to pay one of your healing masters. So that's good news. But the French nobles, they're discussing numbers that would—well, it would give us five years. They have an amount of money that is hard for me to comprehend."

"That's amazing," Kip said. "Well done."

"It's not done yet." Emily rose. "We've one more day, so we have a chance to find one more donor."

"If there's anything we can do to help," Kip said, "just ask. I don't have anything to do tomorrow except see Victor's demonstration."

"Oh, yes." Alice leaned against Kip's side. "What is that about?"

"I don't know. Nobody will tell me, least of all Victor."

"Take my advice." Malcolm leaned forward. "Don't go. You don't need to give him the satisfaction."

"I don't want to go, but I don't think I can stop myself. What if I don't go and he ends up showing something powerful that we need to be warned about? Maybe he wanted to show off to me?"

"He's always felt inferior." Malcolm tapped the table. "And with good reason."

"He's not incapable or useless," Kip argued. "He just doesn't have the one thing he really wants."

"If he had it, he wouldn't want it any more." Emily gestured around to them. "Now that's enough talk about Victor and enough talk in general. We have one more day, so let's all get some sleep."

Kip and Malcolm spent most of the next day keeping an eye on the students, Kip inside Trippenhuis and Malcolm outside, as the Exposition refused to reverse its rule on the ravens despite Emily's protest. Richard and Charity avoided the Prussian group altogether, making their final day reports on the non-European countries, and Jorey mostly stayed with them, though he did go back to talk to the British sorcerers.

When the time came for Victor's presentation, Kip walked down to the Salon with Richard, Charity, and Jorey, the two humans ahead of him and the squirrel at his side. Charity and Richard talked about an alchemical sorcerer who had fused sand into many-colored glass in a variety of decorative shapes; Richard had met a French apprentice of physical sorcery and had struck up a friendship, but they were struggling to find out how to correspond once the Exposition was over. Jorey remained uncharacteristically quiet until Kip asked what he'd seen, and he said he had seen the fused glass display with Charity and was trying to work out whether he could make something of value with it that the school or his family could sell.

Kip thought this an interesting idea, though he gently reminded Jorey that creating something beautiful required artistic training as well as magic. But he encouraged the squirrel to keep thinking about it as they walked into the Salon and joined the people pushing to get into the hall beyond. Making their way through the small doorway, they found a place together in the exhibition hall near Emily and Alice.

Jorey stayed close to Kip, looking around at the crowd of humans, his nose twitching. Kip made sure to keep the young squirrel in front of him so that he wouldn't lose track of him as he focused his attention on the stage. The crowd was more restless now than at the exhibition on the first day, which Kip would not have expected after three days of walking around. He focused his ears on and caught snatches of conversation around him, people talking about what they were there to see.

Like him, many of them had talked to Victor, and he had told them the same story he'd told Kip. Something "incredible," something "unprecedented," something "revolutionary." Kip wanted to tell them that Victor was probably lying, but part of him worried that the magic-less sorcerer had in fact uncovered something of great interest. Exchanging a look with Emily, he saw that she shared his thoughts.

They did not have much more time to speculate; barely ten minutes after they arrived, Victor strode out onto the stage. The crowd murmur quieted as he made his way to the center of the stage and stopped there, hands steepled in front of him, head bowed. Only when the room was nearly silent did Victor look up.

"Ladies and gentlemen," he said, with a stronger English accent than Kip remembered him having. "Thank you all for coming. I have promised many of you a unique, historical spectacle, and I promise that you will not be disappointed. In a moment I will bring out on stage my two assistants, but before that, I would like to give you a little bit of history to provide the context for what you are about to see."

Lovely, Kip thought, but he kept his ears forward. Beside him, Emily sighed.

"Throughout history, we have understood sorcery to be divided, broadly, into three classes: earthly spells, which include all physical, alchemical, and spiritual magic; ætherial spells, which include summonings and translocation; and Great Feats, which may appear to be earthly in nature but which persist beyond the death of the sorcerer and are therefore suspected to have an ætherial component."

Kip stood straighter and turned to Emily. She appeared to be just as bewildered by this system of classification as most of the sorcerers around them also seemed to be.

"Perhaps you have not heard of these classes." Victor wore the faintly superior smile Kip knew well. "They have not seen broad use, but a few sorcerers in history and today have explored the difference between Earth and Æther. I set myself to this task some two years ago and am pleased to present you with the first fruits of my labors." He waited for the crowd noise to rise, and then said over the loud murmurs, "Today you will witness the first replication of a Great Feat."

The crowd erupted. "Won't be a Great Feat then, will it?" someone near Kip said, while behind him a man said, "Impossible!" in a German accent. These sentiments were echoed over and over until Victor held up a pale white hand.

Slowly, the crowd stilled. "I understand your skepticism," he said. "Believe me, I have faced it many times. I would not be here if I could not answer it convincingly."

Jorey looked up at Kip. "He can't really…?" he whispered, as Victor went on.

"Shh," Kip said. "Judge by the action, not the words."

"Good policy with Victor anyway," Emily muttered.

"You know Master Adamson?" a sorcerer behind them asked with a slight Dutch accent.

Kip and Emily both turned and nodded shortly. The sorcerer said, "I hear he is quite brilliant."

"He kidnapped me once and almost killed me." Alice turned only enough to make sure the sorcerer heard her words.

He subsided, but a moment later asked, "Was this for—?"

They never heard the justification he was going to present for Victor's actions, because Victor finished his spiel and gestured to the curtain hanging at one side of the stage. Two men walked out, one a sorcerer in robes, and the other—

Kip stood straighter. He hissed to Emily, "Is that—?"

"Looks like him," she whispered back. "But it can't be."

Alice squinted and then gasped. "Farley?"

To all appearances, the first man to join Victor on stage was broad-shouldered, dark, sulky Farley Broadside—not as Kip had seen him most recently, a marmot-Calatian in a hooded cloak, but as Kip had known him in school, a stocky bully, fully human.

Emily looked down at the floor and Kip knew her thoughts as surely as if he could hear them. If this demon curse could be reversed, then what of Malcolm's? Could he have his eyes restored? And then: if this was real, would they have to ask Victor for help?

"My very gracious volunteer here will help me demonstrate, and Master Gupta will cast the necessary spells." The second man, a gaunt-faced Indian sorcerer wrapped in a black robe, bowed as Victor spoke his name.

There was only one Great Feat in memory that Victor could be thinking of re-creating, and it didn't take the crowd long to come to the same conclusion Kip did. "He's going to make a Calatian," he breathed, and then he went one step farther. "It's a trick."

"What?" Emily took a half-step closer to him.

"It's not real," he said, as Victor raised his hands and called for silence. Kip lowered his voice so that Emily, leaning in, could hear him. Jorey looked up as well, ears perked. "There's an illusion on Farley. He's just going to take it away."

"Sorcery can make people see what's not there?" Jorey asked.

"It's spiritual magic." Emily squinted at the stage. "It's very hard to do with so many people, though, and at a distance like this."

"Yes," Kip said, "but Chakrabarti told me that in India they have spiritual sorcerers who can affect crowds, at least for a short time." He wrapped his robe around his paws and gathered magic, casting a quick spell to free himself from spiritual holds, on the chance that it might be effective against Victor's illusion. He completed the spell while Master Gupta was still in the process of casting his, and peered eagerly at the stage.

There was no change. Farley remained human, glowering down at the boards. And then Master Gupta finished his spell and raised his arms with a flourish.

Farley let out a cry and doubled over, moaning, arms over his head. To Kip's ears, the moans sounded faked, but when Farley stood up, his face had changed to the marmot-Calatian, his hands were furred paws, and a thin tail uncurled behind him.

The room erupted in noise. "Incredible!" some cried, while others yelled, "Fakery!" For nearly a full minute, Victor held his pale hands up but was unable to calm the crowd. When finally the noise had subsided—though people at the front still agitated, reaching their hands up to try to touch Farley—he said, "I completely understand your surprise and disbelief. For years I have struggled against the same restrictive preconceptions. But I can assure you that this transformation is completely real. Any human can be turned into a Calatian."

Victor seemed to be staring directly at Kip as he said that. Was he challenging Kip to contradict him? Or was he boasting directly to Kip that he had, in fact, changed Farley back and forth from Calatian to human at will? What would that mean to the world and to Calatians if that spell existed and could be learned?

Kip's chest chilled. Jorey tugged on his robe. "It's a trick, right?"

"I think so. I mean, it has to be." He looked over Jorey's head at Emily, who also looked quite worried. "If that's all he has, though, we should take our leave."

He turned, but before he could take more than a step, someone near the front called loudly, "He's going to turn us all into animals!"

This incited an immediate panic. People turned and ran for the exits, pushing past each other. Some translocated out of the room but many either didn't know how or didn't trust themselves to cast the spell while being jostled and shoved. Kip curled his tail around him and held the tip to stop it being trampled; next to him, Jorey did the same, but a moment later Kip had lost sight of the squirrel as a wave of people pushed between them.

Richard and Charity had hold of each other. Kip took Charity's hand and pushed toward the squirrel, the two students trailing behind him. When they got close enough, he put Charity's hand in Jorey's paw. "Side exit," he said shortly, pointing toward the door he'd chased Farley out of two days ago.

They struggled across a stream of people heading for the exit into the Salon, pushing their way through as best they could. Kip spared a glance for the stage, where Victor was hustling Farley and Master Gupta back toward the curtained exit. The question ate at him: was this truly a spell, or just a trick?

They reached the cluster of people forcing their way through the side door as Kip reached a decision. "Go out," he told the students. "Find Malcolm and go directly back to the hotel. No heroics. I'll have Ash watching over you."

"Yes, sir," the squirrel said, and the two humans nodded.

Kip alerted Ash to watch the side door, then turned to make his way toward the stage. Ironically, it was easier to move against the current of people than across them, and in a few seconds he had reached the back of the crowd. A few sorcerers had clambered up onto the stage, headed for the exit

Victor had taken, so Kip followed them up, across the stage, and through a wooden door that hung ajar.

He caught up to them at an intersection in a narrow hallway where they stood arguing in Russian. When Kip reached them, the one nearest him said something sharply and then turned. "You are American sorcerer, yes?"

"Yes," Kip said. "You're looking for Victor?"

They all nodded, and the one who'd spoken, a short dark-haired man with a great black beard, said, "We wish to determine that it is not a falsehood." His brow lowered. "What do you think it is?"

"I think it's a trick," Kip said, "but I think it was a trick to make him seem human before the spell. I know that Calatian. He's demon-cursed."

One of the other sorcerers, a stocky red-bearded man, snapped what sounded like an oath in Russian. The black-bearded man said, "Ah! This explains much. Then why do you follow?"

"Because…" Kip squeezed his tail and let it go, finally. "There is a small chance that it is not a trick."

This set the three men to arguing in Russian again, during which time Kip checked with Ash. The raven had spotted the three students in the street and watched from the rooftops as they made their way to the hotel.

Finally the black-bearded sorcerer said, "Enough! This is Master Penfold. If anyone knows truth about Calatians, it is him. Master Penfold, do you know which way they may have gone?"

Kip lifted his nose to both hallways. Victor's perfume filled the air, but not more strongly in either direction as far as he could tell. "I'm sorry, no."

"Very well. Pasha!" The red-bearded sorcerer snapped to attention. "Take Lyosha and go that way. I will go with Master Penfold down this way."

The two sorcerers left down one of the hallways, leaving Kip and the black-bearded one to take the other. "Please," the Russian sorcerer said, "excuse my terrible manners. My name is Pyotr Petrovitch Koshka."

"A pleasure to meet you, Master Koshka," Kip said. "May I ask why you are so determined in your pursuit of Victor?"

"This exposition is almost over," Koshka said. "Master Adamson may return to England this very night, taking the proof of his spell with him. Do I return to my tsar with the information that we witnessed this great spell and yet tell him that we cannot say whether it was truly cast?" He shook his head. "Better to tell him nothing of it until we make certain, else he may assign us to discovering the means of this magic, which may not even exist."

"Maybe that's what Victor wants," Kip mused as he followed the other sorcerer down the hallway to the doors at its end. "To divert minds of foreign powers to a fool's errand."

They tried the first door and found an exit onto a shadowy street. The other door led to a small storage room, but Kip caught the smell of marmot as soon as the door opened. "They were here," he said. "At least, Farley was.

Victor's cologne is fainter. He might have come in to fetch Farley."

Koshka looked shrewdly at Kip as he closed the door. "You know the Master as well as the Calatian?"

"I know Victor Adamson, and yes, Farley is the Calatian, but he wasn't always one. I don't know the other sorcerer." Briefly, Kip told Koshka about Farley's encounter with a demon and his transformation. "So while it is possible that Victor turned him back…I don't believe Farley would allow himself to be transformed again. I think that third man was a spiritual sorcerer who made Farley appear human and then removed the illusion."

Koshka's companions approached from the other hallway, their footsteps audible before Kip could make out their forms. Koshka did not react if he saw them, only stroked his beard and stared down the hallway. "Then the purpose was to make other nations fear England, to make them believe she has lost nothing by losing the Colonies."

"That seems most likely," Kip agreed.

"Master Koshka," the red-bearded sorcerer called, now close enough for Kip to distinguish him. "There was nothing down that hallway save a storage room and an exit."

"Yes," Koshka said. "I fear we have been too slow, but look at what our energy has brought us: a meeting with a knowledgeable American sorcerer. He and I have developed a theory that I believe true enough to bring back to our tsar."

"That is good fortune indeed!"

Kip was about to reply when a note of panic from Ash drew his attention. He sent his consciousness to the raven, who was scanning a street full of people faster than Kip could parse. The sense of panic and the raven's movements told Kip as clearly as words that she had lost sight of the students.

Koshka was saying something, and Kip interrupted him. "I'm so sorry to interrupt, but I am urgently needed elsewhere."

"Of course." Koshka put his hands together in front of him and bowed slightly. "Thank you for your assistance, Master Penfold."

"It was a pleasure to meet you," Kip said in the few seconds it took him to gather magic and send himself to Ash's side.

CHAPTER EIGHT:

DISAPPEARANCES

A chilly wind cut across the roof where Ash perched. Kip drew his robe around himself and stared down at the street. Taking it in through his own eyes rather than Ash's frenetic searching helped him make sense of what he was seeing, but did not reveal the three students anywhere. "What happened?" he asked out of frustration, knowing that Ash couldn't answer.

Again he got the feeling of panic from the raven. She didn't understand any more than he did. And where were Emily and Malcolm?

"All right, all right." He reached out to stroke Ash's back, forcing himself to be calm so that she would calm down too. The first thing to try was translocating to the students directly. It would annoy them, but at least he'd know they were safe.

Translocating with a person as a destination was difficult and Kip had only recently succeeded in it. He called up his memory of Jorey, the one he was closest to, and pictured the squirrel's smile, his voice and scent, and the feeling Kip had when Jorey was around. Magic flowing through him, he formed the spell and cast it. The spell took hold, reached out for a destination, and—

—Kip remained where he was.

The spell had worked, so that meant Jorey was inside magical wards. There was a small chance that the wards were not related to the students' disappearance, that they were merely in a space that happened to be warded, but he did not feel that that was likely.

"Let's go back to the hotel," he told Ash without much hope. "Maybe everyone ended up there and Malcolm warded it."

She fluttered up to his shoulder, responding to his tone. Having a raven, Kip had discovered, was like having a very perceptive young child, and he'd learned to project calm and assurance even when (as now) he did not feel them naturally. Arabella and Aran responded much as Ash did, though even Aran was now of an age to question his parents rather than take their assurances on faith.

Kip translocated himself and Ash to the front of the hotel, a little above the street because he was worried there would be crowds. Some sorcerers milled about, along with a few others who cried out at the appearance of a levitating fox in sorcerer's robes, but Kip ignored them, lowering himself to the ground and hurrying into the hotel's lobby.

Alice found him before he spotted her and ran to him, with Emily trailing behind. "Are you all right?" Alice asked, throwing her arms around him.

"I'm fine," Kip said. "Where are the students?"

"Wasn't Ash watching them?" Alice looked up at Kip's raven, now scanning the lobby.

"She was, but she lost them somehow. I don't know what happened. I was talking to some Russian sorcerers and only half paying attention to Ash." Guilt tightened his chest. "I tried to translocate to them and couldn't. They haven't come back to the hotel?"

Emily shook her head. "Not that I've seen. Let me try to go to them." She closed her eyes for fifteen seconds, concentrating, and then opened them again. "Nothing. You don't think…"

Kip sighed. "I don't think Farley got to them. The stage exit was the other side of the building from the alley they left by. But I wouldn't be surprised if Victor managed to kidnap them somehow."

"Victor?" Alice startled. "Why?"

Emily nodded. "He's been after Kip for years. The chance of another magical Calatian? One less able to defend himself?"

"Jorey." Alice flattened her ears. "But why the others?"

Kip growled. "Deprive us of all our students. Ruin the college."

"He doesn't know that's all our students," Alice said.

Emily looked toward the doorway. "He wouldn't have to. He would assume we brought the best. Have you heard from Malcolm?"

This was to Kip. "No. I haven't seen him since this morning. I suppose he's still looking for the students too, if Corvi was watching them. Maybe he knows what happened."

"What a mess." Emily kept watching the entrance as more sorcerers wandered in and a few left, none of them Malcolm. The chatter in the hotel lobby rang louder than usual. "Knowing Victor, I feel this is exactly what he wished to have happen."

Kip told her what the Russian sorcerers had said. "He might also have wanted to get foreign sorcerers working toward fool's gold."

"Perhaps. But I feel this was aimed at us, if anyone."

"Us?" Alice asked.

"America," Emily clarified. "We're the country that used Calatians to win the war. This was a notice to us that Britain can create more Calatians if they like. And," she added as though it had just occurred to her, "a notice to our hosts that their new community of Calatians is not as valuable as they had thought? In any case, it has the stench of the Crown behind it."

"Which means," Kip said, "that Victor has a very powerful patron."

"But…" Alice looked between the two of them. "What about the spell? I know you think it wasn't real, but what if it was?"

"Yes," Emily said grimly. "That's also a worry."

After another ten minutes had passed with no sign of Malcolm, Emily suggested they return to their room, as the lobby was very crowded. They made for the stairs, and just as Kip set foot on the first one, his nose tingled and Malcolm's voice came to his ear. "I'm safe. Students gone. Been trying to find them, no luck. Where are you?"

Kip spoke under his breath to the demon. "At the hotel returning to our room. Send Corvi and Emily can bring you back."

"No need. I'm only a short walk. I'll be there soon." Demons often lost the emotional nuance in a person's voice when conveying messages, but Kip could tell just from the short sentences that Malcolm was discouraged.

"Was that Malcolm?" Alice had turned her ears around toward Kip.

He nodded. "He'll be here soon," he said to her and Emily, in front of her, who'd half-turned at Alice's question.

"I know. He told me too," Emily said. "I'll go down and wait for him. You two go up."

"Should we keep looking?" Kip asked.

"If you can think of something to do that doesn't involve leaving the hotel, by all means." Emily kept her eyes on the doors. "But Malcolm will have more information. I'll come up with him as soon as he gets here."

In the room, neither Kip nor Alice wanted to sit still. Alice stood near the bed and walked to the door every few seconds, sniffing for any scent of Emily or Malcolm. Kip paced between the bed and the window. If only he hadn't let himself be distracted, caught up in chasing Victor, he might have kept his eyes on the students. Could the Russian sorcerers have been agents working with Victor to keep him occupied? He considered the thought and filed it away. Perhaps they had been, but it didn't matter now; what mattered was finding the students. At best, they had hidden themselves away. At worst...he didn't want to think about the worst. Whatever it was, it would be partly his fault.

Though he didn't say anything, Alice walked over to him. "They're alive," she said, taking his paw in hers. "And we'll find them."

He drew her into a hug, forcing a smile he didn't feel. At least she was safe, she and their unborn cub. Her scent, he'd been told, would change as the pregnancy moved along, but it hadn't yet. She was still sweetly, reassuringly herself, and he pressed his nose to her fur, taking what comfort he could in that. "I hope so."

It seemed an hour, but the sky had barely darkened when Emily and Malcolm came into the room, so it couldn't have been more than fifteen minutes. Emily closed the door behind them as Malcolm went to sit heavily on the bed, Corvi fluttering to keep balance on his shoulder.

"I lost them," he said before anyone could ask. "Corvi here caught up with Ash when we saw everyone leaving Trippenhuis, and I spotted Jorey easily in the crowd, then the other two. I hadn't summoned my demon, because Victor and Farley were in the hall, and I had the students in sight so I didn't think he'd be needed...We kept sight of them around a corner, down another two streets. The crowd thinned out a bit, so they were easier to keep track of. Then—it happened in a second. This man in a cloak came out and laid hands on Jorey and Charity, and they were gone. Richard barely turned around before it grabbed him and then they were both gone as well."

None of them said a word. Malcolm spread his hands. "And that was it. They were gone. I failed."

"No!" they all protested more or less at once, and Kip went on. "I should have been watching as well. I let myself get distracted." Or, he wondered, had Victor planned the event and disruption to distract him? The shouted voice from the front that had incited the panic, now that he thought back on it, had sounded false, almost rehearsed. If Victor had been behind it, if he'd taken their students...fire simmered in Kip's chest, growing hotter.

"There was nothing either of you could have done," Emily said sharply.

"I could have warded them." Malcolm pressed his hands together. "I should have."

"Why would you have?" Emily asked. "We haven't been this whole time. There'd be no reason to suspect a need."

"Unless it was because there was an event Victor was orchestrating," Kip said, his ears down. "Because if he were going to try something, it would be then."

"It's no good now thinking about what we should have done." Alice swept her tail back and forth. "We should be thinking about what we're going to do."

"Quite right." Emily heaved a sigh.

"If we can't find the students," Kip said, fists clenched, "then I'm going to look for Victor."

Malcolm sat up. "Aye, not a bad idea, that."

"And do what?" Emily asked.

Kip held his paw out and conjured a fire above it, only a small part of the anger burning in him. "Convince him to confess," he said.

Alice slid an arm around his waist, unworried about the fire. "You can't just burn confessions out of people."

"I've never tried," he said, "but I'm willing to learn."

"It's not you." Alice nuzzled his shoulder.

"Besides which," Emily said, "if you attack him with fire and he does have a highly-placed patron, that would give him more leverage to attack the credibility of our school."

The fire died in Kip's palm. "We have to do *something*."

"I know what you and I have to do, though I hadn't expected it to be this difficult. I must travel to Paris next to secure funding for our school, and I think it would be best for you to accompany me. That leaves Alice and Malcolm to find our students."

"Wait!" Kip cried. "I want to look for them! It's my fault—"

"It was my fault as much, if not more," Malcolm reminded him.

"All the more reason we should both look! We came through many battles together."

Malcolm nodded. "That makes sense."

"Quiet, both of you," Emily snapped. "First of all, I'm the headmistress of the school. You think I'm not just as terrified as any of you at what Jorey and Charity and Richard might be going through? But I also have to consider the future of the school itself, beyond this year's class. If we don't secure the funding from M. and Mme. Dieuleveult, there may be no school. Well, apart from one Dutch healer, I suppose, if he wants to sit alone in a room and teach nobody."

"Monsieur and Madame who?" Kip asked.

"Dyoo-le-vuh," Alice said carefully. "They're the nobles who offered us money."

"If they already offered it, why do I have to go to Paris?"

"Because," Emily said, "they haven't promised it to us yet. Mme. Dieuleveult told me this afternoon that there were several sorcerers with 'interesting ideas,' as she put it, and so she has invited all of us to their mansion in Paris for a fête and to allow us to further demonstrate our ideas."

"It's a competition." Alice's ears were down. "So you have to go, Kip. You've got the showiest sorcery and you're the Hero of the Battle of the Road. If anyone can convince them, it's you."

It didn't feel right to Kip that he should leave the students, but he couldn't argue any of the points. When they had all agreed Emily should run the school, she'd said, "You understand that this means you will abide by my decisions where the school is concerned," and Kip had responded that he couldn't think of anyone he trusted more, including himself.

"What's second of all, then?" Malcolm asked.

"Second of all," Emily said with a tight smile, "I'm the headmistress of the school. Kip, you're coming with me to Paris. Malcolm and Alice, stay here and try to find any clue to the whereabouts of the students."

"They'll be in London by now." Kip wrung his paws together.

"We don't know that for sure. Richard fell afoul of that Prussian sorcerer, and something may have happened with him. Or it could be someone none of us know—they talked to dozens of people. If we knew for sure that it was Victor, yes, we would all go to London immediately, funding be damned." Emily took Malcolm's hands. "I trust the two of you to get to the bottom of it. If you discover anything concrete, let us know, and Kip and I can come help wherever you are. I will speak to Master Janssen and ask him what resources may be put at your disposal."

"If you bring us to Paris," Malcolm said, "then my demon and raven will know where you are and will be able to come fetch you if we need to."

"Excellent idea." Emily smiled. "I'll check in with you every day regardless."

Kip sank down on the bed. "I hate the idea of going off to Paris while they're prisoners."

"If it's any consolation," Emily said, "I rather doubt either of us will enjoy ourselves."

They sent Ash and Sleek to fly in circles over the streets around Trippenhuis looking for the students (or Victor or Farley), and Malcolm sent Daravont to look through buildings for any warded space, starting with the street Farley had disappeared in when Kip had followed him. They knew that the students could have been translocated anywhere in the world (and indeed, that street turned up nothing of interest), but it felt better than doing nothing. Kip, Malcolm, and Alice tried to eat at the neighboring public-house while Emily paid a call on Master Janssen, but by the time she returned, they'd barely picked at their meals. "Master Janssen will meet you both in the lobby next door in an hour or so," Emily told them as she sat down. "He wants to discuss matters with some of his masters, and there are other demands on his time, but he understands the urgency of our situation." She stared down at her plate, and then around at all the others, still full of roast pork and onions. "I don't know how much of this I can eat."

"Eat as much as you can," Alice said. "We need to keep our strength up, and it won't help Jorey, Charity, and Richard if we starve ourselves."

"True enough." Emily set her fork to the meal, and that inspired the rest of them to eat a little more.

Kip ate quietly until Alice asked him about Chakrabarti. That set him to sit bolt upright. "Oh no," he said. "I haven't seen him at all today."

"We can't offer him anything until we have the money secured anyway," Emily reminded him, "but you should have a way to reach him when that happens."

Alice smiled. "I'm sure we'll get the money, too. Who can compete with you two?"

"If they play fair," Kip said darkly. "Anyway, didn't you have one master's salary from that von Bismarck?"

"I did," Emily said, "but I promised the spot to that Dutch fellow because of all Master Janssen's done for us. Including help find our students tonight. He's very keen to have close ties between our two schools and he wants his masters to experience the breadth of the world."

It wouldn't make any difference to point out that Kip liked Chakrabarti better. "Very well," he said. "He told me where he's staying; I'll go look him up now and let him know."

Alice offered to go with him, but Emily thought she should stay and hear what Master Janssen had to say, so Kip went alone.

He had to ask three different people but eventually found Chakrabarti and sat down with the Indian sorcerer in his room. After confirming that he was still interested in coming to Peachtree, Kip explained their situation. They arranged to send word via the Sorcerer's Post, forwarded through the Athæneum (as Kip did not trust King's College to forward any correspondence on their behalf).

"I very much hope to have good news for you in a week, or a fortnight at most," the fox said, rising to leave.

"Good night, Master Penfold." Chakrabarti shook Kip's paw with a smile. "I thank the gods for the fortune of our encounter."

"I hope it won't be our last." Kip returned the smile.

The streets between Chakrabarti's hotel and his own had grown more crowded as the night grew darker, filled with sorcerers enjoying the last night of the Exposition. Kip drew his robe around himself and tried to stay to the side of the street, but he couldn't stop himself from watching the revelers in case anyone tried to use sorcery as they had the previous night. As he was also keeping some of his attention on Ash's ever-widening circles, his pace slowed almost to a crawl.

More than once he passed by conversations about Victor's demonstration. If Victor had wanted nothing more than to get people talking about him, he had certainly accomplished that. Kip wanted to stop every person he heard and tell them that Victor was an expert manipulator, that the truth behind his show wasn't what it appeared. And yet…what if Victor had actually found a way to make new Calatians? It would be very like him to stage a demonstration that did not show off any of his actual secrets, and to goad Kip into declaring him a fraud when in fact he would be able to back up his claims.

Frustrated, he called Ash back to him and fixed King's College in his mind, the great towers looming over the Thames with the Isle of Dogs on the other bank. Magic came to him and in a moment he stood in the grass between the College and Greenwich.

"Go," he told Ash, who shook off her disorientation and launched herself from his shoulder. She made a circuit of the five stone towers, but even in the mild spring evening, there was not much activity to see, and certainly no sign of Victor nor of Farley.

Kip stalked back and forth on the grass. Anger had brought him here and left him adrift with no further guidance, or at least nothing more useful than burning the whole college to the ground. As appealing as that sounded emotionally, Kip had close enough control of himself that he didn't even light a small fire. And when Ash dropped to his shoulder, having completed her circuit, he packed away the darkness in his mind and returned them to Amsterdam.

His mood when he returned to the hotel was not good. None of his friends or wife was in the public house, nor the hotel lobby, and when he opened the door to his room, Alice lay alone there on the bed.

She looked up as he entered. "Did you sort it all out with Master Chakrabarti?" she asked.

"Yes," Kip said, and sat on the bed, rubbing the end of his tail.

"Everything's set?"

He nodded. After a moment, Alice sat up and moved to sit beside him. "It'll be all right," she said softly, resting a paw on his knee. "We'll find the students."

"You and Malcolm will. I'm going to be put on display like a show horse while Victor is doing God knows what. I can't do anything. I don't even know where to begin to look."

"You're doing important work—"

Saying out loud that Alice would be searching for the students reminded him of her danger, and worry pushed his anger aside. He laid his paw over hers. "You're as much a target as Jorey was, if Victor's looking for magical Calatians."

"And you'd be even more of a target."

"I'm not carrying our cub," he pointed out.

Alice stiffened. "You don't think I'm going to put our cub in danger?"

"You're going into danger," Kip said.

"I'll have Malcolm with me, and haven't I proven by now that I can look after myself?"

He squeezed her paw. "Yes. You have. But can you blame me for worrying? For wanting to face the danger instead of you?"

"And," she retorted, "don't you think I would be just as worried at the prospect of our cub growing up without a father?"

"There will be a father," Kip said with a half-smile.

"You know what I mean."

He nodded. "I know. I'm sorry. It's not that I think myself more capable."

"Well." She splayed her ears, mollified. "You are the one who won the war single-pawed."

He flattened his ears. "It's that I want to face all the dangers for you."

Alice sighed. "I want to face all the dangers for you, too." When he didn't respond, she leaned against him and smiled. "In just a few months, I won't be able to go on adventures. You've had a cub as surely as we will, only your cub is an entire school, and perhaps even the whole territory of East Georgia. You can't just go off on adventures anymore."

He sighed. "I want to be in two places at once."

Alice lifted her paw and wrapped an arm around him. "For tonight, let's both of us be in this one place, for the last time in hopefully a very few days."

"Yes, you're right." He kissed her and lay down next to her, letting her warmth and scent wash away the problems of the world just for one night.

CHAPTER NINE: PARIS

In the morning, on their way to the small bakery at the end of the street, Kip tried one more time to change the plan. "What if Alice comes with me to Paris," he proposed, "and Emily, you and Malcolm stay to track down the students? You have the best rapport with the Dutch sorcerers, after all."

"I'll be fine," Alice said before Emily could respond. She rested a paw just above Kip's tail. "Emily has to go with you. She represents the school. How would it look if we didn't send the headmistress? And besides, she knows all the money details. I'd be completely lost."

"I promise we'll be exceedingly careful." Malcolm had recovered a little of his good humor overnight. "But I feel we'll be successful. Remember, we're the ones who solved the mystery of the attack on the White Tower."

"I remember that very well," Kip said, and the memory of Coppy, who had been lost in the course of solving that mystery, hung ghostlike in the air around them. After a moment, he cleared his throat. "But that took months, and we haven't months."

"If we don't find anything here today," Malcolm said, "we'll go to the Isle of Dogs. Alice will be very useful among the Calatians who might not entirely trust a human. And I promise that anything dangerous to be done, I'll undertake myself."

"No," Emily said firmly. "Anything dangerous to be done, you'll advise me before undertaking, and Kip and I will come help."

"Yes." Kip wrapped an arm around Alice.

"We'll be fine," Alice said. "And so will the students. I promise."

At the bakery, Emily went inside to purchase pastries for their breakfast, leaving Sleek with Alice. Kip held his wife's paw, not wanting to let her go, and then seeing Sleek on her shoulder gave him an idea. "Why don't you take Ash with you?" he said. "Then you'll be able to contact me—us—right away if something happens."

Alice looked up at the raven, who had perked up at the mention of her name. "If you think she can bear to be away from you for that long."

"She loves you." Kip smiled as Ash croaked, bobbing her head.

"Well…all right." The vixen beamed up. "I'll be glad to have her with us."

"Have who with you?" Emily had come out of the shop with a handful of small pastries.

Malcolm took one from her. "We're to bring Kip's raven along with us, to set his mind at ease. And to make it easier to talk between us," he added, at Kip's glare. "This way you needn't worry about bringing us to Paris."

"Good idea." Emily handed pastries to Kip and Alice. Sleek hopped back over to her shoulder, and Ash fluttered down from Kip's to Alice's. "I should have thought of something like that."

"We're a team," Kip said.

"Cheers." Malcolm smiled and raised his pastry like a glass, and the others followed suit.

"And we're all worried. It's hard to think clearly when we're worried," Alice pointed out.

Emily's grey eyes were cloudy, and though she bore up very well, Kip noticed her quick nod and the way she and Malcolm leaned against each other.

The sweet rolls were delicious, and vanished quickly (a few morsels finding their way into the beaks of the ravens). And then it was time for Malcolm and Alice to go to the Athæneum, and for Kip and Emily to meet their French hosts. They embraced, Kip and Alice sharing a longer embrace while Emily and Malcolm did likewise. "Take good care of yourself," Kip said.

"You too." Alice nuzzled him. "Trouble has a way of finding you, so do try to keep out of its way."

"I'm going to a French noble's estate," Kip said. "But I will do my best, yes. And if you hear anything…"

"Yes, yes. And if you think of anything, tell us."

They kissed and then stepped back from each other. Emily took Kip's paw. "We'll see you two soon," she said. "Good luck."

And in an instant, she and Kip were in Paris.

They appeared in a basement room similar to the room at the Athæneum, for similar reasons, Kip assumed. "I talked to Master Debroussard at the Exposition," Emily said.

"Debroussard?"

Emily walked toward the door. "The one I met on my mission for Abigail Adams during the war. He'd said I could use this room any time I pleased, and I just confirmed it would be available. We won't have time to spend with him, as the Dieuleveults are sending a carriage to meet us here right away."

On the other side of the door sat an apprentice, a stocky young man in white robes eating a croissant. He dropped the pastry as Kip and Emily emerged, and asked their business in French. Kip replied that they were here by permission of Master Debroussard to travel to Paris, and his French must have been bad, because the apprentice wished them well in English. "There are riots and fights today again," he told them. "Be sure to tell your driver to avoid the center of the city where possible."

They emerged into what looked like a historical reconstruction. There had been old buildings in Amsterdam, but here the entire city was made up of hundred-year-old square greyish-tan buildings, darkened with streaks from the drizzling rain. Identical tall rectangular windows stretched along the façades in a regular grid, a few open but most closed and reflecting the cloudy sky.

The French school resembled a large fortress; even in an old city, it looked ancient. Kip studied it for a moment before Emily drew his attention to the carriage waiting in the street. A velvet-clad footman stood smartly before it while a black-cloaked driver, hooded against the rain, sat on the driving board. Two jet-black horses waited patiently in the harness before the carriage.

The footman, watching the door, straightened as they approached. "Miss Emily Carswell?" he asked, and when Emily nodded, he opened the carriage door and spoke in French-accented English. "Mme. Dieuleveult regrets that she could not be present to meet with you herself, but the demands of an estate leave her very little time to herself. She asks me to present her most sincere apologies."

"That's all right." Emily stepped up into the carriage. "Thank you. Ah, the apprentice there said there was some trouble in the city center and we should avoid it?"

The footman stayed standing in the light rain. "Yes, we saw it on the drive in. We will conduct you safely, do not worry. Have you no luggage?"

"I've taken it home," Emily said as Kip joined her in the carriage. "When we arrive, I will go fetch it again. It's safer there than being driven."

The footman nodded and then stepped back, preparing to close the door. "If you would prefer privacy, I would be pleased to ride with the driver."

"Oh, no." Kip tucked his tail around to one side of the hard cushioned seat, attempting to wipe away the moisture his wet fur had left. "Please do join us. There's plenty of room."

"Thank you very much, sir. It would be my pleasure to describe the wonders of Paris as we drive, if you and Miss Carswell would prefer."

"That would be lovely," Emily said with a glance at Kip. "Master Penfold has never seen Paris."

"Oh!" The young man sat beside Kip and pulled the door closed from the inside, then rapped on the ceiling. A moment later, the carriage jerked into motion behind the clop-clop of horse hooves.

"Fortunately," the footman said, "the most spectacular sight will be early on our journey. There." He pointed out the left-hand window. "You can see the Hôtel de Ville, the center of Parisian government, and beyond it the towers of Nôtre-Dame de Paris, the great cathedral that ministers to more souls than any other church in the world."

It was easy to claim such a thing, but in this case it might be true. Kip realized that Emily hoped the distraction of the tour would help them both relax, to leave the quest for the students in the very capable hands and paws of their friends, so he made an effort to engage with the footman. "How old is Nôtre-Dame de Paris?" Kip asked, peering out. There seemed to be a great crowd in front of the Hôtel de Ville, perhaps part of the "trouble" the apprentice had spoken of, but he couldn't see details from this distance.

"A church has stood on that spot for nearly a thousand years," the footman replied, "but the cathedral that you see now was completed only a few hundred years ago."

"'Only.'" Emily smiled wryly. "There aren't any buildings in America older than two hundred years."

"The Hotel de Ville is less than two hundred years old," the footman said, pointing. "That is, this version of it was completed during the reign of Louis XIII."

"How long ago was that?" Kip asked.

The footman paused. "Er…I believe in the environment of one hundred and ninety years."

"Practically modern," Emily said.

Kip smiled at the footman's embarrassment. "We are proud of the newness of our country just as you are proud of the endurance of yours," he said.

This seemed to put the young man at ease. "Thank you, sir."

"You're very well educated. What can we call you?"

"Oh! My apologies. I am called Charles, Master Penfold."

"Then proceed with the tour, Charles," Kip said, and leaned back to watch the beautiful old buildings of Paris pass him by.

Charles called out building after building, but Kip began to see groups of people huddled in the mud at the edge of the street, some with arms outstretched, and these Charles did not mention, nor even seem to notice. They crossed a majestic stone bridge ("the Pont Royal, Paris's third oldest bridge") soon after passing the Hotel de Ville and the ancient palace of the Louvre, and thereafter seemed to have left the heart of Paris behind, because the buildings diminished in grandeur on the other side of the Seine.

Emily pointed out a spire that Charles had not described. "What's that?" she asked.

"Ah, that is the chapel of the…" He paused, looking down. "*Hospice des incurables.*"

"Hospital?" Kip asked. "For…incurable diseases?"

"Yes, sir. I apologize for my deficiency in English."

"No, no, you're doing wonderfully." Emily reached over to touch Charles's knee, but this contact did not help; the footman stiffened. Emily withdrew her hand and folded it with her other in her lap.

"Do you know this area well?" Kip asked.

"Sir, I grew up in Neuilly-sur-Seine." He pointed past the hospice. "To the west and north of here. But I know the Hospice—the hospital—well. My mother spent the end of her life there."

"Oh." Emily glanced out again at the hospital and then back at Charles. "I'm so sorry."

"It was not a bad thing. They kept her very comfortable. And it led me to the service of the Dieuleveults and allowed me to be here in the carriage with you." He smiled and pointed out the other side of the carriage. "Here you will see the trees of the lovely Luxembourg Gardens. You cannot see the fountain from here, but if you have the chance, I pray you take a walk and find it. It is lovely and very peaceful."

The trees were visible past buildings, at the foot of which sat another collection of beggars. Kip didn't like thinking of them that way, but there was no other way he could imagine to describe them.

As they left Paris, he thought there would be fewer beggars, but there were not; the difference was that they were walking rather than sitting. Even through a patch of harder rain, the ragged-clothed people slogged through the mud at the side of the road. After the rain had slackened and then stopped, they passed farms where farmers, in tunics that at least had fewer holes, walked through the fields sowing.

Charles continued to speak. "These lands belong to M. and Mme. de Clamart, who are good friends of M. and Mme. Dieuleveult. They are great patrons of the musical arts and have often brought gifted performers to soirees at the Dieuleveult estate."

Emily's gaze, too, rested on the farmers, and when she turned back to look at Kip, he saw that she had the same questions he did about the poverty of the people and the wealth of their lords. He saw too that she held back those questions, because they didn't know if they could trust Charles; any perceived ingratitude might make its way back to the Dieuleveults, and if they were in competition for a donation, they couldn't afford any missteps.

When they passed into the Dieuleveults' land, only Charles's words signaled the change. The farmlands looked just as dreary and the people just as unhappy, although at around this point the rain did stop and the sun broke through, leading Emily to ask Charles with a smile, "Did the Dieuleveults arrange for nicer weather for our arrival?"

"I am certain that M. Dieuleveult prayed for it," he said without a trace of a smile. "To Saint Médard, if I am not mistaken."

"I can never remember all the saints," Emily said. Her eyes flicked to Kip, but she kept her expression neutral because Charles was looking at her. Kip, at the footman's side, did not stop his ears from splaying; he was sure that even if Charles noticed, the man wouldn't understand the expression of bemused surprise.

"Nor can I, but Saint Médard is one that M. Dieuleveult invokes often." Charles waved outside. "He looks after the weather."

"M. Dieuleveult is quite devout, then?" Kip asked.

There was the barest pause before Charles replied, "Exceedingly. He has devoted his life to the Church. The Dieuleveults' chapel contains no fewer than three Holy relics."

"Which ones?" Kip leaned forward.

"I am certain that M. Dieuleveult will wish to show you the relics himself, and he will give a much more thorough explanation than I am able to." Charles pressed his face to the window. "In another few minutes we shall come in sight of the estate."

By "estate," Kip expected to see a large house in the midst of many fields and orchards. But when Charles said, "Here we are," the carriage passed by orderly rows of trees into farms that looked only a little more well-off than the ones they had been riding past. The ground below the carriage wheels did smooth out noticeably, but little else seemed to have changed. Kip searched the horizon for a house, and then asked Emily, who was looking out the other window, "Can you see the house from there?"

"Oh," Charles said with a small laugh, "the Château Dieuleveult is some ten miles down the road."

He pointed out the window, which afforded Emily the chance to mouth, "chateau!" at Kip.

Now Kip didn't know what to expect. He had seen the palaces in Paris and London; would it be a low, sprawling building that impressed with its reach, like the Louvre? Would it be a grand, modern building like Windsor Palace?

It was neither. As it turned out, the Château Dieuleveult bore a closer resemblance to the White Tower than to either of those other great palaces. Calling it a castle might be deemed a slight exaggeration, if not an outright lie; it did have a great round tower from which two men stood guard, and a large wooden gate in its outer wall. But the tops of the outer walls showed wear from the weather, and the area they enclosed was scarcely larger than Trippenhuis.

Just inside the wooden gate, the carriage stopped and two men ran up to take charge of the horses. Charles hurried to disembark so that he could reach up and help Emily down, and Kip followed her.

They stood in a courtyard small enough that the carriage could not have proceeded much further without running into a finely carved wooden door upon which a heraldic coat of arms had been painted. Another carriage sat against the wall nearby, and behind it stood a small stable. The stones of the courtyard glistened with mud as evidence of recent rain, and the mottled grey stone of the outer walls felt very old and plain.

Ignoring the grooms and the driver, who clambered down behind them, Charles tried to take Emily's arm. When she refused, he settled for leading her and Kip to the emblazoned door and opened it for them. "On behalf of M. and Mme. Dieuleveult," he said formally, "I bid you welcome, honored guests. Please enjoy the hospitality of Château Dieuleveult."

The world on the other side of the door could scarcely have been more different from the plain stone courtyard. Blue and gold velvet wallpaper lay behind several immense oil paintings, and a white marble statue in the Roman tradition stood at the center of the room with its arms outstretched in welcome. Beautiful Persian carpets covered the floor, and a couch that matched the wallpaper lay against the wall. A fire crackled in a large fireplace, filling the room with warmth and the smell of wood smoke.

Another servant in livery similar to Charles's hurried up to them with several cloths draped across his arm. "Please," Charles said, "if you would be so kind as to remove your shoes..."

He removed his own, as if to show them how it was done. Emily reached down, but the other servant stopped her with a phrase in French. He motioned for her to lift her leg; she did, and he gently removed the shoe from her foot, guiding her to step on the carpet. They repeated the process for her other leg, and then he knelt to dab at her stockings with a towel.

"This isn't necessary," Emily said.

"Mme. Dieuleveult insists," Charles explained. He barked something to the servant, who ducked his head and finished quickly. "Please notify me if he should touch you inappropriately."

Kip was glad he'd worn shoes; these days he often went without footwear, but for visiting Amsterdam he'd thought it best to look respectable, so he'd brought a pair of shoes made for the shape of his feet by a Calatian cobbler. He did not, however, wear stockings (they caught on his fur), and when the servant had removed his shoes, the man stared for a moment at the bare feet below.

"It's fine," Kip said, meaning that the servant didn't have to clean his feet, but Charles misinterpreted his permission. The footman spoke in French, and the servant replied, "*Oui, oui,*" and set to rubbing a warm damp towel over Kip's fur. The pleasant feel of the cloth on his fur did not make up for the awkwardness of having a servant perform the task.

When this ordeal had finally concluded, Charles led Kip and Emily out of that room and down a long hallway hung with tapestries, many of which looked ancient, several of which depicted saints, if Kip's recollection served him correctly.

Through a sitting room, through a large ballroom, up a staircase, down a short hallway, through a parlor-type room, and then down another hallway—all of them carpeted—to a door that Charles opened for them. "These will be your rooms for the duration of your stay."

Inside, more of the blue and gold wallpaper, more oil paintings, and two more of the long couches. No Roman statue greeted them, but a young woman did get up hurriedly, brushing her skirts down. "This is Claudine," Charles said. "She will attend to your needs while you are a guest here. Her English is not very good, but she understands better than she speaks."

"Welcome, Monsieur and Madame." Claudine's English was heavily accented, but she spoke properly despite being clearly distracted by Kip's appearance.

"Oh, we don't need a servant." Emily stepped into the room.

"Mme. Dieuleveult insists." Charles bowed. "It has been my very great pleasure to make your acquaintance, Master Penfold and Miss Carswell. I hope to renew it soon in the future."

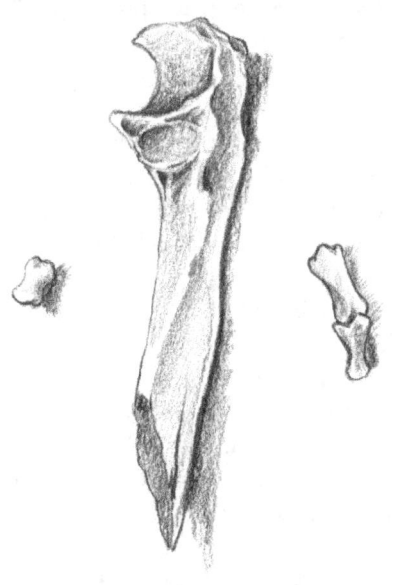

CHAPTER TEN:

THE COMPETITION

After Charles left, Kip and Emily tried to settle in, but it was difficult with Claudine there, even though they'd been assured she didn't speak English. Kip wanted to plan out what kind of sorcery would be most impressive, and Emily had spoken to the Dieuleveults where he hadn't. But he didn't want to discuss strategy in front of a servant of the house, because he didn't want to appear calculating, or showy, or anything else, even though he was supposed to be showy and was being forced to compete for money.

When Emily came back with their bags, she seemed less bothered because of the sorcery, and more bothered because she didn't know how long they would be waiting for the Dieuleveults and Claudine could not tell them. "How long will we be here, do you think?" she asked Kip, staring at the wardrobe. "Need we bother unpacking? Will we cast a spell tonight and be off before sunrise?"

"The sooner the better as far as I'm concerned."

"One good fire spell should do it. Nobody else can do that."

"I don't want to terrify them." Kip paced in front of the window. Claudine hovered nearby. "Summon an elemental?"

"They'll hardly be less scared of that," Emily said. "Do stop worrying about it. Can you please try to ask her again?"

"She doesn't know."

"Just ask her."

"Then will you please tell me what sorcery we're going to do that will—" He looked at Claudine. "I don't know, what are we going to do?"

"I don't know either. We can't do anything until they're here."

Kip tapped his claws on the windowsill. "Who else is here to ask for money?"

"I've no idea. I think they said there was a Dutch school, but not the Athaeneum. Maybe it was a Belgian school."

"I didn't even know there was a Belgian school."

"Of course there's a Belgian school," Emily said. "And there's at least one other. I don't know who they are, Mme. Dieuleveult didn't say."

"What—" He couldn't finish. What else could they do, these other schools? What would be impressive, set him apart? "Where are they?"

"Who?"

"The other schools. The other people. If I could just meet them..." Maybe, he thought, some of the other sorcerers knew spells that could find lost people. Maybe they could help him.

Emily sighed. "Then ask her."

He turned to Claudine. In basic French, he struggled to ask, "*Ou sont... les autres?*"

She brightened, hearing French, and replied very quickly with a string of words that he only caught some of. He asked her to go slower, and eventually nodded his head in understanding so that she would stop.

"I think they're somewhere else on this floor," he said. "I'm just going to go see if I know anyone from them."

He made for the door, but this alarmed Claudine. She hurried to intercept him, shaking her head, and when he put his paw on the handle, she spoke rapidly in French. At least some of those words, he knew.

"What's she on about?" Emily asked.

"I think we're not supposed to leave? She said Charles's name so I think he's meant to come fetch us."

"They can't keep us here." Emily walked over to Claudine, who retreated from her. "Go ahead."

But as soon as the hindrance had been removed, Kip hesitated and withdrew his paw. "I don't want to get us in any trouble. What if this hurts our chances?" He returned to the window, pulled a chair over to it, and sat staring out over what was a very pretty elaborate garden. "I'll see what Alice is up to."

Ash was watching Alice and Malcolm in a small room together. She turned her head and Kip didn't see anyone else there, so he said through Ash, "Hallo."

Both of them turned toward the raven. Alice's ears perked and she beamed. "Hello, Kip. How is France?"

"Confusing," he said. "Have you made any progress?"

"We haven't solved the mystery in half a day, if that's what you're asking," Malcolm said. "How's Emily?"

"She's fine. She's doing well. What have you learned?"

Alice sighed. "Very little, I'm afraid. The Dutch tried to be helpful, but all they could confirm was that someone saw Jorey and the others—"

"We assume," Malcolm chimed in.

"Yes, Jorey is the only one they remember. Anyway, one of the Dutch masters saw him hurrying along with two others and then they were approached by a man in a cloak and then they all vanished."

"Exactly what I saw," Malcolm said.

"Yes. The master did at least say that he didn't know the man in the cloak, and he knows all the Dutch sorcerers as well as a good number of others who were at the Exposition."

"It wasn't Victor or Farley, unless Farley's learned to translocate."

"He might well have, but he wouldn't be described as a 'man' by any stretch of imagination. And for what it's worth, the sorcerer said he thought the man looked British or American."

Malcolm spoke up again. "He may have assumed American because Jorey is a Calatian."

"So not much more than we knew." Kip exhaled. "What next?"

"We go to London, as we'd planned," Alice said. "I'll talk to the people I know there and we'll see if we can't get a calyx to spy on Victor, or at least sniff out the students. I think I can describe the scents well enough."

"And Headmaster Janssen said they will continue to listen for information here and will contact us through the Post to the school if they hear anything."

"All right," Kip said. "Meanwhile, we're waiting for the Dieuleveults to get back so we can start this competition."

"Good luck," Alice said.

"You too."

"Best to Em," Malcolm added.

Kip looked up at Emily. "Malcolm sends his best," he told her.

"Did they learn anything?"

"No."

"I didn't think they would, but I hoped." She turned to Claudine, who was staring at them. "Oh, go on with you."

Claudine shook her head and retreated to a corner, where she stayed for the next half hour while Kip and Emily discussed sorcery in low voices. Kip's fire was the obvious choice for their most impressive sorcery, but controlled in a way that never let the audience feel they were in danger. That "feel" was the hardest part; they never would be, but they couldn't see Kip's control. "A little danger is good," Emily argued. "People like it. But not too much."

"I've trained for years not to allow *any*," Kip pointed out.

They were still discussing this when Charles returned. "Master Penfold, Miss Carswell. You are invited to join the Dieuleveults and their other guests for refreshments in the parlor."

He bowed and waited for their reply. "We would be delighted," Emily said, and she and Kip followed the footman out into the hall.

When he'd closed the door behind them, Emily said conversationally, "Would the Dieuleveults be very put out if we should explore the house unaccompanied? I would very much like to admire the works of art they've collected."

"The Dieuleveults do prefer that their guests be accompanied in the house," Charles replied. "The paintings, tapestries, and statues all have stories and they feel that without hearing those stories, their guests will not appreciate the art as much as they should."

Emily shot Kip a look, and he nodded minutely. As they walked along the hall, he lifted his nose, trying to smell any other people who might have walked along, but most of them were not people he knew. There was one scent that he caught just before the stairs, and it set his ears flat.

He tugged at Emily's sleeve to slow her and then whispered to her, "Patris."

Her eyes widened. "Here?"

Charles turned. "Is something amiss?"

"Not at all." Emily composed herself and smiled brightly.

They descended to a parlor crowded with more paintings, tapestries, and statues than any other room they'd seen. They could stay for a week and still not hear all the stories behind this art, Kip thought. A few caught his eye: a lovely watercolor of a bridge with lilies on the water below; a small statue maybe a foot and a half high of a naked youth fleeing a beast; an oil painting of a haloed saint reaching upward while shadowy jaws snapped around his ankles.

The only other people in the room approached them: an elegant woman with skin made paler by powder, her face framed by a cascade of golden curls trailing down to the shoulders of her mint-green satin dress that shimmered in the afternoon sunlight. Around her pale neck hung a gaudy necklace of gold supporting a large pendant whose center was an emerald as big as an eye.

Beside her and a little behind came her husband, Kip presumed, dressed in a fancy suit that looked to be composed of at least six different layers. Broad ruffles descended from his elaborate collar to the buttons of the vest that strained against their shining fabric, and on his lapel he wore a tarnished round silver piece with the relief of a saint impressed on it. He wore a powdered white wig and a vaguely distant expression that resolved into interest as he focused on Kip.

"Good day, Master Penfold," the woman said in perfect English. "I am Mme. Dieuleveult, and this is my husband. We are so delighted that you have accepted our invitation, and we simply cannot wait to see what marvels you choose to favor us with."

"Never had a Calatian in the house before," M. Dieuleveult said, but more as though Kip were an exotic traveler than an unwelcome guest. He extended a hand at the same time as his wife presented hers.

Kip took Mme. Dieuleveult's hand first, raising it to his lips briefly, and then grasped her husband's warm, sweaty fingers. "His whiskers tickle," Mme. Dieuleveult observed to no one in particular before turning to welcome Emily as well.

"Which saint is that on your collar?" Kip asked as M. Dieuleveult released his paw.

"Ah! Ah! This is Saint Christophe, who looks after travelers. Even when we make our way with the aid of sorcery, I always wear his likeness." He rubbed his mustache and beamed at Kip. "He has not yet failed me. Are you interested in the saints?"

"Very much so," Kip said, "although I confess that between the study of sorcery and the fighting of a war I have had little time to study them."

"Oh ho, well, Monsieur le Renard, if you would like, I could tell you something about them."

"I would be most grateful." Kip let the "Mister Fox" appellation pass. "I was told that you have an enviable collection of relics."

"Oh, that I do, that I do. Purely for the adoration of Christ, you understand, as his works are seen through the lives of the saints."

This disclaimer was delivered so earnestly that Kip felt compelled to reply, "Yes, I understand."

"You are Roman Catholic?"

"Oh, no, we are of the Church of England."

M. Dieuleveult laughed. "Still? You can break free of the Crown, but not the Cross, eh?"

"Well..." Kip gave him a brief overview of the discussions within the Church as he understood them, that the American branch of the Anglican Church was already separating from the British branch and had revised certain prayers (mostly the ones addressing the King as the head of the Church). "But for the moment we go to the same churches and pray to the same God."

"Very wise. God despises rapid change, or at least His servants do." M. Dieuleveult continued to chuckle. "I suppose that if you are interested, you might see some of the relics. I'll have to go with you for safety, you understand."

"I would insist, if only so that you could tell me their stories." Kip was about to ask which saints' relics were represented, but was forestalled by the return of Charles with two black-robed men behind him, both unfamiliar to Kip. They were introduced as Masters Muller and Mahieu of the Brussels Academy of Sorcery, and though Kip did not know them, they clearly knew who he was.

Mme. Dieuleveult made polite conversation between all the parties, in the course of which she firmly dissuaded her husband from talking to Kip about his relics. Muller and Mahieu were alchemical and translocating sorcerers, respectively, and neither had any insight in how to find lost people who might be warded. Muller suggested Kip talk to military sorcerers, which was a good thought, although there weren't many military sorcerers with whom Kip was on speaking terms at this point; the ones he knew had either allied with Master Colonel Jackson and wanted nothing to do with him or belonged to the British Army and still resented him.

And then Charles returned with a man behind him whom Kip did know well, though his wild mane of silver hair and his beard had both been trimmed to almost military shortness.

"This is Master Patris of the American College of Sorcery," Mme. Dieuleveult said. "It's so lovely to have two representatives of our youngest country here. I do wonder which one of them has a more spectacular show planned for us."

Kip and Emily stood stiffly as Patris was led over to them. He showed no greater interest in greeting them than they did him, but they all clasped hands (and paw) politely. "Is it only you here, then?" Emily asked.

"Aye," Patris growled.

"I'm surprised not to see Master Colonel Jackson here," Kip said.

"The Headmaster's time is taken up with many matters. He trusts me," this was delivered through gritted teeth, "to represent the College to the best of my ability."

"Well, we simply can't wait to see what you do." Emily smiled sweetly. Patris moved on without responding.

When he'd greeted everyone, Kip thought they would get on to the meal, but Mme. Dieuleveult kept making conversation, and presently he noticed that Charles had left the room again. So there was one more party.

Kip wasn't worried about outperforming Patris; the former headmaster was skilled in physical magic, which while very useful was not as glamorous as fire. And he was fairly sure Muller, the Belgian alchemical sorcerer, wasn't a fire sorcerer or he would have heard about him before now. A good fire spell, a really showy one, was still their best shot.

And then Charles returned, leading a flaxen-haired young man in a light blue suit down the stair, a tall black-robed man trailing behind him. Kip's ears flattened and he almost said something before Charles said, "*J'ai l'honneur de presenter M. Victor Adamson et Maître Gupta.*"

Victor stopped on the second stair from the bottom, surveying the room from that height before deigning to take the last two stairs down. The sorcerer behind him, whom Kip was sure had been the one on stage at the Exposition, waited a moment and then followed, but remained near the stairs while Victor joined the group.

"Hallo," he said smoothly to Master Patris, who barely touched his hand before jerking his own back. Victor moved on to the Belgian sorcerers, wishing them well in Flemish, Kip presumed, and then the familiar face came to him and Emily. Kip brought his ears up, knowing Victor had at least a little practice in reading his expressions.

Victor's smile widened. "Ah yes," he said. "They did tell me I'd be competing against the Calatian sorcerer. I look forward to resuming our rivalry in a more friendly, controlled environment."

"Perhaps that might afford you the chance to beat us at least once." Emily's tone had sharpened, and Kip presumed that this was because Victor hadn't mentioned her as a competitor, nor was he looking at her.

He didn't even spare her a glance in response, just extended his hand smoothly toward Kip. "I trust you enjoyed my little trick at the Exposition?"

"Which do you mean? The illusion on stage, or the chaos you created to kidnap our students?" Kip restrained the fire in him and kept both arms at his sides.

"Well." When it was clear that Kip wasn't going to take his hand, Victor retracted it and finally allowed his eyes to skip over to Emily. "I see you're here keeping things in line. Mind you don't go popping off to the French shipyards or anything like that."

"No worries," Emily said. "Though it'd be a great help if you could tell us where you've taken our students."

"I'm sure I have no idea what you mean. Have you lost some students? That would certainly be careless. Perhaps a new headmaster would be in order." He glanced over at Patris.

But as casual as his answer had been, Kip had seen the slight hesitation in his eyes. "You think we should replace Emily with the man who lost over a hundred students and masters?" he asked.

Victor inclined his head. "And without even leaving the country. All right, I'd best greet our delightful hosts. So looking forward to seeing what display you choose. Perhaps you'll destroy another Great Feat," he said.

"Cast one and I will," Kip called after him.

Emily drew him to one side, away from Patris's glare. "When I asked him," she said tightly, "he flinched. I saw it. He knows where they are."

"I saw it too." Kip bounced on his heels and then calmed himself. "This might be our chance to find them without even going to London. But we have to be careful. He's always on his guard."

"Oh!" Her fists shook at her sides. "If only we had a spiritual sorcerer here."

"He's no doubt got plans for that." Kip inclined his head toward Gupta. "That's the sorcerer who was on stage during his transformation. If Gupta can cast illusions, he's a spiritual sorcerer."

Emily's eyes widened. "He's not looking into our minds, is he?"

"Probably not from over there. Although we should watch out for that. Maybe you should go back and fetch Peter?"

She scowled. "He's so vulnerable when we do that. I don't like it at all."

"It would only be for a few days."

"Not to mention we leave the school without one of its strongest protectors. But maybe for the competition. Can you tell Malcolm and Alice that Victor's here, and how he reacted?"

"When we're back in our room."

She nodded. "And Kip, keep talking to M. Dieuleveult. He likes you, and any edge we can get, we need."

"I know."

Malcolm and Alice arrived safely in London but had nothing to report that night. Though neither of them had objected to the second inquiry, Kip and Emily had both realized that their constant requests for news were not helping, and that the others would definitely tell them when they'd found something. They vowed to throw all of their attention to this competition beginning the next day.

So Emily went to breakfast with Mme. Dieuleveult and Kip met her husband at sunrise, with fog curling around the stones of the courtyard and, he saw as they left the castle, laying across the gentle roll of the hills. Kip drew his robe around himself. "We're not riding?"

"It's not far." M. Dieuleveult had traded his elaborate evening suit for an only slightly less complicated outfit that consisted of a mix of white linen and soft tan leather with a heavy cloak thrown on over it. He did not wear a wig this morning, but had put on a cap with a feather in it over his thinning brown hair. "And nowhere to attach the horses, you see."

"Of course." Kip didn't mind the chill in the air; it reminded him a little of New England, and after two years in East Georgia, he was glad of that. He had put shoes on out of deference to the clean rugs of the Dieuleveult estate, thankfully, so he followed the short man's hurried steps across stone and dirt and through dewy grass.

Around the side of the castle, M. Dieuleveult stopped and pointed to where a small stone church stood alone amid rough, ungrazed grass and patches of dirt. "This was where the peasants worshipped, back when this land was ruled by lords. Now we are all serving the King, and the farmers have made their worship at the church in town. They never come up here any more. If they wish a gaudy service, they travel into Notre Dame. And we have our own chapel in the house," he waved to the great castle. "So nobody comes out here anymore, and it's perfect."

They set on down the short dirt path. "Perfect for what?" Kip asked.

M. Dieuleveult did not respond until they had reached the door. There he grasped his mustache in two fingers, staring quite intently at Kip. "You're not a Roman Catholic, you said."

"No. Why?"

"Oh, the Catholics, you know, they would…" He waved a hand, still with his eyes on Kip. "They might covet what's in here."

"Aren't we specifically told not to do that?" Kip asked.

"Ha ha!" M. Dieuleveult laughed so loudly that a ground bird fluttered up from near the church. "Yes, of course, God has made his wishes quite clear, but men do not so often take heed, do they? All right, come in, Monsieur le Renard."

He removed his cap as they passed through the creaking wooden door into a small, cold stone room. If this was where the peasants had prayed once upon a time, Kip could well believe they had quit it at first opportunity. Crude wooden pews lined the floor, and very little in the way of decoration enhanced the somber grey stone. The plain windows let in very little light, and there was nowhere in the church for the light to gather; it lay flat on the floor.

Behind the large stone altar, a stone crucifix hung high on the wall, so worn that Kip couldn't make out the Christ's facial features. He clasped his fingers together as the chill of the church seeped even through his fur, and the thought came to his mind, as always happened now when it was cold, *you could make it warm in here very easily.*

He resisted the urge with the ease of years of practice. M. Dieuleveult did have precious objects in here, or at least acted as though he did, and whether or not the relics were real, Kip did not think that conjuring unexpected fire would be appropriate.

"Now, *par ici*, this way." M. Dieuleveult produced a large key from a trouser pocket and unlocked a small door at the back of the church.

Kip followed him into a small sacristy, whose only furniture was a wardrobe with doors hanging open to reveal that it was empty. Dieuleveult stopped him. "Ah, I am so sorry, but please wait outside. I will bring them out to you."

"Of course." Kip backed out, and the Frenchman shut the door after him.

His ears caught scraping noises and then a grunt of exertion and a louder scraping, like a heavy stone being shifted. A pause, another loud scrape, and then silence. Outside, birds sang and clouds drifted across the newly-risen sun.

If Kip went to listen at the door, he could hear more, but he did not feel that was prudent nor necessary. So he remained at the altar, arms resting on the cold stone, ignoring the whispers of fire in the back of his head until the Frenchman reappeared, holding an ornately carved wooden box reverently in his short arms.

"Yes, yes, the perfect place," he said, and gently set the box on the altar next to Kip, opening it to reveal a white cloth with smears of dirt. Carefully he drew back the top layers of the cloth and beamed down at the contents.

Three bones lay on the cloth, recognizable as human: a narrow bone of the forearm, broken at one end; a large toe bone, and two joints of a finger. Kip studied them with what he hoped was appropriate reverence.

"This," Dieuleveult indicated the long, narrow bone, "is an arm bone from Ste. Colette, Colette de Corbie. She lived only four hundred years ago and looks after sick children and women with child."

He moved to the toe bone. "This is the toe of St. Théodard. He was an archbishop of Narbonne nearly a thousand years ago who dedicated his life to ministering to the poor. The Huguenots stole his relics but I obtained this bone from my grandfather, who had it from his grandfather, whose great-grandfather hunted down many of the Huguenots. They say that Théodard was 'eyes to the blind and feet to the lame,' so having his toe bone is quite apropos, would you not say?"

"Very much so." Kip would have agreed with anything, but he did think it was fitting. He wanted to know whether M. Dieuleveult prayed to St. Théodard to intercede on behalf of the poor people who lived on his land, but felt that the answer to that was fairly obvious. His eyes strayed to the third bone.

"Ah, this one." Unlike with the others, which he'd brushed gently, Dieuleveult kept his hand an inch above this bone. "This…is a finger from Ste. Geneviève. She's the patron saint of Paris and she's cured the city of diseases on many occasions. She lived thirteen hundred years ago."

Kip leaned forward to examine the bone, which alarmed Dieuleveult. "Don't touch it!" he exclaimed. "The man who sold it to me remarked on how fragile it was."

"I'm just trying to get a closer look." Details were hard to make out on the bones, but as Kip's nose drew closer, he made out some scents.

"Ah, yes." Dieuleveult looked at the windows. "Sunrise is the best time to see it, because the church faces east and the sun comes in at these times, but with these clouds…still, you can make it out well enough, no?"

"If you like…" Kip stepped back from the altar. "I can provide more light. I am a fire sorcerer, and I can promise you that the fire that I create will no more consume these relics than it will consume the stone it sits upon."

The Frenchman's face tightened. "Fire? Oh, I hardly think there's need for that, is there?"

"There's no need," Kip said, "but it would provide more light, and I can assure you that your wonderful relics would be completely safe. Why would I want to destroy such precious objects? I wish only to admire them better. Besides," he added as the short noble thought over his words, "it is chilly in this church, and magical fires would be nicely warming."

Dieuleveult exhaled, and then moved the box to one end of the altar, keeping his hand on it. "There," he said, pointing to the far end, "and if there's any sign of it spreading, I shall gather these up and carry them to safety."

"Of course," Kip said. "But you should trust in my power."

He gathered magic and immediately felt an odd sensation that reminded him of when he'd touched the wall of the White Tower and felt magic surge into him. It wasn't as powerful as that, but there was something magical very nearby. He cast the fire spell and set it on the altar, and while Dieuleveult stared at it wonderingly, Kip looked again at the relics.

The Ste. Geneviève bone he suspected to be fake; such a popular saint would have a great market for her relics, and the finger bone did not look quite as old as the other two to his admittedly untrained eye. But the others—one or both of them might be real, and could be the source of the magic he'd felt. Was a spirit trapped in one of those bones as Peter had been trapped in the Tower? Did that kind of spiritual magic exist a thousand years ago?

"Your fire is quite good," Dieuleveult admitted after a moment. "Come, you may see them much more clearly now."

Kip looked again at the bones, though he wasn't sure what he was looking for exactly. Some sign of their power? Dieuleveult likely wouldn't notice unless he himself was a sorcerer (an unlikely proposition), and Kip couldn't see magic no matter how good the light. His nose caught no tingle of demon presence, either.

Then he noticed Dieuleveult's beatific expression, eyes closed and lips moving, hands steepled before the altar. Kip swiveled his ears around and heard a murmured prayer to Ste. Geneviève, very low and discreet but audible to him. His French was not good enough to decipher whispers, but M. Dieuleveult seemed to be praying to the saint to deliver them a "good company."

Or maybe he was thanking her for the good company of Kip? The fox didn't think it wise to flatter himself, and he was fairly sure he'd heard the man say, "deliver to us." In any case, Dieuleveult was most assuredly praying to the relics—facing them and not the crucifix above them—and although Kip hadn't been raised Catholic, he had the distinct feeling that this was not appropriate.

But Dieuleveult had trusted him and it was not his place to call out whatever this might be, from minor indiscretion to heresy. And besides, he was more interested in the small pulse of magic from one of the bones and how it had come to be there.

The most likely explanation was that one of the saints—if the relics were authentic—had been a sorcerer. Did all sorcerers' bones retain magic? Then why weren't the cemeteries outside magic schools repositories of magic? Perhaps this was a saint who'd been trapped in her bones the way Peter had been trapped in the school. He dearly wanted to touch the bones and find out, but not enough to endanger his rapport with M. Dieuleveult.

By the time Dieuleveult had finished his prayer and asked Kip whether he had seen enough of the relics, Kip had moved around and believed that the long, thin bone was the magical one, though they were all so close together that it was hard to be certain. "Thank you for showing me this," he said. "It's fantastic. I never thought I would get to see something like this in person."

"If you'd like to offer a prayer to one of them, you may." The man's eyes sparkled eagerly in the firelight.

The bone he thought was magical was the one Dieuleveult had said belonged to Ste. Colette, who looked after pregnant women. So Kip bowed his head and thought a short prayer, asking for God and Ste. Colette to watch over Alice and their cub. He waited for some response, but none came.

Nobody had known a soul could be bound into stone until they'd discovered Peter some years ago, and they hadn't told anyone. There could well be other rituals that had been lost to most schools of sorcery. It would be nice to be able to study the bone; maybe if the Dieuleveults became sponsors of the school, they would allow select masters to visit here from time to time.

"Very good," Dieuleveult said when Kip looked up. He folded the cloth over the bones and then closed the lid of the wooden box.

"Have you…" Kip started the question and then realized it might be offensive, but the Frenchman had stopped politely, so he went ahead and asked it. "I mean no disrespect—often I get no response to my prayers. Do you get a response from the saints?"

The man's face broke into an affectionate smile, as though Kip had asked him about his children. "Sometimes. One must look for the answers, is it not so? They can come in signs in the world around us, or sometimes in dreams."

Dreams. Kip cleared his throat. "Have you ever had a dream over and over again?"

Perhaps it was the atmosphere of unreality around the saints that made him comfortable enough to ask this of M. Dieuleveult, where he could not bring himself to ask it of another sorcerer. The French noble, after all, could not go into Kip's mind with sorcery.

"On occasion." M. Dieuleveult set down the box on the altar and looked steadily at Kip. "Would you like me to listen to your dream? I may be able to tell you which of the saints is trying to communicate with you."

The fox took a breath. "There are three different parts to it. All of it

ontaining his relics again. "I will study my history of the saints. If I can find
the one whose story matches your dream, it may be instructive."

"Thank you," Kip said as M. Dieuleveult walked back to the sacristy.
When the door closed behind the Frenchman, the fox swished his tail and
walked over to warm himself by the fire. Staring into its ever-changing red
and gold depths always calmed him and helped him organize his thoughts.
He had not gotten any particularly useful insight into his dreams, but Emily
would be pleased that he had made this connection with M. Dieuleveult;
perhaps their performance should have some connection to saints? Or
perhaps not, not if this were a private thing that M. Dieuleveult wouldn't
want exposed in front of the other contestants. But something religious,
something that hinted at the school's connection to a higher power.

The door to the sacristy opened just a little. M. Dieuleveult slipped
though, and a small rip announced that the space had not been quite wide
enough for him and all his clothes. But he did not even acknowledge the tear
he closed and locked the door. He slipped the key back into a pocket and
turned to Kip with a bright smile. "Thank you for indulging a fellow. I can't
show them to everyone, so I do want to make sure to share them with people
who will be properly appreciative."

"I don't know as much about the saints as I should," Kip said, "and I'm
quite honored to have been able to see these parts of their history." He hoped
he was acting with proper reverence.

"Yes, very much so," Dieuleveult said. "Now, back to the house. Much
to today! The merchants will be arriving for tonight's affair and I must
present to meet them. If Pierre deals with them he will give away all our
possessions with bad bargains."

"I understand." Kip was still thinking of the bone, and then, as they
within sight of the main doorway, he realized what the other had said.
"Tonight's affair?"

"The competition!" Dieuleveult cried. "Oh, it shall be grand. We have
invited many of the neighboring lords and ladies to see the spectacle. It's
months since we hosted a gala. The Duponts held one in February, and
Marquis de Balincourt gave a spectacular one just last December. Oh,
you would have seen it! All the servants held candles and they performed a
Everything was beautiful."

"It sounds lovely." Kip didn't think it would be helpful to ask how the
servants felt about holding burning candles all night.

"But ah ha ha, they did not have sorcerers! Who's a second-rate house
He rubbed his hands together as they reached the door, where he
for Kip to open it. "So you must provide us an excellent show."

Kip obligingly pulled the heavy door open, his mind racing at this new
addition to the competition. "What kind of thing do you think would be
work well with fire, but we can provide other kinds of…" He didn't

seems to take place in a golden city."

"Actual gold, or a gold color?" M. Dieuleveult shook apologize for the interruption. Please go on."

"Gold color," Kip said. "Walls of stone, but the color of one dream, I'm on a ship approaching the city. I know people but I'm apart from them. It's not my city, and though it's apprehensive—" He paused, not sure whether the Frenchman that word. "I'm worried about what will happen to me there. I in the city—I think it's the same one—in a great palace, full gold, statues of strange creatures, and flowers and pools. The supposed to serve, but I know he's cruel and I'm planning else to overthrow him. And in the last…" He looked up at th being marched through the streets. The people around me loose white robes, all of them, and mostly they're silent. Th me are on horses and—I think—camels. I don't remembe camel before, but I found a picture of one and it matches marched through the street because—because a friend betra

M. Dieuleveult nodded throughout Kip's recital. Wl took a moment to think, and then said, "Your city could be It has been described as golden in ancient times. And the who were martyred for their beliefs, for believing in the g in that pagan country. One of them may be seeking to sh: with you, although I can't say which one it might be with(cannot think of a saint who was brought to Rome on a sl

"So you think it might really be a vision from—fron

The Frenchman smiled. "I understand that not all He gestured to Kip. "You are a stranger to many hum: your headmistress has told us of your success in the w might easily imagine sorcery as a shining city and yourse brought into it."

"That's what I thought at first," Kip said. "But th back, not always exactly the same, but close."

"And then there is the matter of the camel. From arise?" M. Dieuleveult shook his head. "No, 1 suspect the attention of a saint who is trying to warn you of a

"Close?" Kip asked.

"Pardon my English. I mean close in time. Soon!' lit up. "A betrayal soon."

"But I've been having these dreams for alm was betrayed by Master Colonel Jackson, in a sens happened?"

"Perhaps. Or…you know that God has said a th to Him. Perhaps to the saints, it is similar." He smile feel right saying "entertainment," so he said, "distraction," which also wasn't the right word but at least didn't make him feel like a court jester.

"Ah, I would not know how to judge!" M. Dieuleveult's excitement had shifted from religious veneration to the joy of a child presented with a well-wrapped gift. "Please do not let my limited experience restrain your imagination."

"All right." Kip wasn't sure whether any of this information would help them decide what to cast, but Emily would be a good judge of that. And then he thought of something simple he could do. "If you need help moving things into the kitchens, or—or where they need to go, I can help with sorcery."

"Oh, no, I wouldn't dream of it. Besides, they may not arrive for an hour or more, and I would detest making you wait."

"There's a cart approaching right now," Kip said, ears flicking.

"Eh?" M. Dieuleveult hurried to the door and looked out. "So there is! How extraordinary. Did you perceive it through sorcery?"

"Er..." Kip was saved from having to choose between lying and disappointing his host by M. Dieuleveult getting a good look at the cart for the first time.

"Surely there was to be more wine than only three barrels," he muttered, forgetting his question to Kip as he hurried out to meet the horses and driver.

Kip followed behind, ready to make good on his offer even though it did not seem that three barrels would be worth casting a spell over. M. Dieuleveult forged ahead quickly. "*Qu'est-ce que c'est?*" he called as the horses drew level with him and stopped, huffing. This was followed by a stream of French too quick for Kip to follow completely, the gist of which seemed to be that three barrels was definitely not enough.

The driver of the cart—the merchant, presumably—answered slowly enough for Kip to understand that the rest of the shipment was "not available." The reason seemed to be "people."

He thought he'd misheard, but M. Dieuleveult repeated the word incredulously. What 'people'? he wanted to know.

People, the merchant replied, just people. He gestured vaguely. There had been many of them and they had taken his wine. No, he had not informed the royal soldiers; he had hurried to deliver the wine he could escape with.

This was impossible, M. Dieuleveult fumed. Heads would be separated from rebellious bodies. He exhorted the merchant to come inside and tell him whether any of the scoundrels were known to him, while this fine fox would unload the wine and bring it to the kitchen.

As there was no mention of sorcery, the merchant looked skeptical but followed them into the castle. A steward stood waiting in the courtyard and through sign language and broken French, Kip made him understand that he would be taking charge of the wine. The steward thanked him and pointed to the door through which the wine needed to be sent.

When Kip cast his spell and lifted all three barrels from the cart, the merchant snapped his head up from his conversation with M. Dieuleveult and swore an oath. The noble could not hide his smile as he said that oh yes, this was the sorcerer, it was no great matter for him to be here carrying wine for the Dieuleveults.

Kip gritted his teeth, reminding himself of the importance of his mission, and moved the wine into the kitchen behind the steward, who more than made up for his master's nonchalance with his unending stream of gratitude.

to the door through which the wine needed to be sent.

When Kip cast his spell and lifted all three barrels from the cart, the merchant snapped his head up from his conversation with M. Dieuleveult and swore an oath. The noble could not hide his smile as he said that oh yes, this was the sorcerer, it was no great matter for him to be here carrying wine for the Dieuleveults.

Kip gritted his teeth, reminding himself of the importance of his mission, and moved the wine into the kitchen behind the steward, who more than made up for his master's nonchalance with his unending stream of gratitude.

feel right saying "entertainment," so he said, "distraction," which also wasn't the right word but at least didn't make him feel like a court jester.

"Ah, I would not know how to judge!" M. Dieuleveult's excitement had shifted from religious veneration to the joy of a child presented with a well-wrapped gift. "Please do not let my limited experience restrain your imagination."

"All right." Kip wasn't sure whether any of this information would help them decide what to cast, but Emily would be a good judge of that. And then he thought of something simple he could do. "If you need help moving things into the kitchens, or—or where they need to go, I can help with sorcery."

"Oh, no, I wouldn't dream of it. Besides, they may not arrive for an hour or more, and I would detest making you wait."

"There's a cart approaching right now," Kip said, ears flicking.

"Eh?" M. Dieuleveult hurried to the door and looked out. "So there is! How extraordinary. Did you perceive it through sorcery?"

"Er..." Kip was saved from having to choose between lying and disappointing his host by M. Dieuleveult getting a good look at the cart for the first time.

"Surely there was to be more wine than only three barrels," he muttered, forgetting his question to Kip as he hurried out to meet the horses and driver.

Kip followed behind, ready to make good on his offer even though it did not seem that three barrels would be worth casting a spell over. M. Dieuleveult forged ahead quickly. "*Qu'est-ce que c'est?*" he called as the horses drew level with him and stopped, huffing. This was followed by a stream of French too quick for Kip to follow completely, the gist of which seemed to be that three barrels was definitely not enough.

The driver of the cart—the merchant, presumably—answered slowly enough for Kip to understand that the rest of the shipment was "not available." The reason seemed to be "people."

He thought he'd misheard, but M. Dieuleveult repeated the word incredulously. What 'people'? he wanted to know.

People, the merchant replied, just people. He gestured vaguely. There had been many of them and they had taken his wine. No, he had not informed the royal soldiers; he had hurried to deliver the wine he could escape with.

This was impossible, M. Dieuleveult fumed. Heads would be separated from rebellious bodies. He exhorted the merchant to come inside and tell him whether any of the scoundrels were known to him, while this fine fox would unload the wine and bring it to the kitchen.

As there was no mention of sorcery, the merchant looked skeptical but followed them into the castle. A steward stood waiting in the courtyard and through sign language and broken French, Kip made him understand that he would be taking charge of the wine. The steward thanked him and pointed seems to take place in a golden city."

"Actual gold, or a gold color?" M. Dieuleveult shook his head. "I apologize for the interruption. Please go on."

"Gold color," Kip said. "Walls of stone, but the color of the sun. In one dream, I'm on a ship approaching the city. I know people on the boat but I'm apart from them. It's not my city, and though it's beautiful, I'm apprehensive—" He paused, not sure whether the Frenchman would know that word. "I'm worried about what will happen to me there. In another, I'm in the city—I think it's the same one—in a great palace, full of gold, actual gold, statues of strange creatures, and flowers and pools. There's a king I'm supposed to serve, but I know he's cruel and I'm planning with someone else to overthrow him. And in the last…" He looked up at the crucifix. "I'm being marched through the streets. The people around me are dressed in loose white robes, all of them, and mostly they're silent. The people behind me are on horses and—I think—camels. I don't remember having seen a camel before, but I found a picture of one and it matches. And I'm being marched through the street because—because a friend betrayed me."

M. Dieuleveult nodded throughout Kip's recital. When it ended, he took a moment to think, and then said, "Your city could be Rome, of course. It has been described as golden in ancient times. And there are many saints who were martyred for their beliefs, for believing in the godhood of Christ in that pagan country. One of them may be seeking to share his experiences with you, although I can't say which one it might be without further study. I cannot think of a saint who was brought to Rome on a ship."

"So you think it might really be a vision from—from a saint?"

The Frenchman smiled. "I understand that not all dreams are such." He gestured to Kip. "You are a stranger to many human institutions, and your headmistress has told us of your success in the world of sorcery. One might easily imagine sorcery as a shining city and yourself as a stranger being brought into it."

"That's what I thought at first," Kip said. "But the dreams have come back, not always exactly the same, but close."

"And then there is the matter of the camel. From where did that vision arise?" M. Dieuleveult shook his head. "No, I suspect that you have caught the attention of a saint who is trying to warn you of a close betrayal."

"Close?" Kip asked.

"Pardon my English. I mean close in time. Soon!" The Frenchman's face lit up. "A betrayal soon."

"But I've been having these dreams for almost two years. And I was betrayed by Master Colonel Jackson, in a sense, so maybe it already happened?"

"Perhaps. Or…you know that God has said a thousand years are as a day to Him. Perhaps to the saints, it is similar." He smiled and picked up the box containing his relics again. "I will study my history of the saints. If I can find the one whose story matches your dream, it may be instructive."

"Thank you," Kip said as M. Dieuleveult walked back to the sacristy. When the door closed behind the Frenchman, the fox swished his tail and walked over to warm himself by the fire. Staring into its ever-changing red and gold depths always calmed him and helped him organize his thoughts. He had not gotten any particularly useful insight into his dreams, but Emily would be pleased that he had made this connection with M. Dieuleveult; perhaps their performance should have some connection to saints? Or perhaps not, not if this were a private thing that M. Dieuleveult wouldn't want exposed in front of the other contestants. But something religious, something that hinted at the school's connection to a higher power.

The door to the sacristy opened just a little. M. Dieuleveult slipped through, and a small rip announced that the space had not been quite wide enough for him and all his clothes. But he did not even acknowledge the tear as he closed and locked the door. He slipped the key back into a pocket and turned to Kip with a bright smile. "Thank you for indulging a fellow. I can't show them to everyone, so I do want to make sure to share them with people who will be properly appreciative."

"I don't know as much about the saints as I should," Kip said, "and I'm quite honored to have been able to see these parts of their history." He hoped he was acting with proper reverence.

"Yes, very much so," Dieuleveult said. "Now, back to the house. Much to do today! The merchants will be arriving for tonight's affair and I must be present to meet them. If Pierre deals with them he will give away all our possessions with bad bargains."

"I understand." Kip was still thinking of the bone, and then, as they came within sight of the main doorway, he realized what the other had said. "Tonight's affair?"

"The competition!" Dieuleveult cried. "Oh, it shall be grand. We have invited many of the neighboring lords and ladies to see the spectacle. It's been months since we hosted a gala. The Duponts held one in February, and the Marquis de Balincourt gave a spectacular one just last December. Oh, you should have seen it! All the servants held candles and they performed a dance. Everything was beautiful."

"It sounds lovely." Kip didn't think it would be helpful to ask how the servants felt about holding burning candles all night.

"But ah ha ha, they did not have sorcerers! Who's a second-rate house now?" He rubbed his hands together as they reached the door, where he waited for Kip to open it. "So you must provide us an excellent show."

Kip obligingly pulled the heavy door open, his mind racing at this new dimension to the competition. "What kind of thing do you think would be best? I work well with fire, but we can provide other kinds of..." He didn't

CHAPTER ELEVEN:

VICTOR'S SPELL

Emily was predictably annoyed that their competition had been turned into a spectacle. "You realize what this means," she said. "A gala like this is planned weeks ahead of time. They never had any intention of giving us money at the Exposition, only to lure a few sorcerers here to put on a show for them."

"I hadn't thought of that," Kip said honestly.

"When you have as much money as they do, you expect everyone to just fall in line." Emily's eyes flashed. "And we need their money, so we'll have to make the best of it. I suppose one benefit is that our sorcery tends to be showier anyway, so we must make it as visually impressive as possible."

"And what does that mean?" Kip asked.

She sighed. "What benefit does our school have? Calatians. So I'm afraid I can't get around the idea that you should summon a demon. The Dutch showed off their ability to do it at the Exposition; if you show that you can do it without a calyx, that would be impressive."

"They won't understand what it means to not use a calyx," Kip objected.

Emily ran a hand over Sleek's feathers. The raven sat on her arm rather than her shoulder, preening, and made a soft throaty croak when Emily touched her. "So tell them. But unless one of the others brought a calyx—and I don't think any did—none of them will be able to replicate it."

"I really don't like summoning demons," Kip said.

"If I could do it, I would."

"What about fire? M. Dieuleveult was quite impressed with my fire, and nobody else can do that either."

She nodded. "We'll start with fire. But have a name ready, and if we judge that we need something extra, you'll be willing to do it, right?"

It would be just one summoning, brief, just for show, and then it would be done, weighed against the possibility of years of education for Jorey and Richard and Charity (they would find them, of course they would, and tomorrow he could join the search) and others like them. "Yes," he said, though he resolved privately that he would try every other avenue first.

"Good." She lifted her arm and Sleek fluttered to the window. "Then let's practice some of your fire sorcery. I know you don't need the practice to cast, but maybe I can help you see what looks best to an audience."

Thinking of the students made him want to look in on Ash to see how Alice and Malcolm fared. He wanted to tell Alice about M. Dieuleveult's relics and his strange obsession with the saints, and to ask whether she'd spoken to Coppy's family yet. But he restrained himself and worked instead on giving his fire as much theatricality as he could.

They found that lamp glass, levitated, could do a great deal toward containing and shaping fire, so Emily suggested she visit Boston in the afternoon (Boston's morning) to see if she could find any interestingly-shaped glass from a shop. Kip practiced summoning and binding a phosphorus elemental, which would be hopefully more entertaining than a demon, because the gregarious phosphorus elementals enjoyed talking to people and could be fed bits of paper or anything else flammable. Summoning elementals was not as difficult as summoning demons, and Patris certainly could, but perhaps the others would not think it worth showing off.

He and Emily worked hard to come up with something related to M. Dieuleveult's saints, but sorcery kept itself secular by design (Kip had been taught very briefly about the Holy Roman Wars of the 1300s in which the Catholic Church had challenged the faltering European monarchies and lost, after which for three hundred years sorcerers were not permitted to join the priesthood) and they could not come up with any good ideas that did not seem blasphemous.

Emily thought they should also demonstrate what use they would make of the money, which led back to worrying about the students. "Let's worry about getting this done," she said, "and then we can go to London and join them there," and the way she said it made it clear to Kip that she was telling herself as well as him.

Charles brought them a small lunch with the news that the gala would begin shortly before sundown. Claudine set the table for two, despite Emily and Kip's invitation to Charles to join them. "How far away is sundown, would you say?" Emily asked as Kip helped himself to a delicious buttery roll with cured ham on the side.

"I would guess about three hours," Charles said.

"That gives me time to go to Boston. I don't know where there are glassblowers there, but I know the market area and I should be able to find one."

Charles asked politely whether he might ask her why she wanted glass and if there were anything he could provide. Emily explained what they were looking for, and he nodded thoughtfully. "There is nothing like that here," he said, "but if you can take me along with you, I know where there is an excellent glass merchant in Paris who will have what you need."

"That sounds lovely." Emily took one of the rolls. "I haven't any French money, though. Oh! I believe M Deboussard might give me some in exchange for our coin. I would have to go back to the Academie anyway, so I could ask him."

Charles smiled. "I believe Mme. Dieuleveult would happily purchase your glass for you, if it is in service to tonight's competition."

"I will accept that offer." Emily took a bite of the roll. "Oh, these are lovely. Very well, Charles, would you like to go now?"

"I have a small number of duties to attend to," the footman said, "but I will return within the half hour with traveling clothes and would be delighted to accompany you then."

"We won't be out of doors," Emily reminded him. "I intend to travel by sorcery."

"We will have to leave a building to meet the glass merchant," Charles said, "and it will be twenty minutes to walk from the Academie."

"I'll prepare myself. Thank you, Charles."

The footman bowed and left. Emily finished her roll and wiped her fingers on the lavender napkin. "I'm rather excited to see Parisian glass," she said. "I don't know that Boston's glass is all that special; it's simply where I knew to go. Having a guide around Paris will be wonderful. You're coming along, aren't you?"

"I, ah, I rather thought I would stay here and practice spells."

Emily looked shrewdly at him. "I do think it's important you come along with me and test the lamp glass to make sure it's tempered well enough to withstand your fire." When he searched for a response to that, she said, "Malcolm and Alice are doing the best they can."

He splayed his ears. "I was…"

"You were thinking you might pop in and help them out. So have I. I hate that we have to do this and not devote all our attentions to finding our students."

Kip sighed, and then perked his ears up. "We'll be going to the Academie, right?"

"Of course."

"Then perhaps we could look for a spiritual sorcerer who might come back with us and protect us from Victor's sorcerer? Or—" Excitement set his tail wagging. "Or maybe look into Victor's mind himself. If we could get him to just think about where the students are…"

"That's an excellent idea," Emily said, "and I won't deny that I've had similar thoughts. So you'll come along?"

"Yes," Kip said. "Let's go."

When Charles had returned and they had finally dressed for travel, Emily took Charles's hand and Kip's paw and cast her translocation spell.

The basement of the Academie was nothing like the peaceful room they'd seen the day before. Directly in front of them, two sorcerers argued in French, while near the doorway another strode out of the room clutching a burlap sack that looked heavy.

"What—" Emily looked around as the two sorcerers near them jumped back. "What's happening? I had to correct to stop running into you!"

They stared at her as she pulled Kip and Charles out of the way, then shouted in French. Emily asked, "Charles, what are they saying? Tell them I'm sorry."

He called her apology to them and then, as they reached the door, said, "They are arguing about where to go. One of them wants to go to Spain, the other to Russia. They said—I do beg your pardon—'are you crazy, don't come here.'"

Two more sorcerers appeared in the room behind them. "They're leaving?" Kip asked. "What's happening?"

"Let's go upstairs," Emily said grimly. "I want to see if Master Debroussard is here."

Charles followed the two sorcerers, and fortunately most of the traffic inside the Academie moved in the same direction, as sorcerers appeared and left the translocation room. "Where are they coming from?" Kip asked.

"I cannot say for certain," Charles said. "But two of the sorcerers had a royal crest on their robes."

Emily forged on ahead up two flights of stairs. As they reached the ground floor, outside noises became clearer. "You hear that?" Kip asked.

All three of them stopped on the landing. "Shouting," Emily said.

"And fighting. Glass breaking—there." He listened. "They're saying 'Vive la France' and something else I can't make out."

Charles went pale and staggered back against the stone. "They are calling for death to the king," he said.

Kip searched for a window, but the narrow ones in the stairwell had been built to fire arrows out of and gave only an incomplete view of the chaos on the streets outside. When he put his nose to it, though, the thin acrid smell of smoke came to him, and when he sent his awareness out he found fire everywhere.

"Burning," he said shortly. Emily had already started up the stairs, but Charles was waiting for Kip.

"This building?" the footman said.

"I don't think so. It's stone; it'll take more than fire. But—"

Charles hurried past him, which Kip initially took as eagerness to catch Emily, but the footman stopped at the next window. As Kip reached him, he stepped back. "So much smoke," he said, pressing fingers to his eyes.

From this window, Kip could at least see buildings and the skyline of Paris, and indeed, multiple columns of thick black smoke coiled up into the air. "I could stop the fires," he offered.

"The fires are not the problem." Charles pointed down at the street.

Kip had to angle his muzzle downward to see the crowds in the streets. Dressed in dirty, patched clothes, they were clearly the same type as the beggars he'd seen the previous day, but where those beggars had seemed apathetic, these were energized. They broke windows and rushed into buildings. As he watched they pulled a man from a house and set to beating him.

"We cannot stop this any longer," Charles said. "We should return immediately to the Dieuleveults' estate."

"I can stop some of it." Kip reached out with magic and lifted the man away from his assailants into the air. He couldn't fit him through the window, but he could deposit him on a roof far from the crowd, and did so.

This caused most of the attackers to look up and point and cry out, "*Sorcier!*" They ran toward the Academie, gathering others as they came.

"That was maybe not a good idea." Kip backed away from the window.

"I thought that the riots would die down," Charles said. "Where are the royal guard? They are meant to be fighting!"

"I don't know."

They reached the second floor, where shouted arguments took the place of running feet. Emily stood at a door knocking, but stopped when they arrived. "I don't know where M. Debroussard is," she said.

"If he's a translocational sorcerer, maybe he'll be downstairs helping others evacuate."

At that moment the neighboring door opened and a dark-haired man with an olive complexion stepped out into the hallway. "Debroussard?" he asked, and then rattled off a sentence in French.

"He says," Charles translated, "that M. Debroussard went to help the royal sorcerers and will be downstairs coming and going."

"Thank you," Emily said to both the sorcerer and Charles, and made for the stairs.

Kip hung back. "Can you tell him please that the mob is coming here and maybe he should leave?"

Charles nodded and spoke to the sorcerer in French, and got a curt nod in reply before the man disappeared back into his office. "He did not seem terribly worried."

"Most sorcerers can translocate themselves," Kip said. "I can take another person, so don't worry, I'll keep you safe."

"Thank you, sir," the footman said. "Shall we follow Mlle. Carswell?"

They hurried down the stairs, catching up to Emily just after the ground floor. Kip cleared his throat as they descended. "We think the rioters are headed this way. There may not be much time."

"We can go back as soon as it's dangerous," Emily said without breaking stride, "and if they try to burn us out, I trust you can take care of that."

"Yes," Kip said, "but I'd rather it not come to that. Can we find a spiritual sorcerer and maybe go back? Or stay and help the sorcerers leave… if they need the help."

When they got to the basement, there were more sorcerers and more arguments. They stopped for a moment and then Emily called, "Monsieur Debroussard!"

A tall man, sandy-haired with a small nose and full beard, turned from a conversation he was having. "Mistress Carswell," he called, and asked the sorcerers he was speaking to for a moment, then came to join them, pulling them to one side of the room.

"This is a very bad time," he said. "I am needed to help our sorcerers leave the palace and the military barracks. But quickly, what are you doing here?"

"We came to Paris to—never mind, it doesn't matter now. Can we help at all? What's happening?"

His mouth set in a grim line. "The crowds this morning assaulted the palace. There were skirmishes and the guards were overpowered. The King ordered his sorcerers to kill the crowd and they did not wish to be murderers so they refused. He threatened them and they offered to take him to his wife's relatives in the Russian court, but he refused numerous times. So we are bringing all the sorcerers back and sending them to their homes."

"If anyone needs a refuge," Kip said, "our school is open."

Emily and M. Debroussard both gave him considered looks. "For some refugees that might be appropriate," the French sorcerer said.

"But," Emily continued, "for royal or military sorcerers, it would look like our country was taking sides."

"Still," Kip objected. "If it's a matter of their safety."

"Yes," M. Debroussard said. "I thank you for the offer, Master—Penfold, yes?"

"Yes."

"*Bien sûr.* I would be pleased to make your acquaintance at some future time. For now we must secure the safety of our sorcerers."

Before Kip could answer, a deep pounding echoed through the room, coming from upstairs. "Ah," M. Debroussard said. "They are at the doors."

"We should go."

"They are defended, but yes." He took Emily's hand and brought it quickly to his lips. "Travel safely."

"Come to our school when you're able," Emily said as he waved and hurried back to the sorcerers he'd been talking to.

All around them, sorcerers had been appearing and disappearing, but now the crowd seemed to thin out. "I think they have gotten most of them out," Kip said.

"We can wait another moment." Emily looked upstairs.

The pounding continued from upstairs, then silenced. A moment later, a sorcerer ran downstairs and shouted a question in French. One of the others responded, and he nodded, then he caught sight of Kip and Emily. "*Américains?*"

They both nodded. He frowned and growled several quick sentences at them in French and then ran back upstairs.

Emily turned to Charles. "What did he say?"

"Please excuse me," the footman said. "He said that this is your fault."

Kip startled guiltily. How could this sorcerer have known that he'd brought the mob to their door?

"The American Revolution showed that kings are not invincible," Charles went on. "You showed them a path to freedom, and now they are charging violently along it." He coughed. "That is what he said."

Relieved of immediate guilt, Kip considered. "He's not completely wrong, I suppose. We might have revolted even sooner if someone else had done it first."

"No." Charles shook his head. "The country has been very poor since Napoleon's defeat. The first year we had food, but after that it grew scarcer. Those of us who live with nobles do not experience hunger, but many of us have families and friends who do, even when we provide food to them. For many years now the people have made do with nearly nothing, and now the price is being paid. Last month the bakeries ran out of flour and there was no bread for a week. And then when all the sorcerers went to the Exposition, fights started. Now my country is dying."

He did not look pleased or satisfied, but spoke hollowly and slowly. "We should go back and get the Dieuleveults to safety," Emily said.

"If one of these is a spiritual sorcerer…" Kip looked around, but Charles cut him off.

"The Dieuleveults will not leave their castle," he said. "The gala will go on. The riots are in Paris and it will take them a day or two to travel south."

"We can't take that chance." Emily either had not heard Kip or was ignoring him. "They may be in danger."

"I know Mme. Dieuleveult," Charles said. "I will ask her, but I am certain that unless the castle is besieged, she will insist that the gala proceed. And," he added, "they do have money and will hold to their agreement to give it to your school, even if it is from exile, should it come to that."

"We'll have another chance at Victor," Kip said, but at that moment the pounding resumed from upstairs.

"We haven't time." Emily looked around the room, which had mostly cleared out. "In another five minutes they'll all be gone, and we should be as well."

"All right," Kip said, and Emily took his paw and Charles's hand and brought them back to their chambers.

Claudine let out a shriek as they appeared, and even after Charles spoke to her, she crouched nervously by the window. "I will go inform the Dieuleveults of the situation," Charles said. "Please plan to participate in the competition." He paused. "I am sorry you could not procure your glass."

"It's all right," Emily said softly, and Charles bowed to her and then left.

Kip made his way to the fire and sat. "I made things worse," he said, and told her about moving the man to the roof and the crowd's resulting surge toward the Academie.

"I wish you hadn't," Emily said, "but I can't fault you for saving a life, and I suspect you hastened things by only a short time."

"A short time in which we could've found a spiritual sorcerer and had a better chance to save our students."

"We've got Peter, if it comes to that." Emily stared into the fire. "We'll just have to keep a very close guard on him while he's here."

"I suppose that's right." Kip rested his elbows on his knees. "I thought we were done with revolution. I thought France was doing well. I don't know anything about international politics, I suppose."

"Napoleon upset things." Emily brushed her hair back from her eyes. "He was outside the lineage of kings, a regent who took power but actually listened to the people and led France to glory. Fleeting, but glory. When we defeated Napoleon, we put a king back on the throne because that was the old way, but many people look at this king as the embodiment of their defeat. So it's easy to rise up against him."

"Plus he was starving them. George didn't go that far with us."

Emily didn't say anything, but rested her head on his shoulder. "Everything is so tenuous," she said, her voice cracking. "We need this money, and our students are in danger, and if it all falls apart then it's my fault. France is crumbling and we're no closer to finding our students and I feel so powerless that it doesn't seem fair that it's on my shoulders."

He put an arm around her. "How can it be your fault? The students were kidnapped on my watch, and the revolution has been brewing for a while, you said."

"It doesn't matter." She leaned into him. "I'm the headmistress. If the school fails, that's what's recorded."

The feeling of powerlessness was relatable. There was only one thing they still could control, and that was the competition. "Let's make sure we win this competition, then," he said. "If we don't have glass, maybe I can... make shapes from the fire? Some of the Chinese sorcerers were making frost shapes in the air."

Emily didn't move. "That sounds intriguing. What can you do?"

He stared into the fire and imagined it shaped to fabulous creatures. It was but a step from that to actually casting the spell and bringing wings of fire out of the fireplace. Behind them, Claudine uttered another oath, but he ignored her. He couldn't hold a shape well, but with a little practice he hoped the shape of a phoenix would be clear, something to reassure the nobles that France would rise again. "We'll make do without the glassware," he said, "and the Dieuleveults are going to give us money."

"Before the mob takes it away," Emily said.

"Before then." Kip searched for a way to make her laugh. "We'll ask for it in gold."

She did laugh, and then straightened up. "I suppose we must go through with it. And we'll find a way to get the truth from Victor. If he didn't do it then I don't know where we'll look."

The wings collapsed back into the fire. "I really don't think we'll have to worry about that," Kip said.

From the fireside, the view through their window allowed them to watch the carts arrive with food for the gala. Neither of them spoke as they watched the dirty people in ragged clothes drive carts loaded with vegetables and loaves of bread along the road past their window and into the palace. They exchanged a look and then returned to staring into the fire.

Kip had removed his robes so they wouldn't get singed by the fire, and had not yet dressed when Charles returned, announcing that Mme. Dieuleveult requested their presence before noticing Kip's plain tunic and stopping mid-sentence. "Will you need help in dressing, Master Penfold?" he asked.

"No, thank you." Kip stood and fetched his robe.

"Master Penfold has been working with fire," Emily said. "He didn't want to risk burning his clothing."

"Of course," Charles said smoothly. "As I was saying: the other sorcerers are gathering in the parlor to prepare for the gala. The first guests have already arrived."

Emily stood. "We can find our own way if you have other duties to attend to."

"My current duty is to bring you to the parlor." Charles smiled.

"Should I bring Sleek?" Emily held up her arm with the raven on it. "She can as easily stay here."

Charles examined the raven and nodded. "If she is not essential to your demonstration, then that might be best. Some of the nobles might not understand her presence."

Kip finished the last fastenings of his shirt and picked up his robe. "We're ready," he said. "Let's go."

Servants had been busy at work in the parlor: blue satin ribbons hung from the windows and walls, fastened by rosettes of the same satin with additional white and red. Glittering decorations of crafted glass spun in front of each window, and the large chandelier now bore lit candles that cast playful light around the room.

All the sorcerers present wore more formal attire than Kip and Emily, but the fanciest was Victor Adamson, who had added a peacock feather boutonniere and a stylish top hat to his elegant light blue suit. He stood next to Mme. Dieuleveult in close conversation with her, but as Kip and Emily entered the room, his blue-grey eyes met Kip's and his mouth curved up into a smile.

Kip didn't hold the look for long. "After this," he murmured, "the sorcerers will likely have time to prepare their shows. We can try to get Victor then."

"Mmm." Emily rubbed her chin.

M. Dieuleveult looked ill at ease at the side of Master Patris. "Come on," Kip said, walking in that direction. "I'll introduce you again. Victor might have the ear of his wife, but we'll at least get our feet in this door."

"All right," Emily said, "but I do want to talk to Mme. Dieuleveult as well."

"Yes." Kip didn't look over toward the noblewoman. "I don't want Victor to think we're worried about him."

"No, I agree. Let's build on your work this morning."

As they approached M. Dieuleveult, the man brightened. "Ah, it's Master Penfold! How have you spent the day?"

"Planning to give you a marvelous show." Kip smiled, ignoring Master Patris's glower. "You remember Mistress Carswell, the headmistress of our school?"

"Indeed I do!" M. Dieuleveult grasped her hand and brought it to his lips. "A most formidable lady. I imagine that between the two of you, you can accomplish much."

"We have done the best we can." Emily smiled her warmest smile. "We hope that with your help, we will be able to do much more."

"Of course, of course!" The Frenchman laughed. "Although, you understand, my wife will make the final decision. I may add my opinion to the matter, but she runs the estate."

"Oh." Kip and Emily looked over to where Mme. Dieuleveult laughed at something Victor said.

"Yes." Following their gaze, M. Dieuleveult's smile vanished. "We have a saying in the court about the peacock and the rooster, and that is a rooster for certain, for all his finery and that feather."

"He doesn't even—" Kip stopped to get control of his voice. "He's funded by King's College, with the Royal Treasury behind him. He doesn't need money."

"No, but it would please him greatly to keep us—or Patris, for that matter—from getting it." Emily's tone, clipped and short, matched the tightness in Kip's chest.

"As I understand it," M. Dieuleveult said, "he has been telling my wife that our money will be safe overseas. He says that this can soothe our relationship with the British Crown and that he alone of all the schools promises to return the money once his research is complete."

"Return the money?" Kip stared. "How does he mean to do that?"

"He's not spending it to educate," Emily answered before M. Dieuleveult could. "He's spending it to make some kind of sorcery that people will pay for. A weapon, I suppose."

"Or else he's lying," Kip rubbed his paws down his robe and turned to M. Dieuleveult. "I'm sorry. Victor has been less than truthful with us in the past."

"You and he have a story?"

"We have history, yes." Emily drew in a deep breath and let it out. "Out of impotent jealousy at our accomplishments, he has tried to wield some political influence to tear down what we've built."

"He's kidnapped Calatians and tried to frame me for murder," Kip said.

"Oh, dear." M. Dieuleveult clasped his hands together.

Emily gave him a bright smile. "We hope that our performance convinces your wife that ours is the worthiest cause."

"Yours is by far the worthiest cause," the Frenchman said unexpectedly. "What could be more worthwhile than teaching young students sorcery? And of all the schools here, yours is in the most dire straits. We have made inquiries. But alas, worth may not win the day."

"Then what—" Kip stopped as Emily laid a hand on his arm.

"We understand and we'll do all we can," she said.

Kip thought back to the morning and the visit to the church. "Which of the saints would hear our prayers, do you think?" he asked.

"Grégoire le Grand," M. Dieuleveult replied promptly. "I believe in English he is called Gregory. He was the Pope who spread Christianity throughout Europe, Gregory the First. I have read a little of his Dialogues, and for a while I hoped to obtain one of his relics, but they are held close in Saint-Pierre de Rome. But yes, he is the patron saint of teachers and students, and there are even whispers that he was a sorcerer himself."

"I had not heard that." Kip wasn't sure whether Saint Gregory would approve of their secular education, but he accepted the recommendation because M. Dieuleveult's smile returned as he was giving it, which was his purpose in asking.

"He has one line that I refer to often with our servants here who do not have their letters…'Illiterate men can contemplate in the lines of a picture what they cannot learn by means of the written word.' He meant, of course, that you can illustrate the Gospel to reach those who cannot read, but it is a reminder to me that simply because one cannot read doesn't mean one is," he tapped his head, "unintelligent."

"Very true," Kip said.

"Now, speaking of the servants, where are those hors d'œuvres?" The noble looked around the room. "Charles told me that the carts arrived as planned. And where is Charles? I beg you excuse me while I see to this. I hope there will be refreshments soon."

He walked briskly toward one of the doors. Kip tugged on Emily's sleeve. "Come on," he said. "If Madame is the one to convince, then let's go do the convincing."

Emily stared at the noblewoman and Victor and then said, "In a moment. I need to straighten my hair."

"But—" Kip had time only to utter that word before she vanished through one of the doorways.

He calmed himself until she returned, and to his eye her hair looked the same as it had when she'd left, but he didn't say anything. "Ready?" she said, and walked on without waiting for an answer.

Mme. Dieuleveult was still talking to Victor when Emily strode up boldly with Kip in tow. "Hallo, Victor," she said. "It is so delightful to see you again."

"Miss Carswell." He half-bowed.

"Headmistress Carswell, actually." Emily's smile didn't crack.

"Yes, I've heard." Victor turned to Kip. "And Master Penfold."

"I can't wait to see what trick you've decided to use to entertain the guests tonight," Kip said.

"Oh, I was just telling Madame Dieuleveult that I think we can do better than a trick. Of course I can't expose our research to every sorcerer at the Exposition, but here in more refined company, we can be more free with our sorcery."

"By 'we,' I assume you mean Master Gupta there. The one who can actually cast spells?" Kip indicated the other sorcerer, standing by himself looking down at the floor, his lips moving.

"The magic comes from him, but the research and the spell are, I assure you, all mine." Victor's smile didn't crack.

"Master Adamson claims that he can really do what he showed at the Exposition," Mme. Dieuleveult said. "Isn't that wonderful? To replicate a Great Feat here, in my house!"

If a Great Feat could be replicated, it would by definition no longer be a Great Feat, but Kip didn't think their hostess was in a mood to hear such technicalities. It occurred to him that if Victor did succeed in creating Calatians, he would have destroyed a Great Feat, although with much less destruction than Cott had.

"It will indeed be remarkable, if it happens," he said.

Victor just smiled. "If you'll excuse me, I do see some more people entering that I should greet." He took Mme. Dieuleveult's hand and brought it to his lips.

"One moment." Emily took Victor's hand as he released Mme Dieleveult's. "I did want to ask, since you mentioned our students yesterday, whether you'd seen anything that might be of use to us in finding them. After all, it was immediately after your demonstration that they disappeared."

"I see. As I'm sure you're aware, a demonstration at an exposition takes a great deal of planning and focus. Oh, but you didn't give a demonstration, did you? I—" His fixed smile cracked, and he pulled his hand away from Emily's. For a moment he stared at her and then he called over her shoulder, "Master Gupta!"

Emily wore the same neutral expression, but beneath it her teeth were clenched. Kip wanted to ask what had happened, but was forestalled by Victor, smoothing his smile into place again and addressing the bewildered Mme. Dieuleveult. "I thought," he said, "that we might give you a small taste of tonight's spell, since Master Penfold is here."

The Indian sorcerer arrived at Victor's side, and Victor pointed to Kip. "The fox," he said, "just for these people here."

Master Gupta nodded and lowered his eyes in concentration. Kip took a step back. "Wait," he said, drawing magic into him in case he needed it. "I haven't agreed to anything."

"It won't harm you," Victor said. "Master Gupta is an accomplished spiritual sorcerer whose specialty is illusions, the ability to convince people they are seeing what is not real. He is going to demonstrate the spell I am working on and, with your support, will be able to complete."

Emily took Kip's paw in her hand. He grasped it, glad of the comfort, and felt a small stone from her ring pressing into his paw. But Emily didn't usually wear rings—

A voice echoed in his head. *Kip, I am here.*

He nearly jumped. *Peter?*

I will guard you against any spiritual sorcery, have no fear.

All right. Thank you. He breathed evenly and relaxed.

Mme. Dieuleveult stared intently at him and then her eyes widened. "*Mon Dieu!*"

"Yes," Victor said. "You see, the foundation of my research is to examine what gives a Calatian their essential nature. What if you could separate the animal from the human and allow them to live normal, fruitful lives unburdened by the curse of their birth?"

The noblewoman shook her head, still staring at Kip. "I am not sure I see the value in this."

Emily took a step back, also staring at Kip, and then a frown crossed her face and she shook her head. Kip wanted to throw the illusion off of him like a cloak, but had no way to do so. "We don't regard it as a curse," he said to Victor, "but a gift."

"A gift that keeps your people in cramped, filthy housing."

"The way that people treat us doesn't determine our nature," Kip said.

Victor turned to Mme. Dieuleveult with mock sadness. "You see that sorcery is not the only obstacle. We must also convince those in need of our help that it will benefit them, when they have constructed an entire belief around worshipping their affliction."

"Perhaps," she said, still doubtful.

Emily pulled Kip away before he could retort, and that was a good thing given how tempted he was to start a fire, either real or verbal. "Kip," she hissed, "come here!"

He followed her to one side of the room. "That...that...son of a—"

She cut him off with a low whisper. "He kidnapped them, Kip."

"It's a good job you brought Peter," he said, and then her words penetrated his anger. "What?"

"That's why I brought Peter. Not to protect you, although he came in handy there too, thank you, Peter. It occurred to me that he would be more on his guard later, among just sorcerers, and if I could surprise him—which is why I didn't tell you either, I'm sorry about that—we might have more success. And we did."

Kip's ears perked up and he gripped Emily's arm. "Where are they?"

"He caught on," she said. "Peter saw him picturing the students—all three of them—in stone cells, and then Victor pulled his hand away. But it's in King's College somewhere, Peter's sure."

"Then let's go, right now." He had magic in him already, singing to be used.

"We can't. Kip, look, Victor was our strongest competition and she doesn't like his spell. We can get their money in just another hour, and with Victor here, nothing's going to happen to them. Peter said they were all alive in Victor's mind."

He clenched his jaw. "Yes, you're right. But the moment Victor leaves—"

"We'll leave too."

"No." Kip lowered his voice further. "He knows where they are."

Emily took his meaning in a moment and set herself to object, then changed course. "You're right. He's kidnapped American citizens. As soon as the gala's over, we'll take him back to Peachtree."

"He may be trained to resist spiritual magic readings," Kip said. "But even then—"

"We've had those trainings too. We know how they can be broken," Emily said darkly.

"I don't mean…" Kip stared across the room at Victor. "Ruin his mind. I mean, we could negotiate with the Crown for the students' return."

"Well," Emily said tightly, "that's another option. Now I'm going to go put Peter back to make sure the school remains safe. Stay here and stay calm, for God's sake."

His tail had curled up tightly against his side; he let it relax. That simple action helped his mind relax as well. "All right," he said. "But hurry back."

"I will." She left through the nearest door.

Kip leaned against the wall and watched Victor talk to two other nobles. His mind moved from a pleasant imagining of Victor telling them where to find their students back to the spell Victor claimed to be working on. It should have been clear to Kip the moment Victor brought Farley out on stage. Most of the audience would not have recognized Farley at the Exposition or understood his importance, but Kip and his friends did. This sorcery, if it were true, was a serious threat. If that spell got out and many sorcerers learned it…Calatians could be gone from the world in a generation. Many might choose to give up their magical nature in exchange for a less troubled life as a human.

Before he worked himself into a state over this, he wanted to see Victor— or Gupta—actually perform the sorcery, not just a simulation of it. He still doubted it was possible. Victor had a long history of claiming feats he could not or had not actually performed. That would be another thing they could ask him about after tonight.

Whatever happened, they were close to finding the students. The information sat here in the room with them, and likely they would have an answer before the night was out. He took heart from that.

Emily returned a moment later and took him by the arm. "There's still time before the competition," she said, guiding him back to Mme. Dieuleveult. "Can you tell the story of the Battle of the Road one more time?"

Kip splayed his ears. "As many times as the school needs," he said, and when they reached the noblewoman, he obediently launched into the story, giving it as many thrilling notes as he could.

The telling gathered three or four more nobles, and at the end of it, Mme. Dieuleveult called several more over to hear Kip tell it again. This second time, he started with the arrival of the British ironclad rather than starting the story in the middle of the battle, and the French audience grew merry to hear about the defeat of the great metal ship. "These British think so much of themselves," a Marquis said, "and yet they fall and perish like everyone else."

"They have learned nothing from Babel," another noble replied, and the answering murmur contained some laughter in it.

That merriment carried over into the part where the Road was destroyed and people burned to death in the boiling water, even though Kip tried to paint it somber. The nobles spoke French among themselves, and quickly, so Kip had little idea of what words they were saying, but their tone and laughter between remarks left no doubt of the meaning. In English, they only said, "Such a British thing to conceive one miracle and ruin another! What fools!"

As much as this boded well for their competition against Victor, the idea that people were laughing at such horrific deaths disconcerted him and made him lose his place in the story. He didn't want to emphasize the horror of the people burned to death, so he skipped to the end and then searched for a reason to excuse himself.

"Your husband hasn't come back," he said to Mme. Dieuleveult. "Perhaps someone should go look for him?"

"He'll be fine," she said. "Duchess Trévise, was that not the most marvelous tale?"

The Duchess, a short woman wearing a large wig and an excessive amount of scented powder, agreed that it was, and then another Marquis wanted to ask Kip questions. He bore the conversation under Emily's gaze, knowing they needed to curry favor, but after several questions he excused himself, saying that he would find M. Dieuleveult.

"Please do," Mme. Dieuleveult said. "We should begin the competition momentarily."

"Don't be long," Emily hissed at him.

Kip nodded his head toward Victor. "Keep an eye out," he replied, and hurried to the side door where the Frenchman had exited.

Once the door was closed behind him, he leaned against the stone wall. The noise of the gathering faded to a murmur, though he could still pick out a loud phrase here and there. If he had to tell that story over and over again to secure the future of the Lutris School, he would, although he hadn't realized it would be so much harder when the audience didn't react appropriately, not to mention having to watch Victor, knowing that their students sat in stone jails somewhere.

He felt better just being away from the crowd for a short time. What Emily had said about people with money resonated with him, and he made a silent vow not to be a terrible person if ever he acquired enough wealth to move in these circles. Thus calmed, he placed a paw on the door handle to return and then he remembered that he had said he was going to find M. Dieuleveult. He should at least try to do that.

The noble had been going to check on the food, he'd said. This small room held two sideboards on which food could be prepared before being brought out to the party, but both of them were bare. One of the two doors at the back of the room was open, and as he approached, the sounds of activity and a low murmur of voices came to him. "Monsieur Dieuleveult?" he called out.

The voices fell silent. His fur prickled in the stillness. This didn't feel right. He gathered magic and advanced cautiously on the door. Beyond he could see only an empty room with a large wooden table and part of a stove. Another step, and another, and then he saw the feet of a man lying on the floor, the fancy shoes the same color as the coat he'd seen M. Dieuleveult wearing.

CHAPTER TWELVE:

REVOLUTION

More than ever, Kip wished for Ash or a demon, someone he could send around the corner to see what awaited him in the room. He had to reach M. Dieuleveult, but whatever had struck the noble down could easily be waiting for him as well. So he stared at the far corner of the kitchen, the empty spot behind the wooden table, and translocated himself there.

It was risky because it exposed him to attack from anyone who could see him appear in that space, but he had that moment to spare and more. The group of four ragged men holding cudgels and iron bars remained focused on the doorway Kip had been calling from, standing over a prone form that was definitely M. Dieuleveult. Oddly, though this was a kitchen, there was no trace of the food he'd seen brought in on carts earlier that morning.

He cast a physical magic spell to hold all four of the men; it was difficult but he caught them before any could turn around. When he was sure they were immobilized, he walked around the table and knelt beside M. Dieuleveult under their impotent eyes.

The Frenchman had a mark on his forehead, an ugly red welt and a cut that had bled quite a bit, but he breathed well and appeared to be only unconscious, not in any serious danger. Kip straightened and met the eyes of the four men. "Now," he said, "does one of you want to tell me what this is about?" He unbound, carefully, the head of one of them and called on his limited French. "*Qu'est-ce que passe ici?*"

Before he'd even finished the sentence, the man cried out, "*Le sorcier! Tirez! Tirez!*"

"*Tirez!*" The call echoed outside the kitchen.

"What?" Kip approached the man. "What did you say?"

"*Vive la France!*" the man cried, and then spit at Kip.

The fox dodged the projectile and was about to respond when a familiar smell tickled his nose. Behind the man lay an empty sack that smelled faintly of pitch.

Pitch implied fire. Kip sent his awareness out into the castle and yes, there were fires, but the mansion was full of candles and fireplaces. New ones sprang up, and he reached out to pull them back when he felt them starting, but he could only reach out to one at a time and they were spreading fast. And while he could quench fires from anywhere, he couldn't see what other things the attackers might be doing in the castle. He and Emily had to warn everyone and get everyone to safety.

But he couldn't leave M. Dieuleveult lying here, could he? He decided in an instant: the man was safe enough with the attackers immobilized. He'd come back for him.

He ran through the staging room and burst back into the party, seeking out Emily and Mme. Dieuleveult, who fortunately stood together in a small crowd of people. Kip pushed his way through nobles. "There's an attack," he gasped out. "Everyone's in danger. M. Dieuleveult is hurt."

"What?" Mme. Dieuleveult looked bewildered.

Emily was more used to acting in a crisis. "Where?" she asked tightly.

"Back in the kitchen," Kip said. "But there are more of them. I don't know how many or where. There's fires starting all through the castle."

"We need to get out of here." Emily turned to Mme. Dieuleveult. "Come with me."

"I will not leave," she said. "We are in the middle of a gala."

"They've attacked your husband." Kip gestured toward the kitchen. "Emily, where can we take him?"

Emily brushed an invisible strand of hair back from her face. "Nowhere in Paris. Amsterdam?"

"What about our school? We know it well and know it's safe."

"Now, listen," Mme. Dieuleveult said. "You will not take my husband anywhere."

"Come and see for yourself, but he needs—" Kip stopped. They didn't have a healer at the Lutris School. "He needs to be somewhere safe."

He strode for the kitchen without waiting for permission. Behind him, Mme. Dieuleveult made an exasperated noise and then spoke loudly in French to the room, saying something about the competition beginning soon. Then she and Emily followed Kip into the small room and on to the kitchen.

At first, Mme. Dieuleveult saw only the immobilized attackers. "Who are these ruffians and what has been done to them?" she asked.

The one whose mouth Kip had freed said something in French, and the lady replied, "*Ne dit pas des bêtises*," which Kip understood to mean "don't say stupid things." She was about to say more, but then she took a step further and shrieked, "Bertrand!"

She ran to her husband's side and called his name again. Kip hurried over. "He's alive," he said.

"We must get him to our bedroom. We have cloths there, and he'll be more comfortable. We can send for the doctor."

"Can't you smell the smoke?" The odor stung Kip's nostrils. "It's not safe here."

"Can't you keep us safe? I thought you were a fire sorcerer," she snapped.

"I can stop fires, but there are attackers all over the castle," Kip retorted.

Emily stepped forward. "We can put out the fires, perhaps even stop this attack completely. But the riots are going on all over Paris. It's not going to be safe anywhere for nobles, maybe not for a long time."

In the ensuing silence, they heard shouts from the gala; the smell of smoke must have reached them. Mme. Dieuleveult half-stood, staring off in that direction, then knelt next to her husband again. "Bertrand," she said softly.

"I can take him to our school in America," Kip said. The smoke drifted into the room, visible now. He could sense the warmth and strength of the fires around him. "You and Emily go back to the gala and get everyone out."

"I can bring three people at a time back to America," Emily said. "It will be safer there than anywhere in France, I think."

"What do you know of France?" Mme. Dieuleveult shot back, but her eyes were wide and afraid.

"I have been to the Academie today," Emily replied calmly. "Almost all the sorcerers have fled Paris. Only a few remain to guard the King himself."

Beneath her makeup, the noble lady paled. "I—then—There are a few things I want to fetch."

"We haven't time—"

She cut off Emily's protest, standing. "I have a good deal of jewelry. If you wish to receive any payment from me, we will go to my room."

"I don't care about payment," Emily said. "I want to save your life."

"You can take me as easily from upstairs as downstairs, *non*? Then we will go upstairs. Come." She turned to Kip. "Take my husband."

Kip nodded and knelt, resting a paw on the unconscious man's chest.

Behind him, the attacker spat something in French, to which Mme. Dieuleveult responded coldly. They went back and forth twice more before he began to shout curses at her.

"They do not speak English," she said to Kip in a tone just as cold. "I told him they will be left here imprisoned to burn."

"I won't do that." Kip looked up at her.

She nodded back to him. "I know you will not." And then she swept her dress around her and gestured for Emily to follow her. "Come."

When they'd gone, Kip locked the door out to the salon with a spell so the attackers couldn't follow when he unbound them. To help with the damage as much as he could, he reached out to the largest fires he could feel and drew their fierce hunger into himself, extinguishing them. Then he visualized Emily's office and pulled himself and M. Dieuleveult there.

He put a paw over his eyes to shield them from the bright afternoon light streaming through the windows. M. Dieuleveult lay before him on the carpet, still unconscious. Kip sat back on his heels. If this were the only casualty of the attack, they would be extremely lucky. He should go back and put out the rest of the fires.

The image of the kitchen swam back into his mind and he released the four men he'd bound as his wartime instincts ran through the situation to find the best place for his talents to help. Emily would be helping get the nobles out of the Salon and probably could handle that on her own; if he put out fires then the revolutionaries would keep setting them, or would attack in other ways.

What they really needed was a healer to treat M. Dieuleveult and any other injuries. De Koning might be available in Amsterdam, but Kip had been to Chakrabarti's hotel and could go back there directly. Perhaps the sorcerer had stayed in Amsterdam to visit the city? He'd said something of the sort to Kip, or maybe Kip was only imagining that. At any rate, it was easy to send himself to the hotel lobby.

The clerk at the desk almost jumped when Kip appeared. "Yes?" he said crossly.

"Is a sorcerer named Chakrabarti still staying here?" Kip asked. "I'm sorry for the appearance. It's an emergency."

"Can't your master contact him directly?" The clerk pointed toward the stairs. "The Indian sorcerers are still here. Some of them, at least. I don't know whether yours is one of them."

"I'll go look, then. Thank you." There wasn't time to correct the clerk about Kip's "master," nor to ask him to look in the record. He remembered Chakrabarti's room, so he hurried up the stairs.

To his immense relief, the sorcerer answered the door himself. "Master Penfold?"

"There's an emergency," Kip said. "Can you come with me?"

The man took only a moment before saying, "Yes, of course."

He reached out and took Kip's proffered paw, and Kip transported them back to Emily's office.

Emily and Mme. Dieuleveult stood by Emily's desk, the latter holding a large valise which she released to the ground. "You left my husband alone!" she cried.

"He was safe here," Kip said, "and I went to get a healer for him. This is Master Chakrabarti. Master, this is Mme. Dieuleveult and that is her husband, who was struck on the head."

"We are no longer in Europe," Chakrabarti observed, kneeling next to the unconscious man.

"We are in America, in East Georgia at the Lutris School," Kip said, and then, to Emily, "What happened to the other guests?"

"We had to retrieve the valuables first," she replied, keeping most of the disgust out of her tone. "Some of the other sorcerers rescued guests, others just left. I'm going back to see if anyone else needs help."

Without waiting for anyone to give permission or contradict her, she vanished. "Really," Mme. Dieuleveult said. "What am I to do now?"

"I suppose we should find you a place to stay." Kip ran through possibilities in his mind. "My parents have an extra room in their house. Or you could stay in my bedroom until arrangements are made. My wife and I will be away for a few days." The missing students would not be found soon nor easily, he suspected, now that they'd lost their chance with Victor.

"I certainly do not imagine I will be here longer than a day." Mme Dieuleveult looked out the window, shielding her eyes. "I have family in Rheims and they will have a place for us to stay while this unpleasantness passes."

"I can heal this man," Chakrabarti said, "but he will remain asleep. If you wish, you may wake him afterwards."

"Let him sleep." Mme. Dieuleveult's voice softened. "The less he must experience of this, the better."

As Chakrabarti worked, the Frenchwoman asked Kip, "How did you chance to meet this sorcerer?"

So Kip told her of their meeting at the Exposition, and that Chakrabarti was one of the sorcerers he was hoping to bring to the school with her money. "I'm certain he will be a great teacher."

"He's a competent healer," she said. "Bertrand has no more mark on his head."

"No." Chakrabarti straightened and joined them. "The blow was not strong. His injury was not severe."

"I'm very glad to hear that." Mme Dieueleveult returned to looking cross. "What an inconvenience this is. Could they not have waited one more night? We would have given such a lovely gala."

"What has happened?" Chakrabarti asked, so Kip and Mme. Dieuleveult took it in turns to tell him, until they were interrupted by Emily returning with two more nobles, a Marquis and Marquise.

"There are two more couples." Emily patted the nobles, who looked terrified. "I'll be back shortly. Kip, I think Bryce should be aware that we will have some French nobles with us for a period of time."

"I'll see to it," he said.

She took him aside. "I looked for Victor," she said in a low voice. "He was gone, of course, at the first sign of trouble. Patris at least stayed around to help get some people to safety."

Mme. Dieuleveult came over to them, color rising in her cheeks. "It will not be 'a period of time.' A day at most, until we can meet with my cousins. I cannot speak for everyone else."

"Fine," Emily said. "Please excuse me." And with that, she disappeared.

Mme. Dieuleveult stared for a moment at Kip and then turned back to the other French nobles. "Marie, Jean, you have family around Lyon, do you not?"

The Marquis and Marquise slipped into French, and the three of them chattered away. "I hate to ask this," Kip said to Chakrabarti in a low voice, "but can you remain here for a few moments until I return? I have to get our mayor and secure accommodations for these people."

"Of course." Chakrabarti smiled. "I am pleased to be helpful in whatever way I can."

"Thank you so very much."

"Please." The other sorcerer bowed his head. "This adventure may not measure up to some of your tales, but it is quite thrilling for me. To be in the story of a revolution!"

Mme. Dieuleveult heard this and turned. "This is not a revolution," she stated. "It is an uprising, and it will be put down in due course. We have lived through others."

Kip did not have a great experience of uprisings, so he did not feel qualified to say whether this one was different. They might not know for days or even weeks; if the King survived and held his power, then Mme. Dieuleveult might be correct. But from what Emily had said, it sounded like the French sorcerers did not believe this was just another uprising.

Regardless, his immediate duty was to accommodate their visitors (he did not want to think of them as refugees yet). So he translocated to the town square and set out to find Bryce Morgan.

The hedgehog spent most days in his office, and Kip found him there in discussion with a pair of squirrels in some kind of dispute. "It's an emergency," Kip said. "I'm so sorry to interrupt."

One of the squirrels looked put out by the interruption, but they agreed to return later in the afternoon. Kip explained the situation to Bryce, and the hedgehog snorted. "Bringing refugees back here again? I thought you'd broken that habit, Penfold. All right, let me see what room we have here."

"It's only a few of them." Kip smiled as Bryce walked to the wall to consult the map of the town. "French nobles, needing to stay here while the government deals with an…uprising."

"Only an uprising?" Bryce turned around. "You made it sound like a revolution."

"I think it is. But I don't know; I only saw the attack on the estate we were in and the riots in Paris."

"Riots are not revolution. When we did it, we planned out our actions."

"We also lay across an ocean from the King," Kip pointed out. "We had the luxury of time. These people look up at the palace every day. At least, some of them do. I don't know where the French king lives, to be honest."

The hedgehog went back to the map. "I hope for their sake it is just an uprising. Let's see here."

He pointed out four families who might have room, and Kip offered that some of the rooms in the school might also be available. Between them, he felt they had enough space set aside by the time he returned to Emily's office.

She sat behind her desk with her head on her arms as the half-dozen people in the room (not counting M. Dieuleveult) chattered rapidly back and forth in French. Chakrabarti had retreated to the window behind Emily, but perked up and came forward when Kip reappeared.

Mme. Dieuleveult also made for Kip as soon as he returned, and she arrived first. "I have decided," she said, "that we will accept your generous offer to share your quarters with us. May we go there immediately? My husband needs rest."

"Of course," Kip said, and raised his voice. "For everyone else, there are rooms here at the school. If they are not to your liking, there will be families in town with space. Our mayor is going around to ask them to provide quarters for any of you who wish them."

A few of the people stared blankly at him until Mme. Dieuleveult spoke in French. "I have said your words to them," she told Kip, and then, as they crowded around, said, "They have questions."

Most of the questions were easily answered (everyone wanted to know when they could go home, and Kip had to explain that he and Emily could only go to places they'd already been), but one particularly flushed and angry man kept demanding, according to Mme. Dieuleveult, "why the Americans have ruined our country."

Like the sorcerer, this noble claimed that since the American Revolution, the riots and "uprisings" had grown in scope and frequency, with this one being the last straw. "Without the Americans," the Frenchman said through Mme. Dieuleveult, "they would not be so bold as to steal our food and burn our homes."

Her voice faltered as she relayed this last part, and without waiting for Kip's response, she strode to Emily's desk and rapped on it. "Miss Carswell," she said. "Miss Carswell!"

Emily raised her head and rubbed at her forehead. To Kip, she looked pale. "Yes?"

"We must go back. There are paintings that must be saved."

Two of the others who spoke English hurried up behind her, chorusing that they, too, needed to save heirlooms and jewelry from their estates. Emily put her hands up to quiet them. "Your house is burning," she told Mme. Dieuleveult. "It would be dangerous to go back."

"Then bring your fire sorcerer." The lady pointed at Kip. "Miss Carswell, I pledge my support to your school, but we must save as much as possible."

"I will support your school!" the man next to her cried.

Emily shook her head. "I don't know where you live," she said. "Unless it's in Paris somewhere, it would take hours to get there. And Madame…it's not just the fire. There are revolutionaries—uprisers—all over."

"They'll have fled the fire." The woman leaned closer. "Please."

Emily shook her head and was about to speak when a voice from the floor floated up to them. "Fire?"

M. Dieuleveult had sat up and was rubbing his head. "Our house? On fire?"

His wife hurried to kneel by his side. "Yes, but it's all right. The sorcerers here are going to take us back to reclaim our valuables."

M. Dieuleveult's eyes widened and he sought out Kip. "Master Penfold. Please, you must take me back."

His relics. If anything was priceless, they were. Kip hesitated, and into his silence, Emily said, "It's simply too dangerous."

"I can take him." Kip turned to Emily. "Just me, and only him. We can retrieve a few things, and if the situation isn't too bad, we can fetch more."

She started to object; he could see that. But she reconsidered and gave him a nod. "Use your judgment," she said.

"Wait." Mme. Dieuleveult straightened. "Take us both."

"I can only take one. And it has to be me so I can deal with the fire," Kip said. "And I have to take your husband because he knows where—certain valuables are."

"What, his old bones? Those are—" She broke off, aware of her husband's gaze. "We have many valuables. Why should they be first?"

Kip leaned in close to her. "I have examined them," he whispered, "and at least one of them may be a truly unique relic."

She did not appear visibly moved by this, but extended a hand to help her husband to his feet. "Very well, Bertrand," she said. "But when you've done your errand, do retrieve the Greuze if nothing else."

"Of course, my dear." He stood, a little shakily. "Master Penfold, I am at your disposal."

The first place to go was the sacristy in the little stone church. Kip warned M. Dieuleveult before they left, "I am going to attempt to take us to the front of the church, near the altar. If I see that we are in a dangerous situation, I'm going to bring us back immediately."

"Understood." Despite Chakrabarti's healing, the nobleman seemed a little unsteady still, but he had just woken up, after all.

Kip grasped the man's shoulder, visualized the church and the altar, and sent the two of them there.

They appeared in front of the altar looking out over the main body of the church, where three men in ragged clothes worked to carry a wooden pew out the door. The one facing Kip dropped his end of pew and shouted, pointing their way.

Kip visualized Emily's office, but before he could cast the spell, M. Dieuleveult slipped out from under his paw and ran to the sacristy door. Cursing, Kip followed.

Inside the room, a man jumped to his feet and brandished a small knife at them. Kip pushed the door closed behind him as he grabbed the man with a spell and lifted him off the ground. The man continued to shout in French, arms and legs flailing helplessly at the air as he sought for any kind of purchase.

Outside, more shouts answered, so Kip flew the man across the room and pinned him against the door. "Please hurry," he entreated M. Dieuleveult, who knelt next to a stone in the wall and was pulling at it.

"I don't think they have discovered them," the man replied, pulling the stone away, and indeed, when he reached in, he pulled out the wooden box, cradling it reverently. He said something in French with a tone of "thanks be to God" and stood. "We may return now."

"Your wife asked you to look for one of your paintings," Kip said. "Should we not do that?"

"And risk these items without price?" M. Dieuleveult shook his head. "No, we should leave."

The man against the door, jarred by the pounding and pushing against it from outside, now stared at Kip and shouted. Kip didn't catch any of the words except for "*Americain!*" and M. Dieuleveult seemed unconcerned. "I'll take us outside," he said, "and we can see the state of the house."

"No," the Frenchman argued, but Kip had already grasped his shoulder and translocated them outside—not to the ground, but to a point fifty feet above it. M. Dieuleveult shrieked and clutched at Kip's arm as they fell.

"I've got you," Kip said, releasing the man in the church as he cast another spell to hold both of them in the air. "And the relics too. I caught them in case you dropped them."

"I would never!" M. Dieuleveult's eyes were wide enough to show a good deal of white. "What are you playing at?"

"We're safe up here unless they have guns, and we can get a better view of the house." That view, here where they could see over the stone walls, was still obscured by a great cloud of smoke. As they watched, a crash came from inside the house and a great billow of black smoke joined the others.

M. Dieuleveult's complaints died away as he watched the house burn. "Saint Médard," he murmured, bowing his head, and then a few words in French. Kip caught "rain" and "fire," and that was enough to puzzle out what M. Dieuleveult was praying for from the saint who supposedly controlled the weather.

When he'd finished, his head remained bowed. Kip touched him gently on the arm. "Your wife spoke of a particular painting. Where is it?"

"The…The Greuze." M. Dieuleveult's eyes searched the castle and he pointed to a place from which smoke issued thickly. "You can…put out the fire?" he asked in a husky whisper.

"Yes," Kip said, "but not repair what has already been burned."

"Nothing is left," the man said, and turned away. "Take us back."

Kip set the image of Emily's office in his mind, and then a patch of light caught the corner of his eye. He turned his head, already casting the spell, and saw that the moonlight was reflecting off a large, thick bank of thunderclouds. Had they been there before M. Dieuleveult's prayer? He didn't know, and a second later they were replaced by the walls and carpet of Emily's office.

"We could not save the Greuze," was all M. Dieuleveult said to his wife when they returned. She asked more questions about the state of the house and got rather sharp when she saw that he'd saved his relics, but none of it penetrated M. Dieuleveult's stolid demeanor. He asked Emily if he could keep the relics somewhere safe, and she told him that for the time being they would be safest in her office, so he placed them in her desk before following his wife and Kip out the door.

At his house, Kip introduced them to Abel, who took the unexpected guests in stride. "Keep your door closed," he said, "and I'll do my best to keep the children quiet when they get home from school."

When the Dieuleveults had gone upstairs to Kip and Alice's room, Abel pulled Kip into their sitting-room and insisted on hearing the story. Kip, grateful for a respite, gave him a short summary of the Exposition, Victor's display, and the revolution. "I think it's more than an uprising," he said to the other fox. "They burned the estate. The sorcerers have fled. I don't know how long the king can hold out."

"And they had some planning." Abel sighed and put an arm around Kip. "I'm glad you're out of there. I know you can account for yourself, but I much prefer that you don't have to."

"I do too." Kip leaned against the other fox. "I wish I could stay to see Arabella and Aran, but I have to get back. And I have to get to London to see what Malcolm and Alice have been doing."

He sent his mind to Ash, finding her in a house by herself with moonlight coming through the window. "I'll find them later," he said in response to Abel's questioning look. "But I'm glad I got some time with you."

"I am too. I wish it could be more. Tell me if there's anything I can do."

Kip looked at the ceiling. "Be nice to them. They're good people, and they've just lost their home."

"I will." Abel clasped his paw and pulled him close. "Be careful."

Kip kissed him on the muzzle. "I'll be back before you know it, with Alice and Malcolm and all the students."

He walked back rather than translocate, because the afternoon air was pleasant and it was nice not to be in a hurry for once. As he walked past the gates, still leaning against the stone posts, he saw Emily waiting outside the front doors and went to meet her.

She waited as he approached, looking over the gardens that were still only little shoots that barely had their leaves. "You're going to say that we need to go to London," she said. "I won't argue. But I think I will stay here. For one thing, the Dieuleveults know me best, and the others know me at least a little."

"And you're human."

"And I'm human." She sighed. "I tried to translocate to Victor, but either I don't know him well enough or he's warded, or possibly both. It has been some years. Perhaps you'll be able to find him now that we know he's in the College."

"I'll do my best."

"And I'll go back to Paris in a day or two and perhaps see if things have calmed down or gotten worse."

"It's all right." He'd been working himself up to argue that he should go to London, and to find that he didn't have to was an immense relief. "Abel wants to help here too."

"I'll go see him now." Emily rested a hand on Kip's shoulder. "Thank you, Kip, for all your help. I don't know what's going to happen to the school, but we did the right thing, I think."

"I think so too." He reached out to hug her. "I wish we'd gotten Victor, though. If only those revolutionaries had waited one more night."

"I suspect they were aiming for the night of the gala." She hugged back.

"One question before I go," Kip said, reminded by thinking of Victor and the gala. "When Master Gupta did his illusion, what did you see?"

Emily shook her head, her mouth in a twisted smile. "Most likely Master Gupta's fanciful imagining of what you would look like as a human. Sharp-nosed, red-haired, but of a darker complexion, not quite his but certainly not as light as mine or Malcolm's. It wasn't flattering, but I only saw it for a moment, and it's of no consequence anyway."

"All right." He smiled. "I was only curious."

She touched the fur of his cheek. "It was by no means an improvement on your current form, which I'm very fond of. Now go. Give my love to Alice and Malcolm. Find those students and come home soon. And take Sleek." The raven hopped from her shoulder to Kip's. "That way you can at least tell me what's going on."

The weight of Sleek on his shoulder reminded Kip how much he missed having Ash around, and by extension how empty the town of Peachtree felt without Malcolm and Alice and the three students. "I'll report in every day," he promised. "And even if they don't appreciate it, you did a marvelous job getting those people to safety, and you've led us all through this better than anyone else could."

"Thank you." She smiled and looked around the quiet, peaceful school in the late afternoon light, the sky beginning to tinge with orange and the scent of the gardens giving everything a tranquil air. "I'd hoped we were done with revolution and could get on with the business of living," she said.

"I don't know that we'll ever be done with revolution. Not until we reach our reward." His eyes traveled up.

Emily gave a short laugh. "At this point I don't know what our reward will be. Depending on whom you listen to, we're as likely to wind up down below as up above. I prefer to worry about making this world better."

"Doesn't that mean we're always waiting for a revolution?"

"Change doesn't have to come in big, violent upheavals," she said.

Kip splayed his ears. "I'd like to believe that, but...it always seems to, doesn't it?"

CHAPTER THIRTEEN: REFUGEES

The Isle of Dogs was quiet, the air cool and almost as humid as in Peachtree, though with the smell of rot from the Thames instead of flowers. Kip appeared in the house where Ash was perched and reached out to her with his mind to wake her. She croaked and tried to fly to her customary shoulder, only to find Sleek there. This prompted a lot of fluttering and more croaks that Kip tried in vain to quiet, after which Sleek flew to a perch and Ash took her place.

One of the shapes lying on the floor stirred and sat up. Kip's eyes had adjusted enough to recognize the ears of a fox, and Alice's scent came to him a moment later. "Kip?" she whispered.

"Yes."

She got all the way up and hurried to him, throwing her arms around him and disturbing Ash again, though this time the raven bore the disruption quietly. "What happened? Did you get the money?"

The outline of the curtain shimmered with moonlight. "It's complicated," he whispered, moving in that direction. "Let's go outside."

They left the house to stand outside, remaining against the wall of the house so as to stay out of the way. Calatians walked purposefully up and down the narrow street but did so without much talk or noise. Kip leaned back against the stone wall and Alice followed. "We didn't get the money," he said, still whispering. "I don't know if there is money anymore."

"What?" Her ears went back.

Before he could explain, the curtain rustled and another shape joined them. "Having secrets from the rest of us, are you?" Malcolm said with a smile. "Loud as rain on a tin roof, you two."

Kip turned to hug his friend. "We didn't want to wake anyone."

Malcolm patted Kip's back. "Sure, I've slept enough that I can miss an hour to hear from you. How was Paris?"

"Burning," Kip said, and then explained the riots to them, the chaotic fleeing of the estate, and his return and the burning house.

"Is all of France rioting?"

"I don't know, but all of Paris seems to be." Kip straightened. "But we have some news. We used some sorcery to get Victor to admit that he took Jorey, Charity, and Richard. He's got them in a cell somewhere."

Both Malcolm and Alice made noises of outrage, and Malcolm said, "Ay, well, no surprise there, but I suppose we hadn't known it for certain until now, had we? Did you get anything more out of him?"

"We got distracted getting people out of the burning castle." Kip clenched his fists. "We should've just taken him right then."

"You couldn't have known." Alice laid a paw on his arm.

"Would be nice to have him to tell us where to look, for sure," Malcolm said. "But there's a reason Alice and I came here and not to Madrid or Moscow. We knew it was him."

"We knew but we didn't have proof." Kip sighed. "Now we do and I don't know if I feel better or worse about it. How have things been going here? I know it's only been a couple days, though it seems longer to me."

"The problem is that we can't send people into the College," Alice said. "We can only ask calyxes to spy for us when they're called, and only one was called yesterday."

"You'll be pleased to know that our old friend Grinda is running the show here." Malcolm kept his voice low. "At least, the show behind the scenes. Blaeda's still the mayor, but with Abel gone, the rebellious ones have aligned behind her. And she still doesn't like you much, as she made certain to remind poor Alice here."

"She doesn't like me much either," Alice said, "but at least she was civil to me and agreed that the next time someone comes for one of the foxes, I can take their place."

"What?" Kip spoke louder than he'd intended. "No."

"Kip—"

"It's too dangerous."

Alice and Malcolm shared a look that told him they'd discussed this and had known he'd react this way. Malcolm stepped closer to Kip. "The way Grinda is," he said in a low tone, "we had to talk her into it for an hour, and only won out because of the help of one of her associates, a beaver. She said

put him in the empty room next to Master Argent. When they're all awake, I'll introduce them."

"That's good." Kip's ears perked, surprised. "Does he know we might not be able to pay him?"

"He knows. He says he believes his school will provide at least money for his food if we can promise to help them with flooding. Every rainy season—I'm not sure when that is—some of their villages have problems with water and mud and they think that having a few extra sorcerers could save many lives. I said yes, because we really do need a healer, and Alice is good with mud and water."

"Of course," Alice said immediately, and Malcolm and Kip echoed her.

After that, it was back to watching the windows of the College through Ash and waiting for the call for a calyx. An hour passed, then another, and finally Kip said, "If we don't hear something today, I'm going to go to the College tonight and look around myself."

"Kip, no," Alice said.

"I'd go right now if the College weren't so crowded during the day. We can't wait any longer. Every day gives Victor more chances to do something to the students. He's been occupied in Paris, and today is his first day back. I don't want him to have time to—"

Alice put a paw on his. "I know," she said. "But you can't just go snooping around the College. You'll get caught."

"What if Malcolm goes along to keep me warded?"

She folded her arms. "Then I'm going too. If he's focusing on the wards, and you're doing magical snooping, someone has to keep an eye out in the physical world for you."

"Ash and Corvi can do that."

Alice glared at him. "I'm not sitting here alone while you two go off into danger. All right, I shouldn't go by myself, but neither should you, and neither should any of us. We should all work together whenever we can."

Kip gave Corvi a beseeching look, and Malcolm shook his head. "Nah, mate. I'd make the same argument to Emily and I'd get overruled just the same. It's dangerous, aye, but she's more than earned her place with us. An' I venture to say that if she were the sort to meekly sit home while you went out into danger, your marriage would be a sight less successful."

Alice looked very pleased at this, and Kip had to smile as well. "All right," he said. "Yes. It'll be the three of us."

"Good." Alice's ears went up. "Now if you're done having Ash look around, why don't you come see this wall that Malcolm and I have been helping with? We started doing it because we didn't want to just sit around doing nothing."

She led them through narrow streets and past mice, hedgehogs, foxes, and other Calatians to the western shore of the Isle, and then about fifty feet along it to a place where the old stones that marked the edge of the Isle fell away. "Here," Alice said, sitting on the edge of the breach. "The wall here fell down last year, Varwen told me."

"Varwen?"

An old otter in a long threadbare tunic walked toward them from one of the riverside houses. "Him," Alice pointed. "Hello, Varwen."

"Hallo, young miss." The otter smiled. "And Master sorcerer, and this'll be your husband the other Master sorcerer, I suppose, Master Penfold."

"That I am." Kip smiled. "It's a pleasure to meet you."

"Many on our Isle adore you, and a few despise you." The otter drew closer, so that Kip could make out the grey on his muzzle and the cloudiness in his eyes. "And me, I've not met you yet, so I'm reserving my judgment."

"I'll be on my best behavior," Kip promised.

Alice pointed to the breach. "So the wall fell down and many of the stones are in the river now. I've been trying to feel around down there and find rocks..." Lined up neatly in front of the breach rested a pile of stones. "But I only found a couple that I could put in place and I'm not sure how to secure them. I figure just getting the stones up is helpful, and if we can put them in place that'll be even better."

"It's a good idea. Did you go underwater to look?"

"No; I tried to call a water elemental but I couldn't make it work." She splayed her ears. "Still. But I found out I could 'feel around' under the water, and I can tell when something is about the right weight to be a stone from the wall, and then most of the time it is. Once it was a rusted metal thing and once it was a dead dog." She shuddered. "But I found a lot of the stones, and if we find more we could maybe repair the wall, or at least help them to do it."

"The river don't come up t'here," Varwen said, looking down over the breach, "but without t'wall, it eats away at the Isle on this side." His paw swept out. "Current come down from London proper."

"We can help get it fixed," Kip said. "Can you get mortar?"

"Aye. Least, I know someone who can." The otter sat down on the wall beside Alice. "Will it be a bother if I watch?"

"Not at all." Alice gestured to Kip. "Want to try?"

He took a seat on the other side of her from the otter. At least from here he could see the College and keep Ash occupied flying around it looking for Victor. "I'll be happy to."

For a short time they explored the river bottom looking for stones to lift up. Kip hadn't found any to Alice's two when Sleek croaked loudly and then said in Emily's voice, "Malcolm! Kip! Alice!"

Kip let go of his spell and stood. Malcolm, closer, also stood and said, "We're here," his face creased with worry.

"Charity came back."

Alice jumped to her feet. "What?"

"She came back." The raven clacked its beak. "She's here."

Malcolm held out his arm for Corvi, and Kip took Alice's paw as Ash came to his shoulder. "We'll be there in a moment."

"Where?" Kip asked.

"I'm taking her to her room," Sleek said, flying up to Alice's shoulder.

A moment later the three of them stood in the Welcome Hall of the Lutris School, a warm, cheery space with windows that opened onto the flower gardens and a large fireplace that held only a lone phosphorus elemental. The lizard perked up when they arrived and chirped a greeting to Kip, which he returned, apologizing for the hurry as he followed Malcolm and Alice to the student quarters.

They met Emily at the door of Charity's room, and floating next to her in the air was indeed Charity herself. She looked almost as she had when they'd last seen her at the Exposition, her tunic a little less white, her face streaked with dirt, and under her arm she carried a small wicker box that she kept her eyes downcast to. But when she heard them approach, she looked up and held her arms out to Alice.

Alice ran over to her, and Charity threw her other arm around the fox and hugged her, keeping the wicker box clutched tightly to her.

"Shh, shh," Alice said. "I've got you. You're safe now."

Charity burst into tears. "We're not safe," she sobbed. "We're none of us safe."

Kip reached out to take the wicker box from her. "I can get this," he said.

She clutched it tighter, then registered that it was Kip reaching for it and let it go, but stared after it. "Don't let him out of your sight," she whispered.

The box felt warm and had some weight to it. Kip hefted it, and in that moment whatever was in it moved around, shifting the weight of the box and making Kip put both paws on it. The lid pressed up against his grip, and a high-pitched chattering sounded from inside it.

"What is it?" Emily asked, beckoning them all into the room.

Charity gulped and pressed her face into Alice's shoulder as Alice carried her forward. Her words came so muffled that Kip's ears didn't pick them up, but Alice's did, and lay flat against her head.

"What?" Kip asked. "I didn't hear."

Alice set Charity on her bed and Emily released the spell so that the girl could sit properly. They waited for her to repeat what she'd said, but she shook her head and looked at Alice.

The vixen turned to the others, her eyes on the wicker box. "She says that's Jorey in there."

CHAPTER FOURTEEN:

LESS THAN HUMAN

Malcolm and Emily stared at the box as well. Kip cracked the lid and peered inside. Certainly the animal that was in there was a red squirrel, but there was nothing to identify it specifically as Jorey. What had he been looking for? A tiny sorcerer's robe?

"It's Jorey."

He looked up to see Charity staring at him. "I saw—" Her voice broke. "I saw him cast the spell."

"Who?" Alice sat on the bed and put an arm around the girl.

"Master Adamson."

"He's not a master," Kip said sharply. "You mean he directed someone else."

Charity shook her head. "Well—I suppose in a way. There was—I think—a demon there. He told it what to do and it did it? But he spoke the spell." She shook her head. "I didn't hear it. He didn't let me hear. But his lips moved." She shuddered. "He made me watch."

"You don't have to talk about it yet," Emily said.

"No, I should." Charity took a breath. "I want to tell you."

Emily sat on the student's other side, and Kip and Malcolm sat cross-legged on the floor, Kip still holding the wicker box. Charity looked around at all of them and took a breath. "It feels a little bit like a dream now that I'm back here," she said. "This is real. You're all real."

But then her eyes fell on the box and tears welled up in them again. "But...that's real too." She looked up at Emily. "I'm sorry. If I'd been quicker..."

Emily took Charity's hand in her own. "Just tell us what happened."

Charity nodded. "We left the Exposition in that chaos, but we weren't worried. The crowd was excited but not violent and we thought we'd just get back to the hotel. Besides, we knew that the ravens were watching us. And—and we thought we didn't need to be watched. We had made our own way up until then.

"He came up behind us, and we didn't touch him—like you taught us." She looked at Malcolm. "But he said he had been talking to Headmistress Carswell and Mrs. Penfold about giving the school some money, and... then he grabbed all of us and translocated us to a prison. And right away another sorcerer—the one who was on stage with him, I think, the Indian one, touched us all and took our magic away."

"Master Gupta," Kip said tightly. "The spiritual sorcerer Victor carries around to do his sorcery for him."

"He can do sorcery," Charity insisted.

"Yes, tell us about that." Emily laced her fingers together.

Charity looked down at the floor. "I don't know how many days we've been gone. It feels like a week."

"You were taken about four days ago," Emily said gently.

"The first couple days we didn't see Adamson. There was only a rat-Calatian of some sort."

"A marmot?" Kip asked.

"Maybe. Jorey tried to ask him questions but he didn't talk at all." She didn't ask, but went on. "They fed us a little bit. Scraps. After a bit—a day?—they put us into separate cells, Richard next to me and Jorey across from both of us. We talked whenever we thought we were alone, tried to come up with ways we could escape, but there were no windows and no fresh air at all. Our magic had been taken away, and we didn't know what else to do. Richard tried to scrape at the stones in his cell, but they were all very solid. We figured that eventually they would have to let us out of the cells and we agreed we would all be ready for that moment."

She took in a breath. "And, uh, that's when Master—when Adamson came in. He talked to us a lot. He said that we were going to see some sorcery that was more important than anything we would learn at your school, that what he was doing would change the world. He talked about you a lot, Master Penfold. He said there was an imbalance but he was going to correct it, and that there were many different kinds of power."

"He's said that before," Kip muttered.

"I don't remember all the things he talked about. I was waiting to see if he'd let us out. I think we all were. But then he came back one time and this time the rat-Calatian, or the marmot, and that other sorcerer was with him, the one who approached us, not the Indian one. And he cast some kind of spell so Richard and I couldn't hear anything that was happening, then he—or someone, maybe it was the marmot—summoned a demon, a kind of old man made of fire. I wasn't scared of it, and neither was Jorey. He was very brave. And then Adamson's lips moved, and the demon nodded and stared at Jorey, and then…and then…Jorey just *shrank*."

The room was silent. Charity choked back a sob, and Alice put an arm over her shoulders. "He…he disappeared into his clothes, and then the marmot came forward with that box and he cast a spell that lifted Jorey and dropped him into it."

It was a trick, an illusion. It had to be. That spiritual sorcerer had to be around somewhere where they couldn't see him, hiding and casting the illusion so that the real Jorey couldn't be heard. To remove the magic from a Calatian…that shouldn't be possible. Kip stared at Alice and saw the same thoughts in her eyes. What if this spell were real? What if they could be reduced to the animals from which they'd come hundreds of years ago?

"And then the silence spell lifted and Adamson held out his hands and they were glowing."

This didn't prove anything. Adamson knew what magic looked like and what it would look like to a couple of students.

Emily leaned forward. "Did he cast a spell?"

"I…I think so." Charity's eyes skipped from Emily to Malcolm to Kip and Alice. "He said, 'Not as much as I'd hoped,' and then lifted himself off the ground. He floated away without saying anything else to us."

Jorey was safe. They'd translocated him somewhere and brought in a squirrel.

"Richard and I talked about what we'd seen. It was like what he did on the stage, but worse. And Jorey—the squirrel—kept scratching around in the box, and every time he did I thought, that's my friend, and we have to find a way to put him right."

Nobody said anything, but Emily put a hand on Charity's knee. Charity turned to her. "There's a way to do that, right?"

"If there is, we'll find it," Kip said, trying not to think about Malcolm's eyeless face. "Can you get back to the prison?"

The girl's eyes widened in horror, and Alice held her more tightly. "Not this minute," Emily said, "but do you know it well enough to translocate back there?"

"Probably?" Charity sniffed. "But I can't take another person."

"It's likely warded anyway," Malcolm said, "but perhaps Chakrabarti can get the location from you and we can try ourselves."

"How did you get away?" Alice asked.

"Oh, yes." Charity wiped her eyes. "Adamson came back later. I don't know how much later; I'd slept a little and we'd gotten a meal. He told me and Richard that we had only seen the beginning of what he hoped to accomplish. He talked like he had been studying sorcery forever and had found things nobody else had."

"He was in school with us," Kip said.

"He sounded very impressive and scary." Charity folded her hands in her lap. "He had that fire-demon with him and he ordered it to pull Richard to the bars of his cell. I couldn't see what was happening, but that other sorcerer, the one from the stage, he went up to the cell. Adamson said they had to be very careful with the timing, and the other sorcerer touched Richard and then Adamson said a spell. I could see from the side of my cell the way they did it, and the demon did something but I didn't know what.

"Richard fell. I heard the thump. And then Victor's hands glowed again and he told the demon that he could do the physical magic this time. He cast a spell and pulled me to the bars."

She stopped and looked around, sitting up straighter. "He'd taken something from Richard and then he had magic, so I figured the other sorcerer must have given Richard his magic back and then Adamson, or the demon, took it and put it in Adamson. So I'd get my magic back for as long as it took him to cast his spell.

"I stared at Jorey's cell, and as soon as that sorcerer touched me, I pulled magic and translocated there. I didn't know if I could, I only knew...I was good as dead if I couldn't." Nobody spoke as Charity drew in a rasping breath. "I wanted to get Richard but I can't take another person, and as soon as I bent down to get the basket, they'd turned around and I only had time to come back here." She swallowed and rubbed her eyes again, making them redder. "I had to leave him behind."

Then she leaned into Alice's shoulder and all the weight of her ordeal fell on her and she began to cry.

Alice wrapped both arms around her and held her. "You were very, very brave," she said.

"I'm so proud of you," Emily added, and Kip and Malcolm echoed her.

"You," Charity gulped, "you, you can save Richard, can't you? And set Jorey right?"

In Alice and Emily's faces, Kip saw the determination he also felt. "Absolutely we can," Malcolm said before any of the others could speak. "An' we will."

Movement behind Kip tickled his whiskers. He turned to see Chakrabarti standing in the doorway. The sorcerer inclined his head and coughed delicately. "Headmistress," he said. "You requested my presence here?"

Charity looked up at the voice and jumped when she saw Chakrabarti.

"You!" A second later, she sank back to the bed. "No, you're the sorcerer we met in Amsterdam," she said. "I'm sorry. For a moment you looked like— like Adamson's sorcerer."

"I assure you," Chakrabarti said, "I have never met this Adamson, and he does not sound like the sort of fellow I would work with."

"He isn't." Emily rose. "Charity, Master Chakrabarti is a healer and a spiritual sorcerer. I asked him here so that, with your permission, he can see if Adamson did anything to you and can help with it."

Charity looked up at Emily. "And see where the prison is?"

"Yes."

The girl nodded. "If you say it's all right, Headmistress, then you have my permission."

"Very good." Emily smiled at her. "Thank you, Charity. You've been through a terrible ordeal, but it's going to be all right. Come on, the rest of you."

Kip and Malcolm got up, but Charity clung to Alice, and the vixen said, "May I stay with her?"

Emily nodded and shooed the others out of the room, then closed the door behind them. They walked across the Welcome Hall and up the other side to Kip's office, which was nearest. "Well," Emily said when they were inside. "What now?"

"He still has one of our students," Malcolm said. "Two if you count what he did to poor Jorey."

"It was a trick," Kip insisted. "It has to be. He can't undo a Great Feat. Look what happened to Cott when he did. It would be..." He groped for words.

"A lot of magic released into the world?" Malcolm asked.

"Yes, but—" Kip stopped. He believed still that Cott had died from the undoing of the Great Feat, and what little research he'd managed to do into Great Feats had led him to another conclusion, little more than suspicion at this point: that the casting of a Great Feat would similarly kill the sorcerer. There were no records of Calatus surviving to guide Calatians into society; the creator of the Road had perished after his work was complete. It made a sort of intuitive sense to him; magic was a product of will, and if you poured enough of yourself into making your will permanent, none would remain to keep you alive. But Great Feats were so rare that he could not, and likely never would, prove his theory.

When he didn't articulate an objection, Malcolm went on. "Maybe if you undo just a small part of a Great Feat, you get just a small bit of magic. And maybe he can funnel that into himself somehow."

"Ugh." Emily shuddered. "Like drinking someone's blood." She caught Kip's expression and a stricken look passed over her face. "But worse. Like drinking all their blood."

"I'm not going to argue that the calyx ritual isn't grotesque," Kip said. "It's probably where Victor got the idea. I'm sure he thinks we'll believe this is real because it's based on a reality like that."

"I hope it's not real," Emily said, "but we have to behave as though it is. If it isn't then what is he after?"

"I don't know. Why was he asking French nobles for money when he's already funded by the British Crown?"

"I wouldn't put it past him to simply be keeping money away from the American schools. He's already tried in other ways."

Malcolm nodded. "And the Crown would be happy enough to watch us fail."

Emily ran a hand through her hair. "They can't know we're close to failing."

"He can," Kip said. "The one thing he was good at, if not sorcery, was finding things out."

"Regardless." Malcolm rested a hand on Kip's shoulder. "We have at least one more student and more Calatians to rescue."

"Two students," Emily said. "Whether that's Jorey or not, we have to rescue him."

"Agreed." Kip sighed. "And we can't leave the Isle Calatians now, or Grinda will be right about me."

"Would that be so bad?" Emily asked. "Why does one person's opinion matter so much?"

"She has a voice. And..." Kip searched for the way to articulate his concern. "If we want to remain on good terms with the Isle Calatians, to have them send students here, then she's an important ally. But it's more than that. She's pulling me to be responsible for all Calatians, not just the American ones."

"But you're American," Emily said, "and they should be your primary responsibility."

"Yes, but...I took responsibility for all of them during the war. I still feel I need to live up to that."

"For how long?"

Kip spread his paws. "I don't know. Maybe the rest of my life?"

"That seems a bit much," Malcolm said. "Even our President Adams has said he won't hold that office more than a few years."

"If someone else comes along to take charge of the Calatian race, I'll gladly step aside," Kip said.

Chakrabarti came in, followed by Alice. "She is sleeping now," the Indian master said, and went to Emily. "I took the location of the prison from her, with her permission, and I can convey it to you if you would like."

"Please." Emily extended a hand to him and reached out her other arm to Malcolm and Kip, who both grasped it. "We'll have to try."

They stood still for a tense moment and then Emily shook her head. "It feels like a horrible place but I can't go there. The wards are too strong."

Kip let go of her arm. "All right. Let's go back to the Isle and tell them what's happened. We'll search for Victor from there."

"I'll stay with Charity," Emily said, "and I'll send a note to Philadelphia advising them that Americans have been kidnapped by a British citizen. But I don't expect anything to come of that in time to be of use."

"We need to try every possible avenue," Kip said. "We won't give up until we have Richard and Jorey back as well."

"And Victor behind bars," Malcolm added.

"Or in an ocean," Emily said darkly.

CHAPTER FIFTEEN: DESPERATE
MEASURES

When Alice, Kip, and Malcolm returned, everyone was hurrying to the landward side of the Isle. "What's happening?" Kip asked, shading his eyes against the late afternoon sun.

"News!" a dormouse cried. "There's a crowd over on High Street."

The newspaper sellers didn't come to the Isle, but if the Calatians stood on the landward side they could hear across the water. Kip and Alice started in that direction and then stopped themselves. "We haven't time for this," Alice said. "Whatever it is. We've got to tell Grinda."

"I'll send Ash," Kip offered, and the raven took off from his shoulder. They moved out of the main street into a smaller one as he contemplated sorcerer-hating Grinda's reaction to the news that Calatians could possibly be unmade. "Is there nobody else we can work with?" he asked. "You two have been here longer; is there someone Grinda trusts who is more sympathetic to us? Who might temper the news before it reaches her ears?"

"Not that we've been able to find," she replied. "Your friends the otters like you the most, but she doesn't place a lot of faith in them, not that I've seen. Maybe that beaver; she trusts him and he seems reasonable. Besides, if you want her to trust you, you should go talk to her directly."

"I know." Kip shook his head. "I worry that if we tell her what Charity said about Jorey that she'll distrust us even more. And especially if it's just a trick, we'd be scaring her—and everyone—to no purpose."

"Do you really think it's a trick?" Alice asked.

"He as much as admitted in Paris that the Exposition spell was a trick. What if he intended Charity to escape and tell her story?"

Malcolm frowned. "To what end?"

"To scare us? I don't know. I can't imagine what game he might be playing at."

"Well," the Irishman said, "trick or not, I agree we should wait for proof before scaring people."

Alice nodded. "As long as we don't outright lie."

"We won't." Kip stopped and listened through Ash. "Ah, the news they're calling is that Paris is still in flames."

"Still?" Malcolm asked. "Or is this the first they're hearing of it?"

"I don't know." Kip shook his head and brought his awareness back to himself. "Let's go on to Grinda."

Alice led him to a small house that smelled strongly of wolf, where Grinda, three other wolves, and a beaver looked up as they pushed aside the curtain. When Grinda saw them, she sprang up. "How dare you enter my house? Get out, out!"

"We have news," Alice said.

"I'll hear it in the street. Is it about Paris burning? I've heard that already and we don't need your help to understand it, thank you very much."

Understand it? What was there to understand? But Kip, Alice, and Malcolm retreated out into the street. Behind the curtain, Grinda said, "All of you stay here. March, you come with me."

A moment later, she pushed the curtain aside and came out into the street trailed by the beaver. "Now, what is it?" she demanded.

Kip let Alice speak, as she had the most goodwill with the wolf. "One of our students has come back," she said. "She escaped. And she said that Victor Adamson had imprisoned her."

Grinda's ears perked up. "Did she see any other Calatians there?"

"No." Alice hesitated. "Only our student."

"Did he escape too?"

"Um…we aren't sure."

The wolf folded her arms. "So you've come to tell me you're returning to America, and the missing are our problem to deal with once again?"

"No!" Alice took a half-step back into Kip as though anticipating that he would object as well, but he kept silent. "We're going to stay and get the others back."

"All right. We'll have another meeting tomorrow morning, then." She glared around at them. "Unless there's something else?"

Now Kip did speak up. "What does the news from Paris mean to you?"

Grinda's ears went back and she narrowed her eyes. "It means that the world is changing even more than it did two years ago, more than you could imagine."

"We changed a lot two years ago."

"For some of you. Not for most of us." She turned and pulled aside her curtain.

"We really want to help," Kip said.

Grinda huffed and then went back into her house. But the beaver, March, remained outside. He studied the three of them the way one would examine fruit to see if it was rotten, and then said, "Oh, you want to help, aye? Do you not understand what she means? What this news means?"

"It means that the monarchy in France is in danger. But it wasn't very stable to begin with," Kip said. "It was put back in place after Napoleon took over."

"It means," March said, "that power is shifting, from those who live in the towers to those who live on the streets. So maybe you understand now why she turns her back when you look down from your towers and offer to help."

"March!" Grinda called from inside.

"We don't live in towers," Malcolm said pleasantly. "Modest rooms in a two-story schoolhouse, and a small house down the road from it." He indicated himself and then the foxes. "And me da used to say, the road is hard, aye, but harder still if you leave your friends by the side of it."

"You've yet to prove yourselves friends," March said, "and people have been betrayed by supposed friends before. What good is it to make the road easier if your self-styled 'friends' lead you to the gallows at the end of it?"

"You think so little of us?" Kip asked.

The beaver opened his mouth and then shut it again. "Honestly? You're children. You've done some good things, aye, but you still don't understand much. You may not live in towers, but you're idealists all the same, with no idea what life is like for those in the streets."

"We lived in the streets too," Alice said quietly. "I've been kidnapped and threatened with death."

"You've seen both worlds," March agreed. "But you're sorcerers now. If it came to tearing down the College, would you side with us or with them?"

They hesitated, and he nodded. "Aye."

"We'd make sure it didn't come to that," Kip protested.

The beaver shook his head and went back inside.

"Well," Malcolm said. "Want to go walk around the College in twilight or have you any other ideas to find Victor's secret prison?"

"We can wait until it's darker." Kip eyed the lavender and orange of the western sky. "But I still want to go. It sounded as though it was underground, so maybe we can find it by walking around the outside of the towers. That wouldn't be too suspicious."

"I don't know that I can sense wards that far away, though I'm willing to try," Malcolm said. "We'd still need to find a way in, unless you've learned how to summon an earth elemental in the past day or think a large excavation of dirt wouldn't be noticed. Whatever's been done to Richard has been done, and maybe to Jorey as well, and Charity's safe, so there's perhaps no great need to hurry."

"Unless the other Calatians are still in danger."

"Charity didn't see them."

Alice cleared her throat. "Sending in someone as a calyx would still give us the best excuse to have someone in the College. But whatever we do, we should check with Grinda. I know, Kip, she's being really terrible and all, but she's also organizing and doing things and if we don't tell her what we're doing, that could be really bad for both of us. For all of us."

He scuffed his foot along the ground. "If she wanted to know what we were doing, she could have asked us."

"Trust, Kip. It takes time."

"I know." He breathed in and out the thick, humid air. "They don't have it as good here as we do, or even as good as the Amsterdam Calatians. I wish I could do something about that, but what?"

"Listen to what they want," Malcolm said. "Did you never have well-intentioned charities come to New Cambridge to help with the plight of the poor Calatians by giving you blankets and lamp oil, or other things you'd no call to use?"

"Once." Kip flattened his ears. "But I think those groups mostly tried to help the Calatians in the cities. In New Cambridge we were farmers and lived well enough. Except for when some of us would...disappear."

Alice nodded. "But we knew who was doing that, and there wasn't anything the humans would do about it."

"So you take my meaning," Malcolm said.

"But what they want is to be free of the sorcerers, and if not for the sorcerers, we wouldn't be protected at all." Kip waved back in the direction of the stone pillar on the Isle that marked the site of the Blackstone fire. "We'll be killed openly, not in secret, and nobody will care."

"Sure, I'm not saying it's an easy problem to solve." Malcolm clapped Kip on the shoulder. "And that's even more reason to listen to all the people trying to solve it."

"I know, I know." Kip squinted ahead. "But they're not listening to all sides."

"All right. I'll go walk around the outside of the College looking for a warded spot. You two occupy yourselves here, and then around sunset we'll go back to Grinda and tell her our idea and plan. Maybe she'll be in a better mood then. Maybe I'll know where the prison is."

They had come to the fallen wall. Kip eyed the stones and the Thames beyond them. "And maybe the rocks will leap out of the Thames and assemble themselves on the wall."

Malcolm laughed. "That's the spirit. Always think positive."

After a productive hour, the light faded, but Kip and Alice continued working. Even when Malcolm returned with the disappointing news that he had sensed several warded locations both above and below ground, and there was no way to tell which might be Victor's, Kip put off going to meet with Grinda.

There had been Calatians in New Cambridge who hadn't wanted him to pursue sorcery, but that had been because they worried that the humans would resent a Calatian seeking power. At least, that's what he'd thought their problem was. If there had been a movement in New Cambridge to topple sorcerers, he'd never encountered it.

"Should we go now?" Alice asked.

"A little longer," Kip said.

But barely fifteen minutes later, the ravens alerted them to a beaver coming down the street purposefully toward them, and when he called out, "Ho, sorcerers," they recognized March.

"Good evening," Malcolm said. "We were planning to come seek you and Grinda out in a short while here."

"Grinda would like you to join a meeting," the beaver said. "So come seek her out now."

Kip blinked. "She wants us?"

"Aye." The beaver gave him a slight smile. "Someone mighta told her it'd be more useful to know what you might be doing rather than leave you to your own devices."

"Funny," Malcolm said. "We had thoughts along those very same lines."

"Well then, with our goals aligned, let's get back to the meeting house. One of our calyxes returned today and said nothing happened and he couldn't find out anything about the missing ones."

They asked him more questions but he said that was all he knew. So they sent the ravens to the roofs nearby to watch out and followed him into the large house.

Grinda saw them enter but didn't acknowledge them, occupied in conversation with a black rat in a blue tunic. Pierce waved them over to sit near him, so they took seats on the floor around him. "That's Mace," he said. "He went up yesterday and they thought he'd disappeared, but he said Master Cross just asked him to stay because he was casting several spells."

"He doesn't know anything?" Kip whispered.

"Not that he's said to us, but he might be saying more to Grinda now."

They conversed in quiet tones about life on the Isle; Pierce, though he wanted conditions to improve, generally seemed very happy with his life. He thought that the Calatians who'd gotten to go to Amsterdam, like the Cottons, were very lucky and only wished he could visit more easily. Passage on boats was more than most could afford unless they worked, and it was hard to secure working berths on ships because there was a lot of competition for them.

"All right," Grinda called after a few minutes. "This won't be a long meeting, but I wanted to talk to everyone now that Mace is back. He didn't see anything out of the ordinary, and he tried to explore but didn't get anywhere. It doesn't feel like asking calyxes to find our missing brothers is useful."

The rat shook his head. "Nah. We can't wander around the school or we're seen right away."

Grinda looked at the sorcerers. "So if we're going to find them, it'll have to be with sorcery. We have three sorcerers here who claim that they're willing to help us. What sorcery can they provide?"

Through Ash to Corvi outside, because Malcolm couldn't see, Kip said, "Go ahead and start. I should speak last."

Malcolm turned a fraction and nodded in understanding. "We haven't a spiritual sorcerer here, so we can't look into minds or anything like that. I can put wards up around someone, Kip can work with fire and fire elementals, and Alice can summon air elementals. Though an elemental on its own wouldn't be able to get through a ward."

"But," Alice said, "if the calyx breathed it in, it could travel through a ward that way maybe?"

"Oh, interesting." Malcolm rubbed his chin. "We could test that."

March leaned forward from Grinda's side. "What about summoning a demon? Could you do that?"

"Demons are detectable by other demons," Malcolm said smoothly. "And our student told us that Victor has a very powerful demon there. It's unlikely that one would be able to do anything useful before it was found out and imprisoned or destroyed. We couldn't use a more powerful demon because it would be too hard to control from a distance and for that length of time."

March nodded and settled back. "It's not much," he said. "Haven't you any sorcery that finds people?"

"Not through wards. Those are to stop people from being found. We can find people through translocation—sometimes—but that can be stopped by a ward. The good news, such as it is, is that one of our students is still in there, so if we can get around the ward, we can get there through translocation."

"Yes." Grinda cleared her throat. "How did one of your students escape but not the other? It was the human who escaped, wasn't it?"

"One of them," Malcolm said. "The other human is still there."

"And the Calatian?" Malcolm paused, and Grinda half-rose. "Why the hesitation? You said earlier you 'weren't sure' if he'd escaped. What secrets are you keeping?"

"Ah, now," Malcolm said, "we think our student was told some lies about Jorey and we're still sorting out what's real. We don't want to spread Adamson's lies for him, if that's what they are."

"Why don't you let us judge the truth of them?" The wolf folded her arms.

Malcolm, through Corvi, said, "What should I do?" to Kip.

"I don't know," Kip replied through Ash.

Alice touched his arm and when he met her eyes, she mouthed, "Trust."

If only Malcolm hadn't paused. If only Victor hadn't hit on the most dangerous rumor to spread. If only Kip had been better at looking after his students in the first place. He would have to tell them now, because otherwise they would never trust him. Not that Grinda would anyway...

His ears, which had splayed to the side, perked up. "We would be happy to tell you in private, Grinda," he said, "and then you can decide whether it is worth telling more people before we have determined the truth of it."

Her ears flattened back. "If it's something you can tell me, you can tell this whole room. Don't try to divide us."

"We aren't," Alice said. "But it really is a thing we don't know is true. If it isn't, then why tell everyone?"

"You can tell the people in this room." Grinda swept her paw out in front of her. "We have already sworn that anything said in these meetings remains between us, but we can swear it again if you need to witness it."

Alice splayed her ears. "I think we should tell them," she said to Kip in a low voice.

"As long as it does not go beyond these walls," Kip replied.

When he didn't go on, Alice stood. "Victor claims to have changed Jorey into—a squirrel. An animal."

For a second, Kip thought she would have to explain further, and she must have too, because she opened her mouth to go on. But before she could say anything, everyone in the house seemed to understand all at once. "Preposterous," someone said, as several others gasped and Grinda sank back in her seat.

"You had to wonder whether this was truth?" Grinda asked. "That he could undo a Great Feat?"

Was she calling them stupid? What did she think she knew about sorcery? "We have seen a Great Feat undone," Kip reminded them.

"You have," the wolf retorted.

"Yes. And this isn't an undoing of an entire Great Feat, but merely a small part of one." Kip didn't stand even when everyone watched him. "We think it's a trick, because Victor is good at tricks, but we have to weigh the possibility that it isn't. At least, until we know for sure."

"And how will you know for sure?"

Kip fixed his gaze on the wolf's skeptical expression. "I hope we never do."

"Then answer me another question. If you do rescue everyone from this Adamson, what's to stop him from kidnapping Calatians again immediately? Are you going to kill him?"

"I...I don't know." Kip looked to Alice and Malcolm, but neither of them had any idea either.

"So how are you going to stop him? Take him to the police?"

That wouldn't work, and Grinda knew it wouldn't work as well as Kip did. "We'll tell him we'll come back any time another Calatian disappears," he said, feeling the weakness of the words as soon as they left his muzzle.

Grinda barked a short laugh and the Calatians in the room followed her lead. "Aye," she said, "that's how we dealt with the humans who came for our cubs' tails. Gave them a stern warning."

Abel had told Kip that humans sometimes raided the Isle looking for the tails of fox and squirrel cubs, which they could pass off as wild animal tails and sell to the rich as stoles. But he'd never told Kip that some Calatians fought back. "We can't just throw him in the Thames," he said.

"Then maybe you'd better work out what you can do to stop him." Grinda sat down again. "That's where you might actually be useful." She looked around the silent room. "This meeting is over."

CHAPTER SIXTEEN:

SUMMONING

Kip managed to keep his temper under control until they got back to Ella Lutris's house, where the torrent of words he'd been keeping bottled up exploded out of him so strongly that Ash, newly settled on his shoulder, fluttered to the back of a chair with an indignant croak. "Work out what you can do," he said. "Like it's so simple. What does she want us to do, just kill him?"

"I'll be honest," Malcolm said. "Em's thought to drop him in the middle of the ocean is sounding better and better to me."

"You can't just—kill people. Then we're no better than he is."

"We could send him to Australia," Alice suggested.

Kip shook his head. "He'd find his way back. There aren't sorcerers in Australia, but there are ships."

"You know, when we needed to fight as a country, we didn't shy from some violent acts." Malcolm reached up to stroke Corvi's beak. "Would you not say this is a war?"

"Grinda would." Alice found a crust of bread in the pocket of her robe and broke it into pieces to give to each of the three ravens. When she got to Sleek, she said, "Emily? Have you been listening?"

There was no response. "It can't be more than afternoon there," Malcolm said. "It's only been a few hours since we left."

"She's probably occupied with the French people." Kip paced. The thought of Australia felt like a reminder of something he ought to have thought of, but he couldn't put a finger on what it was.

A few moments later, Ella poked her head in the door. "Meeting all done with?" she asked. "I've got the makings of a stew."

"We're done," Alice said.

So Ella bustled in and set about cooking. Kip lit the fire for her, after which she went on about how marvelous that was until the fish and vegetables were well into the large iron pot. Even after that, he noticed that she gave little looks toward the fire, as though unsure whether it was real.

The stew was delicious, if a little blander than Kip was used to from Peachtree, where after all they had access to several spices that probably never made their way to the Isle. Malcolm and Ella provided most of the conversation, talking about Ella's job at a weaver's shop in London proper.

All through the meal, Kip reflected on the afternoon and the meeting, and about what he could do. When dinner was over, he signaled to Alice and Malcolm. "Can we go to the wall again? There are some things I'd like to discuss."

"Oh." Ella stood. "Please don't mind me. I was going to go to Mum's house anyway. My nieces are there and I'm to help take care of them. You are welcome to stay here if you like."

She ladled the remaining stew into a bowl and carried it out, bidding them good night as the curtain fell closed behind her.

"So," Malcolm said, his voice low, "what brilliant strategy have you come up with to deal with Victor?"

Kip sighed. "None, I'm afraid. But I think I've realized that it's time I summon Nik."

Alice put a paw on his knee. "Why not just summon a different demon?"

"Because I made an agreement with Nik. I said I'd summon her if I needed her, and she said that was fine. Another demon…I'm just imprisoning them. Besides." Kip leaned back against the wall of the house. "I trust Nik. I know that's a strange thing to say about a demon, but I do. If I miss something, I think she'll still do the right thing."

Malcolm nodded, and Alice splayed her ears but didn't object. Still, Kip hesitated. "This is the right time, isn't it? I'm not making excuses? We've thought through everything else we could do."

"I don't think anyone, demon or otherwise, could fault you for thinking there was need right now." Malcolm ticked off items on his fingers. "Students kidnapped, and the future of our school in doubt, and Victor at least claiming to be able to undo Calatians. Sure, you can imagine circumstances more dire. You've lived through them. But that doesn't mean this isn't a time when you call on all the friends you have."

"Victor's calling demons, probably as many as he can," Alice said quietly.

"That's the thing." Kip leaned his head back and closed his eyes. "There will always be someone who's going to use demons, and we can't fight them without demons of our own."

"You say you trust Nik," Malcolm said. "Maybe that's the solution, aye? We can't do without them, but we can treat them better."

"We can't trust all of them. We all know that."

"Me as well as any of you." Malcolm said it lightly, but it got Kip to open his eyes and meet his friend's eyeless smile. "But we've got to start somewhere, if we're to do this, and why not with the one you know?"

"All right. Ash and Sleek, go out to watch the street. Don't want anyone walking in on us."

The ravens strutted to the door and pushed aside the curtain. Kip stayed with Ash long enough for the raven to get to a roof from which she could look down one side of the street. Sleek took the other side, standing next to Ash so they could communicate quickly.

Kip summoned magic, preparing himself. "You remember the spell?" Malcolm asked.

"Yes." Kip recited it to himself to make sure. "It hasn't been that long."

Still, he hesitated before speaking the words. He'd made a promise, and now again he weighed whether the need really was great enough to justify breaking it. But no more options revealed themselves to him. Victor had demons; they did not. They had four sorcerers going against the might of, perhaps, the entire King's College and military of the British Empire. And at stake was not only the future of the school, but perhaps of all Calatians.

He spoke the summoning and then, under his breath so Malcolm and Alice wouldn't hear, the name, "Nikolon."

For a tense half-second, he thought that perhaps the summoning might not work. But then she coalesced out of the air, vapors taking the form of a naked female fox-Calatian.

"Ah, Kip," Malcolm said nervously at his side. Alice didn't know enough about demon summoning and binding to know what Kip had left out.

"Hello…" Nikolon paused and looked around. "Kip Penfold."

"Hello, Nikolon." Kip drew in a breath, dismissal spell at the ready. "You have noticed that you are not bound. I agreed to summon you again only in a time of need, and I hope that by not binding you, you will trust me that this is a time of need for me. If you do not wish to help, I will dismiss you."

She walked up to Kip, growing in stature until her nose was even with his. Alice made a noise, but Kip held out a paw to still her movement, keeping his eyes locked on Nikolon's. He felt as though on a knife point, balancing delicately from falling in any number of dangerous directions. Blood pounded in his ears and he wanted very much to open his jaw to pant, but kept his mouth closed.

"Aren't you afraid I will curse you?" she whispered.

"You said you already have."

Her eyebrows rose and her ears went back, a much better mimicry of a fox-Calatian than she'd previously accomplished. "I said that curses take many forms. I remember those words."

"Did you curse me?" Kip asked.

She held his gaze a moment longer and then stepped back. "Do you need my help?"

Kip closed his eyes for a moment. His tail uncurled and the tip brushed the ground. Beside him, Malcolm uttered a soft oath. "Yes," the fox said. "Please."

He explained the situation as best he could. Alice added some details; Malcolm seemed still too stunned to speak. "So," Nikolon said. "You would like me to investigate the College and find out where your student is imprisoned. And there is a very powerful demon there that I must be watchful for. And this…Adamson. How will I know him?"

"You've seen him before," Kip said. "He was the blond man in the stable when you rescued Alice?"

Nikolon turned to look at Alice, who was trying her best to smile. "I remember…Alice…a little. There was…fire?"

"It was a few years ago," Alice said.

"I remember you, my summoner." Nikolon faced Kip again and her eyes seemed to glow. "What we have done together is very clear. Some of the rest remains, some fades. I remember all my summoners."

"Don't worry about Victor." Kip shifted his weight, his tail curling again. "The first priority is to rescue Richard, and Jorey if he's there. The second is to find out if Victor really can…alter Calatians in that way. But I don't know how you'd find that out unless you happen to see him trying it on a Calatian."

"If the spaces are warded, I will not be able to enter."

"No," Kip said. "I'll go to—I'll go to the top of the Astronomy Tower and wait there, so I'll be nearby when you find a space, and I can come to it and we'll figure out how to get past the wards. I'll leave Ash here so I can talk to you two."

"I'm coming with you," Malcolm said. "If anyone knows wards, I do."

"Then I'm coming too." Alice folded her arms. "We've had this discussion."

"Yes, I know." Kip hesitated.

Alice took a step forward. "You're not leaving me—"

"No, no." He reached out and hugged her to him. "Never."

She hugged back and kissed him, and he held on to her a little longer, breathing in her scent. "It's just—in Paris I acted quickly and I made the situation worse. Now that I come to it, I wonder if I'm doing the same thing here. Grinda is starting to trust us and if we go off and do our own thing… what if we get caught? What if Nikolon is captured or destroyed by the other demon?"

"Can demons be destroyed?" Malcolm asked.

Kip looked to Nikolon, who said, "I have never known a demon who was destroyed."

"They couldn't exactly come back and tell you about it, though, could they?" Malcolm mused. "Look, Kip, we're all for taking the risk. You've not hidden anything from us and if we go, it's our decision."

"But she's right about Victor," Alice said quietly. "Even if we rescue the students, we need to make sure he can't do anything to the Calatians here ever again."

"All right," Kip said. "He's kidnapped American citizens, and he doesn't have any magic. When we find him, we'll take him back to Peachtree and we'll give him to the American authorities for a trial. Mister Adams—President Adams—will be able to work something out."

"And what about Grinda?" Alice asked.

He released her and kissed her muzzle. "If we believe that this is the best way to proceed, we should tell her. But perhaps we can wait—"

Ash squawked outside, and Kip shifted to the raven's view. March the beaver was hurrying down the street toward him. "Someone's coming," he told Nikolon. "Please turn invisible and don't let him know you're here."

Nikolon vanished without any acknowledgment.

"An invisible unbound demon," Malcolm muttered. "Not much makes me nervous, but—"

"Shh." Kip nudged him both because Nikolon was still present in the house and because March was almost there.

"That dinner was splendid," Alice said brightly, artificially loudly.

"We'll have to thank Ella when she gets back," Kip replied, and a moment later March cleared his throat outside the curtain and then entered.

"Sorry to bother," he said. "But Grinda wants to see Master Penfold."

"This late?" Kip perked his ears.

"She said now." The beaver rubbed his paws together. "Summat about that Victor Adamson's magic. Wants to see you in private to ask your opinions about it."

"Should we come too?" Alice asked.

March shrugged. "If you wish. She only asked for Penfold."

The young vixen took one of the chairs and sat. "I'll wait for Ella, so she doesn't wonder where we've all gone."

Malcolm rose. "I have ideas about it so I might as well come along. We won't be long, will we?"

"I've never known Grinda to be slow about anything." March inclined his head and held the curtain for them to come out into the street. Above them, Corvi took flight and followed them along the street while Ash remained on the house, keeping watch.

"What changed her mind?" Kip asked.

"Who can say that it was ever changed?" March slapped his flat tail against the ground. "Maybe she always thought that it was worth more discussion but didn't want to appear weak in front of her people. You put her in a difficult position."

"I was trying to be helpful." Kip flattened his ears.

"Aye, when two sides are far apart the first salvos of trust may fall short in the gulf between them." March held his paws two feet apart. "When I first met Grinda a year ago she wouldn't let me even talk to her family."

"How did you get on her good side?" Malcolm asked, coming up on March's left.

"A lot of work and a lot of dedication. I've convinced her that I put the welfare of the Calatians over my own."

"That's what I'm trying to do." Kip brought his ears up. "That's why this spell of Victor's is so dangerous if it's real. But I think it could also be a trick of his to scare us."

"It could be," March said. "I want to stop him kidnapping more Calatians. It's not just that we can ill afford to lose one or two a month. It's that we've already lost families to Amsterdam, and it's a terrible thing to feel that they can take any of us whenever they want. We have no power, but we don't need to be reminded of it quite so often."

"True enough." Malcolm lifted his head. Corvi's wings fluttered over them.

March turned to Kip. "Though I don't expect you deal with that worry too often."

"More than you would think." Kip breathed in the night air. "You can't solve every problem by lighting it on fire."

"I imagine that solves a good many of them, though." March rubbed his paws together. "There have been cold nights when I'd have given a lot for a simple fire."

"You can make fire or get it from other people."

Malcolm chuckled softly. "Don't sell your power short," he said to Kip. "You destroyed a Great Feat, remember."

"Shut it," Kip said amiably.

"Sometime I'd like to hear that story." March stopped in front of the meeting house, from which the rich smell of fish emanated. "Not tonight, alas."

"Smells like they've had dinner as well." Kip glanced up as Corvi alit on the roof opposite with a sharp clatter of claws.

"They were just sitting down to it when I left to get you." March pulled the curtain aside and called in, "I've got Masters Penfold and O'Brien here."

CHAPTER SEVENTEEN:

BETRAYAL

Something was wrong, Kip thought a half-second before someone grabbed his paw. He reached for magic and found himself cut off from it. Malcolm gave a startled half-cry as the shadowy figure in front of Kip grasped his hand as well. "Get the ravens," a gruff voice said.

Kip found his body frozen by a spell. He'd been in this situation before. *Nikolon*, he called, knowing he wouldn't be able to hear a response, *please tell Alice it's a trap! Tell her to get out!* He said the same through Ash, or tried to; he couldn't see anything through the raven's eyes nor tell whether his words had come through. He tried to tell Ash to fly to London and hide among the shadows in the crevices of buildings, but again, he could not tell whether his orders had been followed.

"There's only one raven." Farley Broadside's voice.

Kip's eyes adjusted to the dim interior quickly, so he could now see the whiskered face of Farley and the face of the Indian sorcerer, the one who'd grasped him and Malcolm. That sorcerer now turned to March, who stood off to one side. "Why didn't you bring all the sorcerers and ravens?"

"Because Mister Adamson said he only wants Penfold. What was I supposed to do, tell them to all come along with their ravens and walk into this dark house together?"

"Have a care with your tongue, water-rat," the sorcerer snarled. "You and the ground-rat here are useful tools, no more."

"I delivered Penfold as I was ordered," March said. "Mister Adamson said that was all he wanted, and the rest of us would be safe. He didn't say anything about listening to you."

"Enough," the Indian sorcerer said, and reached out to Kip and Malcolm again.

Kip woke on a stone floor, his tail and left arm aching because both were pressed under him at awkward angles. Pressure on his shoulder withdrew. "He's awake," the Indian sorcerer said.

"Good." This voice, silky smooth and higher in pitch, was Victor Adamson's. Kip rubbed at his eyes and opened them.

The Indian sorcerer stood back from the metal bars that separated him from Kip. Next to him, crouching, Victor's pale blue eyes stared through the barrier.

Kip scrambled to sit up, discovering in the process that he was naked. He curled his tail around to cover his privates. "Ah, yes," Victor said. "You really have no-one to blame but yourself for your current state of deshabille. Albright warned me that you could conjure sorcery into small items, so we thought it best to relieve you of all possible hiding places for such things. And—well, we'll get to the other reason presently, perhaps."

"Of all the things I thought you wanted me for," Kip said, "I never imagined—"

"Ha ha!" Victor laughed. "Don't flatter yourself. My interest in you is purely scientific."

"Purely?" Kip reached up to brush a paw over his ears and whiskers, which felt out of place from sleeping on them. At the same time, he tried to cover the flare of his nostrils as he sought to find out more about who was with him in the neighboring cells. "I find that hard to believe. You've resented me since we met. Why did you tell March you specifically wanted me?"

"Because you're the most powerful Calatian sorcerer, the rarest of a very rare breed. I did try to make it work with your squirrel, but I regret to say he was insufficient."

"I'm not a naïve student," Kip said. He could smell Victor and Gupta clearly. Farley, too, and Malcolm, and...Richard, yes, and Jorey and Charity too, faintly. At least two other Calatians, but their scent was old. "Don't try to sell your trickery to me."

For a moment, anger clouded Victor's eyes, and then his expression relaxed back into an easy smile. "I suppose that's fair, after the Exposition. Well, don't worry. I'll show you exactly what is a trick and what isn't."

These words chilled Kip more than the stone he sat on. "People know where I am. Kidnapping me will have serious consequences for your country."

"Oh, I'm sure if anyone were able to prove it, that might be true. Which leads me to the question I woke you up to ask, which I am certain you will not answer truthfully: whom did you tell about your kidnapping? I know that your raven evaded us and that your," he waved his paw, "mate was elsewhere on the Isle."

"My wife," Kip said, heartened. At least Alice had escaped.

"I could easily make you think we'd captured them, but you would see through any of my tricks, more than likely." Victor gestured, and the Indian sorcerer came forward and reached through the bars.

Kip scooted back from the touch. Victor clucked his tongue. "Don't make Farley pull you against the bars. He's liable to get a little too enthusiastic about it."

From outside of Kip's view, Farley chuckled. It was not a pleasant sound.

Gupta was a spiritual sorcerer, so he was likely going to read Kip's mind. After his encounters with Master Albright, Kip (and all the masters at the Lutris School) had trained in techniques to keep certain thoughts out of his mind. He hadn't had much call to put them into practice, but here he would have to if he wanted to keep Nikolon's existence secret.

So he approached the bars and allowed Gupta to put a worn hand on his shoulder again. "Now," Victor said, "whom did you alert after your capture?"

"My raven and Alice," Kip said evenly.

Victor turned to Gupta. The Indian sorcerer frowned, and Kip felt the feathery touch in his mind. "He is concealing something."

"Well, find it. Don't worry about damaging his mind. He won't need it for much longer."

That threat, so casually delivered, shook Kip's concentration. "Ah," Gupta said, with distaste. "He summoned a demon."

"Blast. March told us he wouldn't do that!"

"And—he did not bind it?" Gupta withdrew his hand and stared at Kip.

Victor paused for a moment, his face screwed up in thought, and then laughed aloud. "My dear fellow, he's created a false memory to scare us with the idea of an unbound demon flying around. No sorcerer would summon a demon and not bind it. Albright also said he had some facility to resist spiritual magic. Look at him, the trickster."

Gupta continued to stare at Kip, and the fox looked back, hoping to find some measure of sympathy there. Then the sorcerer bowed his head. "You are undoubtedly correct," he said. "I did not see anything else to concern you."

"All right." Victor straightened and stood. "Then we have one more thing to do, and after that the experiment can proceed."

Kip scrambled to his feet, keeping his tail in front of him. "What experiment?"

"Oh, don't worry, I'll explain it all to you in time. And perhaps you'll even remember it afterwards. I haven't been able to ascertain that." Victor raised a hand. "I wouldn't count on it, though."

He swept out of sight. Gupta followed without another look at Kip, and Farley walked past Kip's cell. The marmot paused to gather phlegm in his throat and then spit through the bars at Kip.

The fox got his paw up to intercept the worst of it. Farley stared, and for a moment Kip thought he might try again, but he just laughed and walked on. A moment later, a heavy door creaked and then slammed shut.

Silence for a minute, then two. And then Malcolm's voice came weakly. "Please tell me I'm having a nightmare and that wasn't Victor and Farley laughing at you."

"If you're having a nightmare, we're sharing it." Kip's ears perked up. Though he'd hoped against hope that Malcolm hadn't been taken prisoner, he felt a great wash of comfort at his friend's voice. He pressed his muzzle to the bars of his cell but couldn't see to either side, and the cells across from him were empty. "Are you well?"

"Cold and angry and flat on me back, so not an unfamiliar spot for me."

"Did they take your clothes as well?"

"What? Strewth, no. Have they taken yours?"

"I'm down to the fur." Kip rubbed his arm, sleeking the fur down. "At least it's not skin."

"Shockingly indecent of them. No, they left my clothes but took my eyes. Can't feel Corvi anywhere."

"If you talk to him, he might be able to hear you," Kip said. "I tried with Ash. I hope Alice got away."

"She wasn't alone." Malcolm didn't say more, and Kip understood that while he meant the presence of Sleek and a way to reach Emily, he didn't want to say so aloud where anyone might be listening. "Speaking of being alone, is there anyone in here save the two of us?"

"Not that I've heard. The other cells seem to be empty." Kip listened to the silence, but small noises echoed off the rock and made it hard to sort them out. "I think I hear someone else breathing, but I can't be sure."

"I'll hold my breath and you hold yours and then we'll listen for it," Malcolm said.

They did so, but that only made the silence more deep and dreadful. "I don't hear anything now," Kip said, but just as he said that, from the cell on the other side of him came a small gasp.

"Richard?" he called, but only silence responded.

"Maybe he's asleep," Malcolm said. "Or pretending he's somewhere else."

"Maybe." Kip turned and sat with his back to the bars. Despite his fur, the cold of the stone seeped into him.

Malcolm cleared his throat. "Say, Kip, would you mind describing this place where we are?"

Kip pressed his fingers to the stone floor. "Well, the floor you can feel extends up to the walls and above us. It's a dark grey color with flecks of white in it. Looks old."

"Feels old, too." There came a dull clunking sound. "And these bars are iron. There isn't a latch somewhere that lets one right out that I'm just not seeing, is there?"

Kip had to smile. "No, I've looked."

"Ah. Pity. Victor's a clever fellow, but even clever fellows overlook things now and then."

"True. I should've known that we couldn't trust Grinda."

"Don't lay the blame at her feet. Or paws. She might not even know. It could be March all alone. Remember him talking about how he had to gain her trust?"

"Aye." Kip wanted to blame Grinda, but he had to admit that they had no proof that she'd betrayed them. "You may have the right of it."

For a short time, there was silence, but Malcolm could never let silence go on too long. "What do you suppose Victor wants to do with us?"

"With me?" Kip closed his eyes. "He wants to take my magic away. Maybe turn me into an animal. With you? I don't know."

"Doesn't seem like he can leave me alive after this." Malcolm mused. "Maybe he'll turn me into a Calatian. What sort of Calatian d'you reckon I'd be?"

"I doubt he'll waste that much energy on you."

"Come on," Malcolm said. "What do you think I'd be? I think I'd make a good rat, to be perfectly honest. They're hard-working and keep to themselves, aye?"

"You'd be a lovely rat," Kip said. "But I think you'd be a better otter."

"An otter? Thing is, I can't swim."

"All the more reason. You'd learn. But otters, they're—they're very talkative and happy a lot of the time." He thought about Coppy and about how the otter would have handled Grinda. He would've somehow smoothed things over; that was something he'd done well. Or if Abel had been here…

"That sounds like a good life," Malcolm said wistfully. "I don't suppose Adamson takes requests, though."

Abel and Aran and Arabella, and Alice and Emily, all the people he would likely never see again, and his unborn cub whom he would never meet. If only he could send them a message, simply tell them he loved them and tell them good-bye, he would feel better about going to whatever fate awaited him. "I don't suppose he does, because there's a lot of things I'd ask for."

"A comfortable bed."

"My clothes."

"Some wine wouldn't go amiss."

"One of those nice French cheeses."

"Oh, did the Dieuleveults feed you well?"

Kip smiled at the memory. It was only days ago but felt like months. "For the day we were there, very well. Their cheeses have such an interesting different taste from the ones we get."

"What were you going to do for them?" Malcolm asked. "For the competition?"

"Something with fire and glass, or fire and shapes. It was going to be very pretty and very useless."

Malcolm tapped the stone floor, a short rhythmic sound that Kip found calming. "You know," his friend said presently, "of all the spells you've cast, the one you did just before we left Ella's house was the one that impressed me the most."

"Oh?"

"I've never seen anything like it. It's something to be proud of."

Still avoiding specifics in case they were being listened to. Kip wasn't sure that "proud" was the right word for him; having Nikolon prove worthy of his trust made him ashamed of how he'd treated her in years past. "I wish I'd cast something more useful, like a ward."

"You don't think that spell might still prove useful?"

An unbound demon well-intentioned toward him? Perhaps it might be useful, but even if Nikolon could get through the wards into this dungeon, what could she do? She couldn't restore magic to them, and she couldn't translocate them. He'd asked her, years ago, and she'd said that her power was only sufficient to take people to the demon plane. She had never done that and did not know, nor did Kip, whether people could survive such a trip, much less return to the physical world from it.

It would be nice if she could send Victor to the demon plane and let him find his own way back. That would be better than dropping him in the ocean. Except—what if Victor found a way to harness the energy of the demon plane? Maybe he couldn't reach magic from here, but he might be able to from there.

It was all academic anyway, unless Nikolon showed up. "It might," he replied cautiously to Malcolm. "But I wouldn't count on it. I'd much prefer to rely on our friends to find us. They have more information than we did yesterday, at least about people involved."

"They do," he said, "and if anyone in the world can do something with that information, I'd put my money on those two. All the same, I don't know as we can count on anything we can't hear right at the moment."

"I'm out of tricks, I think." Kip sighed. "The best I can do is talk, and I don't think Victor's inclined to listen to me at all."

"I always knew that giving him power was a terrible idea. Wish I had just a moment with the fellow who employs him. You know, before I go to whatever fate he has in mind for me."

"Suppose old King George wouldn't put up much of a fight," Kip said.

Another pause. "You think he works for the King?"

"If not for the King, then for a highly-placed government official with the King's knowledge. At the Dieuleveults, he told them that if they funded him, it would 'soothe relations' with the British Empire, or some such. And here, when I said that kidnapping us would be a problem for his country, he didn't deny the association. It isn't a lot, but..."

"With Victor, he lets so few scraps drop. Yes, I tend to agree with you, but then, I've a dim view of British monarchs in general, and this one certainly knew about the attacks on the American schools even if he denied it in public."

"I shouldn't be surprised if this is somehow meant to bring America back into the Empire." Kip wrapped both paws around his tail and shifted again on the uncomfortable stone. "I can't quite see how, but it would explain quite a bit."

"But as well, you know..." Malcolm scooted along the stone, and his voice came from closer. "Victor works for himself first."

Kip got up and sat against the wall that separated his cell from Malcolm's. He reached an arm through the bars and toward Malcolm's cell as far as he could, tapping as he went. His claws found the edge of the wall and a first bar. "True enough. Did I tell you that Patris was there too?"

Malcolm shifted, and then fingers found Kip's claws, and his friend's hand grasped his. "You did."

The touch helped immensely. Kip smiled. "You remember how he and Victor were so friendly all the time? Victor barely talked to him. As soon as someone better came along, Patris was tossed aside."

"Couldn't happen to a more deserving fellow." Malcolm squeezed Kip's paw. "Tell me again about the event."

So Kip recounted as much of the Dieuleveults' soiree as he could remember, including the attack at the end. While telling it, he remembered that M. Dieuleveult had recommended he pray to Saint Gregoire, and so after he told Malcolm that, they both fell silent for a short moment. Kip said a prayer to that saint and any other who might be listening, and guessed that Malcolm was doing the same.

He'd almost forgotten his nakedness until the door clattered open a little while later. He and Malcolm let go of each other, and Kip withdrew his arm into the cell.

Footsteps clomped down on the stone, and Farley's voice called, "Feedin' time."

The marmot came into view and stood in front of Kip's cell. In front of him floated three cups and three plates accompanied by the aroma of old bread. "Get back now," Farley said.

Kip got up as the marmot's paws glowed lime green. He knelt and braced himself; the glow disappeared and he was thrown against the back wall of the cell. A thump from either side told him his cellmates had suffered the same rough treatment.

Farley deposited a plate and cup in front of each cell and then came back to Kip's and kicked the cup over, sending splashes of water over the stone. "Aw, look at that," he said. "Spilled your water, I did. Let me fill that up again."

He knelt in front of the cup, reached under his robes, and fixed Kip with a gleeful look. A moment later a stream of piss hit the cup with a rattle and then a splash as the cup filled. "And that bread looks a bit hard," Farley went on. "Let's soften it up, shall we?" He guided the stream back and forth over the two pieces of stale bread on the plate.

Kip held Farley's gaze, doing his best to remain stoic even as the stench of the urine reached him. He was not too hungry, so the loss of the bread didn't bother him, but he would have liked a drink of water.

Farley finished up and stood. "Next time, maybe I'll have something else to drop on your plate," he snarled at Kip, his whiskers flaring. "And you," he said to Malcolm, "your food and water is outside the bars. Have a care you don't tip your water over. There won't be any more 'til evening."

He strode away. The spell holding Kip to the back wall released him, dropping him to the floor. Farley's footsteps continued on, and Kip, spurred to hit back somehow, called, "Victor's only keeping you around because you're useful. Once he has magic, you won't be."

The footsteps went on, and Kip thought Farley might just ignore him. But that would have been the wise thing to do. "Think I dunno that?" he retorted, stopping somewhere past Malcolm's cell to judge by the distance of his voice. "You lookin' out for me now?"

Kip wanted very badly to say, "Well, we're both Calatians," but he caught sight of the cup of urine in front of his bars and imagined Farley coming back to do something worse if antagonized. "He's always been using you," he said. "You'd still be human if not for him."

Farley made a grunting noise. "Listen 'ere," he said. "You can say what you like. I'm not stupid like you think. I know what he is. We got a deal. He's gonna make me human again."

"Like he pretended to at the Exposition?" At least Farley was listening to him, talking to him, and Kip had to sow as much doubt as he could. He had no illusion that Farley would ever be friendly to him, but at least he could perhaps sour his relationship with Victor. "He's a Boston city boy, thinks he's so much smarter than everyone else. He's good at tricks."

"When I'm human I'm done with him. I got a word there's trade down to the Caribbean and I'm gonna go live there. And guess what?" Farley's voice had been sharp and angry, and now it turned cunning. "I just thought of this right this minute. After he's done with you, sucked all the magic out of you and left just the animal you are, I'm gonna ask him if I can have you. I'll take you with me and keep you chained, and when you die I'll wear your skin around my neck. How you like that? That make you want to keep talking?"

"Why retire to the island and deprive the world of a future diplomat?" Malcolm chimed in, perhaps to stop Kip from talking, though the fox had no intention of saying any more words.

Farley just laughed. "You. When he's done with you, you won't even be worth chaining up. Take a look at the other if you want to see what's in store. Oh! You can't, can you?"

"Sometimes it's a real blessing not to have any eyes," Malcolm replied lightly.

There was a pause while Farley processed that, and then his tone got sharp again. "What's that mean?" Malcolm stayed silent. "Oh, you'll look at a stinking fox but not at me? Maybe you want some of what he got." Footsteps came back toward Malcolm's cell, and Farley's robes rustled.

There was silence for a good long while, and then the robes rustled again and Farley grunted. "I'll get you next time," he said, and tromped away down the hall. This time he didn't stop, and the door creaked open and shut.

Malcolm's exhalation carried over to Kip's cell. "Aye," Kip said.

"It was worth a try," his friend replied. "Can't save a rotten apple, but you can maybe chuck it back at Victor. Maybe you got him to think."

"That would be more impressive than any spell I cast." Kip eyed his soiled bread and edged toward the bars, pressing his eye to them. "Can you find your meal? I can just see the edge of the plate."

"I'd be much obliged for some help."

So Kip directed Malcolm as best he could, and Malcolm eventually found the cup and plate just within his reach. "Would you like the rest of my water?" he asked. "I believe I've heard what became of yours."

"Drink what you want and then I'll take the rest." Kip extended his paw through the bars and over to Malcolm again. "My paw's where it was before."

"Give me a moment." Malcolm took a drink and then shifted around. The metal of the cup touched Kip's fingers. "Careful now."

Kip grasped the cup, keeping it upright. "Thank you," he said, bringing it back.

"What do you think he meant by 'the other'? Is it Richard?"

The water was warm and stale, but it was wonderful. Kip licked his lips. "That person we heard before is in the cell on the other side of me. I think it's Richard but I don't know for sure."

"Richard?" Malcolm called.

They waited, but again there was silence. "What do you think Victor could have done to him?" Kip whispered.

"No telling." Malcolm kept his voice low as well. "But if he's turned Calatians into animals…"

Kip's imagination took that speculation and went in some very unpleasant directions with it. "Ugh. Richard," he called again. "You can talk to us. It's all right."

The only response was movement and then the slow scraping of the cup and plate across the stone. Crunching and drinking followed a moment later.

"Maybe that's not Richard," Malcolm said. "Richard would share."

"I suspect that even if it used to be Richard, maybe it's not anymore."

"Ah, come now. You're not after believing in Victor now?"

"No. But he's done something to Richard, and spiritual sorcerers can already ruin someone's mind. Even if the rest of his magic-draining spell is all a trick, he's still working with a spiritual sorcerer and they're crazy enough."

"There is that. There is that." Malcolm tapped the bars of his cell.

This reminded Kip to return his cup, so he reached across with it. "Had any brilliant ideas about how to get us out of here?" he asked as Malcolm took the cup back.

"None yet, but the day's still young. I suppose it's day because he said we'd be fed again in the evening. This bread isn't quite the consistency of the stone I'm sitting on. I should've saved some of the water to soften it."

"Thank you for sharing it," Kip said quietly.

The crunching paused, and then Malcolm said, "Ah, he ruined your bread too, didn't he?"

"It's all right. I'm not hungry. And I don't suppose I'll be here long enough to get hungry. That's Farley, though. Thinking of the worst thing he can do right now, not thinking ahead."

"Seems like he was thinking a little bit ahead."

"Fantasies. Whatever Victor has planned for us, it doesn't seem like we'll survive. Any of us, and I mean Farley too."

Malcolm was quiet. "You know, if it wasn't for the manner of going, and the missing of Em and leaving her behind, I wouldn't be too troubled by passing from the mortal coil at this stage. We've seen and done much, enough to fill a life for sure. I'm sure I'll find ways to fill the years, and there are many left that I could do something with, but…I've fought demons, helped rescue thousands of Calatians, won a war, and started a school. I met a good woman and…well, I wish I had more time with her, and with all my good friends. But if that's how my tombstone reads, I'm well content with it." He paused. "I really only wish my departure wouldn't give Victor any satisfaction."

"I agree." Kip eyed the tin plate and wondered whether he might break it or crack it enough to have a sharp edge. "But I don't wish it hard enough to do something about it."

"No, and that's a mortal sin anyway."

"True enough." Kip leaned his head back against the wall and closed his eyes. "Then we keep our ears open for an opportunity and we hope that there's something Victor overlooked."

"Faint light is still enough to see by in the middle of the night, me da used to say." Malcolm shifted around. "And truth be told, though I'd give anything for you to be somewhere else, I'm glad to have your company."

Kip's breath caught in his throat. "I wish you weren't here, too. And I'm grateful that you are."

CHAPTER EIGHTEEN:

KIP'S GAMBIT

Kip and Malcolm talked over the next several hours, and when they didn't talk, they fell into dozes. The mysterious person in the other cell continued to make some noises without speaking, and at this point Kip hoped it wasn't Richard, remembering the suave good humor of his student.

The school, the students. At least they still had Charity, but if this turned out the way it looked to be going, they would have lost all their other students and two of their masters. Emily would carry on the school, but without the Dieuleveults' money, they would be in worse shape than Prince George's school had been after losing all their apprentices to the attack.

But from that attack had come himself, Malcolm, and Emily, and indirectly Alice. Things might look bleak now, and perhaps he wouldn't live to see the next upturn, but if anyone could steer the school right, Emily could.

Of course, nothing could last. Look at France: from stable monarchy to brief shining empire to puppet monarchy to revolution, all in Kip's lifetime, or just about. America had had an insurrection almost fifty years ago now, and another one just two years ago and now was a fledgling country trying to get its feet under it. Change came quickly; it could benefit you one day and crush you the next, like the great Wheel that Chakrabarti had talked about as part of the Hindu faith.

The change that seemed to be coming throughout the world now was people rising up against governments and tyranny. Kip had seen America go through the idea of rejecting their king in favor of a more representative government (an idea that had not fully taken hold yet), and France was going through the same motions now, albeit more violently. India…he wanted to know more about India. Sorcerers going out among the people had sounded like a strange practice when Chakrabarti had first mentioned it, but now it felt almost vital. Grinda accused him of being out of touch with Calatians; the Dieuleveults and other French nobles had been out of touch with their people. Perhaps he should spend more time talking to other Calatians, not just a visit to a pub in Amsterdam or occasional visits to the Isle. After all, that he had access to magic was an accident of his birth. It didn't make him better than anyone else. If anything, he should be using his power to help those who weren't as fortunate.

Thoughts of those less fortunate reminded him of Nikolon. He sent out a call to her every so often, but the demon never answered. Kip believed that the wards were preventing her; although she could be doing anything out in the world, he thought she would be looking for him.

Malcolm answered when Kip talked to him, and agreed with his thoughts on the changes in the world. "Sure, those with power will always take what they want from those without, but the purpose of a king is to protect those under him. Without the king, they're vulnerable."

"I'm not sure they are. An army is made up of a lot of people."

"But who commands it?"

"The person most qualified. Not the King's nephew or something like that."

"It sounds good, but…" Malcolm grunted and shifted. "How do you start this happening? If you go the American way, you wind up arguing for years. If you go the French way, you're likely to be regarded as vandals and nobody will listen to you."

"They're burning Paris *because* nobody was listening to them. The world is listening now. But things shouldn't have to get to that point. There has to be a way. Maybe in India or in Persia, someone has found it."

"When we've disposed of Victor, we'll visit all those places."

"Aye." Kip paused. "Any new ideas on how to do that?"

"None over here. Still working on it, though. I don't suppose you can get Ash to bring you one of those talismans Victor was so worried about?"

"If she knew where we were. And if there were a way for her to get in."

"Right. I keep coming back to that part where nobody knows how to get to us."

"It's the big obstacle."

"Still nothing from your spell?"

"Nothing yet."

"Ah well. Perhaps he'll forget about us. I'll look for loose stones in the wall. In a year or so we might break through to the outside."

Kip smiled. "Better to be doing something than simply waiting."

For his own part, when he wasn't calling to Nikolon, he went over and over the places where Victor might be weak. Master Gupta was the most obvious; Kip had connected with him briefly over the matter of treatment of demons, and if he had the chance to speak to him, he might be able to solidify that connection. But Victor would never allow that; he had sent Farley to feed them in part because he knew Farley would be cruel, but also because he knew Farley would never listen to anything Kip had to say.

Victor himself was the most accessible weak point, but Kip had only ever gotten the best of Victor by going around him, never by out-talking him directly. He was unlikely to fall for anything Kip could concoct on the spot. His main desire was to have magic, and he had already found the way to do that, so unless Kip could offer him an alternative…

An idea took shape, very unlikely to work but the only idea Kip had been able to come up with. He didn't even tell it to Malcolm because there wasn't anything Malcolm could do to help, and he'd be certain to object to one part of it.

Hours of reflection yielded no other ideas, nor any response from Nikolon, so when the door opened again in what Kip presumed to be the evening, he was stuck with just the one faint sliver of hope.

"Everyone still here?" called out Victor's cheerful voice. It sounded like two other people were with him, to judge from the footsteps, and that was good. Master Gupta's presence increased his hope from vanishing to slim.

But the first person who came into view past the bars of his cell was March the beaver. Kip sat up, startled, and only after a second realized that the beaver floated immobilized a foot off the ground.

March stopped in front of Kip's cell, hovering there, and then Victor stepped into view, waving to Kip. "Good evening. I trust you've had a pleasant day to think about—well, I suppose you'll have been wondering about my claims and whether I can do what I say."

"Since you haven't actually said," Kip replied with as much coolness as he could muster, "I haven't given it a single thought." His tail twitched with the urge to cover himself again, but he restrained it. To do so would be to announce that his nakedness bothered him, and would give Victor some satisfaction.

Victor's face clouded for a moment, as Kip had hoped. "I would have thought that your student told you what she saw, and no doubt you dismissed it as illusion. It's true that Master Gupta is an accomplished master of illusion, which is something of a lost art here in the West. But I assure you that my spell is real, and I have come up with a delightful way to both convince you of that and tie off one of the loose ends that had been worrying me."

Kip jumped to his feet and grabbed the bars. "Don't hurt March. Don't hurt anyone else. It's my power you want."

"Of course it is." Victor smiled at him, composed again. "But more than that, I want your respect. No—I want you to understand how very completely I *deserve* your power." His jaw tightened as he said that, his eyes hard despite the smile. "You wave your hand and set things afire, a force of unchecked destruction. I have learned how to manipulate the very fabric of magic itself."

"That's all well and good," Malcolm called from the other cell, "but have you learned how to cultivate real friendships? Because the only people I've seen you with have been, well, me ma used to say, it doesn't matter if you walk out of the gutter if you still carry its stink around with you, and—urk."

"Thank you, Farley," Victor said. "Release him. He'll understand what will happen if he interrupts again."

Malcolm drew in several harsh breaths. "Strewth," he gasped.

"Now." Victor addressed Kip. "If you don't wish Farley to throw you against the stone again, please go stand flat against the back wall and remain there."

Kip stared into Victor's eyes. "Don't do this. I believe you."

"I've told you already, I have to do it regardless, and I want you to watch. Now go." He shooed Kip with a delicate motion of his hand. "Farley, deal with the clothes, would you?"

The fox turned and walked to the back wall where he stood and faced the sorcerer. Victor produced a key and opened the door to Kip's cell. Behind him, Farley cut through March's clothes with a knife, struggling through a few of the seams but eventually tearing everything away. He pushed the beaver into Kip's cell, and as soon as Victor had shut the door, March dropped to the floor.

"You said you'd stop," he rasped to Victor. "You said that all you wanted was Penfold."

"I said I would stop taking Calatians," Victor replied, "once I had performed my experiment on Penfold. Which, as you can well see, I have not." He replaced the key in his pocket and drew out a thick white rock, which he tossed through the bars. "Penfold. Take that chalk and make a mark on the beaver's fur or tail, somewhere, anywhere, and don't tell me where it is. Gupta is nowhere around."

March turned toward Kip. "I'm sorry," he said. "I had to do it. He said he'd stop. I thought I was saving my people."

"Oh," Victor said silkily, "now you're making me feel like I didn't have to also give you so much money to infiltrate the rebellious group. If I'd known you would have done it merely to save your people, I'd have treated myself to…well, a moderately fancy dinner, at least, instead."

March hung his head and sat motionless on the stone floor. Kip remained where he was, trying to figure out how his plan would work if Gupta wasn't here. "I'm not going to put a mark on him," he said.

"Ah, well." Victor leaned against the bars. "You see, it's rather important to your understanding that you do. I'm trying to remove any possibility that this might be an illusion so that you'll understand how real it is before understanding is removed altogether. It's quite important to me."

"I already told you that I believe you."

Victor's smile tightened. "Put a mark on him, or I'll have Farley begin to break bones in O'Brien's body. He's very good at that, you know."

"Don't you worry about me," Malcolm called, and then was silent, whether of his own volition or Farley's, Kip couldn't tell.

"I have another idea," Kip said. "You don't have to do this to him. Or to any Calatians."

Victor's smile disappeared, and he put his hand up to the bars. "What I don't have to do is listen to you," he said. "Pick up the chalk, now, or O'Brien suffers."

"But I—"

Victor turned to his right. "Farley, go ahead."

"All right!" Kip hurried forward to pick up the chalk. He knelt next to March, who was mumbling to himself with his paws clasped together in front of him, and said, "I'm sorry," as he rubbed the chalk on the beaver's knee.

March did not acknowledge having heard him. "…and forgive us our trespasses," Kip caught before his words were lost in breathy sobs.

"Is it done?" Victor's tone had grown impatient.

Kip dropped the chalk. It had left a white smudge in the fur, barely perceptible. "It's done." He sat back on the floor, heart pounding, dreading what was going to come next. "Please, don't."

"Ah, as much as I love hearing you beg, I'm going to enjoy showing you how foolish you've been even more." Victor gestured Farley over. "Summon it."

Farley spoke a summoning spell, and out of habit Kip listened for the demon's name. It wasn't familiar to him—Poatancia—but he committed it to memory as a whoosh of air and the smell of burning plants signaled the arrival of the demon somewhere out of sight. A sharp tingle in Kip's nose told him that the demon was likely around a third-order demon. Not the most powerful, but powerful enough.

When Farley had finished the binding spell, though, instead of the litany Kip knew from every demon summoning, Farley said, "You will obey every command of this man, Victor Adamson. You will make no move save on his order, speak no word save on his order, use no magic save on his order."

"Thank you, Farley," Victor said pleasantly. "Now, Poa, you will look into my mind only enough to see the spell I am holding there, and you will take that spell exactly and cast it on the beaver right here."

"Yes, master." The demon came into view then, a small crooked man with smoldering skin like that of a phosphorus elemental and wisps of hair around the crown of his head that gave off a constant stream of smoke. His eyes, at the level of Victor's chest in height, glowed the bright yellow-orange of a fire, and he moved with deliberate slowness, as though his body were made of stone.

Victor rested one hand on the bars and focused. "This spell," he said. "You have it?"

"Yes, master." The demon's voice hissed and popped like a slow-burning fire. It walked through the bars as though they weren't there, its body parting and re-forming around them, and then reached a hand down to March's shoulder.

The beaver cried out and flinched, but the demon's hand stayed pressed to his fur. A moment later, the demon's other hand reached back through the bars, and Victor grasped it. For a heartbeat, nothing happened, and then March made a choked cry and his body—his body collapsed in on itself, legs shortening, head sinking down into his neck, the whole of him shrinking as Kip watched in horror. The beaver-Calatian let out a long low moan, swinging his head from side to side, now the size of a child. Now he was smaller, short and squat.

Kip backed away on the stone floor, unable to look away. Now the demon lifted his hand from the body of a beaver, an animal the size of Kip's chest. The beaver wobbled on his legs for a moment, then looked around as though he had just woken from a nap. He took two steps forward and sniffed at the stone wall, then ambled curiously along it.

"Your mark is still there," Victor said. "Go look." When Kip didn't move, Victor's tone grew steely. "I said, go look."

His arms glowed, Kip saw now, but with a dark kind of light that hurt his eyes to look at. Turning back to the beaver, Kip tried to get close enough to see the fur where he'd placed the chalk, but the beaver raised his head in alarm and ambled away as Kip approached.

"I'll just hold him still for you, shall I?" Victor spoke a basic physical sorcery spell, and the beaver lifted from the ground, his legs waving around and head turning in alarm. He rose to the height of Kip's head and then remained there. "Go on now."

Kip drew close enough to see the white smudge on the fur, unnecessary now because he believed in what Victor had done. He stared at the beaver that minutes before had been a person and imagined himself reduced to a fox, an animal bereft of understanding. What would he experience? Would it be like dying, his consciousness snuffed out in a moment? Or would he simply be stricken of reason and retain whatever limited intelligence was allowed in that form? He imagined Alice and Abel and Abel's cubs as foxes running around Peachtree on four legs, and his eyes closed against that future. He would do everything in his power to prevent it, for as long as that power lasted.

"Have you verified that it's there?" Again the impatient, bored tone.

He swallowed his visions of the future, turned to Victor, and nodded. His idea seemed foolish and impossible now, but he had no other recourse, and possibly only minutes before even that was lost to him.

"Good. Now you know. You should have befriended me years ago, you know. You could have been my apprentice, could have helped me and shared in the glory I'm going to receive from this."

"Glory?" Kip choked out the word. He could feel Malcolm wanting to mock Victor, so he spoke quickly, as much to forestall his friend as to work his way around to his desperate plan. "You've managed to perform a, a basic physical magic spell. And not very well, I might add." His limited experience as a teacher helped him here. "Your levitation was uneven and wobbly."

Victor scowled, and the beaver dropped five feet to the floor with a thud. Kip flinched, but a moment later the beaver shook himself and hurried away from Kip without even a noticeable limp. "Of course the magic from a single Calatian is limited," he said. "That's why you're here."

"And you don't still have the magic, do you? You spent it all on one spell?" The more he focused on the academic and distanced himself from the reality of what Victor wanted to do to him, the calmer he became.

"I told you, the magic is limited." Victor grew more annoyed. Kip hoped that it was because he wasn't suitably impressed or scared, and that gave him a little more courage to keep going. "I've learned to hold back a little of it." He lifted his arms so that Kip could see a little of the dark light flickering around them, and then even that vanished as Kip rose a few inches from the floor and hovered unsteadily there.

"So every time you need to cast a spell, you'll need to sacrifice an entire Calatian? That's not very efficient. You'll use them all up, and then what will you do?"

Victor's grin returned. He gestured, and Kip dropped to the stone floor. "I've thought of that, of course. I've been studying this for a year. I think you'll be interested to see the solution."

He walked to the other cell, the one that didn't hold Malcolm, and went out of Kip's view. A lock turned, a door opened, and Victor said, "Come on out, there's a good lad."

Shuffling footsteps followed him, and when Victor reappeared he held a pale hand, leading someone forward. Kip's breath caught; he knew it was going to be Richard before the red-headed boy dragged his feet into view behind Victor.

He wore the same clothes that he'd been wearing at the Exposition, dirtier and torn in places that Richard would normally never have tolerated. The clothes were not the worst thing about him, though. He walked listlessly, with a vacant expression that took in none of the world around him. Even when he turned to Kip, there was only a fraction of a second of hesitation before his eyes passed with equal interest to the beaver behind Kip in the cell.

"It turns out that humans have a small amount of magic in them as well." Victor spoke as conversationally as though he were presenting at the Exposition, as though the creature he led by a hand had not once been a bright, promising student. "Moreso if they can access magic. And while the supply of Calatians is limited, there are more humans than there have ever been. Besides which, he can still eat and perform simple tasks. He could likely be trained to carry a weapon for an army. He's by no means as useless as a used-up Calatian will be."

The words were clearly intended to apply directly to Kip. He quashed the vision of a four-footed future again and tried not to look at Richard, because unlike March, Richard looked almost exactly as Kip remembered him, and it was impossible not to connect that past Richard to this one. "It still seems very inelegant." He'd stored that word as one that might annoy Victor in a subtle way, which was safest in his current situation. "I'm surprised you haven't managed to simply forge a connection to magic the way sorcerers have."

Victor's smile curled up at the corners. "But my dear animal, that's exactly what you're going to help me do. The spell I've conceived has failed with inferior levels of power, but the amount stored in your body should be enough to break through."

"'Should be,'" Kip echoed. "And if it isn't?"

Victor waved a hand carelessly. "You still don't understand. The magic contained in you is only half of what I want from you."

"You've held a grudge for this many years?"

"It's not a *grudge*." The smile slipped, his thin lips straightening. "That implies that you've wronged me. But it's not you that's wronged me; it is the fickle nature of fate that chose to give such a great gift to an animal while leaving my superb mind unable to touch it. If there is a grudge, it is not against you, but against the universe. You are merely the symbol of injustice, and indeed the injustice that any of your race exist at all, that magic was spared to help animals upright and give them speech when that magic could have gone to good men, to improve the world."

"By selling magic to their fellows?" This was Malcolm, unable to restrain himself, but Victor did not signal Farley this time.

"By taking magic from those who cannot use it properly and giving it to those who deserve it."

"Deserve," Kip said, and would have gone on, but Victor was at the bars in a step, and his eyes blazed.

"Yes," he hissed. "*Deserve.* I have spent the last three years listening to what a wonder you are, simply because of the accident of your birth, that an animal can control magic, and what wonder, understands fire! Fire, the simplest of the elements; it is merely consumption and no more. And then that you have destroyed a Great Feat. All you can do is tear down: the school, the American Army, the British Empire, the Road. I would have built. I would have made the British Empire a nation of sorcerers, with magic to take the Union Jack to every corner of the world, bigger than the Roman Empire, lasting longer than the Zhou Dynasty or the Holy Roman Empire."

"With you at its head."

His eyes glittered. "I've better things to do than manage dozens of quarreling colonies. I will be its indispensable backbone, sorcerer to the sorcerers."

Kip noted the change from "would build" to "will be," but let it go. His heart pounded but he kept his demeanor as calm as he could, ears up, tail still. "I suppose that since you are so emotional about my death, it's not worth proposing a bargain to you."

The clear blue eyes stared, and then Victor stepped back and laughed. "Ha! Bargain!" He supported himself with one hand on the bars and doubled over laughing. "Do you hear this, Broadside? The fox wants to bargain. With what? He hasn't even clothes to offer me, and the only thing of his I want I can take at any time."

"Shouldn't listen to him," Farley said. "He'll talk and talk. Best is to just take what you want."

"Well, now, maybe that was true when you were holding his snout down in the mud and anyone's parent might walk by. But there are no parents coming to rescue him now." Victor stepped back and folded his arms. "I think it fitting that his last words will be an amusing pathetic plea."

Kip shook his head. "You know, I've changed my mind. I'd rather die knowing that you never got the chance to have this knowledge."

Victor nodded. "Very well, then. Demon, come here."

The old fire-creature shuffled toward him, and for a moment Kip really thought Victor was going to ignore his taunt. But then Malcolm said, with perfect tone and timing, "Good job, Kip. I was afraid you were going to tell him."

Victor glanced toward Malcolm's cell in irritation and then back at Kip. Uncertainty passed over his expression. "Go on then," he said. "Speak your bargain."

"Have Master Gupta come down here and read it in my mind if you want to hear it so badly," Kip replied. Victor wanted it now, thanks to Malcolm, and it annoyed him more that he couldn't just have it.

Victor's eyes flicked toward the demon—just for a second, but it was enough for Kip to realize that Victor didn't want Master Gupta here for a very specific reason. It could be because he had summoned a demon; if the Indian sorcerer shared Chakrabarti's beliefs, he would not approve of the way Victor used demons. There was more in Victor's look, however, enough to give Kip a clue about his further intentions. "Oh," Kip said. "You're going to use my magic to cast a spell to steal the demon's magic. That'll probably kill it, shouldn't you think?"

The demon shifted only enough to let Kip know that it had heard and understood. "Because you're hoping to get magic from the demon plane," Kip went on.

"Enough," Victor snapped.

"It's just interesting," Kip went on, "because that was similar to my line of thinking when I was trying to figure out how to give magic to more Calatians."

Victor's expression froze. "Oh yes," Kip said. "You think I was merely teaching students, traveling around to government officials, and trying to build a school? I'm trying to preserve my race. If all Calatians had magic—well, you laid out the scenario very clearly. But replace British Empire with Calatian Empire."

Farley made a growling noise. Kip leaned over to see what he could of the marmot. "You could be part of it, Farley, if you stay in this much preferable form."

"When you're an animal," Farley growled, "I'll choke you with my shit."

Kip returned his attention to Victor. "I can see why you like him." The more he asserted his control of the situation, the calmer he felt. If indeed he were going to die in the next minute, then it didn't matter what he did. "Did you also discover the truth about the demon plane?"

He had no idea, honestly, what truth he might be talking about, if any. He only wanted to goad Victor into bringing Master Gupta down, because Victor would be much more likely to believe Kip's idea if he heard Master Gupta read it out of Kip's mind. If Kip spoke it, it would sound ridiculous. It might still work, but he felt the chances were slimmer.

Victor, however, stopped and narrowed his eyes. "I discovered something," he said. "What truth did you discover?"

"Ask Master Gupta."

"I rather think I'll have Farley ask O'Brien if you don't tell me. I'm getting tired of having to make these threats."

Malcolm made a strangled noise, probably a stifled plea to Kip not to worry about his well-being. And now Kip had to make up something, something relevant and interesting. He connected the two most recent things Victor had mentioned: that he wanted to be able to draw magic himself and that he was going to do it through a demon, and he remembered something

Chakrabarti had told him about a sect of Hinduism and their beliefs. "That it's where our magic comes from," he said.

Victor's eyes widened, and Kip felt a jolt of relief. "How did you come to that? The papers of Master Alia had not been viewed in decades."

"Oh, Master Albright and I had some interesting conversations before he tried to kill me." Kip had the desperate feeling that he was staying just one step ahead of Victor, and if he made one mistake, he would be a four-footed fox a moment later, his life as he knew it gone. "He told me about Alia's work and also about some other research he'd done." Here was a good place to throw in a nugget of truth, and so Kip did. "He once told me that the knowledge I was pursuing was dangerous, more so than I knew. Did he not tell you about it? Perhaps that's why."

Albright had said that during the war, when Kip mentioned the name of the demon Master Windsor had called to destroy the American schools. Another master had pointed Kip to an old text in a library that mentioned this demon, but Kip had failed to understand the context. Still, the name itself was enough to unnerve Albright, who had killed the master who'd given Kip that clue.

"He did mention that you were seeking knowledge you oughtn't." Victor rubbed his chin and went on, more peevishly. "And he won't tell me what it was. But you'll tell me."

"Why should I?" Kip inclined his head toward Malcolm. "Because you'll make him suffer? For how long? We can both bear it. You're going to kill us both anyway, and I can assure you that it would give me a great deal of satisfaction to go to my grave with a piece of information that could have helped you, knowing you willingly threw it away."

Victor drew in a breath, glaring, but no words came from between his clenched teeth. Farley, to the side, said, "You want I should pull his tail off? Open his stomach?"

"All right," Victor said in a low, taut voice. "Name your bargain."

CHAPTER NINETEEN:

ON DEMONS, AGAIN

Here was his moment. Kip drew in a breath. "I'll share my knowledge. You will promise to release me, Malcolm, and Richard, and to never harm us nor anyone from our school again."

Victor raised his eyebrows. "A modest assurance."

"I wanted to ask for a promise I can trust you to keep."

In the next cell, a choking noise came again. Both Victor and Kip ignored it. "Very well," Victor said. "I will leave everyone associated with your precious school alone."

Kip flicked his ears. "And release myself and Malcolm?"

Victor raised a finger. "There we may have a difficulty. You see, you've already seen enough to make things very difficult for me, and I will not insult you by asking you to promise never to reveal what you've learned here. Therefore, I will not agree to that. If your information is useful, you can spare your loved ones."

"Deal," Malcolm rasped from the other cell.

"All right," Kip said. "But you'll give us a chance to say good-bye to each other first."

Victor rolled his eyes theatrically. "You can do that now."

"In person."

"Yes, fine, very well. Go on, already."

Kip crossed his arms and took a breath. "You're sure you don't want Master Gupta here to read it from my mind? Or to confirm that you're going to keep your promise?"

"Tchah. The fact that you're willing to subject yourself to that is enough. As for me..." Victor gave Kip a beatific smile with cold blue eyes. "You have no choice but to trust that I abide by my word. But I promise you that I always do, and I will."

"Very well." The sudden fear that Victor would laugh in his face and cast his magic-draining spell in the next moment seized Kip, paralyzing his chest and throat. He struggled to pull in a breath, squeezed his eyes shut, and opened them again. "Have you never tried traveling to the demon plane?"

For a moment, it looked as though Kip had told Victor a joke that he hadn't understood, and then the blond man scowled in disgust. "I have to give you credit. For a moment you had me thinking that you had actually made a breakthrough. But Farley was right; you were merely stalling for time. Well, now your time is up."

"I've done it," Kip lied.

Now Victor did laugh. "You're making it worse. Yes, I've looked into it, of course I have. So have a dozen other sorcerers and I've read all their notes. Here is the problem, or rather the two problems, which I will lay out so you may see how idiotic your made-up 'discovery' is: first, while in the Æther you would be at the mercy of thousands of unbound demons, and second, even if by some miracle you were able to survive, most sorcerers believe that you cannot simply translocate back from the demon plane, otherwise demons would infest our world. In fact, many believe that you cannot translocate to the demon plane at all. So you see, Penfold, you are not nearly as cunning as you believe you are."

"In the first place, if a demon brings you to the plane, they will guard you against others. And in the second—"

"Nonsense," Victor scoffed. "Your binding spell would not survive the transition. Demons who are dismissed without being unbound do not return bound, as Master Halis discovered a hundred years ago and his students recorded. All that work to pull apart the dismissal and unbinding spell, and for nothing."

"That's why you need an unbound demon to take you. One you can trust."

"You can't trust a demon. There are two accounts of sorcerers who thought they could trust their demons, and both of those accounts are written by other people after those sorcerers disappeared."

Kip flicked his ears. "To the demon plane, perhaps, as I did."

Victor's scowl remained, but his tone grew less dismissive. "And how did you manage to come back, then?"

"A summoning spell. But it has to be someone who knows your sorcerer name."

"Ridiculous." But Victor said it more softly and he turned to look at Farley. "And you have a demon you can trust, do you?"

"Master Gupta told you that I summoned a demon and didn't bind it. You didn't believe him."

"I still don't. It's a fairy story. You're trained—you would never do something like that." Now Victor paced back and forth. "This demon...it's still out there?"

Kip's heart gave a leap. He had Victor now, hooked on the idea. "As far as I know. I haven't any magic, so I can't feel the link."

"It's being kept away by the wards." Victor stopped his pacing. "Is this a trick to get me to drop the wards? You should know that I have altered the spell slightly. The few seconds that allowed your student to escape have been eliminated."

"Then what are you worried about? That I have somehow worked out a signal with Emily that at this precise time she should attempt to translocate to us? Malcolm and I don't even know what time it is beyond your pronouncements of 'morning' and 'evening.' And we haven't any magic to contact her."

"Very well," Victor said, clasping his hands together. "If you've been there, describe the Æther to me."

This, Kip had been ready for. He had 'seen' the plane of fire elementals, and had talked to Nikolon about what her home was like. "It's like floating in a sea of power. You can perceive the demons all around you but there are no physical features to distinguish them. But you can sense the difference. A little like when you dream of someone and you know who it is."

"Conveniently vague. So the question is whether I trust you, a desperate cornered animal, or my own studies and research." Victor turned to the fire creature. "Demon. Does this description sound accurate to you?"

"I cannot judge what the fox may have seen on his trip to the demon plane. I cannot even say how another demon would perceive it."

"Would you say that this description aligns with your own perception?"

"Depending on how one chooses to translate the perceptions of senses that do not exist on this plane, it might or might not."

"You're as useless as he is," Victor snapped.

"Do you know Saint Gregory the Great?" Kip said quickly, before Victor could turn further away from going to the demon plane. "He said, 'Illiterate men can contemplate in the lines of a picture what they cannot learn by means of the written word.' I think that's very profound, don't you?"

The cell fell silent. Farley coughed. "Is 'e calling you illiterate?"

"In a sense." Victor rubbed his chin thoughtfully. "I suppose that the only real danger is that I try it and I can't come back. So since you've been there before, we'll send you first and then Farley will bring you back. Once I see that, I'll go."

"What if he comes back with magic and burns us all up?" Farley asked.

"Mmm. Yes." Victor smiled. "This is quite the fascinating puzzle to solve. A pity it's likely to be for naught. We'll go together, then. If he gains magic, I will too. And Farley, if you can't bring me back tonight, bash O'Brien's head against the wall and then go to Peachtree and kill as many as you can." He turned a bland gaze on Kip. "Does that sound fair to you?"

"Except in that it rests on Farley's competence as a spellcaster," Kip said. "But I've seen him summon demons, so I suppose he can cast that spell, at least."

"Don't imagine I'll be bringin' you back," Farley sneered.

"You bring up a good point, though. All right, then, another safeguard. Demon!" The fire-creature inclined its head toward him. "Go to the top of the tallest tower in this building and remain invisible. When the first rays of the morning sun reach you, go to Peachtree in America and kill as many of its residents as you can."

"Yes, sir." The demon disappeared.

Victor turned to Kip. "There you are. Now, are you still going to insist on this story?"

If the wards were lowered, he could tell Nikolon to warn Emily or Alice, and could try to speak through Ash for a moment. He still held out hope that Victor would be trapped with him in the demon plane, unable to return, and if his hope was in vain, then at least he'd spared his family. "I'll take you to the demon plane, where you can forge a link to magic, and then Farley will summon you back. When you're back, you'll call off the demon."

"I still say it's a trick," Farley said. "Don't just go on his say-so."

Victor turned to the marmot with an expression of open disdain for Farley. It must be no secret between them. "I don't trust him, but I do trust his pathetic savior complex as regards his people. If he, knowing that their destruction is at hand if he lies, continues to hold to his story, then that convinces me more than even Master Gupta's reading would. People may cloud their thoughts, but put their backs to a wall and find what they value most, and you will get the truth out of them every time."

"Hang on," Farley said. "You say you can give anyone magic. How is it you only got one student out of all them Callies?"

Victor turned back to Kip with raised eyebrows. Kip took a moment to think of a reasonable answer. "You don't imagine we'd bring all of our magical students to the Exposition, do you? It works best on younger people and many of them aren't ready for schooling yet."

"See?" Farley smacked his fist against the bars. "He got an answer for everything. Just let me break one of his paws and he'll tell you the truth all right. Or one of O'Brien's, don't matter to me."

"Enough." Victor glared at Farley. "I have anticipated all of the risks, and he is willing to risk his home. I am tired of explaining to you why I believe that." He half-turned to Kip, still talking to Farley. "Maybe, given enough time, I could draw you a picture."

In truth, Kip was only sure that Nikolon could take them to the demon plane. He wasn't sure what would happen afterward. But he had thought about what he would do as soon as the wards were down.

Farley shook his head and opened his mouth again, but Victor snapped, "I said that's enough. Summon your demon back here."

"What, cast the spell again? Just tell it to come back."

"I'm not linked to it," Victor said patiently. "Say its name and tell it to come back."

"You can't just say 'Poatencia.' It isn't—"

Victor interrupted, his face reddening. "Not aloud! Not in front of others, especially other sorcerers!"

The marmot shrugged. "What they gonna do? They got no magic."

Victor looked like he wanted to choke Farley. "Fine. Then cast the spell again, just be quick about it."

"What, the summoning spell?"

"No, you imbecile, the spell to fly you up to where the demon is so you can tell it to come back." Victor pressed fingers to his forehead. "Yes, the summoning spell."

Farley grumbled but cast the spell again, and the demon reappeared with a pop and a sharp tingle in Kip's nose. "Yes, master?" he said.

"Go find Master Seric and tell him to drop the wards for fifteen minutes. That should be enough, wouldn't you say?"

Kip's ears flicked. Nikolon couldn't get to America and back in that time, but hopefully Emily had come to the Isle to look for them, or Alice was still there. Or anyone he could trust. "It depends on how far my demon has wandered in the time you've had me a prisoner here."

"It will have been looking to return to you, will it not? It knows you are around the college, so it should be able to find you."

"She's unbound," Kip said. "I don't know what she's been doing. I couldn't talk to her without magic anyway." He hoped Victor would not question the lie.

"Fifteen minutes it is." Victor turned to the fire-creature. "Demon, go now, and then resume your wait at the top of the tower. Return here in fifteen minutes."

"Yes, master." The demon vanished again.

Victor crossed his arms. "Now, you had best hope your demon is worthy of your trust."

Kip was already calling out silently to Nikolon, telling her to find Emily or Alice on the Isle if she could, and to tell them to summon him with the demon summoning spell in half an hour (Emily knew his sorcerer name, as he knew hers), and also to tell them that a demon might be coming to attack them at sunrise in London time, and then to come find him and make herself visible. And to please hurry because the wards around him would only be down for fifteen minutes.

He repeated that message as Victor checked his timepiece, and then repeated it again, over and over, reciting it as though it were a spell he were casting without magic out into a silent void.

"Ten minutes," Victor said casually, looking at his timepiece again.

Kip tuned him out, reciting his plea over and over again. Every moment he hoped to hear a pop in the air and see Nikolon's form.

"Five minutes."

Please hurry, Kip thought, and started his request over again.

A pop, a sharp tingle in his nose, but the shape on the other side of his bars was not a female fox-Calatian. Victor looked at his timepiece and gave an approving nod. "Very punctual."

"Wait!" Kip cried. "Just a few more minutes."

Victor slid the timepiece back into his pocket. "I am a little disappointed," he said, "but the consolation prize is quite worthwhile. Demon!"

"Yes, master?" the demon said, smoke trickling thinly from its smoldering "hair."

Victor pointed at Kip. "Read the spell in my mind and cast it on that fox."

Kip called out to Nikolon one last time, and then closed his eyes. He prayed to Saint Gregory and to God to keep him and his family safe.

"Wait!" Malcolm called from the other cell. "I can—"

Hunger gnawed at the fox's stomach. He spun on the stone floor, disoriented, while around him large humans made noises, some loud and rhythmic, some almost soft and musical. They smelled terrible, and one of them had marked this area with his piss, a thick rank odor that the fox backed away from.

He knew those odors, though; they were familiar, as though they frequented his home. And when he backed away, he caught movement behind him and found a beaver scuttling away. Hunger drove him forward a step, but beavers were only prey for the desperate: heavier than a fox and good fighters, they might easily injure him. And besides...this beaver's scent too held something familiar that made him pause. Even were he starving, it would not be prey.

The large humans stood to one side of the large open area, and one of them held up paws that glowed with a dark light that hurt the fox's eyes to look at. Another, a strange creature that looked like a burning human, hurt his nose if he got too close to it. Their noises and scents scared him, so he bolted to the far side of the bars and darted through and down the hall.

They made barks of alarm behind him, and a moment later he found himself floating in the air, his legs kicking at nothing. He yelped in alarm, and this brought the rhythmic barks from them again. The rank one whose urine he'd smelled came closer—but he was not walking; the fox was floating toward him. Though the fox flailed, he couldn't move, so he bared his teeth.

The human wasn't deterred. He reached out a great paw, and the fox tried to bite it but found he couldn't open his jaw. He growled as the meaty paw touched his fur, grabbed his tail, and pulled. He was pushed against iron bars beyond which another human lay on the floor, one with a disfigured face, and there were more barks all around as he struggled to gain his freedom.

There was a pop and the sharpness that hurt his nose again. The human holding him let go with an alarmed bark as another human with the coloring of a fox appeared.

The fox-human barked in a high, melodic voice, and the other human responded. They barked back and forth while the fox struggled to find a foothold on anything and the rank human remained with its paw on his neck, occasionally making a bark of his own. At one point the paw tightened enough that the fox's breathing became labored, but then it loosened again.

This went on for some time; the fox lost track until it felt as though there was only the air and the hunger in his stomach. And then the fox-human took him in her arms, and after a reflexive struggle, he relaxed, at ease even though his nose stung enough that he sneezed twice. He trusted her more than any of the other humans here.

She murmured something into his ear. The melodic human—not the rank one—came to stand beside them. And then the world turned inside out.

CHAPTER TWENTY:

THE GREAT FEAT

Smells suffused the air, more variety than the fox could remember experiencing, and his nose stung so badly that he rubbed it with a paw. He was floating again, but without the unbalanced feel that he'd had floating in the air. This was more like swimming, but his fur felt different, more sensitive, as though his body were whiskers all over and motion registered from all sides.

The female fox-human was still with him, though he couldn't say how he knew that, and the other human was nearby as well. After a moment he picked them out in the fog around him, even though their appearances and smells had changed. She was a sandstorm larger than him or maybe just very close up, smelling of a sharp spice; the human was bright blue with a silver cord trailing behind him like a tail, off out of the fox's sight, and he no longer smelled flowery, but just of meat and earth and fear, though the acrid <leffikfar> scent was dissipating.

The sandstorm came closer to him and enveloped him, and noises thrummed through him, not in his ears. He turned to find the source of the noise and saw a silver tail extending from the end of his own tail, stretching away. He tried to curl it, but it would not respond to him.

The noises in his mind grew different, familiar enough that he forgot his tail. They drew his attention as though they were smells telling him something.

...understand me. Please tell me when you understand me.

He understood. He could not figure out how to make a noise back, but the first noise he wanted to make was the fox-human's name, and he thought it. *Nikolon?*

It worked! Do you know your name?

I'm...Kip. Kip Penfold. Awareness and memory came back in patchwork form, sparingly at first and then stronger. *Victor stole my magic?*

He's restored it. For the moment. But he is...he is attempting something great and terrible.

Who is? Victor?

The bright blue spoke with Victor's intonations. *Welcome back, Penfold, and thank you. With this power, I can complete the charge laid on me by the Crown. When Broadside summons me back, I will undo Calatus's Great Feat and take in all the magic he wasted. I thought it would take decades, but—*

No! Kip cried. *You promised!*

I will keep my promise, Victor said. *I will leave you and yours alone— entirely alone. You will be the only Calatians left in the world, and when you have passed away, there will be no more. America's power will crumble, as will Spain's, and the British Empire, with my magic, will reign supreme. Perhaps in two or three decades, I will summon you, so you may see—*

He vanished.

The sandstorm around him retreated and radiated concern with a voice like a fluttering breeze. *I tried to help. I did what you asked.*

Having his awareness come back to him in this bizarre place made everything else seem unreal. The—not air, not water, but the medium, the æther, perhaps—that he floated in brought new odors to his nose every moment, some of them physical odors like pine and apples, some of them specific, like the smell of a desert morning (which Kip recognized despite never having been to a desert), and some of them curious, like a smell that made him think of the color of Alice's ears, or one that smelled like a song Arabella had sung.

Similarly, except for the sandstorm and his own body, which looked approximately like a nude fox-Calatian made of violet light so far as he could tell, nothing that his "eyes" focused on for more than a moment remained the same. Here a patch of green that looked like a far-off hillside melted into a school of silvery fish; there a chimaera of horse and lizard shifted into a giant serpent which then birthed a bird that grew and changed from brown fur to golden feathers; there a wall of stone became glass and then loam with worms crawling out of it.

So Kip focused on Nikolon. *You gave Emily my message?*

Emily was not on the Isle. Neither was Alice. I searched for a long time but could not find either of them. That is why I was late.

And Victor made you bring him here?

I agreed to bring him if he would attempt to reverse the spell on you.

He brought a "hand" up in front of his "eyes," a glowing violet appendage that moved approximately in line with his thoughts. Having something to focus on comforted him as he turned his head around to find a part of the sandstorm he could talk to. *It seems to have worked.*

Here, Nikolon said. *Perhaps I can make you more comfortable.*

Kip's surroundings brightened and gained a sense of up and down. He sat on a warm surface, invisible at first but which became warm ocher stone that resisted his fingers with a gritty texture. In front of him, a golden fountain sprayed sparkling water into high arcs from the mouths of a nude young man and three water-serpent creatures that played around him, and the water even smelled real. Around the fountain spread a garden of flowers in bright colors and patterns Kip was sure he had never seen, and yet he knew the flowers and knew this place.

A nude vixen appeared on the bench next to him. Nikolon swished her tail. "Sometimes I create this place to sit in."

"This is the garden from my dream. Did you put this dream in my head?"

"When I was unbound, yes." She bowed her head.

"And that's what you meant by 'curses take many forms'?"

"I am cursed with these fragments of dream. I shared the curse with you."

In the fountain, a fish surfaced briefly, drawing Kip's attention. "Is this a place you were summoned to a long time ago?"

"I am not sure. I confess I hoped you might know the place and help me understand what it means." Nikolon folded her paws in her lap. "If you wish to be clothed, you need only imagine yourself so."

Kip looked down at himself, his body appearing the way he'd always known it, and then back at Nikolon. "I've been dreaming about this and the march through the streets and the boats for two years. I still don't understand it, except for the feelings of betrayal."

"This is the happiest of those three dreams." Nikolon stared ahead at the fountain.

"Perhaps you had another master, one you could trust, or thought you could, but he betrayed you? A long time ago?"

She nodded. "Perhaps."

"What is the earliest thing you remember?"

The vixen smiled. "Time does not proceed as you know it. I remember certain masters I have had, and I remember scenes, important points, and spells I've done. But the order..." She gestured with a paw. "It comes and goes. I remember helping you rescue Alice, but that feels like many years ago. I also helped a sorcerer during the wars against the Frenchman, which could have been yesterday. I remember very clearly the fabric of the French uniforms."

"How do demons come to being?" Kip asked. "Do you have children, or..."

Nikolon's laugh sounded like the bright splashing of the fountain. "New demons appear. Sometimes old demons fade away."

"Then maybe these are memories around a sorcerer who summoned you. Is that why you trust me?"

"I trust you because you trust me. And because when I think of betrayal it makes me uneasy. I don't like it." A cloud passed over the illusory sun. The flowers drooped and their scent acquired an acrid tinge.

"I'm glad that you trusted me." Kip closed his eyes. "Even if it was all for nothing."

"I'm sorry," Nikolon said. "I did not know he was going to do that."

"He must have hated us for years. Or he accepted us when we weren't a threat and hated us when we were. And the British Empire wanted us exterminated, all for a few more years of power." The flowers had perked up and their scent was sweet again. "I thought that having our own place would be protection enough, but it wasn't. I don't know whether anything could have been."

Nikolon remained quiet. The stillness and peace of the garden made Kip loath to speak again, but finally he did. "This is very nice," he said. "Do you mind if I sit here with you now and then over the next few decades?"

"I cannot keep this here for very long," she said. "At least, I don't think so."

"Do you spend time with other demons?"

"Some of them. There are two whose names I remember. I saw one of them recently." She paused. "I think."

Would his memory also be affected? Would he start to lose the faces and scents and voices of his family and friends? He searched for them in his mind and found them still there, and that was a comfort. A more recent memory was hazy, though. "Was I really a fox? An animal fox? I—I remember it, but it feels like a dream. Then again, this all feels like a dream too."

"You were a fox. I could feel that it was you, but the barest flicker of you. There was enough that I thought with magic, you could come back."

"And I did."

"I'm...glad." Nikolon looked down at her paws again. "I did not want to betray you."

"You haven't. You've been...a revelation. Trusting you was terrifying— you saw how Malcolm behaved, let alone Victor."

Nikolon nodded. The soft sounds of the fountain continued to wash over them. "May I ask what you thought would happen when you and Victor were brought here?"

Kip drew in a breath and only then realized that he had not been breathing. He could not hear his heartbeat. The realization disturbed him, but in the grand scheme of things it was rather minor. "I thought the most likely scenario was that we would be trapped here. That would have been fine. He would have been away from where he could hurt anyone, and I would have been here but I would have saved everyone else. If you told Alice about the demon, I feel that she and Emily would have handled it, and perhaps Farley would have killed Malcolm—probably—but he was at peace with dying as well.

"I hoped that if Farley did summon him back, that Emily would be able to summon me as well. But Victor got summoned back, and that means that Alice is…" Emotion choked off his words, even though he wasn't physically breathing.

In front of him, a four-legged fox appeared. It walked around and then sat, curling its tail around its feet and watching him.

"Did you do that?" Kip sat up straight.

Nikolon shook her head. "You did."

He wished the fox away, and it vanished. He folded his paws together and sat staring ahead at the fountain and the flowers.

After a little while, Nikolon said, "If Emily summons me, I might remember to tell her she can summon you. I will try very hard."

"I don't know if she knows your name. Malcolm did." He called a raven into being. "I wonder what happened to Ash. Malcolm's probably dead by now or drained of magic."

"He can drain humans also?"

Kip nodded and told Nikolon briefly about Richard's dull, unintelligent state. The demon considered this. "It is in some ways like the way demons are treated. Our will is taken from us and we are bound to another's service."

"It happens all over," Kip said. "Those who can bind others do so. People in our country still own other people, not with magic or anything, just because they have power over them."

"We have so much power here, but take us out of this realm and we are easily bound," Nikolon said.

"It's funny." Kip tried to place a peach tree in flower next to the fountain and got a misshapen blob with a few defined patches of leaves and flowers. But the scent was perfect. "Victor said everyone should have access to magic, which I think is right. But what he meant was: humans who can afford to pay him should have access to the magic he can give them." Kip shook his head. "I suppose I should be grateful that he was so determined to be the only one with that power that he hasn't told anyone else about his spell. Imagine if he had a whole army of sorcerers who could take magic out of people."

"He has enough magic now to do it all himself."

Kip reflected back to Victor's last words. "This would be small consolation, but...he doesn't really know what happened at the Road. Do you remember that?"

Nikolon nodded. "That moment was extraordinary."

"I've thought about it a lot. I think that everyone assumes that Cott died because there was so much heat and boiling water and the ship almost capsized, or else they think I killed him. I didn't," he hastened to add.

"I know."

"I think that what killed him was the amount of magic he used to undo the Great Feat. And I did a little bit of research about the Great Feats. The sorcerers who accomplished them never did anything again after that. The ones I could find records on died; the others disappeared, except for one Chinese sorcerer who toured the country after creating the terracotta army, but there are several reports that say that he wasn't the one who did that, just someone who took his name to profit from."

"I don't know what a Great Feat is."

"It's a magical spell that remains permanently in the world and hasn't been duplicated. There are only—well, I thought five, but I think there are more in India and so there are probably some elsewhere too."

"To remain permanently in that material world requires a binding of a sort."

Kip nodded. "I think that the sorcerer dies when he casts a Great Feat. Like maybe somehow his life becomes the binding. And undoing one also works the same way except that it takes a life to remove a binding. So... maybe my people will all be reduced to animals, but Victor will die from trying it. I would never have taken that bargain, if offered." The reality of it all still felt very distant. He worked on his peach tree, firming up the visual aspects of it until it more closely resembled an actual tree. If he stopped paying attention to it, it would lose definition.

"We know the spell can be reversed," Nikolon said. "And the other demon knew Victor's spell. And you know that other demon's name."

"We know that, and we're stuck here," Kip said. "There's no way out except being summoned."

"For a demon." Nikolon pointed behind him. "No demon has that."

The silver tail streamed out from his tail, like a silken cord floating in water. "Victor had that too."

"What does it feel like to you?"

He reached up to it with a paw, but his paw passed through the silver without breaking it. He focused on it like the peach tree, trying to manipulate it, and encountered resistance. "It feels like not part of this world."

"Maybe it's a link back to your world."

"Maybe." Kip stared at the silver stream again, and then a small pop sounded, faint, but one that resonated all through him, as though he were a water elemental in a pond and someone had thrown a stone in.

In a moment, the garden and fountain vanished, replaced by the ever-changing chaos again. This time more demons swirled around them, fish-tailed people and clouds of formless yellow smoke and dragons and a giant bird with snakes for feathers and still more. And near them was a brightly glowing blue outline of a human.

A demon is appearing. Nikolon moved toward it as many other demons did, closing quickly. *I have only seen this a few times. Hurry!*

Kip moved behind her, matching her speed. As he approached, a darker light that hurt his eyes showed in patches beneath the blue. *Victor?* Kip asked before he could help himself.

The human outline turned toward him, staring through the crowd of demons closing in on it. It had no face, no features except for a mouth that moved. *I know you, I think,* it said in Victor's voice. *You're Penfold, the one who stole everything I wanted from me.*

Small bits of silver rose from Victor like embers and fizzled out in the void. Some of the demons that had arrived first raced to capture them before they dissipated. *I got boats!* one of them called. A great schooner came into being around that demon and sailed away.

Another said, *London has changed so much,* and melted into a human dressed in formal wear.

Nikolon captured a spark and uttered a cry of revulsion. She loosed the spark into the void, where it faded out. *Cruelty,* she said.

One silver spark floated toward Kip. He grasped it and into his head burst the image of the King's College library, the smell of dusty old books, his fine white-skinned hand reaching down to turn the page.

What did you do? Kip asked Victor.

I did what I had to do to restore balance to the Earth. I—I— The blue shape turned around, only now seeming to notice that it was giving off sparks. *I have magic.*

Did you cast the spell? Kip noticed now that there was no silver behind Victor, nothing trailing off into the distance.

The blue featureless face studied him. *You're Penfold,* it said, as if just realizing this again. *I don't like you.*

One particularly bright spark drifted up from the blue form. Victor cried out and reached for it, but his ill-formed hand missed it. Kip reached out and took the spark and—

He stood in the hallway where he'd recently been a four-legged fox, and less recently a prisoner. The smells were dull, muted, but every fleck of rust on the iron bars, every crack in the stone walls and floor, stood out in sharp relief. Power flowed through him, more than he'd ever felt, more than he'd imagined was possible. He took a step back and looked down at Malcolm, lying against the wall of his cell. "I'll deal with you after," he said in Victor's cruel voice. "For now, count yourself lucky. You are one of the few to witness a Great Feat." He reached deep inside himself, felt the power there, and drew it up to send out into the world. He knew how spells were cast, knew the strength of his own will, knew that the Calatians were the rust of the world, the cracks in its stone over which good men like himself tripped, and he set about to mend them. The beaver, the squirrel, the polecat, the rabbit, and most of all, the fox, all the ones he'd drawn magic from burned bright in his memory, his successes, but now he did not have to patch each crack laboriously by hand. Now he could feel them all out there, all of the worthless animals given magic by a fool, and he gathered them up in his grip. A few he left alone, mindful of his promise and savoring the pain they would feel, but the others...he flexed his power, squeezed...and nothing happened. Impossible. He had the power, he had the will, this would work. It had to work. Fury built in him, desperation, conviction that he was the only one who could repair this terrible wrong—and power crackled around him, and all the Calatians in his grip, he could feel them squirming like worms and he tightened his grip, and magic flowed out of them, all over the world, from them into him—and the spell ended, he had done it, he had— he had—darkness flooding into him, his awareness fading? He collapsed to the ground, death's hand around his heart as surely as he had held the Calatians a moment before.

Kip struggled free from the memory with a cry. *You filthy—*

Victor's shape, still undefined, managed nevertheless to radiate pleasure. *Have I done something to offend you? Good. I should never have restored you. You were better as an animal.*

Nikolon, again a whirling sandstorm, enfolded Kip. *Leave him,* she said.

They sat again in the garden next to the fountain. Kip's peach tree remained there, but Victor was nowhere to be seen, nor were any of the other demons. The fox's paws shook. "That—that—" he said. "He did it. He erased the Calatians."

"Not you," Nikolon said.

Kip wasn't breathing, not as he remembered it, but imagining the slow rhythms helped calm him. He knew that he should be trying to find a way back, to undo Victor's monstrous act, but another realization struck him. "And then he died. He unbound a Great Feat and he died. And then..." He pieced together what he'd just seen. "That was a demon. Victor...became a demon."

Nikolon nodded slowly. "I have seen that before, the giving off of memories. We take the ones we can because they are something new, something interesting. I never knew where they came from. I thought the demons bore the memories of their creator, perhaps."

Kip stared at the fountain, still trying to process this. "He came here and lost his memories, and he'll be here. Not in Heaven, not in Hell, but... but in the Æther."

The two foxes sat in silence while the fountain went on burbling and the sweet smell of peach blossoms filled the air. Kip thought again about all the Calatians in the world and turned his mind away from those thoughts. There was nothing he could do until someone summoned him back. "Then those memories you have," Kip said. "Those are yours. You were human once."

"Was I?"

"You lived a long time ago, to judge from the boats and the city. I've never seen anything like them."

"Perhaps I did. I don't recall."

"Were you a sorcerer? Are all the demons spirits of sorcerers?"

Nikolon shook her head. "It could be so. Every demon I know is familiar with magic."

"I wonder if I could find Cott. Or Coppy." Kip's mind raced. "Do you know how to find a demon by name here?"

"No. We can find other demons we know, sometimes, and we can see other demons near us, but I cannot just call a name and have the demon answer. This world is vast."

They could summon the recently dead back from the demon plane, they could raise the spirits of sorcerers long-dead...and then Kip remembered the sparks coming off Victor, the way his spirit had lost bits of memory just in the short time Kip had seen him. Would he want to raise Coppy or Cott, knowing their spirit might not even remember him or understand an apology? Just imagining it made the garden dim and the peach tree wilt.

So he reached over and took Nikolon's paw. "We solved your mystery. Those images you remember: they're from your life. You were human, you were brought to another city and made to serve a king, and a friend betrayed you."

She met his eyes and nodded. "So it seems."

"Does that help you?"

"Not really." She smiled. "I understand the images but that doesn't help them become part of me."

"Were you a female sorcerer?"

Again she shook her head. "I took on female guises to tempt sorcerers. But I liked it. Some time ago I began to keep them even when I was back here. That much I do remember." Her paw felt warm in his, and malleable like the surface of water. "Thank you. For trusting me and for helping me."

"You've repaid my trust and help a hundredfold. If not for you, I'd still be running around King's College on four legs looking for a mouse to eat."

She laughed. "I feel that somehow, even on four legs, you would have managed to be an extraordinary fox."

"Thank you." He splayed his ears. "There are so many four-footed now, former Calatians. I hate that I'm stuck here with no way to help them. We restored me, so once I get back I can work on a spell to restore others, but who knows how long that will be?"

Nikolon motioned for him to turn around. "Now perhaps I may help you. Look at that silver trailing from you. No demon has it. Tell me about it again."

Victor had lost his silver cord but Kip still had one. If it was indeed a hallmark of someone living sent to the demon world, then perhaps Kip could follow it back to his world. He turned his head so he could see its brightness stretching away from him to an unseen end. "I feel it, but I can't touch it. It's like...someone holding my paw, but I can't let go and I can't even figure out what paw they're holding."

"What else?"

He shook his head. "It's just...there." He tried speaking to it, as he did with Peter in the stones of the Lutris School, but nothing responded to him. "I can't talk to it. I can't grasp it."

"Can you cast spells here?"

"You can alter this world by thought. What good would a spell do?" But he tried, reciting the simple fire spell he'd first learned years ago. Fire burst into being in front of him before he'd even finished the words. "Hang on," he said. "I'm thinking about the fire, not the spell." He extinguished the fire and tried again, but with the same result. "I don't know. I can cast spells, maybe, but magic is all around me and there's no need to channel it. I just take it and shape it and it's done."

"I brought you here with a spell," Nikolon said patiently. "I can't go back with a spell, but maybe you can."

"Oh!" Kip stared up at the silver cord, shimmering as it stretched away. He envisioned the hallway outside the cell where he'd been kept, where Malcolm and Richard still languished, and channeled magic into it.

The stones of the cell came into being around him. He turned to look for Malcolm and saw the shimmering trail of the silver cord. When he turned back, Nikolon sat next to him. She looked around. "I remember this place. You wanted to go here?"

Kip nodded. "I want to rescue Malcolm. Let me try again."

This time, he stared at the silver cord and imagined himself traveling along it, following it back to the place where the worlds joined. The stones of the cell melted away, leaving chaotic colors and shapes in their wake. As soon as Kip pictured his destination, they re-formed—and Nikolon was there again with him.

"Again."

He imagined the silver cord as a road, and himself walking along it, running along it, back to the material world.

"Again."

A different destination, more familiar. Pulling himself along the silver cord rather than running.

"Again."

He pictured Alice, Emily, Abel, as though translocating to them. Each time, they appeared in front of him and his heart leapt until he saw Nikolon as well, and then he banished the simulacrum with a growl.

"Again."

After some number of fruitless attempts, frustration boiled over in him. Even if Victor had kept his promise to leave Alice alone, would Abel be four-footed now? Regardless, the rest of the Calatians were animals. Emily (and maybe Alice) was all alone with no idea what had happened, and he, the only one who could offer even the smallest amount of help, was trapped here. If he couldn't figure out a way back, all of his friends were going to be doomed forever.

"Again."

Jorey and the Cottons and Ella Lutris and even Grinda, all of them, all the Calatians gone now. Alice and Abel and his family would maybe survive longer, but alone in the world, dying out and taking his race with them. His cub might be the last Calatian ever born, ever.

He prayed to whomever might be listening, and then remembered M. Dieuleveult and his relics, the one relic that had shimmered with magic. If some saints were sorcerers, and sorcerers became demons, then maybe M. Dieuleveult's prayers to the saints had been calls to the Æther, and the relic—the real one—the conduit through which those calls were passed.

He pictured the old bone, the feel of it and the magic in it, and searched for it, and there—maybe—was a faint echo, a reply. He held onto that hope as the need to return burned in him, consumed him until all the restraints he'd learned and practiced for years fell away, leaving nothing but the fire of need, desire shaping him into a hard diamond of purpose.

This time when he tried he felt a rushing sensation and then a compression, as though he were being squeezed into the narrow cord to fit through a small opening with it. He made himself small, kept his emotions burning bright in his mind, and pushed his way through the constriction.

Color and scent disappeared. Darkness closed around him, a tight fist that he wriggled through like the first licks of flame through a pile of wood. Even the silver cord vanished from his sight. No smells reached his nose; no sounds reached his ears.

And then light grew ahead of him and the world unfolded and he landed with a thump on the carpet of Emily's office.

CHAPTER TWENTY-ONE:

RECONSTRUCTION

The carpet lay cool and solid under his paws. Moonlight leaked through the closed shutters, and the office was empty. Nikolon was nowhere to be seen, and Kip felt solid. He smelled Emily and Sleek and Chakrabarti as well as Emily's carpet and all her old books, and realized that he was breathing, and his heartbeat sounded in his ears.

He reached for magic, but the block was still there. So he scrambled to his feet and hurried out the door.

The school lay quiet and sleeping around him. Emily's chambers were one floor up, and all the way down the hall and up the stairs Kip heard no movement. When he got to Emily's door, however, her voice floated through the door to him. "Feeling better? That's got to be a good sign. Maybe there's hope after all. Come on, you want to eat a bit?"

Relief washed through him. He rapped on the door to alert her and then opened it and practically ran inside.

Emily stood staring at the door, her fingers resting on a perch with a raven on it. Another raven stood on the small table just below it. As Kip stepped inside, Emily ran over to him and threw her arms around him. "Kip! Oh God, we feared—Alice told me—"

He hugged her back as tightly as he could. "Alice. How—where is Alice?"

"I sent her home. Where's Malcolm? Is he with you?"

"No, he—" Kip rested his head on her shoulder. "He's still with Vic—well—he's still a prisoner. I don't have magic right now. Is Chakrabarti around? No, wait. I need to find Alice first. Have you been here all night?"

Emily stepped back but kept her hands on Kip's shoulders. "Alice and I were going to go back to the Isle first thing in the morning to keep looking for you two, so she went to get some rest."

"Victor cast a spell—" He made for the door. "I have to go find her and Abel."

"Hang on." Emily held his arm. "The first thing you have to do is put on clothes."

"I've got clothes at my house!"

"I've got a tunic here somewhere, just wait."

As she stepped over to the wardrobe to look, the raven standing on the desk jumped toward Kip, fluttering, but did not stay airborne, landing on the carpet and walking the rest of the way. Kip knelt to collect her, and she jumped into his paws. He couldn't reach her mind, but he knew her smell and feel. "Ash?"

"Yes." Emily turned with a tunic. "We brought her back with Alice, and she was worried but seemed healthy until an hour ago, when she fell off the perch. I forced her to take some water, but she wouldn't eat. I thought—" She held the tunic out to him. "I thought you'd been killed."

"Wait here just a moment," Kip said to Ash, setting her back on the carpet. He stood to take the tunic and pulled it over his head. It smelled like Malcolm and came down to mid-thigh, so it would do. "I—had been. In a way."

"You can tell me in a moment," Emily said. "Alice will be so relieved to see you."

Kip collected Ash and held her in the crook of his elbow. Emily put a hand on his shoulder and in a moment they stood outside the front door of his house.

What would they find? He hesitated before opening the door. Right now Alice was still the Calarian he knew, pregnant with their cub; she and Abel and his cubs were still the family Kip loved.

"You don't have to knock." Emily reached out and opened the door, and the two of them walked inside.

The house was as silent as the school had been. Emily whispered, "The Dieuleveults are up in your room so…"

"Alice will be with Abel," Kip said, walking slowly up the stairs with his eye on that door. Emily trailed behind him.

He padded past his own bedroom to Abel's and stopped there, ears perked. Only the low sounds of breathing came from the other side. He eased the door open.

On the bed, outlined by the light of the moon, two shapes lay under the blankets—the shapes of Alice and Abel, their heads resting on separate pillows, not four-legged foxes but still the people he loved. He ran to the bed and put a paw on Alice's shoulder, calling her name and then Abel's.

She stirred, and on the other side of the bed, Abel did too. But Alice rose first, blinked sleep from her eyes, and then seized Kip, holding him tightly against her so that Ash was knocked off his arm and fluttered to the floor. "You're safe," she cried, muffled by his fur.

Abel lifted himself to his elbows on the other side of her and reached over as well, grasping Kip's shoulder with a smile. Kip nodded back, pressing his muzzle between Alice's and Abel's. The memory of Victor casting the Great Feat felt dreamlike now. Maybe Victor hadn't succeeded? "I'm safe, and—and so are you."

"You warned me, so I came back here. Emily and I were going to go find you in the morning."

"She told me." He nuzzled her again and then reached out to grasp Abel's arm. "I'm so glad you're both all right."

"Both of us?" Alice released him. "Me and Emily?"

"You and Abel." He picked up Ash and stood. "I still don't have magic. We need to find Chakrabarti and then we need to go rescue Malcolm."

"I'll get him," Emily said from the doorway. "You three take a little time. And be presentable when we get back."

"We will." The urgency had left Kip now that he'd seen Alice and Abel safe.

"And don't tell them anything until I get back." Emily closed the door behind her.

Alice hugged Kip again, pressing her nose to the tunic, and then drew back. "Why are you wearing Malcolm's clothes?"

"Because Victor took mine." Kip climbed up onto the bed so he could embrace both of them. "I'll tell you everything later, and I need to get dressed—"

"As do we all," Abel said with a smile.

"But I just want to be here with you, for a short time."

"A short time now, but a long time later," Alice said, and those words were all that Kip wanted to hear.

Some fifteen minutes later, dressed appropriately, the three of them sat downstairs waiting for Emily and Chakrabarti. Kip's apprehension had returned despite the dreamlike feel of the memory of Victor's spell. Was the rest of Peachtree now a forest of animals? Without magic, he couldn't send Ash to look, and he didn't want to leave Alice and Abel, worried that the moment they were out of his sight they would be in danger again.

And even beyond the fate of the Calatians, Malcolm still languished in a cell somewhere thinking Kip was dead or trapped in the Æther, if he retained any intelligence at all. It felt selfish, in the face of all that, to sit with one paw held by Alice and one by Abel, but without magic, there was not much else he could do. It reminded him a little of the stillness of the garden he'd shared with Nikolon. Perhaps the true selfishness was in being glad that he had this time during which he couldn't do anything but be with the people he loved.

There was one thing he could do, it occurred to him. He could go next door to the Warner household and see if the dormice were all right. They weren't part of his family; they would not have been excluded from Victor's spell.

So he stood, and the other two stood with him. "I want to go next door. Have you seen the Warners, or anyone in town, in the last hour or two?"

"Not since we went to bed," Abel said. His ears folded down. "Why?"

"I hope I'm wrong." Kip led them to the door. "But please, let's go wake them up."

"If you think it's important," Alice said.

"I hope it's not," he replied, and stepped out into the cool Peachtree night.

Had he ever been out in town this late at night? The moon sat high in the sky, bright in the field of stars, and while he could hear the rustling of mice and other nocturnal animals through the grasses and bushes around the town, no other noises came to him. Was that normal for this hour?

They walked the short distance to the small wooden cottage where the Warners lived, two young dormice recently married who'd moved down to Peachtree from Boston. Abel knew them better than either Kip or Alice, so he walked up to the door and rapped sharply on it.

"Edward? Sharon?"

All three foxes listened intently. No sound came from the other side of the door.

Abel knocked again and called out, and still there was no answer. Kip sensed movement and spotted Emily and Chakrabarti at the front door of his house. He waved and called out softly, and the two sorcerers came over to them.

"What are you doing here?" Emily asked as Abel knocked again. "Did something happen to the..."

"Warners," Kip said.

Alice lifted her ear from the door. "I don't hear anything at all."

"Let's go in." Kip looked around. "Please. The magic Victor did on Jorey, he might have..."

Abel looked confused, but Alice's ears lay back against her head and she pulled the door open and strode inside before anyone else could move. "Edward!" she called. "Sharon!"

They followed her into the silent house. Kip's fur prickled at the stillness, made worse because none of them spoke. Even Alice stopped calling out names once she stepped into the dark parlor.

Alice checked two doors before she found the bedroom, and then she stepped back with a sigh of relief. "They're not here," she said. "Maybe they're spending the night somewhere else?"

She opened the door more widely so that everyone could see the empty bed, sheets disheveled. Emily put a hand on Kip's arm. "Why don't you let Chakrabarti look at you?"

Kip stared at the empty bed and then walked forward and pulled the sheet back. There, curled up in two little pockets of the sheets, lay two small dormice.

They stirred and then, as the foxes and sorcerers gaped, made high-pitched squeaks of alarm and bolted for different edges of the bed. "Alice!" Kip called. "Catch them!"

Still shocked, Alice nonetheless recovered in time to lift the dormice in the air and hold them there. Kip watched their flailing forms with sympathy. "We need to find a secure place to keep them. And we need to go around to all the other houses and do the same for all the other residents."

"Kip." Emily's voice shook. "What *happened?*"

Time pressed upon him. "Victor trapped us with the help of that beaver March, kept us in cells, used Farley to summon a demon, and turned March into a four-legged beaver, all because he believes he deserves to have magic. I convinced him he should let my demon take him to the demon plane and get magic there, hoping he'd leave us alone, but he made me come with him, and he said he was going to use the demon's power to steal magic from all the Calatians all over the world and then Farley summoned him back." He stared at the dormice. "And then he did it and I came back. Too late."

For a long moment, nobody said anything. "Oh my God," Emily breathed. "I suppose it's too much to hope that he made you imagine all of that."

Kip shook his head. "I didn't want to believe it was real, but it was. It is."

Alice sat heavily on the bed. "Why weren't Abel and I affected?"

"He promised not to harm me or my family or anyone associated with the school. He thought it would be amusing for us to be the last ones."

"There will be foxes left, at least," Emily said.

"Maybe more. I have an idea, but I need...magic, first." At his words, Chakrabarti came over. "But Emily, you need to go to Amsterdam and tell them to do the same in Dierenpark as we're doing here. Go to all the Calatian residences and keep the animals safe. Don't let them escape. And then Boston, New York, Philadelphia, Savannah..."

"I'll get Argent to help," Emily said. "New Cambridge, too. We still have friends in the college there."

"God, yes, New Cambridge. And Spain. I don't know anyone in Spain."

"I do." She stood. "I'd better get going, then. I'll take Ash and you take Sleek and we'll stay in touch with each other that way."

Kip held out Ash, who didn't want to leave him but reluctantly did so, and took back Sleek. Emily nodded grimly to him and was gone.

"What about the Isle?" Abel asked.

"I'll take care of the Isle after I rescue Malcolm." Kip hoped he could do both of those things.

"I'll go around the town," Alice said. "I'll collect as many as I can."

Kip leaned over to kiss her on the muzzle. "Thank you. I'll be back as soon as I can. I have to rescue Malcolm first."

Abel stood. "I'll go with her, then, if I won't be of use here." He leaned in for a kiss from Kip as well. "What if this Victor changes his mind and comes for us?"

"He won't." Kip set his jaw. "You have my word on that. He is not going to be a problem anymore."

At the door, Alice turned. "What did you do?"

"Nothing. He did it to himself. I promise, I'll tell you all about it later," Kip said.

"All right. I'll hold you to that."

And then she and Abel were gone, leaving Kip and Chakrabarti in the empty bedroom. "All the Calatians? In the world? This is quite extraordinary," Chakrabarti said.

"It is." Kip's tail swished. "And it's not over yet, I hope. Can you restore my magic?"

"Headmistress Carswell has been telling me of the problem. I have never done it," Chakrabarti said, "but I know of the practice. I believe I can help."

It took several minutes of trying, with apologies, but when Chakrabarti finally found the right method, magic flooded back into Kip and he felt whole again for the first time in days. Ash's awareness burst into his mind with such relief that he took a moment to turn his head to Sleek, now perched on his shoulder. Through Ash, he saw Emily's hair and Master Argent facing her, his eyes wide and horrified. "I have magic again," Kip said through Ash. "I'm on my way to London for Malcolm."

Emily turned, though he couldn't quite see her expression. "Thank you," she said. "I've just explained the situation. Master Argent will go to New Cambridge to get help there and in the northern American cities, Master Vendis will take the southern cities, and I'm on my way to Europe."

"Master Penfold," Argent rasped. "Is this really possible?"

"It is possible and it has happened," Kip said. "And we have to act quickly if we're to have any chance of saving the Calatians."

Argent nodded. "Then I will." And he disappeared.

"All right," Emily said. "I'm off to Amsterdam. Good luck."

"To you too."

He pulled his consciousness back from Ash and focused on Chakrabarti. "Would you be so kind as to accompany me to London? I may need your help to restore magic to Malcolm as well, and...I don't know what else might come up."

"I am happy to," the sorcerer said with a smile. "In addition to wanting to help however I may, I am most anxious to put right this great wrong."

"As am I." Kip took the sorcerer's hand. "Let's try the direct route first."

He closed his eyes and pictured Malcolm, felt his friend's presence, and cast the translocation spell.

For a moment he thought the wards were still up and he'd have to try another solution, because the spell seemed to take a few seconds to "find" Malcolm. But then the cold stone where he'd spent some of the worst moments of his life appeared around him, and the rank smell of Farley's piss (mixed with Malcolm's and his own) flooded into his nose. And there, in the cell with him, lay Malcolm.

"I can feel that someone's here," Malcolm said, "And you've appeared in my cell, unless I miss my guess, so I'm thinking you're not Victor nor Farley."

"It's me." Kip knelt next to Malcolm and took his friend's hand in his paw. "And Chakrabarti's here. He's going to give you magic back."

"Kip?" Malcolm said faintly. "You're—-you again?"

"I'm me again. We've got some work to do."

Malcolm gripped his paw. "Kip, he did something terrible, I think. Farley summoned him and he came back, and Farley said, "Now do it, like you said," and he said, "Yes, you've more than earned this." Then he did something to Farley, I don't know what, but Farley was gone suddenly, and then Victor laughed, and it wasn't a nice laugh. He told me he'd deal with me after, but then there was..."

"Kind of a silent explosion?"

"Yes! But magical."

Chakrabarti came over to kneel on Malcolm's other side. "Congratulations," Kip said. "You're now the only other sorcerer alive to be present at the destruction of a Great Feat."

"What?" Malcolm sat up.

"Victor turned all the Calatians back into animals." Every time he said it, the images flooded into Kip's head no matter how much he wanted to avoid seeing them. "All except me and Alice and Abel. Maybe my parents. I haven't checked on them."

"What are we doing?"

"What happened after he cast the spell? After the explosion?"

"My head hurt. And I think someone fell outside my cell."

"I'm going to go look. Chakrabarti, can you restore magic to him?"

"I am doing it," the sorcerer said.

Kip walked to the bars of Malcolm's cell and called up fire to eat away at the metal. He stepped through the gap and saw, to his right in front of the cell he'd been kept in, the body of Victor Adamson lying on the stone.

"What's there?" Malcolm asked, standing.

Chakrabarti stepped out to join Kip. "That is Victor Adamson, is it not?"

"It is." Kip walked over and examined the body. "He's dead, Malcolm. Undoing a Great Feat killed him. Careful! The bars might still be warm."

Bracing himself and feeling his way along the wall, Malcolm had approached the front of his cell. Kip hurried over to lead him out. "Ah, you've melted them. Nice trick, that," Malcolm said.

"Where's Corvi?" Kip asked.

"Somewhere in a cage." Malcolm focused. "They caught him, I think. But the room looks empty. Hang on."

He vanished. Kip turned to Chakrabarti. "For the next part of this, I have to summon a demon. I know how you feel about it and if you don't want to watch, you don't have to."

"I thought you had decided not to use demons." The sorcerer frowned slightly.

"I had. I have. This is a special case. And it's not only because the stakes are so high. I'll explain to you later, but...you're right in your belief. And I think we can still work with demons, but differently than we have been."

The frown turned to confusion. "I don't think I understand."

"I'm not sure I do either, not completely. But...stay if you want, or go if you want. We will need help rounding up all the animals on the Isle if this doesn't work the way I hope it will." He paused. "And maybe even if it does. I don't know."

The other sorcerer looked off into the distance. While he was pondering, Kip walked down the row of cells, past the tray of stale bread and the now upended cup and the beaver sleeping behind the bars, to where Richard had been. His student was still there, face pressed to the bars, but he jumped back as Kip came into view and then edged forward, never taking his eyes from the fox's. "Richard?" Kip said. "Can you understand me?"

The young man frowned and then tilted his head. "It's Master Penfold," Kip went on. "Do you remember me?"

Still the blank, uncomprehending stare. Kip reached out a paw, and Richard tentatively reached out his hand to meet it. They clasped fingers until Malcolm returned, when Kip had to pull his paw away because Richard would not let go on his own.

Chakrabarti stopped his pacing then. He didn't ask what Kip had been doing, and Kip did not think this was a good time to tell him that Victor had also learned to steal magic from humans. "I think," the sorcerer said, "that I will withdraw for the moment. I will be most interested to discuss the matter of demons with you later, but it sounds like the discussion might be better saved for after the resolution of this situation."

"Understood," Kip said.

"Where would it be most useful for me to wait?"

"Go back to Peachtree, and Malcolm will come get you when we're ready."

"Aye." Malcolm brushed a hand down his robes, black and clean.

Chakrabarti vanished, and Kip shook his head at Malcolm. "Did you steal someone's robes?"

"They stole my raven. It seemed a fair trade to me. Besides, I was tired of smelling filthy. If only they fit better." He rubbed hands down the voluminous folds again. "So what are we doing here?"

Kip drew in a breath. Malcolm and Farley were the only witnesses to Victor's summoning, and Farley was gone. "Do you happen to remember the name Farley used to summon Victor?"

"He tried three times before using one that worked, and aye, I took note of it. Always remember what demons someone summons in front of you."

Relief flooded Kip. Every step of this was an uncharted challenge, but this was one more success. Next came the actual summoning. "That was Victor's sorcerer name. So…I'm going to summon and bind Victor."

Malcolm eyed the body. "From beyond the grave?"

"I was in the Æther when he died. I saw him reappear there." Kip stared down at his paws.

"Hang on." Malcolm pressed a hand to his head. "You're telling me that the demon plane is the afterlife? That demons are…"

"Spirits of the deceased, yes. At least some of them. They lose their memories when they arrive."

"We don't go to Heaven nor Hell, but…"

"Maybe later," Kip said. "Nik did say that sometimes demons disappear. But yes, it looks like demons are the spirits of the deceased. Maybe only sorcerers."

"Jesus, Mary, and Joseph," Malcolm swore. "If I didn't know you'd witnessed it, I'd be calling your mind into question. As it is…"

"I'd take you there if I thought we could return easily." Kip put a paw on his shoulder. "But in the meantime, I'll hope to convince you by summoning Victor as a demon."

Malcolm shuddered. "I'll trust you won't play foolish games with leaving him unbound."

"No. I hope he'll be able to help me reverse what he did."

"Even though he might have lost his memories and might appear as a centaur with serpents for legs?"

Kip stifled a nervous laugh. "I would be delighted if that happened. But he remembered me, at least. I think he'll remember restoring my magic."

"*He* did that?" Malcolm shook his head. "We're going to have to have a good long tea with Em and Alice when we get back and hear what we've all been through."

"You don't know the half of it," Kip said, and then reflected. "Actually, you know more than half now. But yes. What was the name Farley used?"

Malcolm told him, and Kip pulled in magic. It seemed to come more easily to him now, but this attempt had to work, so he scraped his paw over a jagged edge of the bars of Malcolm's cell and tasted the blood from the cut. There did not seem to be a difference in the level of magic he could hold, as far as he could tell; maybe traveling to the Æther had expanded his capabilities.

There would be time to think of that later. He gathered himself and spoke the words of the spell, reaching out into the demon plane with newfound familiarity. When he spoke the name, he felt the familiar catch as the spell pulled its target up and into the real world, reminding him of the crushing feeling he'd felt on his own return.

A blue mist rose in front of him. It coalesced into a human figure, which groaned as it assumed Victor's features. Quickly, Kip spoke the binding spell, with no small measure of satisfaction: "Make no move save on my order; take no action save on my order, but you may converse with me."

"Penfold," demon-Victor said.

"Ah, you know me. Good. I was worried you might not."

"How could I not? It's thanks to you that I'm here."

"And thanks to you that I'm here." Kip gestured to his body. "Don't think I don't know that you restored me even though you talked so much about wanting to see me humbled."

"I wasn't the one who wanted you on all fours in a collar. That was…" The cloudy smoke that defined his features shifted. "That was someone else."

"Broadside."

"Of course, of course."

Kip studied the familiar and yet eerily changing face. "Tell me honestly: do you remember Farley Broadside?"

Demon-Victor answered promptly. "Yes."

"Do you remember restoring my magic to me?"

The smoky eyebrows lowered into a glower. "Yes."

Kip pointed to Richard, behind the demon. "Can you cast that spell on him?"

"I can, yes."

"Then do so."

The demon turned to Richard and then back to Kip. "It is done."

"Richard?" The young man slouched with the same vacant expression, and did not respond to his name. Kip turned on Victor. "Why didn't it work?"

"It was a spell to restore a Calatian from animal to Calatian state. He is not an animal."

The fox clenched his teeth. "Cast another spell to restore him to exactly the state he was in before you drained the magic from him."

"I do not know what state that was. I don't remember him."

Kip reframed words in his head. "Can you restore to him the magic essence that was taken from him?"

"Not without knowing how much was taken from him."

Kip closed his eyes. "Can you restore to him the amount of magic that is in Malcolm O'Brien here?"

"How can I know how much that is?"

"You may observe only without taking any other action—if Malcolm gives you permission. And tell me when you've finished." Kip turned to his friend.

"I don't know, Kip," Malcolm said. "Let Victor into my head?"

"I can have him find another human sorcerer somewhere," Kip said. "There are—"

"No. I'll do it. Rather me than some poor unsuspecting fool." Malcolm took a deep breath. "But as soon as I say 'stop,' he gets out of my head."

Kip repeated the order, and then Malcolm gave his permission. All was still for perhaps two heartbeats, and then demon-Victor said, "I have finished."

"Can you restore to Richard the amount of magic essence that is in Malcolm?"

"Yes."

"Then do that, and that only, and tell me when you've finished."

Demon-Victor bowed his head. The clouds making up his form roiled more intensely, and then he said, "I have finished."

"Richard?" Kip called.

The wait stretched on forever as Kip and Malcolm stared past the bored demon-Victor, the fox with his ears cupped forward. Finally a shaky, familiar voice said, "M-Master Penfold?"

Malcolm strode quickly down to Richard's cell, gathering magic, and the gate flew open and away as he arrived. He reached in and brought Richard out, the young man rubbing his forehead with a perplexed expression. "I...I thought I was dreaming. It was as if I was in a fog. But now I think perhaps it was real?"

"Can you take him back to Peachtree?" Kip asked Malcolm. "I'm going to set to the bigger task. Oh, and bring Jorey back."

"Of course. I'll return in a moment." Malcolm and Richard vanished.

Left alone, Kip stared at demon-Victor. "Now," he said, "I'll need you to do the spell you used to restore me, but on a much larger scale." The demon's eyes darkened, turning from blue-grey to charcoal. "Victor, restore all the magic that you stole from the Calatians to the Calatians you stole it from, each and every one, leaving none of them out. Do it now."

"Alas," the demon said, "I cannot. My power is insufficient."

"How can it be insufficient?" Kip cried. "You're the one who took it from them in the first place, and now you're a demon!"

"Power is enabled by will. If I were moved by the fanatical determination that the spell needed to be cast, then perhaps my power would be equal to it." The eyes brightened to silver. "Now you, Penfold, you surely have the determination to enact such a spell."

"Perhaps I do," Kip said slowly. "But if I sacrifice myself, and the spell doesn't work, who is left to make things right? No; this just means we will have to do this a more difficult way."

Malcolm reappeared in time to hear this last sentence, holding the wicker box that contained Jorey. "What difficult way?" he asked.

"First, let's see if this works." Kip grasped the red squirrel with a spell and let the box fall away.

Jorey hung in the air, scrabbling wildly for purchase. "I'm sorry," Kip murmured. "I remember how that feels." He turned to demon-Victor. "Tell me the spell you used to restore my intelligence and form."

In a grating voice like the scraping of metal over stone, the demon spoke the words of the spell. Kip ordered it to share the memory of the casting with him and Malcolm, and it did so, again as unpleasantly as it could, sharing the chaos of the Æther and the disdain it felt for Kip as part of the memory of the spell. But Kip thought he could piece together the casting of the spell if he had to, and until then...

"We will call this spell the Calatian Restoration spell, and when I use those words, you will cast that spell," he ordered demon-Victor. "Now cast the Calatian Restoration spell on this squirrel and allow Malcolm and me to feel the casting of it."

Demon-Victor resisted, but Kip's binding held fast, and a moment later, he felt the energy flowing from the demon to Jorey. For a brief second, nothing happened. Had he misspoken? But no, Jorey's form stretched and grew, expanded just as March's had shrunk, until the squirrel as Kip had known him hung in the air.

Jorey looked around, bewildered, and then made a sound. His ears went back and he tried again. "Mas—Masters?"

Malcolm exhaled, a long breath. Kip lowered Jorey to the ground and ended his spell, whereupon the squirrel's legs gave out and he fell to the floor.

"I'm so sorry," Kip said, though he couldn't stop smiling. He extended a paw. "Are you all right?"

"I'm—" Jorey took the paw and tried to stand, but ended up falling into Kip, who wrapped an arm around him for support. "I haven't been all right, but I, I think I'm all right now. I can talk. I can walk. I'm not in a box."

"Sorry about that," Malcolm said, "but we feared you might run off."

"No, I, I would have." Jorey ran a paw through the fur between his ears. "I was an animal."

"You're not anymore." Kip kept an arm around him even as the squirrel gained confidence in his movements. "Can you stand?"

"I, ah, I think I can, but also, sir, I'm very sorry, but I'm not decent."

Malcolm snorted a laugh. "You're a sight more decent than you were a minute ago. Come on, son, let's go back to the College and dress you. Kip, I'll find you later."

"You think you'll be able to cast that spell?" Kip asked.

"Ah...not so's I'd trust a life to it." Malcolm squinted at demon-Victor. "But if we have no other options, well, me ma used to say, if you've only half a cup of sugar, that'll have to do."

"I feel the same," Kip said. "I hope we'll have time to learn it."

"And no cause to use it." Malcolm took Jorey by the paw. "Here we go, lad, prepare yourself." And a moment later, they were gone.

Demon-Victor watched them go and then said, "You cannot intend to have me cast the spell on every single Calatian."

"Every one we can find." Kip lifted the beaver that had been March with magic. "Come on. Let's go down to the Isle."

The Isle of Dogs was in chaos. The first place Kip visited was the bridge to the mainland, where terrified guards had thrown boards and rubble across the street to stop the animals from crossing into London proper. Kip and Malcolm improved on the barricade, sealing it with river mud and stones to keep in all the animals from the wolves down to the mice. Demon-Victor continued to resist his orders, but Kip's binding held; he collected the larger animals first and made demon-Victor restore magic to them.

Once the restored Calatians had been made aware of what had happened, they helped round up the remaining animals on the Isle. Most of them, anyway; some of the mice and dormice were never found, and at least one of the rabbits was killed by a predator (though nobody claimed to remember doing it). Several otters, too, had apparently slipped into the Thames and never returned.

But there was also a moment when Kip presented demon-Victor with a number of mice gathered by magic, and the demon said, "Two of those were not Calatians."

"Which ones?" Kip asked, but Pierce, now at his side while Malcolm was fetching more Calatians to restore, drew him away.

"Why not see if it can make them Calatians?" the otter asked. "There's nobody here but us, so if it goes wrong, we just...change them back. But it could be a marvelous thing."

"It seems wrong," Kip said. "Nobody's asked them if they want to be Calatians."

"Nobody asked us at first either."

"So we should perpetrate the same callous act on others?"

Pierce snorted. "Callous? Don't you feel it's been a blessing? You've fought harder than anyone to preserve our race."

"I know. I think we should have debates, discuss the idea with others. The two of us won't necessarily see all that might result if we go down that path. Let's restore the ones who need it first."

"Why not just see if it works?" Pierce said. "Then we'll know where we are in the discussions. Look," he said when Kip hesitated. "Think about what it would mean. Think about how many of us stay here on this God-forsaken Isle only because we're sure to find a mate here. You've started us spreading around the world. This could be…" His eyes shone in the dim room. "The beginning of a new age of Calatians."

"A revolution," Kip murmured. The thought appealed to him. He knew that this was a momentous thing, something that more people than just him and Pierce should be privy to, but he was also curious to know how it would work from a magical standpoint. In addition, there was a little part of him that wanted Victor, who had tried to eradicate his race, to be the instrument they could use to strengthen it. And yet, did he or anyone have the right to change the life of an animal like that? "Let's wait until all the Calatians have been restored, and then we'll talk about it again."

So Pierce took the non-Calatian mice and kept them aside. They worked all through the night and the next day, Pierce providing Kip with food and tea to keep him awake, Sleek providing him with news of the other cities with Calatians. Sorcerers had been mobilized to help keep the animals all in one place, but they suspected they had lost many of them, especially the smaller ones. In Amsterdam and Madrid, Emily had alerted the sorcerers who were now doing the same, and Amsterdam merchants had made available a number of wire cages for mice and rats.

It helped that as Kip had, the animals seemed to retain an awareness of their familiarity with each other. There were incidents, but few deaths, and once the sorcerers took control, the predators were kept apart from the prey. In Amsterdam and New Cambridge, sorcerers called first-level demons to help them look for escaped former Calatians, and once Kip had finished with the Calatians of the Isle of Dogs, he dismissed demon-Victor and summoned Nikolon, again without binding her, to ask her to help the other demons look, since she knew what to look for.

Kip could no longer keep his eyes open, so he went to Ella Lutris's house. Thankfully, Ella was one of the otters who had slept through most of the ordeal and had not sought refuge in the Thames, so she and her family had been restored. She still had an empty pallet on the floor where Kip gratefully lay down to sleep.

He slept through the evening and night and woke at the glimmers of dawn. Ella and Malcolm slept near him with Corvi and Sleek nearby, heads tucked under their wings. He translocated to Alice and found her asleep in a small room in Philadelphia in the middle of the night. He sat down next to her, intending to stay in her presence only for a short time, but she woke.

"Are you finished?" she asked.

"With the Isle, maybe. The rest of the world needs me, so I thought I'd go to Amsterdam first, then Peachtree and New Cambridge as they wake up."

"Did you sleep at all?"

"Hours and hours. I'm fine. I could stay up another day and night. How are things going here?"

She rubbed her eyes. "I fear we've lost a lot of them. Victor might not have succeeded as he thought, but he's done a great deal of damage."

"I know. The Isle is well-contained and there are still almost a hundred missing from it."

"Where's Emily?"

"Boston, I think. No—she said she was going to Boston, then Richmond, so perhaps there."

Kip nodded and rubbed at the base of his ears. "I'd best get back to wake everyone up. Thousands more to go."

"You're not having any trouble with the binding?"

"On Victor?" He laughed shortly. "I'm very cautious. He's about a second-order demon, which I know would annoy him to no end. So I can hold him for as long as I need to."

"Doesn't he fight you?"

"Constantly, but that's how I know when the binding is weak. A cleverer demon acts very docile so the sorcerer gets complacent and then tests the bindings sharply. But Victor never had much experience of demons, and even less in being one."

Alice was silent, staring past Kip into the dimness. "I still don't know what to think about our spirits turning into demons."

"You haven't told anyone else, have you?"

She shook her head. "But I talked to Emily about it after Malcolm told us. Was—was the demon plane a very terrible place?"

"No. It could be very peaceful. But you lose a lot of yourself when you go there."

"You didn't."

He glanced over his shoulder. "As long as we maintain a connection to this world, maybe that helps anchor our memories. I don't know. It's a lot to think about, and we have thousands more Calatians to rescue."

She leaned over and kissed him. "Go do that."

"Hug Abel and the cubs for me when you see them." He kissed her back and then returned to the Isle.

Amsterdam, Peachtree, New Cambridge, Madrid, Boston, New York, Philadelphia, Richmond, Savannah. Over the next several days Kip visited each city, sometimes with Emily, sometimes with Malcolm, sometimes with Alice. They talked to the sorcerers in charge, Kip summoned demon-Victor, and they set about restoring the Calatians they could find. He had a sense now of how long he could bind demon-Victor, and though the demon never stopped struggling or trying to find a loophole in the things he said, the restoration spell worked every single time.

But in every city, Kip heard before he left that there were some still missing. He returned to the Isle to find that two mice and two rats had been found, and one otter had returned, climbing up the bank and over the broken wall. In Amsterdam, four more Calatians waited for restoration when he returned there, and in New Cambridge, six.

Somewhat to his surprise, the expatriate French nobles threw themselves into the relief efforts in Peachtree, scouring the town for stray animals and helping tend to the ones that had been found before Kip returned. Mme. Dieuleveult brushed off his thanks when he first returned to restore the Calatians. "You've taken us in and now you find yourselves in trouble? What would you think of France if we declined to help?"

"And besides," her husband said, standing beside her, "it makes us understand that there are worse things than losing your home and possessions. I have prayed to St. Francis for all of you."

"Thank you," Kip said. He decided this was not the time to tell M. Dieuleveult about the properties of his relics. After all, he still was not sure whether the relic had brought him back from the demon plane, if he'd simply used it as an anchor, or if it had not mattered at all and his desperation had proved the difference. He might never know, and at any rate there were more pressing concerns, so he went about his work.

In Amsterdam, Master Janssen himself met Kip and thanked him for his efforts; in Madrid, Master Galena, who had asked Kip about the story of the Road at the Exposition, found him and did the same. Master Patris had gathered the New Cambridge Calatians; Master Odden had done the same in Boston, Master Sharpe in New York, and Master Warrington in Philadelphia. All the sorcerers pressed Kip about the manner in which the Calatians were being restored (with Master Sharpe adding his conviction that Kip had arranged this all for the Calatians' benefit somehow), but Kip told them over and over that he was simply reversing an existing spell, not creating a new one. He did not have the original spell, he told them, but this demon was the one that had been used to cast it (a semi-truth) and remembered enough to reverse it.

In Richmond, Master Vendis helped him, and in Savannah, Master Argent and the young Dutch healer de Koning had taken charge of the Calatians. To Argent and Vendis, Kip was a little more forthcoming, though he hid the truth about his demon's identity. He would want to discuss it with all the masters at his school first before they made any decisions about disseminating the information more widely.

In every city, throngs of people crowded around the Calatian neighborhoods, having heard of the crisis and wanting to help. They brought mice and rats by the hundreds, occasionally larger animals. Only twice were any of these animals Calatians, but Kip found himself genuinely moved by the crowds of people and their earnest efforts. One thought that Calatians and humans had not integrated all that well, that New Cambridge was the exception rather than the rule, but here were hundreds of humans stricken by the loss of their Calatian neighbors. He made sure to point this out to the sorcerers in every city, and to the Calatians once they were settled from their ordeal. In some places, he hoped, people and Calatians would begin to mix a little more readily.

By the time he'd finished his second tour in every city, ten days later, he felt as though he'd been doing this work for months. But there were few other people, if any, he reflected, who could say they'd personally met every Calatian in the world.

CHAPTER TWENTY-TWO:

ANOTHER REVOLUTION

They closed the school for a day because the Great Hall, the wide, airy gathering room on the ground floor which was normally a public space, was the only room large enough for Kip, Malcolm, Emily, Alice, Chakrabarti, Argent, Vendis, and the young Dutch sorcerer de Koning to sit comfortably and have a conversation. Before admitting de Koning, Chakrabarti, and Alice, the other five had discussed whether they should be privy to the discussion. Kip and Malcolm had argued that Alice had seen much of what they were about to discuss already, and that Chakrabarti and de Koning had already shown a great desire to become part of the school. They would no doubt bring this information back to their home countries, but Emily, Kip, and Malcolm all believed that that would happen anyway in time, and it was better that they include their new colleagues. Masters Argent and Vendis, who had seen how much Chakrabarti and de Koning had helped in the recent crisis, agreed quickly.

Emily began the meeting by standing and welcoming Chakrabarti and de Koning and thanking them for their help. Then she turned to Kip. "Master Penfold has promised us a full accounting of his recent adventure, and he and I have discussed a proposal that I think will help the future of the school. The two are quite separate, but you all should hear both of them, so…here we all are. Master Penfold?" She sat.

Kip nodded to her and stood. He cleared his throat. "I suppose this all began at the Exposition, with Victor's trick…" He told that story quickly, how the stage show had been both a trick to spread fear about the British Empire's capabilities and a diversion to get their students separated. How Victor had been kidnapping a Calatian here and there to experiment on but wanted Calatians with access to magic, hoping they would give him more power. How he'd somehow bribed March, or maybe March had been his agent all along—March had been restored and was in Grinda's custody on the Isle.

Kip did not tell them about his conversation with Grinda, her sharp, "I suppose you want to be thanked for saving us from this trouble you caused," and her back turned as others stuttered apologies on her behalf, apologies that Kip waved away because he felt that she was at least partly right. He had not committed the great crime himself, but he'd taunted Victor and he'd underestimated the threat the magic-less young man presented. He should have known after all these years that Victor was capable of great evil because he wanted so badly to be great at any cost. Kip would never be able to repair all the damage, restore all the losses. Grinda hadn't lost any family members (wolves were easy to keep track of), but she felt the pain of others who had and wanted to be sure Kip did too. He did, but the other sorcerers here didn't need to.

He did tell them about being captured, about being reduced to an animal (that part was hard and drew gasps from even the ones who knew the story), and about how Victor had done the same to Richard. He told them about Nikolon's help and the journey to the Æther, how he had seen Victor there, then gone, and then back again without his silver cord, memories sloughing off of him to be snapped up by other demons.

"Wait," Chakrabarti said, looking distinctly uncomfortable. "You said 'other' demons."

Kip nodded. "The demon I've been summoning to restore Calatians is—was Victor. He remembers the spell he used, at least, and he knows he doesn't like me, though he doesn't remember many specifics about it."

Argent stared blankly ahead and de Koning's mouth hung open, but Vendis spoke. "So when we die, we become demons?"

"Some of us, anyway." Kip pressed his paws together to keep them from shaking too much. "I, ah, I've thought about it a lot, but I haven't actually had the chance to do much more study."

Vendis laughed, sounding as nervous as Kip felt about this whole subject. "Do you think you could go back to the demon plane? The Æther?"

"Perhaps, but…I'm not actually very keen to, you understand."

Now everyone laughed. "No, of course not. But…this changes everything we know about demons."

"Not to mention Heaven and Hell," Argent said.

"It does. But..." And Kip told them about Nikolon, without revealing her name, how she had not betrayed him at the Battle of the Road, how he had summoned her without binding, how perhaps, just perhaps, there might be a way for humans to work with demons without the pain of binding them.

"Is that your proposal?" Chakrabarti asked.

"No. Well—perhaps, but I rather want to let Emily explain the other thing. I've been talking for quite a while here." He sat.

Alice reached over and took his paw as Emily stood again. "Yes, well. You all know that we've been rather desperately trying to ensure the survival of the school." Murmurs and nods. "We'd hoped to get some money from the Dieuleveults, and that hasn't gone very well." The revolution in France had not died down; the king was in prison, while multiple nobles and two sorcerers had been killed. Paris, reports said, was still burning in many areas. The powers of Europe had withdrawn to see how this would all turn out. "And we're hoping that the American government will see fit to fund both magic schools, but they seem to place the American School at a higher priority than ours. So Kip and I have been talking the last few days and I think we've come up with a good idea."

"Not just to save the school," Kip interjected, "but a good idea in general."

"Yes." Emily smiled. "It was partly inspired by talking to you, Master Chakrabarti, about the practices in India, where sorcerers have to go out to the towns and help people. It was partly inspired by talking to the Calatians of Amsterdam and the Isle, providing a great service to their sorcerers and receiving nothing in return. And it was partly inspired during the past week as Kip and I and many others, you included, watched hundreds of humans give their time, as well as some material benefits like food and shelter, to help restore Calatians to the world.

"When Kip was expelled—unjustly—from school, he lived at an Inn and paid for his room and board with small sorcery jobs. When I suggested out of desperation that we try something of the sort again, he did not think it would work. Sorcerers might barter our services one on one, for favors, but to codify that sale of services feels wrong. I agree with him on that."

The sorcerers around the room nodded. Emily went on. "But in talking over the last few days, with all of these new experiences, we wondered if we were perhaps viewing our problem incorrectly. Sorcery colleges in the British Empire have always been funded by the Crown, and in return they do work for the Crown. We have been hoping for funding from our new government, but the American College has taken what little of that there is. We were hoping for funds from one or two benefactors, but that route has been thrown into chaos, and it is difficult to imagine a scenario in which we could offer equal value for an investment. A charitable donation, yes, but then we would find ourselves beholden to a few wealthy donors."

Kip spoke up. "Just as we were pressed to take the Dieuleveults back into a dangerous situation when their house was burning."

"Quite. So we tried to think more creatively. We are a young country, and our military and civil sorcerers are stretched very thin. East Georgia, again, seems to be last on their list of stops, and everywhere south of Virginia in general feels neglected, at least according to many of the politicians I've spoken to. So we, the sorcerers of the Lutris School, will go help people in the surrounding cities and states. Savannah, Charleston, Richmond, maybe farther if need be."

"It sounds like we're selling our services." Argent frowned.

"Not exactly. We won't be funded by the country's government, but we can approach cities and states and territories for help, and maybe to point us to areas of greatest need. The government of East Georgia has offered a little money, and we can take barter: food, woodworking, whatever people can spare. The sorcerers of the Athæneum can perhaps begin to offer their Calatians travel home to see family in exchange for their services, but if not, we can help them too."

"We used to have sorcerers come down into New Cambridge to help the town." Kip appealed to Master Vendis. "You remember."

"The idea," Emily concluded, "is that we shall become part of our community rather than sitting apart from it, as King's and the American College do."

"New Cambridge supplied calyxes to us," Vendis said. "We didn't take any money from them."

"I'm not saying this will be easy to work out." Emily's grey eyes surveyed the room. "But if anyone else has a suggestion, I will be happy to entertain it."

No-one spoke. Kip leaned in again. "If people see us as something of value to them, they'll be willing to support us, we hope. Nobody has a lot, but a lot of people have a little, and a bit of food here, a bit of coin there... it could see us through the next several years."

"It still feels like whoring ourselves out," Vendis grumbled.

"If I may?" Chakrabarti looked between Kip and Emily, and Emily nodded to him. He stood. "In my country, this going out into the town, as Headmistress Carswell said, this is regarded as a great pleasure, a gift to the sorcerer. It is true that not all sorcerers perceive it in this way." He chuckled gently. "Still, many of us find it very rewarding, a reminder of how important our great power is, at how much a small gesture may make a large difference to another."

"There will undoubtedly be some who will think that their donation entitles them to preferential treatment or services," Emily said. "We are right now only a few, including the students. But we are starting this from whole cloth and it will require some tailoring as we go along."

De Koning, who had been very quiet during this part, raised a hand. Emily acknowledged him. "Er. I am only here a short time," he said, "and I had thought I was here to teach healing and spiritual magic to students?"

"You are." Emily inclined her head. "If you would prefer not to participate in our school's new work, you will not have to."

The young man sat back, looking around at the rest of the sorcerers. "Oh. I did not mean—that is, of course I will be happy to help. But will I be mending small cuts for children?"

"I don't think so." Emily smiled. "There will be enough serious injuries for healers to tend to, and only two of them here at our school."

"Even basic physical and translocation spells can be immensely useful," Kip said. "Moving a stone in a field could save a farmer an entire day. Translocation needn't just be for London Calatians and their Amsterdam families; there are many farmers who have left one territory of this new country to find work in another who also miss their families."

Emily nodded. "President Adams has spoken often of the need to bring all the former colonies together in the new country. But I do hope that we can make this work beneficial for all of us as well as our friends and our country. Master Chakrabarti has told us that the work reminds us of the world we live in so that our own work, the research and exploration we do in the world of sorcery, can be done with that in mind as well."

"If we know what people need," Kip added, "we can make sorcery beneficial to everyone, not just the governments. Kings controlling sorcerers, that's only how it is in Europe, not all over the world."

"We're starting a new country," Emily added. "There's no reason to keep all the old traditions without examining them."

"Especially," Malcolm added, "if the old traditions don't pay you the same under the new government."

"Quite. If we were getting as much money as the American School— or even half as much," Emily said, "we wouldn't have to do this. But after talking to Master Chakrabarti...I want to." She stood straighter. "More than just helping the people around us, I want to help this country. I want to do it in small and large ways that we can see in repaired roads and buildings, in the smiles of people greeting us as we go from one city to another..."

"And in the coffers of the school," Malcolm said, which was met with a round of laughter.

"That too, of course." Emily smiled. "There are five masters plus an accomplished apprentice here."

"I make it six masters," de Koning said. "I will join you. After all, I am here to learn, am I not?"

"So are we all," Kip said.

They discussed more particulars, and everyone had something useful to add to the plan. But when Emily seemed ready to dismiss the meeting, Master Argent stood. "Master Vendis and I thought there would be one more topic discussed at this meeting." He looked at Kip, and the fox knew what he was about to say. "We have witnessed remarkable feats of sorcery these past few days. Not only the draining of magic essence from the Calatians, but its restoration to them. And I believe every sorcerer has asked the question: has Penfold been creating new Calatians as well as restoring them? Can he do that?" He smiled. "Master Vendis and I discussed this subject at length two nights ago, and now we are in the fortunate position of being able to ask the master himself."

Kip nodded and stood. "A friend of mine brought this to my attention on the Isle, the first night we were restoring Calatians. We talked about it there, and I have discussed it with Calatians in New Cambridge, Amsterdam, and here in Peachtree. We have reached an agreement of sorts." He did not feel it necessary to go into the hours of argument that had preceded the agreement, between people who wanted to expand the ranks of Calatians as much as possible and those who preached necessity and caution. Bryce Morgan, the Calatian mayor of Peachtree, had done an excellent job of crafting a compromise. "We will ask each of the major Calatian communities to provide a list of the species most in need of new blood, and once a year we will visit each of those communities to create new ones. We thought that around the Feast of Calatus might be appropriate."

Vendis rocked forward, almost standing. "So you've tried it? It works?"

"No, not yet." Kip pressed his paws together. "It was important to decide how we were going to approach this before we even tried it. But I think it will work. The thing we don't know—we can't know—is how these new Calatians will react to their...new state. That may be the piece of the Great Feat that we just can't replicate. And if we do create new Calatians, they might not like their new state. They will be offered the option to return to their animal state if they prefer it."

"May I be present when you do try?" Vendis asked. "I would dearly love to witness this."

"As would I," Argent said, and Chakrabarti and de Koning chorused their agreement.

"It would be helpful to have other sorcerers present, but I will have to ask the others. We have agreed that all the decisions will be made by this group."

"You've made a ruling council of Calatians," Argent observed with a smile.

"No," Kip protested, but Emily cut him off.

"They have," she said, "and it's about time, if you ask me."

Vendis nodded and smiled. "Truly this is a time of many changes." He rubbed his hands together. "If I'm honest, I have been a touch bored without a royal commission to work on. Teaching students is lovely, but there aren't many of them, and even a talented apprentice," he inclined his head toward Alice, "can only keep one's mind occupied for a portion of a day. So let us go out to the townspeople! I welcome this challenge."

"If you'll all come with me," Kip said, "there's a thing I want to do that I'd like everyone to be here for."

He led them out of the College, where Ash swooped down to his shoulder immediately, and down the front path to where the large iron gates rested against the brick gatehouses. "We built these because it was traditional; we were modeling it after the new buildings at the American College, back when it was Prince George's. But as Emily and I were talking over this new way we wanted to conduct our school, it made less sense to model our school on the American School. And one of the things that we decided we don't need are…"

He called magic and lifted the gates carefully away from the brick, moving them to either side. Everyone remained quiet as the large wrought-iron pieces floated away, leaving the path between the college and the town clear. Kip set them down in the grass to either side. "These gates. Our school is open to everyone."

"Well said." Malcolm patted the shoulder that did not have a raven on it.

"Come on." Emily gestured to the road down to Peachtree. "I'll buy everyone a drink at the Buried Crown."

"No need to offer twice." Vendis fell in behind her, and the others with him.

Alice took Kip's paw. "It's going to be an exciting few years."

"I hope not," he said fervently, and walked with her out through the gate houses and into the town.

EPILOGUE: A PHILOSOPHICAL

DISCUSSION

TWO YEARS LATER

Kip found the Welcoming exhausting, and not just for the expenditure of magical energy. There had been satisfaction in using demon-Victor to make more Calatians at first, but this year, summoning the creature brought more and more distaste, a reminder of a period Kip would rather forget. He and Malcolm had been present at most castings of the spell, and perhaps next year they would try it without demon-Victor before the blue specter could become a tradition at these rituals.

This year they had chosen all baby or infant animals, which decision had been the subject a good deal of discussion. One group argued that infants could not understand their right to have the transformation undone, and so using them was immoral, but the other group, who won the day, pointed out that they had already placed the need of their race ahead of the immorality of the transformation and that only one adult had exercised their right to reversal. Besides, everyone could see that the youngest from last year's new Calatians had adapted best of any of them. A few of that group, cubs and adults, had attended this year and helped greatly; even though they only had a few dozen words of spoken language, they knew very well what it was like to find themselves in a new body, and they knew the body language of reassurance and comfort.

Even without their help, though, Kip thought this Welcoming would have been more successful. He knew better what a successful transformation felt like and had improved this year over last. Next time would be better, and the one after that better yet. Perhaps one day he would be able to replicate what Calatus had done four hundred years ago—creating fully functional adult Calatians from animals—but in the back of his mind, he suspected that the price of that achievement would be his life, so he was content with his small progress.

He left Abel with the Welcomers on the Isle. The fox had shown quite the talent for bringing new Calatians along in Peachtree, so had asked if he could come to the Isle this year, and Kip had been glad to bring him. He hadn't told Abel, nor anyone else, of the other purpose of his visit to London this spring, the one that had taken him a year and a half to arrange.

A soft misting rain hung about in the springtime air as he crossed the bridge to London proper, showing his papers to the guards who remained stationed there. Moving from the Isle into streets full of humans was slightly jarring to his eyes and nose, but he was well used to crowds of humans and he strode forward confidently, Ash bobbing on his shoulder and occasionally croaking when someone stared too long at her.

As he walked, he pulled out the small pamphlet Pierce had given him, with the crude drawing of a fox-Calatian and what he supposed to be King George, judging by the crown on the otherwise generic human's head. Underneath, the title, "The King's Master," brought a smile to his muzzle. Emily would like this newest addition to her collection, he thought as he tucked it back in his pocket.

He stayed mostly to the banks of the Thames, looking as he often did for otters in the river, just in case after two years any of the missing returned toward their home. Here and there he had to cut inland, past narrow dirty homes and merchants' shops. At the entrance to a public-house, a young hedgehog in a dirty apron sweeping the front stoop looked up as Kip walked by, then down again. But Kip had barely gone three more steps when the broom clattered to the stone and the hedgehog rushed up behind him to clutch at the arm of his robe.

"Excuse me, but…"

As soon as Kip turned, the hedgehog's words dried up. Kip smiled down at him. "It's all right," he said.

"You're…" The hedgehog swallowed. "You're Master Penfold?"

"I am."

For a moment, the young hedgehog just rubbed his paws down the front of his apron, seemingly frozen, and then the words poured out of him.

"I never got a chance to say thank-you, years ago, but I remember you and everything you did. For me and my family, I mean, and really, well, all of us."

"You're most welcome." Kip inclined his head.

"And I came out to Peachtree to see my friend. Er, Barton, his name is."

"Oh!" Kip's ears perked. "The marten."

"Aye. Barton the marten, we call him." The hedgehog chuckled nervously. "We thought we might get to thank you on that occasion, but Barton said you was busy."

"Yes, I remember, he told me. You came out, and there was a mouse with you as well?"

"A dormouse, aye, sir. That'd be Jenks. We had such a lovely time, and we both think we might like to live in Peachtree one day, if we can find work."

"You'd leave the Isle?"

The hedgehog glanced up. "I live over the pub now. There's many of us living out in the city. Peachtree feels like it might be a touch warmer."

"A touch," Kip said. "We are a growing town and there is often work. Ask Barton to keep his nose to the wind for you. Was it Jorey who brought you to visit?"

"No, sir, it was Mistress Penfold. She brings a lot of us from the Isle to Peachtree."

Kip tried not to smile too much. "Yes, I know."

"Of course you do." The hedgehog tsked at himself. "I'm sorry, sir, of course you'd know."

"What was your name?"

It took the hedgehog two tries to get it out. The first came out as a raspy wheeze, and then he said, "William, sir."

"Well, William, it's been a great pleasure to see you. I'm afraid I have an appointment, but I'll see you again in Peachtree, I'm sure. Barton will be able to bring you back there himself in a year or so, I shouldn't wonder."

"Yes, sir!" William clapped his paws together. "It's so wonderful, him being magical and all. I still can't believe it. My friend, a sorcerer!"

"Just a student right now, but hopefully an apprentice next year." Kip smiled.

"Indeed." William bowed. "I'm so sorry, sir, I won't keep you any longer."

He hurried back to his public-house stoop, and Kip walked on with a little more bounce to his tail.

The four spires of the Tower of London rose ahead of him, seeming to be a short walk away, but each street brought him only a little closer. By the time he finally stood at the grounds of the great castle, the rain had soaked through his robe and dampened his fur, his tail twice as heavy with the water in it. Though the drizzle remained steady, the sun peeked through a crack in the clouds, setting one wall of the tower shining white as though a fire glowed beneath it, and then the gap closed and the castle went back to its dull wet gleam against the dark sky.

After ten minutes of walking around the grounds, Kip came to the gate house, where a uniformed soldier came out, his bored expression changing very little. "Business?" he asked.

"Official." Kip produced the oilskin pouch that held his papers.

The guard read them and replaced them. "That door there," he pointed as he walked across the moat bridge to open the gate. "You'll find the Yeoman Warder on duty there. He'll direct you further."

Kip followed the guard, then passed through the gate and walked on by himself to the small stone building. As he approached the door, a raven alit on the roof just over it and cawed down at them. Ash looked up and answered, an instinctive reaction, nothing that Kip understood. But it made sense to the other raven, who quieted and watched them.

Inside, amid the strong smell of tea and unwashed men, an older man in a dark blue uniform with red trim stood from a chair by a crackling fire to greet Kip. His uniform resembled Kip's robe in form except that the upper half, above the wide belt, was all of a piece rather than being clasped together as Kip's was. The man smiled over spectacles as he brought a squat top hat with a red circle on it to rest on his head. "What can I do for you?" he asked.

"Here to see one of the prisoners." Kip held out the oilskin again.

The Yeoman Warder took the paper and read it. "Ah, yes, this fellow. You know, you're the first Calatian to visit the Tower?"

"Indeed?" Kip stood awkwardly, aware of his robe dripping on the floor.

"Oh, aye. We see them on the streets, but none have been important enough to be imprisoned here or to visit anyone. You're the first. So far as I know, but I been here thirty years and I've never heard of another."

"I'm honored, I suppose," Kip said.

The Warder replaced the paper in the pouch and handed it back to Kip. "All this seems in order. He's warded, you understand, so if you had any thought of casting spells they wouldn't work. Our Master Dryden is quite adept at that sort of thing."

"Ah," Kip said. "Is that whose raven greeted us as we came in?"

"Could be, but we've a score of rooks living on the grounds, so more likely it was Jerry. She's the curious one about visitors. Speaking of, you've a fine specimen with you there."

"Thank you." Kip touched Ash's beak, and the raven rubbed back against his finger. "She's been with me for years."

"Lovely." The Warder turned to his right and hollered at a doorway. "Oi! Fergens! Escort, if you'd be so kind." To Kip, he said, "Warder Fergens will take you up to the prisoner."

"Thank you," Kip said. "And to be clear, I've no intention of using sorcery or anything else. I just want to talk."

The Warder nodded. "That's all they ever do, is talk, but they do it often enough. Never sent a Calatian before, though." He turned back toward the open door. "Fergens!"

Another Warder appeared, fastening his belt, a young man whose reddish hair stuck out at odd angles underneath his dark blue hat. "All right, all right," he grumbled. "Tower ain't gonna fall down, is it? Cor!" He spotted Kip and stopped. "I'm escorting a Calatian, am I?"

"If that's all right," Kip said, wary.

"Oh aye!" He strode across the room and extended a great ruddy hand. "Name's Fergens. Pleasure to meet you, Master Fox."

"Penfold." Kip shook the hand.

"Master Penfold. All right, let's go on." Fergens took a ring of keys from the other Warder and then examined Kip. "Want to hang that robe to dry by the fire?"

Kip took off the wet robe, causing Ash to hop on top of his head while he pulled the wet cloth from his shoulders. He hesitated a moment; he could easily burn away the water with a simple spell. But he didn't want to do sorcery here, even a minor harmless spell, even at the cost of not wearing his sorcerer's robe to this meeting. So he gave the robe to the older Warder, who hung it by the fire, and, dressed only in his tunic, the fox followed Fergens down a hallway and into the Tower.

It had been clear to him when he first saw it that this White Tower had inspired the design of the White Tower at the American College two centuries ago. That White Tower didn't have the spires at each corner and it was smaller, maybe a fifth the size. But the shape of it called across the ocean to its eponym, and the founders had clearly tried to find stone that matched as well as possible to the Kentish rag-stone that Kip brushed with his fingers here.

"There's ghosts here," Fergens said unexpectedly over his shoulder.

"What?"

"There's ghosts. You know all the history here? How King Henry VIII housed his wife Anne here the night before their wedding and then later had her imprisoned and executed here? How King Henry—another one, before, the fourth, I think—was murdered right in the chapel here?"

"Whose ghost did you see?"

Fergens lowered his voice to a dramatic whisper. "A young boy, about ten. Well, I saw a shadow, but it was about that height. And a door closed when I was the only person in the room. Swear to you. Other blokes seen him too. Sometimes two boys."

"Two boys?"

"There was two princes who disappeared, a long time ago." They came to a locked door. Fergens withdrew a key and unlocked it. Behind lay a staircase which the Warder began to climb. "Some of my mates claim they seen old headless Anne, but I never seen her. Hear things, though. Wailings."

Kip did not think the Warder would be very impressed with his story of the actual ghost he had met in the American White Tower, so he kept it to himself as they mounted two flights of stairs, instead making the appropriate noises of interest and horror at the stories Fergens delighted in telling him.

"Here we are," the Warder said as they arrived at a landing that let onto a small room with three doors, all of them thick-looking oak with viewing slits two thirds of the way up. "You'll want the middle one there." He pulled the keys from his pocket again and stepped forward to open the middle door, then pulled it open for Kip.

Beyond was a tiny room, barely large enough to stand in. Another door stood at the other end. "Here." Fergens held out a key to Kip. "You can unlock that door when this one's shut. When you're done, come out and knock, then lock that one so I can see you. I got to see you with my eyes." He pointed to his eyes as though Kip might have thought he meant some other eyes, perhaps on his elbow. "If he attacks you, yell, and maybe I'll get in there in time."

"I'm not worried," Kip said.

"Aye, suppose you can defend yourself well enough even without sorcery." Fergens eyed Kip's teeth and then stepped back and closed the door. His face appeared at the viewing slit as the lock clunked shut. "In you go, then."

Kip fitted the key he'd been given into the lock in front of him and turned it. With some resistance, the lock gave way and the door creaked open outward.

He stepped through, going from the bare cold stone of the tower into a different world, a carpeted room filled with the warmth of a fire, almost as abruptly as if he had translocated there. A glass-paned window looked out over the grounds and the city of London, and paintings of landscapes hung neatly on the walls. Two upholstered chairs, worn but comfortable-looking, sat on either side of a small table. A curtain hung across the doorway that led further into the apartments.

"Hello?" Kip called.

"One moment," came the call from the other room. A creaking sound followed and then heavy footsteps, and then the curtain was pushed aside and Master Albright strode into the room.

He looked heavier than when Kip had seen him last, the black hair and beard streaked with grey now. He carried a bowl in one hand and a bottle in the other. "I do apologize. They didn't tell me when to expect you."

"I didn't know myself when I would be here." Kip hesitated as Albright put down the bowl, which contained an assortment of nuts, and then the bottle on the little table between the two chairs.

"It doesn't make much difference to me these days. I'm glad of any relief from watching the boats," he gestured back toward the other room, "or the ravens," and he gestured to the window in this one. "I will say I was quite surprised when they told me you'd be visiting. I'd no idea you even knew I was here. Please, have a seat."

"My tail is quite wet." Kip held it awkwardly but could not prevent it from dripping on the floor.

Albright laughed. "I'll move the chair closer to the fire when you leave. It will have ample time to dry before anyone else comes to sit in it, believe me."

Kip held his tail around his hip and sat in the nearer chair as Albright fetched two glasses from the small cabinet below the brighter of the two landscapes. "I didn't know you were here until almost a year ago. It took that long to get the Crown to admit that you were alive. And then another six months to agree to allow a visit. And nearly as long to schedule one."

The other chair groaned as Albright sank his weight into it. "If you'd come later in the day, you might have gotten some of Bridget's lamb from The Darby. Though I suppose you can go there whenever you like."

"You must be very valuable to the Crown," Kip said.

"I have my uses. When you have heard the things that I have, been part of the meetings I have, the government is loath to let that information pass from the world. Especially when the deeds I've done are in their name. Mostly."

"I'd prefer not to be reminded of the things you've done."

"Fair point." Albright poured wine into each of the glasses. "Will you join me?"

"I think I should not." Kip eyed the glasses.

"Very prudent. Exactly right. It's no wonder you've survived to this age." He lifted one of the glasses in a toast and then sipped from it. For a moment he looked hopeful, and then he set down the glass with a sigh. "And you haven't missed anything special. I regret to inform you that this claret is quite sharp. It has not aged enough, in my opinion."

"How tragic."

"It is my lot." Albright took a handful of nuts and leaned back. "Now, before we get to your question, I hope you will answer one of mine." When Kip inclined his head, Albright went on. "How did you know I was alive to pester the Crown about my location?"

Kip allowed a slight smile to touch his muzzle. "I tried to find you in the demon plane and couldn't."

The hand that had been bringing nuts to Albright's mouth froze, and slowly sank back into his ample lap. "Well. There it is, then."

Kip nodded. "Azmelqart, the name I could only find in the text as a powerful Phoenecian sorcerer—he was Windsor's demon. That was the secret you were trying to protect."

"Yes." Albright stared straight ahead.

"My question is, how did you come to know it?"

Now the bushy beard and unruly hair turned toward Kip. "Because I was the appointed one. King's College has had one sorcerer ever since the summoning of demons was discovered who knows the secret, knows where the names come from. We trace that tradition back to Master Capitum who compiled the first lists of demons."

"So are you still the person, or does King's have another now?"

Albright ate the remaining nuts from his hand, chewed slowly, and then laced his hands together across his stomach. "I have passed on that responsibility. It seemed fitting, as I am no longer a member of the College nor even able to cast a simple spell."

There was no real way to feel sorry for this murderer living in a luxurious apartment complaining about the quality of the French wine he was brought, and Kip was not even tempted to try. "So we've known what demons are all this time."

"Of course we have. What, do you think someone wrote down a list of names and a sorcerer just found it, created a summoning spell, and never asked where these creatures came from?" Albright snorted. "Capitum left behind an instructive and nearly indecipherable text that each Keeper of Demons re-copies and updates before passing it on to the next one. It is not yours to read, but I can tell you that at least Master Capitum understood the power that lies in people, guessed that that power might attach to the soul after death, and found the spells to harness it. And of course, stopped people from writing down their sorcerer names where anyone might come across them."

The power that lies in people…Kip's ears came up. "Did you tell Victor about that as well?"

Now Albright's eyes widened, and for the first time he looked slightly surprised. "We had many discussions along those lines, but I never revealed the secret of demons to him. Do you know what's happened to him? The people I talk to know only that he disappeared around the time your people had that unfortunate trouble. My compliments on your performance in the face of that, by the way. Long overdue, but then…" He waved a hand around his gilded cage.

"Victor caused that." Kip saw no need to dress up the truth. "He cast a Great Feat and it killed him. But he also became the instrument of its reversal."

Another look of surprise and then Albright broke into laughter. "Ah ha ha! My dear boy—my dear colleague, I should say, for you have proven yourself many times over—that is delicious. Delightful! I am doubly, triply glad for your visit now. I suppose that unpleasant rat Calatian he dragged around with him everywhere has perished as well."

"Most likely," Kip said evenly. Farley had not been seen since that night, and his fate remained a mystery. But it was true that last year there had come to his ears a rumor of a pirate from Haiti who was able to fling cannonballs with magic, whom, it was said, had been stabbed in the back by his captain and thrown overboard. It was also true that over the last year, people on the Isle of Dogs and at King's College had told Kip that the marmots around Greenwich had grown bold and aggressive, and the phrase "nasty as a marmot" had begun to make its way into common usage. Kip and his friends occasionally wondered which of these had signaled the end of Farley's life, and always decided that they didn't care.

"Don't get me wrong. I liked Victor a great deal. But he was driven by a sense of injustice that was entirely of his own devising. Brilliant fellow, and if he'd had a touch more restraint, he might still be alive and hailed as the most innovative sorcerer since—well, perhaps Capitum himself, or old Calatus before him. Between us, he talked about you much more than he ought. I think your heroics quite put him out."

"Yes, I also got that impression," Kip said.

"Speaking of, you haven't tried to raise old Calatus, have you? Might be able to—his sorcerer name is recorded. Ask him why he created you, you know?"

Kip nodded. "I thought about it a lot. We have discussed it, but…first of all, demons don't hold on to memories very well. I was lucky with Victor; I caught him early on so he remembered the spells he'd cast, and they were very important to him. Who knows what Calatus might remember four hundred years on?"

"True, true." Albright ran fingers through his beard. "And second?"

Kip tilted his head. "Would you want to talk to God and find out why you were made?"

"I know why we were made. They wrote a whole book about it."

"I've read it. It tells you how you were made. Not why. The closest it comes is that God says He made you—us—to rule over all the animals."

Albright looked pointedly at Kip. "A job we have done increasingly poorly in recent years."

"That all depends on whether you consider Calatians human or not. The Church says we are."

"Yes, yes, true enough." Albright sank back into his chair.

"Our pastor also used to say that God made us to worship him and to know His plan."

"I have not consulted the Bible in many years, so you will have the advantage of me there. However, I seem to recall a conversation with a bishop in which he said that God made us to love Him, but we are under no obligation to. I remember because I thought it quite sad that our all-powerful Father could do anything except make us love Him." He gazed out the window. "Of course, that is not the point. The point is that we ourselves must come to a place where we love Him in our lives."

Kip flicked his ears back. "And if you could ask Him whether that is truly why He made you, would you?"

Albright returned his gaze to the fox. "If it comes down to it…yes, I would like to talk to God, but I confess I am quite willing to put off that conversation."

"My point is," Kip said, "that it doesn't matter why we were created. What matters is what we do with the life that's given us. You say 'talk to God,' but when you die, you're going to the Æther and you'll lose your memories, as will I. So we won't get a reckoning at the end of this. Or maybe we will. Maybe demons can die somehow, and at the end of that we'll meet God. But maybe not."

"But surely." Albright became a little more animated. "You owe your life to your Creator. If you were created for a purpose, should you not attempt to follow that purpose to the best of your ability? If He laid down rules for your life…"

"Thou shalt not kill?" Kip asked archly.

"Ha." Albright wagged a finger at him. "I never said I was very good at following rules. But in that case I was placing my country before my God. Both of them, in a sense, created me, so to whom do I owe allegiance?"

"To yourself," Kip said. "To yourself and the people around you, to do the best you can to improve everyone's lot, to make the best of what you've been given."

"Doing good for yourself by necessity means taking good from someone else. There is not an infinite reservoir of good in the world."

"Our school is surviving—in fact, we have a small surplus this year—by doing good for the community. We give our time and talents to people who need it, and those who can afford to help us survive and teach more students. We have a new class of twenty students this year," he added proudly.

"And by giving your good to the community, out of necessity, I presume, you are taking away the good from the work you might be doing for your country. Exploration, research, discovery, an American Empire, all pushed to the side in the name of taking poor old Mrs. Gallivant down the road to the market."

Kip snorted. "Our country's government has not seen fit to spare the funds to pay us until this year, and we took only some of the money offered. We would like to be seen as a partner to the government as well as to our citizens. Sorcerers in the British Empire have always been beholden to the Crown, but it is not so around the world. We are merely trying something that others have already invented, changing it here and there to fit our peculiar needs."

"Peculiar indeed." Albright took another handful of nuts and washed them down with wine. "I presume that the British government is already well aware of this experiment and the dangerous precedent it may set around the world?"

"Dangerous?" Kip perked his ears. "They are aware, yes, but how is it dangerous?"

"Look at France. Two bloody years and they are no closer to settling the people."

"They've formed a provisional government. Emily—sent someone to speak to them a month ago."

Albright waved a hand dismissively. "A provisional government. All they learned from you lot was how to topple the throne. They have no leaders of the caliber of your Mr. Adams, or even your Master Colonel Jackson. Of course, those leaders were shaped by the British Empire."

"France will be stable soon." Kip had had this assurance from Emily and didn't know whether he believed it, but he believed it more than Albright's British exceptionalism.

"I do hope so. And I hope that your American experiment survives as well, and that someday down the road, you find your way back to loving His Majesty." Kip made as if to speak, but Albright went on quickly. "Penfold, I never wished to end your life. I do wish you had joined me so that I could feel as proud of what you've accomplished as I am impressed by the means with which you accomplished it."

"Thank you," Kip said, and searched for a compliment that would be truthful. "Coming from such an accomplished sorcerer as yourself, that is high praise."

Albright smiled and finished his glass of wine, then reached for the other. "You're sure you won't have anything to drink?"

"I really must be leaving," Kip said, rising from his chair.

"Ah, so soon?" Albright made no attempt to rise, but picked up the second glass and sipped from it.

"Regrettably so. I have many obligations, as I'm certain you understand."

The sorcerer nodded. "It has been a pleasure speaking with you, especially about philosophy and sorcery. Should you wish to return again, I would welcome the company. Speaking on nothing but foreign affairs is engaging but ultimately rather repetitive."

Kip made a short, perfunctory bow. "Should I have the time, I will investigate the possibility."

Albright let out a sigh and stared down at his wine glass, and did not say another word as Kip left and locked the door behind him.

He had meetings at King's College that afternoon, first a debriefing with the Headmaster about what he'd talked to Albright about. Kip related most of the conversation truthfully and told Headmaster Cross that there were certain topics related to the position of Keeper of Demons that he could not divulge, which the sorcerer did not like but did not challenge. Kip left room in the conversation for Cross to say, "Perhaps you should talk to our Keeper of Demons," but he did not.

Meetings concluded, he took a late lunch at The Darby, where he complimented Bridget on her lamb chops, and then walked out behind the building and translocated back home.

The sun seemed to retreat from overhead to just over the eastern horizon as The Darby vanished and Kip's home replaced it. Noises from inside told him the household was awake, so he walked inside.

Alice sat in the back yard watching Kira stack wooden blocks on top of each other. The eighteen-month-old fox cub sang, "Ba ba ba," as they stacked, and then when they tumbled down, she laughed and clapped her paws together.

When Kip opened the back door, both foxes looked up. Alice smiled and stood gracefully as Kira tottered to her feet. "Da!" she called, and ran toward him with her arms out.

Kip scooped her up. "Oof!" he said. "You're getting big! I'm going to have to use magic to pick you up soon."

"Da!" she said, and pushed her little nose against his.

Alice brushed her dress free of dirt and came to kiss Kip's cheek. "Morning," she said. "Or, afternoon, or whatever it is for you. How are the new Calatians?"

Kira turned toward Alice and reached a paw out to her whiskers. "Ma!" she said, and then touched Kip's muzzle with her other little paw. "Da!"

"Yes," Alice said, "Ma and Da are both here, and Ba will be back tonight."

"They're the same as here," Kip said. "A little better than last time, still a way from being...you know. But they're getting better, and last year's definitely helped. How has your day been?"

Alice stretched. "Chakrabarti had some interesting thoughts about bringing Calatians to India, but using native Indian animals. We talked about it well into the night. Then I got up a few hours ago to go to the Dieuleveults' farm to help with the planting. Kira came along but slept through most of it. Now I'm tired and she's full of energy."

"You can take a nap if you like. I'm here for a bit and I haven't seen her in a day." He bounced her up and down and she laughed, wagging her tail. "Playing with blocks today, are you?" Kip asked the little cub, still trying to grab his whiskers.

"She cried until I brought them out." Alice smiled. "She won't play with anything else. Maybe she'll be an architect or a builder when she grows up."

Kip looked into his cub's blue eyes, their pupils almost vertical lines in the sun, and he shifted his grip to hold her more securely. "We'll teach her all we know," he said, rubbing his nose against hers. "And after that, she can do anything she wants."

ACKNOWLEDGMENTS

This book was supported in part through Patreon. My page at patreon.com/timsusman features sneak previews of upcoming work, often early drafts that will never be released otherwise. Many thanks to my Patreon supporters for this volume: Brandon Nedrow, Furlia, John Hawley, Marcwolf, Shader, and tav fox.

Thanks to Renee van Amerongen for help with the Dutch language, including linguistic history that I had to restrain myself from delving more into. Thanks also to Ned, who helped with some little aspects of the Christian faith, and to Malcolm Cross, who helped with some of the more troublesome plot knots.

Thanks to the Happy Little Comets writing group, specifically Alisa Alering, M. Milks, Dayna Smith, Brooke Wonders, and Becky Wright, who broke out this story with me and provided extremely useful critiques on an early draft.

Thanks to the Unreliable Narrators, Ryan Campbell, David Cowan, and Watts Martin, for their invaluable feedback on early drafts.

Thanks to Mark and Grant for believing in this series and giving it a wonderful home at Argyll. Their support has been crucial to the development and release of the books.

My deepest thanks to Laura Garabedian, whose art has graced all four books. She made them look exactly as I'd hoped, and then made everything better. I love the extra dimension her art has brought to the series.

And of course, as always, my love and gratitude to Mark, Jack, and Kobalt, at least two of whom did not actively resent me spending so much time at the computer and not throwing a ball in the back yard. They have been and continue to be the best family a fox could ask for.

ABOUT THE AUTHOR

Tim Susman started a novel in college and didn't finish one until almost twenty years later. In that time, he earned a degree in Zoology, worked with Jane Goodall, co-founded Sofawolf Press, and moved to California. He has attended Clarion in 2011 (arooo Narwolves!) and published short stories in Apex, Lightspeed, and ROAR, among others. He has also published many more novels and short stories under the name Kyell Gold and has won several awards for his fiction under both names. You can find out more about his stories at timsusman.wordpress.com and www.kyellgold.com, and follow him on Twitter at @WriterFox.

ABOUT THE ARTIST

My childhood was spent moving, changing locations and school environments. My constant companions became a dragon's horde of fantasy novels and my animals. This connection to creatures through the lens of fantasy has always been a touchstone for my work.

Through the years, I've experimented with many different media, wandering many paths. Now I've settled into the twin focuses of watercolor and oils. I find the dichotomy of their approach refreshing, and each time my hands move from one to the other I approach my work with new ideas and a cleaner view of where I should go.

Art is a way for my to communicate my love of the natural world and the fantasy I see within it. I think that the creation of a narrative around wildlife and fantastical animals can lead people to see the world and the many lives encompassed within it with more compassion and joy, returning the wonder of childlike curiosity to their lives.

I enjoy employing abstract backgrounds with minutely detailed subjects. The duality of the abstract work with small areas of focus lets the viewer fill in parts of strange color fields with their own story. My inspiration from nature and the narratives I like to weave around the strange beasts in my paintings lets me tell soundless stories to those who wish to explore them. In my paintings, bears covered in moss and trailing mushrooms emerge from the mist, gryphons dive from heights unknown with jewelry trailing them, and sphinxes ask questions unheard from behind blank masks. Where they come from, and what they want to say is left for those who watch them to determine. I hope through my work people can find a bit of mystery, of that wonder you have as a child making shapes in clouds, imagining what monster is in the closet, and making each walk in the woods a journey that may take them to Narnia, to Middle Earth, or a world of their own making

http://www.fairytaleswithtails.com